Incensed

{THE NOVEL}

To Susan,
The greatest Auntie
ever. Truly.
Love,
Cary
11/11/11
Mill Valley CA

Published in the United States by Strange Boat Publishing, Mill Valley, California.

www.strangeboatpublishing.com

ISBN 978-0-9837612-0-4

Library of Congress Control Number: 2011936252
Published in the United States of America

Cover design by Daniel Cook Design Inc.
Interior layout by Thomas White
Author photo by Joy Evans

Gratitude

This book would not exist but for my fellow writing group members Christine Harvey, Wendy Young Howard, and Tracy Tandy. I wrote in anticipation of your laughter each week, and edited with the guidance of your critiques. Not to mention, thanks a heap for that tacky dolphin candle. I'm sure Dorothea would sell one just like it.

I am grateful for the professional guidance of editor David Carr. I gave one huge sigh of relief when you agreed to work with me, and a second when you told me the book didn't suck.

Much appreciation as well to readers Melody Sullivan, Kylea Taylor, and Ashley Wile for your helpful comments and, of course, your friendship.

A big thank you to Daniel Cook for the cover design. Your work, as always, is both inspired and inspiring.

Reader, if you don't think this book is funny enough, blame my family. They have always encouraged my dumb sense of humor by laughing, or pretending to. Thank you for your love and support: Alice, Pat and Finnley; Susan and Reva. Most especially to my mother, Patrice: Because you are first an artist, I learned to value my own creativity, wherever it led. Thanks and love also to my dad, Bernie, under any circumstances.

Gratitude is also due to many others, more than I can name here. In particular, though: Christina and Stan, for the opportunity to work with you all these years and for the honor of your friendship. And Glenn Wilson, who has always been there and always will be.

For a lot of years now, I've shared a household with two unbelievably great guys: my son Bryn and my husband Tav. I am most grateful to them for putting up with me, though maybe if they weren't so much fun to hang out with, I'd have finished this book sooner. Tav, you must surely be the most supportive partner ever. "Write books," you tell me; "Buy horses," "Take a sabbatical." You are either insane or destined for sainthood. Either way, I couldn't love you more.

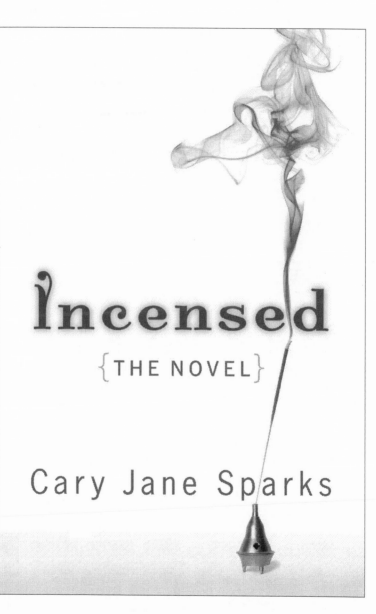

Incensed

{THE NOVEL}

Cary Jane Sparks

1
Mill Valley

What likely put Michaela Thomason over the edge, believe it or not, was a radish. It was a summer radish: a small, deeply red one with a crisp white interior; a little on the fiery side but not too much. It was meant to go into her salad.

Instead, the damn thing disappeared.

Michaela stood at her kitchen counter, ingredients at hand. She had rinsed, dried and torn an organic romaine heart and dropped it into the oversize wooden bowl. She had chopped and added sugar snap peas, ripe tomatoes, scallions, and tiny Persian cucumbers, all from Sunday's Marin farmers market; six pitted Kalamata olives out of a jar from Trader Joes; and radish number one, when radish number two made its mysterious disappearance.

She only had to add feta cheese and a handful of fresh pine nuts just out of the toaster oven, and finish with her special balsamic fig and toasted sesame oil dressing. Then she would have a lovely, relaxing salad to go with the sourdough baguette and hand churned butter – also from the farmer's market – and the glass of Sauvignon Blanc already poured and waiting.

But she couldn't finish the nice, relaxing salad because the goddamned radish was nowhere to be found. She had washed two of them, she was certain. Michaela always sliced her vegetables one at a time, and had automatically set radish *numero dos* down nearby, in order to cut *uno* and put it in the bowl.

She checked all around the cutting board. No radish. She systematically moved all the items still in front of her, putting away whatever she was done with, and removing the rest across the room to a bare counter where she had already established the radish wasn't. The plastic container of feta and small blue bowl of warm pine nuts; the glass flagon of dressing ready to be poured, the stainless steel salt shaker and matching pepper mill, the glass of wine; none were hiding the missing crucifer. She looked on the floor. She returned to the salad bowl, fingered the ingredients, looked and felt for the hard round shape among the leaves and pieces of the already prepared salad.

It was not in the refrigerator. Not in the sink, on the table, nor on any of the other surfaces. Feeling ridiculous, she even checked the bathroom, where, of course, it wasn't.

Finally, frustration and hunger drove Michaela to admit defeat. She would have to settle for a single radish. They were the last two in the bunch, and so that was that. Fine.

Except it wasn't fine. The lack of radish and how it had utterly and completely vanished bothered Michaela the rest of the evening. It drifted in and out of her thoughts while she ate dinner and drank her wine. It was still there while she went into her home office and sent emails from her desktop. While she watched a recorded episode of *CSI: Miami* and the news, flossed, brushed, got into bed and looked at a magazine before she tried to sleep. Michaela simply could not get the lack of radish out of her mind. It was as if the thing had disapparated, a la Harry Potter, out of the physical realm, and reappeared, whole and complete, and completely irritating, deep within Michaela's mental realm. It would not go away. And so, all that night, the next day and night, and for many days and nights after that, Michaela's radish dwelt in her consciousness like a grain of sand in an oyster. And her mind continued to muse upon it at some deep level, of which Michaela was only sometimes, or only partially, aware.

"That goddamned radish. Where in the hell did it go, anyway?" Michaela thought to herself, as she lay awake several nights later. "What could have happened to it?"

For the seventy-ninth time she asked herself that question. But she did not have any better answer than the first seventy-eight times. She pulled the covers up tighter under her chin and sighed aloud. She wouldn't get back to sleep any time soon.

"Damn radish," she muttered aloud, "I refuse to think about it any more."

But, as she realized later, Michaela never really had a choice.

2
Santa Fe

D orothea Light, workshop leader, former therapist, self-professed Sha-Woman, and nearly Ascended Master (she was pretty certain), was working on her enclosed back porch. She sat on the floral-patterned settee with her feet up on the matching ottoman, a pink legal pad resting on her legs. Several of the lined pink pages, covered by Dorothea in zigzags, interlocking circles, and curlicues, had been torn off and gently crushed, and now surrounded her on the cushions like roses. By her side was an expensive, blue-green, handmade ceramic bowl given her by a grateful student. The bowl was two thirds full of personalized M&M's, sent by another student. Each pink, purple and yellow M&M was printed with Dorothea's photo on one side and the word LIGHT on the other.

Dorothea absentmindedly plucked an M&M from the bowl with her manicured thumb and forefinger, and delivered it to her mouth, followed by another, then another. She reached down again, but hit sofa cushion instead. The bowl was gone. A gentle rattle near her left ear let her know husband Dirk was holding the bowl out of reach.

"Now, Dirk," she drawled, still making swirly marks on the paper. "Is that really what you want to do? Put yourself in the role of Daddy, tell me what I can and cannot eat? A lot of pressure comes with that role."

"Thea. You want to stay trim, don't you? You have important service to do in the world, and you'll be taken more seriously if you look good. Being attractive and fit helps bring your message to people who need it."

"Dirk, honey, my people love me. They don't care if I'm a few pounds overweight. That just makes me more motherly. The good kind of mother, not like the ones most of them really had. So they can trust me and let me work with them. Put the bowl back, honey, it helps me think."

"Thea, I don't think you need this. Let me get you some grapes."

"Boo. Grapes are boring. I love my special M&M's. The colors are so pretty, and with my picture on them, it's like eating my own little affirmations. Give them back, now, honeybunch, before I get cranky. I'm right in the middle of an important piece for the new lecture and I need to stay focused."

"Okay Thea, but think about this. What if *Ivy!* comes through this time?"

Dorothea finally raised her eyes to look up at Dirk.

"Hmph," she said. "Okay, then. Get me some grapes. Hurry, before I lose my train of thought."

3
Marin County

M ichaela was a graphic designer, and her specialty was restaurants, particularly menus. She created menus for some of the best chefs and high-end chains in the country. She was not only talented, but was never late and rarely made a mistake. She hated losing a job, and that had not happened for a long time. Michaela was known as one of the two or three best in her field.

Her work was intermittent – a string of twelve-hour days in a row, then a couple of weeks with little to do. Michaela attended to every detail. From the materials, shape and size of the page, book or frame, to the color, weight and texture of the paper, to every aspect of the typeface, all had to be precisely right for the job.

While email and pictures were sometimes enough to ensure every aspect was perfect, often she had to show up in person. She would travel to see a new restaurant during the design stage or a remodel, and get the feel and look the menu should have to complement the food, décor and overall impression the owners wished to make. Her work was often an excuse for a trip to Vegas or L.A. Sometimes her friend Maxine went with her. When they weren't traveling together, they tried to meet regularly for coffee.

"So what's new?" Max asked, as they took their cups from the barista and settled at a small table in the center of the room.

"You know, the strangest thing happened with a radish."

As soon as she started speaking, a roar started up from the oversized blender behind the counter, and Michaela grimaced. These places might as well just install a Slurpee machine and be done with it.

Max raised her voice accordingly. "You have a rash? What kind of a rash?" She screwed up her face as she said the word rash, but it might have been because of the noise.

"Not a rash! A radish!" Michaela yelled.

"So you don't have a rash?" Max said, this time way too loudly because now the machine had stopped. A woman at the next table glanced at Michaela, who stared squarely back to show that she did not have a rash, at least not on her face.

"I was talking about a radish." Michaela said. She wanted to speak loud enough to clarify the situation to whoever might have heard the word "rash."

"A radish? What do you mean? Are you allergic to radishes? I'm allergic to mangos, but I didn't know for a long time. It was, like, every few months the skin around my mouth would break out. I had no idea why, so I went to the dermatologist. He said it might be, like, a food allergy, but I didn't think I had one, so I tried to think, what was I eating that I could possibly be allergic to? Finally I realized: the mangos at Whole Foods. Every time they'd put out a sample, I'd break out. You know how messy they are; they get all over your face. You can't help it."

"Uh huh." Michaela pushed a spilled drop of coffee around with her stirrer to draw a circle with lines coming out, like a child's sun. She added a happy face, then changed the smile to an "O." Now it looked like "The Scream" so she scribbled it out.

"Except, Max, this has nothing to do with a rash. I was making a salad and this radish I was about to use just fucking *disappeared*. That's not supposed to happen. Now I can't stop thinking about it." She saw the skeptical expression on her friend's face and added, "Of course I looked for it, Maxine. I'm telling you this thing wasn't anywhere."

"Under the fridge?"

"Too big to fit."

"So you think it was, what? Some kind of weird cosmic phenomenon?"

"No, of course not." Michaela took what should have been a pleasing sip of her half-caf, sugar-free-cinnamon latte. Except, like everything else for the last few days, the taste wasn't nearly as pleasing as she thought it should be.

"Anyway, what do you mean, cosmic phenomena?" Michaela asked. "Have you ever heard of that happening?"

"Well, it does remind me of a story I heard a while ago about Sai Baba, you know, one of those Indian gurus? A guy I was dating took me to hear this bald dude whose name sounded Indian but I guess he was actually a Jewish professor from Harvard. Rama Dama something; I can't really remember. Anyway, this Sai Baba, you ever hear how he produces this ashy stuff out of his hands? It's a sweet smelling powder called "viboogie," or "gabootie." Something like that. A friend of mine got some in India a few years ago, and he gave me a little bag for good luck or whatnot. The stuff feels and smells like incense dust.

"Anyway, they say it just materializes out of his hands. He, like, produces it. One minute there's nothing and the next this stuff is in coming out of his palms. And he makes, they say, like, tons of it. And he also makes jewelry and other things appear out of the air; and little pictures of him; whatever he wants to give somebody."

"Has anybody proved that's what he's doing? I mean, don't

magicians do that pull-stuff-out-of-thin-air thing all the time? And it's all fake, right?"

"I guess. I don't really know if it's been proven, but my friend spent a lot of time with Sai Baba and he believes it. But there's more to the story. So, like, someone asks Sai Baba about it. He says, 'Baba, how do you do that? Create all this Viboojoo, or whatever it's called, and all these gifts out of nothing?' And the Guru answers, 'I don't create any of it.' So, now, the follower's confused because he's been witnessing this and everybody says Baba makes it. So the guy asks, 'I don't understand. Are you sure?' and Sai Baba answers, 'Of course not. That would be impossible. All exists already somewhere else. All I do is bring it here.'"

"Oh, yeah. So he's not manifesting it…"

"He's just, like, making it disappear and reappear someplace else."

"As if that's any easier or more explainable."

"Exactly. So maybe that's what happened with your radish."

"What? Sai Baba took it out of my kitchen and gave it to one of his disciples?"

"Well that doesn't seem likely, though I guess it's a thought. But what I mean is, maybe you did it somehow. Disappeared it."

"Yeah, I'm sure that's what happened, Max. I'm always doing things like that. I have all sorts of superpowers. I was in the last season of *Heroes*."

Max shrugged and sipped her coffee. "Well, Michaela, you never know. All I'm saying is, that would explain why you couldn't find it."

Michaela snorted, but said nothing. But she was thinking. The truth was, you never did know, did you? Not really. You always thought you did, but mostly you pretty much didn't.

4
Marin

S he should have gone home to work, but Michaela couldn't shake the thought of objects disappearing and reappearing, either spontaneously or at will. A guy she once dated had made her laugh with the rhyme "the spewage of newage is mostly sewage." But after Maxine's story about Sai Baba, Michaela thought the new age bookstore might be useful. If there was any explanation for the radish incident, Michaela wanted it. And as soon as possible, so she could focus on something else. Like planning a vacation, which would be fun and exciting, and make her feel better.

She parked on the metered side street between Third and Fourth Street in downtown San Rafael, close to the store. She approached its wide glass front, which displayed not only books, but also statues in many sizes and forms. She thought most of them were from India, but as for their names and meanings, she had no clue. Some were dark metal and others brightly painted ceramic. There were elephant-headed men, humans standing on other, smaller, humans or animals; and multi-armed characters with more weapons – and hands to hold them – than even one of those video games she watched her nephews play at Thanksgiving.

Michaela swung open the glass door, heard a bell tinkle, and was accosted by the smell of incense, causing her to sneeze. Didn't the owners know some people were allergic?

The store was two large rooms, right and left of the entrance. Bookshelves and display cases lined all four walls, with additional, smaller shelves at the back. To the right of the entrance stood a large glass counter with a cash register. The rest of the room was filled with more books; CDs and DVDs; decks of Tarot and other divination cards; many types of incense; and an assortment of jewelry, stones, and candles.

The bookshelves were labeled by subject, nearly all of which Michaela knew nothing about, with some she'd never even heard of. Chakras, dreaming and shamanism; bodywork, astral projection and tarot; goddesses, symbols and synchronicities; and all manner of healing: vibrational, healing with music, with art, with guided imagery, with prayer, meditation and with breathing. If any of those were about objects vanishing, she'd never know it. This was not helpful. No section or title screamed "edible objects disappearing with no explanation." The closest she saw was some stuff on people who could supposedly "see" objects without using their eyes. (Sure they could.) Was that related to not seeing objects that had to be there?

Since she had the Sai Baba story, she found a small section of books about him, searching for the incident Max had told her about, or anything else. But she was soon distracted by a conversation going on at the front of the store.

A man was talking to the young woman behind the counter, his back to Michaela. He had thick, sandy brown hair, and was of average height and build. Michaela had already noticed the woman, with her knee-length, pink, cotton print dress and long, reddish-brown dreadlocks, which should have been a hideous mismatch but somehow worked.

Michaela was too close to avoid their conversation, but she wasn't really listening until the man spoke.

"Unfortunately, my appointment book seemed to just totally vanish; I have no idea how. I'm certain I left it on the passenger seat, and when I came back, it was gone, even though the car was locked. So I can't check, but I'm sure the meeting was for today."

Michaela's heart beat faster at the mention of the missing book. Without actually moving, she tuned in more closely.

"Gosh, he's not usually here Tuesdays," the clerk said. "I'm super sorry. Can you come back some other time?"

"Guess I'll have to. Is he in tomorrow?"

"He's supposed to be."

"And can I leave these flyers and samples for him? In fact, maybe we can just do the order by phone."

The man placed a black nylon case on the counter and pulled from its pockets a variety of small boxes, miniature plastic bags and colored flyers.

"Cool," she said, picking one up. "I love new incense."

The man pulled the rest of the samples back toward him.

"Oh, I won't use it," she said quickly. "I'll make sure Ron gets it. There's an office in the back; I'll leave it on his desk."

"Thank you," he said, reaching back in the case. "And why don't you try this one yourself. Tell me what you think."

Was he flirting with Dreadlock Girl? Other than the weird hair, she was cute. The girl was smiling at him, too.

"Thanks," she said. "I will." She examined the little beige box. "Mmm, amber rose. Sounds nice."

"Reminds me of your dress," he said. He *was* flirting.

The man closed his case, preparing to leave. But Michaela wanted to hear more about his missing appointment book. She also wanted a better look at him, and he still had his back to her. She replaced the Sai Baba book and followed, pretending to browse titles along the way.

When Incense Man left, ringing the little bell, Michaela waited two beats and went after him. He turned left toward

Fourth Street, and so did Michaela. Then he turned right and crossed the street.

He walked slowly, but was not window-shopping. He appeared to be busy in his own head. Michaela hung back. She wanted urgently to discuss the appointment book, but felt she couldn't just walk up and start talking. If she told him about the radish, he'd probably say she hadn't looked hard enough, or it had rolled away, or give some other logical reason why she couldn't find it. It wasn't likely he'd believe it had just disappeared into nothingness.

For that matter, his appointment book was probably under the seat of his car, or else he left the door open and it fell out, or he never put it there in the first place, or he moved it and forgot. If she didn't think his item had vanished, why should she expect him to believe that hers had?

At the next corner, he turned left to cross Fourth and picked up his pace. Where was he going now? This was annoying. She was probably wasting her time. Either she needed to go up and say something to him or she should forget this whole crazy quest, and go home and do something useful.

Suddenly, the man turned left into a coffee bar, and Michaela automatically followed. Now that he'd stopped, she'd watch him a little longer. He was at the counter, so she got in line right behind him. When he requested peppermint tea, Michaela rolled her eyes.

Michaela ordered coffee, with an extra shot. Incense Man stood right next to her, looking the other way, adding honey to his mug. She still couldn't see his face. He moved to the back of the café, sat at a small table, and began rifling through his case. Michaela took a table just behind his chair.

Okay, this was it. She wanted a good look at him and she wanted to ask a few questions. Michaela was damned if she was going to be intimidated by a guy drinking peppermint tea. And besides, men approached by Michaela were rarely disappointed. She may have a few years on Dreadlock Girl, but instead of a baggy pink dress, her clothes showed off her ultra-fit body and naturally generous cleavage. She wore her light brown, blond-highlighted hair below her shoulders and had often been complimented for her sultry dark eyes, which Michaela thought were her best feature.

She tapped Incense Guy on the shoulder.

"Excuse me," she said.

When he turned, Michaela finally saw his face. Mid-thirties, pleasant looking, he had even features and nice blue eyes. His sandy hair was thick and longish, curling an inch or so behind his ears and down his neck. A tad '70s, but otherwise okay.

As she expected, he seemed pleased by her intrusion, even if he was savvy enough to avoid glancing at her chest, not far from eye-level.

"Sorry for interrupting. This might sound strange, but I was in the bookstore a few minutes ago, when you mentioned, um, losing your appointment book. So, I was just wondering … did you say you're sure it was right there on the seat?"

"Yes. Definitely. Why? Did you see someone take it?"

"Oh, no, nothing like that. I'm sorry. I actually don't know anything about it at all. But are you absolutely sure it was on the seat, and then just wasn't?"

"Yeah, I'm pretty certain." He was looking at her suspiciously, as if he thought she was up to something but he didn't know what. "Why do you want to know?"

"I…well, I…," Michaela started, but he wasn't listening. He was turning to look in every direction – up at the ceiling, in the corners, at the back door. He finally stared back at Michaela.

"You took it, didn't you? Or someone on your crew. This is a trick."

"No, of course not. I only wanted to ask you…"

He suddenly stood up, threw his chair back, and swept his glance around the room.

"Okay! Is this a reality show? Am I being punk'd or something?" the man said.

"Uh, no. Not that I know of. Not by me, anyway. And I don't see any cameras," she pointed out.

He continued to glare around the room. A few folks looked up briefly before returning attention to their assorted collections of laptops, papers, books, snacks and beverages.

After staring a long time at the door, he slumped into his chair and sighed loudly.

"So why *do* you want to know about the book I lost?" he asked, now considerably grumpier.

"Well … ha ha … it's a little embarrassing…" she began.

He stared at her. This wasn't going well.

"You're embarrassed, huh? Then that's two of us," he said. "Go on."

"The thing is, if it really did just disappear like that … I mean, *really* disappear. Vanish, you know, into nothingness. Well, the thing is… I think that same thing happened to me. And I was just in the store looking for a book about it. You know, about that phenomenon. Something to help me figure it out."

"Yeah?"

"So when I heard you had the same experience – or what sounded like it might be the same – I just had to ask. So I followed you."

"You followed me?"

"Um, yeah. I hope you don't mind."

He didn't seem to. In fact, he seemed to puff back up a bit, after the deflation of first thinking he was on camera, and then finding out he wasn't.

Encouraged, Michaela continued to play to his ego.

"I thought maybe this was something that had happened to you before. And I hoped you could tell me something about the phenomenon. You seem like a person who might know a lot about those kind of things."

He settled a bit and reached for his tea, then took a long sip.

"I can't really say that I've experienced this before. Although I've certainly heard of such occurrences. As it happens, I do know a bit about them."

Ego restored, he now seemed willing to open up.

"What happened to your, er, was it an appointment book?" he asked.

"No, not that. A radish, actually."

"Really? That seems significant somehow. You should look up radish as a symbol."

"A symbol? What do you mean?"

"Oh, you know. Like what does it stand for in a dream?"

"What could a radish possibly stand for?"

"Off the top of my head, I have no idea. Crunchiness? Irritation? You'd have to look in a symbol book or a dream interpretation book."

Michaela started to protest.

"I know, I know," he said. "You didn't dream it. I'm not saying that. But if the universe chose a radish to disappear for you, instead of a carrot or a cucumber, well, that might be significant."

Michaela was startled by the thought. If something as big as a carrot or cucumber disappeared like that, she didn't know what she'd do.

"Geez. Well, I guess that makes sense to look it up," she said, not sure that it did. "But what I really want to know is why the universe, as you put it, chose something to disappear at all. For that matter, I'm not convinced any sort of universe chose anything. I don't know if I believe all that stuff. It's just driving me crazy that I can't figure out what happened to it."

While she spoke, he looked at the label attached to the tea bag, then swirled the bag in the heavy white mug. She wanted to ask him what the tag said, and realized she didn't know his name. She put out her hand.

"I'm Michaela."

"Rennie. Nice meeting you … Mik-Ella? What is that, Native American? African? Did you re-name yourself?"

"It's Michael plus an A. I was named after my grandfather."

"Oh." He looked disappointed again.

"So what's it say? The tag."

"Uh, let's see." He read, "'Call on God but row away from the rocks. Indian Proverb.' Whatever that means."

"I'm not a tea drinker," Michaela said. "I like coffee. No proverbs, and you get a better buzz. What about your appointment book? Did you look up the meaning of that symbol?"

Rennie shook his head. "No. I'm afraid I don't need to. It's obvious. I'm not completely happy doing what I'm doing. I want to be a spiritual teacher."

"What kind of spirituality do you teach?"

"I don't know yet. That's what I have to figure out."

"Oh." Michaela wanted to say something helpful but she couldn't think of anything. In her opinion, this was rather an odd ambition and he was going about it backwards. Didn't it make more sense to take something you had an affinity for and then start teaching that to others, rather than trying to find something you wanted to teach? Not that Michaela had given it much thought. She had no interest in teaching anyone about anything, or being any kind of leader either. Not that she was a follower. She hated people telling her what to do. She supposed she must be an independent.

Rennie either didn't notice or didn't care that Michaela hadn't offered him any words of encouragement.

He said, "In fact, I'm probably going to a workshop Saturday called LightWorks Shamanic Meditation Training, with this teacher from New Mexico, Dorothea Light. It's an introductory weekend, but it sounds interesting. Wanna go? I don't know if it'll have anything about, you know, stuff vanishing, but it might."

Rennie rummaged about in his bag, finally pulling out a slightly bent, light blue, three-fold brochure and a pen.

"Take this. They sent me two. If you decide to go, and if you feel like it, give me a call. We could maybe drive together."

The middle-aged woman pictured on the brochure was attractive, though with the slightly surprised expression of someone who'd had recent cosmetic work done. Her wavy, dark hair was longer and more deliberately styled than Michaela's, and she wore a lot more makeup.

"I've got to take off," Rennie said. "I've got an appointment. At least, I think I do."

He laughed, and it made him look more attractive than she'd originally thought.

"I'm glad you came over," he said. "It was good to meet you."

"Mmm hmm," Michaela nodded, waving the brochure in the air. "Thanks for the info."

He dropped his mug in a bus tray on his way out.

Michaela waited a bit, then bussed her coffee mug, too, since it seemed expected. She stopped back in at the store, where she purchased the book on Sai Baba and one on symbol interpretation. She also took a handful of free magazines and flyers from a table by the door. As an afterthought, she went back and bought two types of incense and an incense burner.

"When in *newage*, try the sewage," she muttered.

5
Santa Fe

D espite waking up early, Dorothea, as she often did, remained in bed. A dream lingered just outside her memory. She still felt the dream's emotion, a hint of the warm sensation she had as a small girl visiting her grandmother. She'd be in the kitchen, Grammy wearing her flowered apron, slicing bread she had just lifted from the oven, and buttering a piece to set down before Dorothea on a large white plate.

Only Dorothea wasn't her name then. She'd been little miss Dottie Fimple, of Pineville, Florida, a tiny town in the center of the state. She wanted to go back into the feeling of the dream, but instead it vanished completely, the warmth evaporating into annoyance as she remembered how much she disliked her given name. Dottie. Her ignorant parents had not even made it Dorothy, with Dottie as a nickname that she could have dropped when she got older.

Instead, she'd had to have it legally changed when she was twenty-one. She changed her last name too, while she was at it. She wanted to put her whole unfortunate history behind her. She had been Dorothea Light ever since, even through three marriages, and it was a good choice, the name she was supposed to have. Dorothea meant "gift of god," after all. And Light, of course. That was obvious.

Dorothea's annoyance now changed to satisfaction as she reflected on how far she had risen above her upbringing. Not that there was anything obviously horrible about how she was raised. Her home life hadn't been awful by most standards. She wasn't abused, or anything of that sort. It was just so disgustingly plain and ordinary and uninspiring. Two older brothers and her father, endlessly watching sports, especially football. Her dumpy, boring mother always serving and cleaning up after them, and asking how the game was going. The Miami Dolphins. Ugh. She would be happy if that team disappeared from the face of the earth (why couldn't a hurricane do something useful like that?) so she would never have to hear it spoken of again.

Dorothea had undergone a special ritual five years ago at the Regal Dolphin Swim in Cozumel. She'd wanted to transmute her loathing of the word "dolphin" and all its bad associations in order to appreciate the mystical, intelligent creatures the word was supposed to represent. The dolphins themselves helped her, especially one large, beautiful male who had pushed her around the pool for a good ten minutes before diving under and then jumping completely over her head three times. Dorothea felt him communicating with her psychically. He told her that he had taken his cetacean form in this lifetime in order to be there for Dorothea to work through her trauma around the animals. She was grateful, and telepathically told him so.

The humans called him Calvin, although he told her he had another, real name, a series of clicks and whistles she couldn't possibly pronounce and had immediately forgotten. The ritual had healed her around this issue, and she thanked Calvin for his sacrifice. He had chosen to become a tame dolphin in a pool, when he could have been wild in the ocean, or, for that matter, taken a form in which he could do other important work. She occasionally dreamed about him and his dolphin therapist colleagues. She wished she could write to Calvin, or Clickety-whee-whatever-his-name-was. He would have made the perfect husband.

Instead she had found Dirk. Actually – and Dorothea had never considered it in this context before – the Dolphin Swim was where she first met Dirk. He was in the pool at the same time as she, but she hadn't paid much attention to him. It turned out they were staying at the same hotel too, which made sense since the hotel had organized the Dolphin Swim excursion. The next day he had approached her as she tanned beside the swimming pool. She wasn't attracted to him at first, even though he was considerably younger than she and not bad looking, with curly reddish hair and a bit of a permanent smirk. His butt looked good in blue board shorts, but the rest of him was pale and slightly doughy. For the remainder of the week, he paid her a lot of attention, and wanted to spend all of his time with her. The fact that he seemed to be so smitten improved her appreciation of him considerably.

But wasn't that always the case? People were just drawn to her, and wanted her time and attention. It had been that way her whole life, even in grammar school. She would tell stories about the interesting and special things that happened to her, and the other kids would all be fascinated.

Early on, she also realized she had a special gift for helping people. Even older kids. Even teachers and parents. She knew she was special, and she could make others feel special too, just by allowing them to be around her and putting her powerful, focused attention on them. When she listened and gave advice, Dorothea noticed, she could make people feel better about themselves. And that made them like her even more.

The sad part was when others, who didn't understand, tried to make her stop relating to people the way she wanted to. There always seemed to be one killjoy who didn't want anyone else to be happy and would accuse Dorothea ... Dottie ... of making up stories and manipulating people. Which she would never, of course, do. She told only the stories she knew in her heart to be the truth. It didn't make her statements less truthful, just because events hadn't happened in this reality quite the way she knew they should have.

Like the time she told a group of kids on the playground about the fairylike creature living by the creek behind the school. She hadn't seen the fairy, but she didn't have to. She just knew it was there. She could imagine it perfectly in her head, and she described her vision to the other kids.

They liked hearing about it, too, until a couple of girls got jealous and started telling people ridiculous, untrue things about the fairy. Like saying it was blue, though she knew perfectly well it was white and yellow. When Dottie had logically told them to shut up and stop lying, they'd started a fight with her. Then the teachers butted in, and when the whole story came out, *she'd* gotten in the most trouble of anyone. They said she was "telling dangerous lies." When she tried to explain that she wasn't making it up, they punished her more.

No, she had not been lying. She was focusing on a place more real then this reality, more perfect, where things and beings existed as they should be. The fact that others couldn't, or didn't, recognize it was sad for them. That was part of what made Dottie so special, and why she knew early on what she would do with her life. She would explain the world as she knew it – as it should be. As it *is* in a reality more real than this one. And everyone would love her for that, and she would be respected and famous. And believed. That's right. Loved and believed.

Dorothea knew she had come part of the way to her goal, but she still wasn't there. She was loved by a lot of people. Her books and workshops and CDs had helped accomplish that. And people loved her for a reason. Not just for her natural warmth and empathy, but because she really did aid them in seeing their ideal selves and an ideal world. Even if they couldn't always maintain it when she wasn't around to help and support them.

But there were still many, many people she hadn't yet reached. That was why she wanted so badly for Dirk to get her on the *Ivy!* show. Then, she'd be really famous. And really respected, and even more loved, by more people. And then those nasty kids and dumb teachers, and all the other negative people like them would see her on the show or hear about her.

And they'd say to themselves, "Well, what do you know? We should have believed her. We should have listened to little Dottie Fimple after all."

6

101 North to Petaluma

Rennie made his way back to Petaluma, stopping at another bookstore, two yoga studios, and a tiny Buddhist temple. The incense was a decent business. He had to work steadily and didn't make a fortune, but was able to do what he really wanted: study, meditate, and take a break when he felt like it; to Esalen for a seminar, Tahoe for a ski weekend, or Harbin Hot Springs to soak clothing-free. And every other year he wrote off a month-long trip to India.

Besides his Bay Area customers, he worked with out-of-state distributors, and had a good mail-order clientele. Most recently he was focusing on his website, and that part of the business was growing too. He planned to hire someone to take his routes, so he would have even more time to do what he wanted. But it was a little hard letting go of the connection with his customers. He felt that the personal touch, which he gave each individual he came into contact with, was important for sales. Not to mention for the karma of his operation.

Rennie had a good life, and should have been content, but there was something in the way. While the business served its purpose, Rennie's deepest desire remained unfulfilled. What he really wanted, what he felt was his destiny, would require that he leave the incense behind altogether.

He imagined himself a well-known teacher in some aspect of spirituality or alternative personal growth practice. After reading and thinking about this stuff for years, he must know as much as any of those people writing books and leading workshops.

Once again, he mused over the question: What could be the most perfect, timely and culture-inspiring way to enter the field? To not only to lead workshops, but become famous, maybe working with celebrities, the way Marianne Williamson and that Kabbalah guy did. He wanted a line of health products like Andrew Weil, and his own deck of cards with his sayings, like all those Hay House authors. He wanted to be another Deepak Chopra. He wanted to be quoted by world leaders and presidents. Well, by the cool ones, anyway.

On the other hand, he didn't *want* to want fame and fortune for its own sake. Meditation practice and travel in India pointed him in exactly the other direction. What mattered wasn't what you achieved in the outer world, but your state of consciousness in the inner one. He'd actually had some amazing experiences in meditation, and been a part of some fantastic, worldview-altering occurrences in his travels.

He had learned a lot, but he hadn't dissolved his desires. It was confusing. If he could share all this stuff he knew and had seen, that would help other people, right? And if he got well known for his work, then he could help more people. Was it perhaps more egotistical *not* to share his spiritual accomplishments with others, and to keep it all to himself? So maybe his desire to become known as a workshop leader or spiritual teacher wasn't such a bad thing.

Of course, this was all moot unless Rennie could come up with some really new and provocative way to present his teachings – or whatever he was going to do. He didn't want to be just one of thousands of teachers doing small workshops or seeing a handful of individual clients. In that case, he'd rather stay with the incense gig, have his getaways and continue doing his own practice. He'd have more fun and make more money anyway. So why did he keep feeling it wasn't enough?

7
Marin

Michaela dropped the blue plastic bag of books, incense and flyers on a chair in the living room. She went into her studio and pulled out some sketches. But instead of working, Michaela found herself thinking about Rennie and the bookstore.

Although she'd taken the flyers out of curiosity, she couldn't imagine attending the events: Experience Your Past Life; Communicate with Animals; Connect with Your Sexual Self (Your Eco-Self, Your DNA). Spend a weekend in silent mediation. Bleah.

Of course, if she went to the workshop with Rennie, she could ask him more about the stupid radish. He had seemed rather silly at first, imagining he was on a reality show. But when he settled down, he had some helpful things to say. Still, that workshop was no more appealing than the rest. The very word "workshop" was boring. If she was spending time and money on herself, why do it on something called work? She'd rather be entertained or pampered.

She should be working now, though. She examined the design she'd started. It reminded her of every other menu she'd ever done. Funny, she hadn't felt this way when she took the project. At the time, it had seemed interesting. If she didn't know better, she'd think she was working too hard, but in fact she had been taking it pretty easy lately. That was part of what was great about her life.

In fact, most things about her life were great. And she wanted to keep it that way. She didn't want to make any changes or think about things that upset her worldview. A worldview that did not include objects that existed but couldn't be seen, heard, or felt. Or an item that was supposed to be there, but vanished. She had no desire to re-experience any former lives, if there were any, because wouldn't every past life have ended in a past death? She had no pets she wanted to contact. She didn't need help with men. Nor did she need to be greened, purified, healed, or feng shuied.

And she had never felt the urge to meditate. Why just sit, when the world was overflowing with so many things to do, there wasn't nearly time for all of them?

She had her work of course, and mostly she liked it. She had books and music and plays and movies and TV. If she liked even a small portion of the unending stream of entertainment available, she was set. There were outdoor activities, like hiking or kayaking or going to the beach. She could attend festivals every weekend and celebrate every sort of food, wine, art, music and ethnicity.

She could learn a language or take any of a thousand classes. So why on earth would she want to just sit there and do nothing? What could you expect to get out of that, except boredom? You'd have to be desperate to spend your time that way.

And that was the biggest problem with those workshops. Weren't they full of people with problems, people trying to "find" themselves? Well, that wasn't her. Michaela knew exactly who and where she was.

And yet, and yet...what about the radish? She *had* known, exactly, until the radish. Now her familiar sense of ease was gone, and she couldn't get it back. Her comfortable-fitting life had suddenly become the wrong size.

But why? The radish was lost, not her. The only problem was her obsession with it. It made no sense that the event would bother her so much. Or that she'd be stopping into new age bookstores and following people down the street like a stalker.

Okay, so maybe things had changed since the radish. But they could change back. In fact, if a little meditation would get her back to normal, then she would try it. She was willing to be bored for a short time to get to feel like herself again. Besides, meditation was supposed to be relaxing, and Michaela hadn't felt decently relaxed since Radish Day.

So where was that incense? She fetched the blue plastic bag from the seat of the tomato-red armchair and brought it into the kitchen.

She removed one long, flat, ochre cardboard packet, called Golden Deva, and another called Spiritual Guide. She figured any guidance would be helpful, even from a column of too-sweet smoke. She took out the burner, a long piece of dark polished wood. One end curved up, with a tiny hole for the stick, which hovered above the length to catch falling ash.

She then went back to the living room to the very middle of the floor. She sat, legs crossed, as she assumed she should, and put her hands.... where? What was she supposed to do with her hands? Should she use one of those odd combinations of finger positions, like the statues in the Asian Art museum? Should she circle her thumb and a finger? Which one? Up or down? She'd have to ask someone later. For now, she figured her hands would be okay just resting together in her lap.

She closed her eyes because she knew that was right. And with her eyes closed, legs crossed, hands in her lap and the initial whiff of incense tickling her nose, Michaela had the first great realization of her new meditation practice: she had absolutely no clue what she was supposed to do next.

Since the only thing that seemed worse than sitting around

doing nothing was sitting around doing nothing incorrectly, she opened her eyes, removed her hands from her lap, unfolded her legs, stood up and returned to her office and to the computer, where she knew exactly what to do. She Googled "meditation."

Like everything else Michaela had never considered before, meditation was of great interest to a large segment of the world population. And there were way more forms than she could have imagined. Some were just about what happened in the mind. Some had to do with breathing.

Also, there was a lot of merchandise – supportive, instructional and tangential. Particularly CDs. For a bunch of people who were supposed to be all spiritual, they sure sold a lot of stuff. Maybe people who meditated weren't very good at jobs and careers. So to make money, they created all this and sold it.

Micheala looked at several of the simpler sites, and figured out a few general pointers. The basics were to sit down, close your eyes, and focus on a mantra or your breathing.

She liked that some said it was okay to sit in a chair. That felt more civilized than cross-legged. If you were trying to relax and calm your mind, then why be more uncomfortable than you had to be? She could understand not lying down, because that seemed likely to turn into a nap. But why not a comfortable chair? Maybe meditation had been invented before chairs. Or maybe some people – men, most likely – decided that whoever could overcome the most discomfort while attempting to reach nirvana would be the coolest. Competitive meditation. That was probably it.

Anyway, she had the basics, which would do for now. Later, she could figure out the more complicated stuff. She'd "sit" for a set amount of time, pay attention to one thought or object – they described how to watch her breath going in and out – and observe her mind. It didn't sound hard. Anybody could do that. What's the big deal? Good. She was ready to try again. She should be experiencing some great stuff really soon.

This time Michaela settled into the tomato-red armchair, put both feet on the floor and rested her hands on her legs. The incense smell was quite noticeable now. She closed her eyes.

She opened her eyes. She should note the time. She looked at her watch, then took it off and set it down on the mission-style side table beside the chair, where she could note how much time had passed with a quick glance.

Michaela closed her eyes.

There it was. The inside of her head. Dark. Lighter patches matched the shape of the light coming through the windows. Her throat was a little dry. Should she get a glass of water and leave it next to her watch? That was stupid. She rarely drank water. She wasn't going to sit here that long anyway, just enough to see a little positive result of the meditation. Perhaps just a small, faraway glimpse of enlightenment this time, since she was just starting out.

Okay, no water. What now? Oh, right, her breath. She could visualize it coming in through her nose. She could sort of picture her face from the inside; a dark, face-shaped blob. Her nose. She had never really loved her nose. It was a little too long. She had thought of getting a nose job but hesitated to go through all that. Especially after watching *Nip/Tuck*. What disgusting things those plastic surgeons did, not to mention the surgery. She thought about one of the characters, the handsome one, Christian. He was screwed up, but had a sweet side underneath. She liked him better then the other one, Sean. Poster child for repressed anger. Now there's some one who really needed meditation. Oh shit, meditation. She was supposed to be watching her breath. Not thinking about some dumb TV show.

Breath moving in. Breath moving out. Breath moving in. How much time had gone by while she was thinking about *Nip/Tuck*? Did that count as part of the meditation, or did she have to subtract that from the total time? It was too soon to look at her watch.

She loved her watch. She bought it last year after a nice little win in Vegas. Nearly three thousand. She had made herself walk away from the craps table and had taken a taxi right over to the Forum shops. She found this Ebel Mini-Beluga in stainless steel with diamonds, for only a little more than her winnings. That had been fun. The watch was so pretty.

The watch – the time – damn! She had done it again, drifted off. Well, they said that could happen. And she'd had the good feeling from thinking about winning money, and buying the watch. That should count for something. Probably nothing like nirvana, but it was good, right? But Michaela disliked that she was having such a hard time doing this obviously simple meditation thing. There shouldn't be that much to it. Watch the damn breath, right?

Breath going in. Breath going out. Breath going in, loaded with incense smoke. The smell was getting intense. In fact, Michaela couldn't believe she just now noticed. It was really strong, way too strong. It was driving her crazy. How was she supposed to watch her breath when she could hardly breathe at all? She should really get up and put it out. But then she'd lose more time. But she couldn't stand the smell any more. It was completely distracting. She couldn't possibly continue meditating. She didn't know what to do.

Michaela disliked not knowing what to do. In fact she hated it. Now she was getting pissed off. Why was she even doing this? What was she trying to accomplish? Her life was perfect, she'd had everything the way she liked it for years, with only minor difficulties. At least it *had* been perfect, until the radish, which had started her on this whole mess.

FUUUUUUUUUUCK!!!!! Fuck that radish. Fuck it, fuck it, fuck it.

Michaela's hands flew high up into the air and came banging down as hard as they could on the arms of the tomato-red chair. Holy shit. She was losing it. This wasn't supposed to happen! She was getting further from her goals of relaxation, acceptance, and enlightenment. She was going in the wrong direction. She couldn't even do this stupid little mediation thing. She could barely focus for a single breath. What was wrong with her? She picked up her watch to see how long she had been sitting there.

Seven minutes. *Just seven minutes?* Unbelievable. Well, if this was what meditation was like, forget it. She could relax some other way.

She put her watch back on, went over to the liquor cabinet against the far wall of the room, and poured a snifterful of Remy Martin. Next she headed for the sofa – no way was she going back to that chair – sat down, and took a long sip. She sighed, leaned sideways, rested her head against the cut velvet pillow on the curved end of the couch, and put her feet up. She held the glass against her stomach. This was better. Michaela closed her eyes, thinking about how emotional she had been just a few minutes before. She still felt annoyed. And she realized that for the past several minutes, although it was still going strong, she had completely forgotten about the incense.

8
Petaluma

R ennie drove up to the little house he'd rented for the past
five years. He'd been fortunate to find this place. It was a
short drive from downtown Petaluma, on the back corner of a
large horse ranch owned by a couple he'd met at a retreat. The
house sat in a grove of trees near a creek. Summer, the creek
was nearly dry, but all through the rainy season of winter and
early spring, he could hear the water splashing as he sat on his
back deck, or from inside the house, if it was warm enough to
have the windows open.

Nearing the house, he passed the edge of a large, fenced
pasture that ended about fifty feet from his door. Six or seven
shaggy horses stood grazing or standing in pairs, nose to tail.
They were all retired, lucky enough to have owners willing to
pay for their keep indefinitely, so the animals could live out
their lives in relaxed companionship. Good karma, Rennie
thought.

The house was all he needed. The outside was robin's egg
blue with black trim. The inside was small: a sky-lighted living
room, one bedroom, a den he used as a home office, airy
kitchen, tiled bathroom, and a little laundry room on the back.

The ranch owners had their full-time maintenance person see to its upkeep.

Rennie had hung squirrel-proof bird feeders and ant-proof hummingbird feeders on the trees near his house, and diligently kept them filled. He had wind chimes up in the summer. He had created a small meditation garden not far from the house, where he sat whenever the weather allowed. It was a perfect retreat for him, peaceful and nourishing to his soul, easy to care for and a pleasure to come home to.

But he wouldn't get to enjoy his home for the next few days. This weekend was the workshop he'd signed up for several weeks ago, The LightWorks Shamanic Meditation Intensive. He was only mildly optimistic about going, but was trying it because Dorothea Light's first book wasn't bad. Plus they had more advanced training programs he could take later. If he became a LightWorks practitioner, he might be able to develop his own workshops at some point in the future.

Rennie ran his hand lightly across one of the wind chimes, and went inside to pack. In the morning, he'd be on his way.

◊ ◊ ◊

San Francisco

The LightWorks Shamanic Meditation weekend was at the Hestion hotel in downtown San Francisco. Rennie drove the hour and a quarter from Petaluma Saturday morning for the two-day workshop. He would spend the night at the hotel that evening. Since he couldn't check in until later that afternoon, he parked underground with his overnight case in the trunk, and made his way up to the hotel's main entrance. A sign in the lobby said the workshop was in the Embarcadero Ballroom, one flight up.

A middle-aged couple joined Rennie in front of the sign.

"It's in Embarcadero, Bud, like last time."

Rennie followed them to a bank of elevators.

"Sounds like this isn't your first time," Rennie said.

"Oh, no," the woman answered. "Bud and I have been to four, no, five now. We're studying to be LightWorks practitioners."

"Oh yeah? I was considering it myself," Rennie said. "I guess you must like this work."

The elevator opened, and the woman and Rennie walked off first, Bud trailing behind.

"Oh, it's great. Thea – that's Dorothea – she's amazing. A really special teacher. By the way, I'm Honey, and Bud back there's my husband." She gestured vaguely behind her. Bud reached his hand forward and Rennie shook it and introduced himself.

The couple looked to be in their late forties. Honey had lots of highlighted, honey blond hair in a puffy flip. She wore a flowing turquoise skirt and top, and black leather belt studded and buckled with turquoise and coral. Bud had on jeans and a plaid shirt, set off with a bolo tie, the clasp of which was a silver buffalo with a turquoise eye. The buckle beneath the slight overhang of his stomach was a plate of silver with yet more chunks of turquoise.

Rennie had never met this pair before, yet sensed he knew them from dozens of other workshops and retreats. There were just certain types you saw over and over again, with different permutations. This was the well-to-do couple whose kids were finally out of the house, with enough money and time on their hands for whatever leisure activity they wanted. They had developed or reconnected with an interest in alternative spirituality, and traveling from one experience to the next was their focus in life. Usually it was the wife who spearheaded the effort, but sometimes the husband was even more gung-ho.

They probably collected artwork from their travels, had a personal psychic and several bodyworkers they saw regularly at home, and when they completed this training, would offer workshops in their finished basement. Rennie rather admired this sort of couple, and how they'd found such a positive way to be together.

Much better than the ones who were married but came alone, professing personal growth, but with another agenda – one they often didn't know themselves – of connecting with an attractive person who was not their spouse. Sometimes just flirting, other times a fling, but sometimes an affair, meeting again at subsequent workshops, and going back afterwards to their partners.

This annoyed Rennie in principle, because how serious could they be about working on themselves if coming to workshops was just a way to cheat on their marriages? But it annoyed him personally even more. That made one less possible attractive female for him, a legitimately nice, single guy. And workshops were the main places he had met women over the years.

He didn't see anything wrong with that. He preferred being with someone who shared his interests. Although, most of the women he'd been with weren't as serious about the path as he was. That was probably why none had worked out, because they'd eventually shown less interest in their mutual paths and more in something conventional, like marriage.

Rennie didn't see that for himself. He needed freedom for his pursuit of spiritual advancement. So when it got to that stage, he'd break it off. But he remained hopeful he might find the right woman, maybe even a soul mate. And workshops were the best places to find her.

So when he, Honey, and Bud got to the registration desk where participants received name tags, paperwork, and a nice canvas bag with the LightWorks logo, Rennie chose the line leading to the prettier of two young females. A slim blond in her mid-twenties, she wore a short-sleeved, clingy light-green-and-white print dress with a denim vest and black leggings. Around her neck were several layers of silver chains with turquoise pendants of animal figures, and from her ears hung long silver strands with stars at the ends. As the woman in front of Rennie finished, he stepped forward, offered her a charming smile, and introduced himself. He glanced at the ID pinned above her left breast.

"Lark is a lovely name."

"Thanks," she smiled. "Welcome, Rennie. You're all set, now. Enjoy the weekend."

Not much of a conversation, but at least she was friendly. He'd try again later.

The meeting space was a typical hotel ballroom with a patterned carpet in muted colors. At least thirty-five people were inside, and he guessed another twenty would join them. On the left, chairs in semi-circle rows faced a small raised dais with a leather armchair and a small table. On either side of the dais stood a tall vase with red, lavender and purple flowers.

To the right, tables set up against the wall held merchandise for sale. In the corners were piles of pillows and boxes of tissue. Audio speakers stood on stands in the room's four corners, and two men stood by the sound system in the rear of the room, messing with the controls and talking intently.

Some people sat chatting or waiting quietly, but most stood browsing the books, DVDs, CDs, jewelry and artwork on the tables. Rennie wandered toward the nearest, hoping to overhear something interesting, but they just seemed to be talking about what music Dorothea liked these days. He handled some of the items: jewelry, silver key chains, hair ornaments and money clips embedded with the ubiquitous turquoise and coral, plus malachite, onyx, and other stones. And, of course, books and CDs by Dorothea. He'd read one, *The Light Way of Life*. Her other titles were *The Light Way to Happiness* and *Love and Light*. A large cardboard sign showing a smiling Dorothea announced that her newest book, *Living Lightly*, would be available soon, and could be pre-ordered.

Tee shirts, sweatshirts, caps and mugs rounded out the

offerings. These folks were big on marketing. There was more stuff here than at most of the workshops he went to, and sales were strong. The crowd was excited and positive, and at least half seemed to have been to previous workshops.

It was now past the time they were supposed to start. Outside the room, the lines at the registration table were gone, and only Lark remained available to welcome any latecomers. He expected Dorothea would soon make her appearance, and they would start at any moment.

◊ ◊ ◊

But Rennie was mistaken. Dorothea was not ready to make her appearance. Dorothea was twelve flights over Rennie's head, in her top floor hotel room, debating between two outfits laid out neatly on Dirk's queen-sized bed.

Her own bed was covered with stuff: laptop; nightgowns; colored pages with handwritten notes torn from legal pads; books on spiritual topics, including one of Dorothea's own; the latest issues of *Us*, *People*, and *Star* magazines; entangled necklaces, bracelets and scarves; and, at the top of the pile, an eight-inch-long, plush toy dolphin.

The two outfits were nearly identical. Each had a tunic top with three-quarter sleeves and a mid-calf length skirt in a flowing material. Both were of excellent quality and purchased the prior week at Dorothea's favorite boutique in Santa Fe. One was dark red and the other, a slightly lighter red. Either would show off the necklace she planned to wear, the vintage Yellowhorse spiderwoman squash blossom, made with as fine a turquoise as she had ever seen, the birthday gift she had made sure Dirk knew she would not be happy without.

She held the necklace in front of one outfit, then the other. But before she could choose, the song *MacArthur Park* – her ring tone for Dirk – burst out from somewhere among the stuff on her bed. Dorothea threw the magazines and nighties aside, pushed the unkempt covers around, and finally saw the phone. She glanced at the time. Oopsie.

"Darn it, Dirk, honey, what is it? Why are you calling now? I'm busy here. I have a workshop to lead, you know. Is anything wrong?"

"It certainly will be, if you don't get here in the next three minutes. Please tell me you're on the elevator."

"Of course I am, honey. Well, just about. Well, I might actually still be in the hotel room, but there's a good reason. I've been doing something absolutely crucial for the group. Just tell them I'm channeling an important message for everyone here today, and as soon as I've received it all, I'll be right down."

She turned the phone off so she couldn't hear Dirk's reply, and dropped it in her purse, a large black leather satchel sitting open on the dresser next to the TV.

"Hmmm hmmm, someone left the cake out in the rain…" Dorothea sang to herself.

She decided on the dark red outfit and slipped it on. She reached behind her neck and clasped the necklace shut, added a pair of sterling silver earrings and her favorite watch, stepped into her black and silver studded, pointy-toed clogs, and grabbed the purse.

"…I don't think that I can take it 'cause it took so long to make it…."

She pulled open the heavy hotel room door and, leaving the entire mess for the maid, strolled casually toward the elevator. It was time to focus her mind on the entrance she would make; on her first words to the flock she was about to inspire.

9
Marin

When Michaela picked up a message after working out one morning, she wasted no time returning the call. Roxanne, her sometimes partner, answered on the first ring.

"Where are you?" Roxanne asked.

"Car," Michaela answered, "coming from the gym. I actually have work to finish today."

"Slacker."

It was an ongoing joke. Roxanne was a workaholic. She envied yet insulted Michaela's lifestyle, the stretches of time off alternating with stints of intense but highly paid work.

It was due to Roxanne that Michaela started doing menus in the first place. They'd met as freshmen at UC Santa Cruz. After graduation, Roxanne joined her uncle's restaurant consulting business in San Francisco. As Roxanne began designing restaurants on her own, she brought in Michaela to do the menus. The two had become It girls for many hot new eateries.

"Unlike you, the Ryan Seacrest of restaurant consulting," Michaela replied. "What's up?"

"Nothing much. Just what's about to be the biggest foodie magnet on the planet, that's all. Not that you'd be interested."

"Who says you'd have any idea what's hot?"

"Let's see," Roxanne replied, "that would be the New York Times, Gourmet magazine, the Michelin Guide, and, oh yeah, that little plaque they gave me two years ago at the National Association of Restaurateurs convention. So basically, nobody."

"Don't worry. I'm sure your dog loves you."

"My dog chewed the strap off a four hundred dollar Michael Kors bag yesterday. My dog is in the doghouse, and probably hates me right now."

"C'est la vie de chien. So what's this place?" Michaela asked. "Wolfgang doing something on Fiji? Keller storming Paris?"

"No, it's a new guy. Two guys actually. Partners. One's the chef and one's the money man. And it's local, in the mountains outside Santa Cruz."

"Ah, the old stomping grounds."

"Yeah, right. I remember you got out there in the mountains and stomped every weekend."

"I stomped out a cigarette once," Michaela replied, "when I went for a Sunday drive with Rick what's-his-name. That guy who played lacrosse, with the great body? Does that count?"

"Does what count, stomping the cigarette or having a great body?"

"I already know the body counts. In fact, I know the body count, too. It was four that year. How about you?"

"Junior year? I don't remember."

"Yes, you do, Roxy, and so do I. It was exactly one. You were in love with him all year but you wouldn't tell me who he was."

"I don't want to talk about that. As you know."

"So you're still keeping secrets. That's okay. I'll get the story out of you some day. So what about this hottest-of-the-hot new restaurants? Is that a secret too?"

"A big secret, I hear, which is part of the interest. There's buzz but nobody knows anything definite. Just the name – *Eighth*. Not my client, though. They're doing their own interiors. Rumor is, the design's based on some temple or religious system."

"Feng Shui?" asked Michaela.

"I don't think so. It sounds even more far out, but that's all I know. But what they don't have is a menu designer. That's why they called; wanted your number. I said I'd call you myself and have you get in touch with them."

"Okay, sure. Do you really think it's such a big deal?"

"Yes! Everybody in the business has heard rumors for months but nobody knows what's true. Michaela, you've really got to go down there, check it out, and report back. They're not letting anyone see it and I want to know what's going on. I guarantee you don't want to miss being part of this one. It's going to be a big deal when they open. Reservations will be like getting into French Laundry, at least at first."

"Okay, okay, I get it. If it's that hot, I really do want the job, believe me. I'm not going to miss out on this one. Text over the name and number."

"Call me back after you talk to him. I have to know what happens."

◊ ◊ ◊

Santa Cruz Mountains

Michaela drove back and forth three times before she saw the unmarked turnoff. The address wasn't in the GPS, so she was following the directions of Celia, the person she'd reached when she called. Down 280, across 17, then following increasingly smaller roads. She would have enjoyed the drive if she had been more relaxed, but after Roxanne's buildup, she was feeling pressure to get the gig. Normally she wouldn't worry, but her conversation with Celia gave Michaela the impression that these owners might be a little weird, and that made her tense.

The turnoff was gravel and wound a long way through Douglas firs and live oaks, and even a small stand of redwoods. Finally, she turned a wide corner and drove into a clearing surrounded by more big trees. Michaela could see an unfinished building. The three-story wood and stucco structure had a large dark wood deck extending around the outside, as well as balconies on the two higher levels. Even though the building was still a worksite, long strands of small, colorful flags ran horizontally along the sides of the top two floors.

Further back and to the left through some trees, was a second, smaller, structure in the same style. It, too, had those colored flags running up the sides. To Michaela's immediate right was a white construction trailer. An air conditioning unit on the side hummed loudly.

All around was exposed, uneven reddish dirt covered with wheelbarrows, lumber and piles of pipes. A dirt area to the left held a randomly parked assortment of pickup trucks and dusty cars, with one clean and shiny, low, exotic, yellow number. Hmm, a Maserati.

Michaela tried the trailer first. Celia had said that Michaela would meet with Angelo. When there was no response, Michaela pounded harder, in case they couldn't hear her over the air conditioning.

Finally, she gave up, backtracked down the steps, and followed the path to the larger building. Angelo must be in there. Someone certainly was, based on the banging she now heard. She climbed a stairway to the porch, where a short ramp served as a temporary threshold. She pulled open one of two very tall, wooden doors by its handle, a metal hoop larger than her head. Despite windows and lights, the inside was darker than the bright day behind her. As her eyes adjusted, Michaela took in the unusual room.

The space was open, with the floor divided into three tiers, each encircling the room and each two steps lower than the one surrounding it. She stood on the top tier, looking down. Below the third, innermost tier was an open center, like a sunken stage, about fourteen feet across. Each tier was wide enough to hold tables of four.

To the left of where she stood, two men were installing pieces of stone flooring. Both looked up.

"Angelo?" she asked them. The man on the left pointed toward the far end of the room, lingered on her a beat, then went back to work.

Following his gesture, Michaela saw a wide doorway leading to another room, where more people were working. She followed the top tier around to her right, on the unfinished concrete floor.

Michaela had been around restaurants in construction and recognized this space as the kitchen. But she had never seen a crew quite like this one. A dozen men and a few women were finishing walls, doing electrical work, and coming and going with materials. About half of them looked like guys you'd see on any construction site: in jeans, work boots, and bandannas or baseball caps. The other half all had shaved heads and wore robes of reddish cloth wrapped around their bodies toga-style and draped like scarves over their left shoulders and down the front.

In the center, three men stood talking, one in jeans, one in robes, plus a third man, wearing a casual but well-cut jacket and tie. He was attractive, if a little severe looking, with longish blond hair combed straight back, and very blue eyes. He was speaking and gesturing to the other two as Michaela came in, but when he saw her, he stopped mid-sentence and raised his hand to pause the conversation.

"Excuse me, please, gentlemen. Let's continue this later. I shall need to speak with this lady for a bit, and then I will return. Thank you." He gave a slight bow, returned by the man in robes. Robes and Jeans resumed talking, while Suit walked briskly toward Michaela. He extended his hand and Michaela shook it.

"You are the menu designer, yes?"

"Yes, I'm Michaela Thomason. Are you Angelo? I'm sorry, I wasn't told your last name."

"Yes, of course," he replied, not correcting the omission. "Let's go outside, shall we? It's a lovely day and it will be quieter there. I'll tell you everything you need to know about our project, and you can tell me all about yourself."

He pointed toward the back of the building, and touched Michaela's elbow.

She allowed him to guide her out a back door and down another path. A short distance from the construction area, the ground returned to normal. He gestured for her to continue through some tall trees to a small clearing, where two concrete benches sat close together at an angle, a small table in front of them. Michaela heard a stream nearby. Angelo motioned her toward one bench and sat down at the other.

"Thank you for coming. I'd like to tell you about our vision, but first I have to ask you to sign a non-disclosure agreement. Is that a problem?"

Michaela wasn't surprised. She had been asked to do this before, and from what she'd heard, expected the secrecy.

"Not at all," she said.

Angelo pulled a neatly folded paper and pen from his inside coat pocket, and handed it to Michaela. She glanced at the page, signed it by resting the paper against her skirt-clad thigh, and handed it back. Angelo appeared to be staring into the trees but when she held out the paper, he took it immediately.

"Thank you," he said, refolding and returning it to his pocket. "Now. I assume you've heard very little about our project, and so I will tell you what you need to know. Obviously, it is, in the most obvious and basic sense, a restaurant."

Michaela nodded politely.

"However that is not all it is. Or I should say, we are going beyond merely that, and attempting to express the highest form of restaurant consciousness. The archetype, that is, the ultimate soul of restaurant being-ness, if you will. I'm sure that, considering your success in menu design, you must know what I mean."

When Angelo spoke, he gestured generously with his hands, floating them about in the air. His eyes, too, looked up, as if he could see whatever higher-this and conscious-that he was talking about. Now he paused to look directly at Michaela, so she was forced to nod, yes, she knew what he meant, even though she didn't have the first clue. She hoped he would talk awhile longer. That would help her figure out what he wanted to hear, so she could tell him precisely that. This approach nearly always worked.

"My partner, Jozef, and I connected because we are both spiritual seekers. Separately, we each traveled the world to many sacred places, searching out the most highly evolved sects and sacred lineages all over the globe. But we never met.

"For instance, when I visited a tiny mountain village in Peru, talking to the last in a line of powerful shamans, I was told that another man 'with my voice' had been there the year before. When he went to the sacred Burya lands in Siberia they told him another seeker had just left. We later realized our boats had probably passed each other.

"When we finally did connect, we found that we had meditated at the same Ashrams in India, had audiences with the Dalai Lama a week apart, and many more barely-missed meetings.

"Then, finally, two years ago in Italy, we were in the same temporal and spacial planetary locus. This occurred, not surprisingly, at Damanhur. Do you know of it?"

Michaela shook her head. Damming-her? She'd never heard the word.

"Fantastic, fantastic place. You must go there; the energy is unbelievable. It has been a tremendous inspiration to us. The underground temples are magnificent. Well, Jozef and I met in that heightened vibration and soon realized we were on the same path, not just physically but literally. We had the same vision. You see, he is an elite chef, and I am a businessman who has always wanted to open restaurants. It's quite a long story, with many synchronicities, but you don't need to know all that now.

"Only that what we are doing here is more than just opening a restaurant, you see? Everything is planned with the purpose of spiritual awakening. The architecture, the materials, the intention. And the food – of course, the food. What we take in to our bodies has to be sacred. Every person who works here has been blessed by our Tibetan monks, in addition to whatever personal practices they are also involved with. We don't care what form their practice takes. Even traditional religion is fine, if they truly practice. But they must have one, you see, in order to work here. Consciousness is paramount in all things related to the project."

Angelo paused in his waving around and looked at her again. Michaela was trying to maintain an accepting expression, but it all sounded ridiculous. What difference could it possibly make to have the guy installing the low-flow toilet blessed by some other guy in a red sheet? She supposed she'd have to get a prayer said over her when she started working for them. Maybe she'd see the entire menu in a vision and wouldn't have to work very hard.

"Well that sounds interesting," she said, but Angelo was gazing past her, as they heard someone coming through the trees.

Michaela turned to look, and an instant later a tall, thin person wearing all black emerged into the clearing.

"Ah!" said Angelo, "Jozef! You made it! Very good."

To Michaela, Jozef did not look like a typical chef. Many chefs were, if not fat, then at least rather pudgy, as you'd expect from someone whose entire life revolves around food. Jozef looked like an explosion on a stick. He was tall and thin; not fragile looking but not wiry either, and his curly black hair pointed out in every direction like a headful of exclamation marks.

"Jozef, here is Michaela," was all Angelo said, as if she was an item being presented instead of a person being introduced.

Michaela stood up, said hello, and put out her hand anyway, which Jozef took, but didn't shake. He held it and stared right at her. Disconcerting. This person was not only the oddest chef she had ever met, but one of the most peculiar human beings.

After looking directly in her eyes for a good ten seconds, which caused Michaela to shuffle her feet and peer off into the woods, he finally gave a muted smile and said, "Okay, then," let her hand go, and walked around Michaela to sit next to Angelo. Michaela sat back down as well. They were strange alright, just as she'd expected. But she could put up with them in order to have her name linked to this project. Now she just had to make sure they hired her.

Angelo said, "I was just telling Michaela about our vision." He turned to Michaela, "You see, my dear, what Jozef and I are doing here will take food to a new level. It will be like nothing ever felt or experienced before in a restaurant."

"Organic?" Michaela asked. "Local? Vegan?"

"Well, the first two as much as possible, yes. But not vegan. Not even vegetarian. You see, my dear, we honor and serve all life forms."

Michaela thought there was something odd about that last statement, but he went on so fast she didn't have a chance to figure out what.

"The focus is entirely different from just organic and local. That approach is admirable but not original. Our orientation is quite unique."

Michaela wondered about that. After all, there was only so much you could do to make a restaurant different, unless you were trendy to the point of ridiculousness. Not that it wasn't done. She'd eaten meals where everything served was made of infused foams. And what about that place in London – there was one in San Francisco now too, but Michaela hadn't been there – that featured main dishes made mostly of offal. And in-house charcuteries, once unheard of, were now everywhere. To be truly original, it would have to be an entirely new concept; something that neither she nor anyone else had ever heard of.

Now it was Jozef's turn. He leaned toward Michaela and again stared at her for several seconds before he began talking.

"Everything created at Eighth will be of the highest spiritual significance. We call it the Empyrean Food movement. Yes, as Angelo said – it is beyond fresh, beyond local, beyond organic, beyond merely sustainably grown and raised. All of that, yes. But more.

"For example, our produce. It is grown on small farms, most within 30 miles of here, using water purified by Peruvian shamans. We fly the Shamans in on private planes with barrels of water from a pure spring at the top of the Andes, and they sprinkle it over the fields, raising the consciousness of the local water and soil of which it becomes a part.

"Our fish and shellfish are hand selected by members of an ancient order of Christian fishing monks originally from North Africa. The monks go out with the local boats and, while the fish are still alive, commune with their spirits to determine those of the highest quality of beingness. Those and only those fish are selected for Eighth, and they receive prayers all the way back to the shore, where they are immediately brought to the restaurant. The shellfish is selected from purveyors in a similar fashion.

"Our meat and poultry come from animals raised on nearby ranches, where we've installed pasture with sod sent from Canada. The grass they eat was not only grazed upon first by a sacred white buffalo, but then traditional purification ceremonies were performed on it by Native American Healers. They are butchered in a manner similar to, but even more ancient and sacred than, kosher, with methods interpreted from little-known pre-biblical scrolls.

"We serve teas grown by Buddhists at monasteries on the four sacred mountains of China. Our goji berries are not only pure Tibetan – I can't reveal exactly from where or people might die – but I can tell you they are hand-picked by reincarnated lamas under the age of twelve. We have procured Finnish cloudberries from plants Sami shamans have chanted over for hundreds of thousands of years.

"And our wines…"

"Biodynamics?" Michaela interrupted hopefully. At last she could score some points. She had once attended a wine seminar where they talked about this biodynamic thing, a growing method based on some old German guy's spiritual system. All she remembered was that you put stuff in cow horns and deer bladders and planted it in the soil. There was also something about crystals and the moon. She was certain that would hold great attraction for Angelo and Jozef.

Instead, Jozef waved his hand in a gesture of dismissal and Angelo looked away.

"Puh!" Jozef exclaimed. "Steiner! No, we do not think the biodynamic system goes far enough. I don't suppose you are familiar with the exchange program between a particular mob of Australian Aboriginal people and a small faction of California winegrowers?"

Michaela dumbly shook her head.

"Well let's just say, the vines report they are very grateful to have the Aboriginals to talk to, and are expressing it in their fruit. The wines produced from those vineyards are extraordinary. And some of them will be exclusive to Eighth."

"Those are a few examples, but there is much more. I can't reveal all our plans now, but know that each item used in the meals we serve, as well as the people working with us in every capacity, and all building materials, everything – it is all with the purpose of bringing our patrons to the highest spiritual awareness."

At this point, Jozef wound down and Angelo leaned forward to add, "Of course, the special arrangements we make to ensure the spirituality of each element and ingredient cost a tremendous amount. So eating here will be extremely expensive. But we believe people will feel that their souls are truly being nourished, as well as their bodies, and find it easily worth the price. And Jozef creates transcendent *tasting* food, too, of course, so the meals will be exquisite."

Michaela was astounded. She'd heard of extreme restaurant concepts before – one of her early jobs was for the Skinny's carryout chain, and their focal menu item was Fried Chicken Skins – but this just seemed crazy. But Roxanne had proclaimed it the hottest new opening in ten years, and Roxanne was seldom mistaken. So Michaela figured it could be just weird enough, pricey enough, and exclusive enough to take off, especially among extreme foodies and celebrities. Once word got out *those* people were coming, despite economic fluctuations, the wealthiest of every nationality wouldn't be far behind. Then, second string foodies and wannabes everywhere would be calling for that hard-to-get table and bragging to their friends about how great the meal was, and how much money they spent to eat it.

Which was why she really Really REALLY wanted all those people looking at HER choice of materials, fonts, spacing, and color on the menu. It was a part of, and just as important as, any other element: the architecture, décor, appearance of the servers, attitude of the host or hostess, the tableware, and every other detail. Maybe more important.

Diners enter a restaurant and can gaze around the room and appreciate the decor, or not. Their eyes may be drawn to the attractive rear of the host or hostess, or they can choose not to look. But there is no doubt that after they sit down, the one thing they will surely be ogling is the menu.

Jozef leaned forward. "So now you know something of us and this restaurant," he said. "What about you? Tell us. You do work with a muse, of course, don't you?"

"Well, yes, Joz-*ef*," she answered, careful to put the emphasis on the second syllable of his name, as Angelo had. "I can make the menu as amusing as you like. Part of it's in the way it's worded, and I can help with that too, of course, but mostly I do the visuals. But sure, I can make it amuse, if that's what you're after."

He looked disgusted. "No, no. You misunderstand. I said a MUSE, not amuse."

"Ah, I, ah…." Michaela had no clue what he was trying to say. Amuse or not amuse – was that a question?

Now Angelo spoke up. "Dear girl, we want to know how you create! What inspires you. We simply want to know what type of muse you work with."

Were they really saying muse? Wasn't that some sort of Greek goddess? Or maybe it was some new computer program. Whatever it was, it sounded like they really wanted her to have one. But if she said yes, and they asked her to elaborate, she wouldn't be able to, which would make her look foolish. Then they wouldn't hire her, and that was unthinkable.

Michaela needed to get this meeting back on track, her way. She knew who she was – one of the top menu designers in the country. And, unlike some artists, she was also good at the sales part of her profession. She knew how to give the client what he wanted, no matter how unusual, and she knew how to close the deal. She would take control and get this job.

"Why don't I show you some of my work, and its results? I think when you see the combination of outstanding design and effective marketing, you'll get a better idea what I can do for Eighth."

She opened her portfolio and took out several of her most successful menus and a graph showing sales of restaurants she had worked with in the last three years. When she had not been there from the opening, the chart also showed percentage of sales improvement following the use of her menu. A separate page had testimonials with names they would surely have heard of, at least Jozef. She laid out the menus, placing the graph and testimonials next to them.

Angelo picked up a menu and said, "Yes, it's very nice." He glanced at another. "I noticed this when I ate there last year. Very attractive." He briefly looked at the chart and the praises.

Jozef stared into the trees.

"Thank you," Michaela told Angelo. "I'm sure you'll be thrilled with what I can do for you. The design will align entirely with your vision for the concept and interiors. I can send you prototypes in a week."

It's working, Michaela thought. He can see I'd be perfect.

"My dear, it is obvious you do excellent work. But I knew that before you came here. What I'm interested in is your essence, your spirit. Everything about Eighth has to move the patron toward higher consciousness. You can't do that if you aren't doing so yourself. Your work as a menu designer must transcend the physical plane. Can you do that? What I really must know is, what about your spiritual life, your practice?"

Was he nuts? What practice? What spiritual life? Michaela had not been raised with much religion. She seldom went to church. She didn't care about that stuff. And what did that have to do with this muse business? Why couldn't he just let her create a menu that would simply support people in ordering his mystical appetizers and transcendent desserts, so he could stay in business? What did her spiritual life have to do with that?

But she had to answer, even if it meant bluffing. Michaela struggled to remember some of the titles she'd seen in the bookstore last week, and what she had read online about meditation. There had to be something she make could use of.

"Well," Michaela stated, "for one thing, I exercise my aura

every day. And I follow the, uh, you know, that book, *The Roll of the Shar-min*."

(Was she saying that correctly? Like the toilet paper?)

"And once a month I cleanse my crystals in the ocean and say mantras. Only at the full moon, of course. The incense I use is called Spirit Guide. And I'm trying to find a good ash-ram to visit."

(Another difficult pronunciation, but hopefully she got it right. It sure looked like it rhymed with trash can.)

Michaela wondered if she'd said enough. Then she threw in a final tidbit, since it happened to be true.

"And I do Pilates, which is actually better than yoga in some ways. I'm very flexible."

Angelo was silent for a moment, and Michaela thought perhaps she'd convinced him. Finally he spoke.

"Dear one," he said in a slower, more patient tone. "Just one more thing. Can you tell me about your recent and current transits?"

"Um, sure," she answered, hesitating. Once again she had to wing it. Did he mean transportation? He probably wanted to be sure her perspective was worldly enough.

"I mostly go between San Francisco and L.A. or Vegas, but I've been to most of the big U.S. cities – New York, Dallas, D.C., Chicago, Seattle, New Orleans – and I do go to Europe every couple of years. Mexico, Hawaii. Once to Australia; just Sydney and Melbourne, but I hope to go back."

Jozef was wincing and Angelo now looking positively sorry for her. Really, how rude! So what if she hadn't been to more places. She'd been busy. Okay, so she probably should have gotten to Asia by now, at least Japan. And South America. But you can't do everything. And how did that matter to her design work anyway?

Angelo spoke really slowly, as if she was an idiot or a child.

"My dear, I was asking about your astrological transits, not your travels. But never mind. I don't think it will matter anyway."

He looked at Jozef, who gave the slightest movement of his head, and Angelo nodded in reply.

"We do thank you for coming. As we've said, your work is excellent, and you have the blessings of all the best restaurants. However we don't think it's going to work out. We are looking for someone more in tune with our consciousness and vision."

Michaela did not believe she was hearing this. She couldn't remember the last time she was turned down for a job. All the big-name chefs worked with her. They knew she was the best. And these upstart jacklegs didn't get it! A hot new restaurant without the M.T. signature on the menu was ... unthinkable. It was unimaginable to Michaela that she'd miss out on this one.

For the first time in her life, Michaela actually sputtered. "But I... but I...ah...ah.... That's not... I mean, I would..." She stopped, breathed deeply, and pulled her words back together carefully. Both men were staring at her.

"Listen. I promise you, I will do this design to suit the visions of your consciousnesses. That's what I do. You can see from these examples that each one is unique. Each one expresses the restaurant it represents."

Angelo spoke again. "My dear, the issue is not what you do. Based on your work, we would love to hire you. That's not the issue. But, unfortunately, you are not in touch with your true self. You are not seeking higher awareness, or mindfulness in any way."

Michaela finally blurted out, "What does that have to do with anything! If you like my work, I just don't get what's the problem. I promise you, I'm not hard to get along with."

Jozef gave the final verdict. "The problem is simply this. Everything about our restaurant is spiritual. And you are not."

10

Santa Cruz Mountains

W ith a tight throat and holding back tears, Michaela
gathered her materials and put them in her bag as
quickly as she could.

She stood up. "Well, excuse me then. I should go."

And, without looking at either man again, she rushed out
of the clearing, through the trees, around the side of the
restaurant-in-progress, and through the parked cars.

She didn't hear or see the yellow Maserati spring to life, and
nearly ran in front of it, just as it started to move. The car
grazed her and she sprang back, though she wasn't hurt. It
squealed to a stop, and out sprang a maroon-robed Tibetan
monk, followed immediately by another, then another, until
there were six of them. It wasn't quite as impressive as clowns
coming out of a VW bug, but she did wonder how all those
good-sized men had managed to fit themselves into the car.

"Oh, my dear, we are so very sorry. We didn't see you. Are
you all right? Do you want to sit down?"

She was soon surrounded by monks, and they seemed so
worried about her safety, and so full of concern and kindness
that, even though she was physically okay, she actually burst
into tears. This was unbelievable to Michaela. She couldn't

remember the last time she cried. And in public? It was the most bizarre thing to happen yet, in this bizarre place on this bizarre day, in this completely bizarre month she was having. Nothing was how it was supposed to be.

One of the monks sat her down sideways on the passenger side of their car, with her legs leaning against the open door, and another said he would get some tea, and ran off. A third produced a clean, folded handkerchief and handed it to Michaela. She made a huge, painful effort to stop crying, and used the handkerchief to wipe her eyes and nose.

"Really, I'm fine," she said, aware that statement was false. "I mean, I'm not hurt in any way. The car barely touched me."

"Oh, well, it won't hurt to sit and drink tea for a few minutes. We don't have to hurry off anywhere. Do you?"

Michaela thought, for not being in a hurry, they were driving a really fast car. An un-monk-like car, too, in her opinion.

She was embarrassed about crying, and would just as soon have been on her way. But she also didn't want to be rude to these surprisingly kind and down-to-earth monks. She just hoped Angelo or Jozef didn't come by while she was still here. She did not wish to talk to either of them again, unless they wanted to apologize, and ask her to do their menus. Not likely.

The Tibetans introduced themselves: Gyaltso (the oldest), Darjay (the youngest, and driver), Pabu (handkerchief), Sangmu (just getting back with the tea), Karma, and Pasang.

"I'm Michaela," she said, accepting the warm mug, a napkin, and a chocolate shortbread cookie. She looked up and realized Sangmu was a woman. With her identical robes and nearly shaven head, Michaela hadn't noticed at first. Michaela looked more closely at the others, and saw that at least one was also female, either Karma or Pasang. She wasn't sure which was which.

The tea was pleasantly fragrant and warm, but not too hot to drink, and as Michaela sipped it, she did feel better. In fact, she felt cared for in a way she hadn't in a long time. The thought made her teary again. She touched the corners of her eyes with the handkerchief as the six monks stood around her, smiling and nodding, one patting her on the shoulder.

They seemed in absolutely no hurry to leave, and indeed, Michaela felt she could sit there forever. She had the impulse to ask the monks where they were going, so she could follow them in her car and spend more time with them. But that would be crazy.

Finally, she finished the last sip of tea and crumb of cookie. She wiped her hands on the napkin, and reluctantly said, "Well, that's it then. I guess I should roll. Thank you for the, um, tea and everything. You've been really nice."

Gyaltso, the oldest monk and the only one who hadn't talked so far, now leaned over and patted Michaela's hand.

"Do you have a prayer wheel?" he asked.

"Um, no," Michaela said, once again in the dark as to what someone was talking about. At least these were monks. They were supposed to talk about prayers and stuff. She glanced at the wheels of the yellow car but they didn't seem unusual. Maybe the prayers were inside.

When she looked up, Gyutsu was gesturing with his hands, making a circling motion one around the other.

"I think you would like to have one. You can find them on the Internet, not too expensive. Spin the wheel, speak the words Om Mani Padme Hum. I think you would like doing that."

"Um. Okay." A prayer wheel. Om Mani Padme Hum. Michaela had heard that phrase somewhere before, and thought she could remember it.

"Come back and have tea with us next month," Gyaltso said.

"Okay," Michaela said again, without really thinking about it. She stood up and each of the monks smiled and shook her hand. Sangmu took the empty teacup from Michaela. As she walked to her car, they all squeezed back into their tiny yellow one, and with a roar and a squeal, took off down the driveway.

Michaela managed to get into her own car and start it. She drove off in their dust at a much slower pace, and wondered what on earth she was going to do with herself now.

11

San Francisco

D orothea was being truthful when she said she was
channeling a message. Well, mostly truthful. It was just
that the event had taken place earlier that morning, when she
was doing her own version of daily meditation, and not when
Dirk called.

While Dorothea would sometimes meditate the
conventional way, more often her form of meditation took
place when she just woke up, and was still in her bed. Although
it would appear from the outside that she was just lying there,
it was not that at all. Since she hadn't entered everyday waking
consciousness yet, she was more able to go into a receptive non-
ordinary state. And that way, she could do it nearly every day.
If she had to set aside a special time, place, position, and plan
for the whole thing, it was just too darn hard to get around to.

So while she was "meditating" after awakening in the queen
bed of her hotel room, Dorothea had channeled some new
information that she knew she was supposed to teach to the
group this morning. Receiving channeled information was not
at all unusual for Dorothea. It happened anywhere from a
couple of times a month to several times a week. Some of it
seemed rather mundane, for instance she'd get a flash of what

she should eat that day, or somehow just know that she should soak in their spa for an hour before attempting to do anything else.

But sometimes she got important teachings that she needed to write down to share with the world. The messages could come from different sources, such as past spiritual leaders and historical figures; enlightened masters of various degrees (some of whom had lived previous lives on earth and some who hadn't), nature and animal spirits; and other essences she couldn't quite identify. It wasn't one of those "I see dead people" things. She didn't have to deal with ghosts or anything like that, thank heavens.

So as Dorothea made her way downstairs in the elevator, she was thinking about what time during the morning to give the new teaching – right away, or after she'd presented the material that was already planned for that day. She'd probably do what she usually did; just start with what she had planned, then see where the flow took her over the course of the morning. She had a few things to cover this morning, before the afternoon practices began. The rest of the time she could just let the teaching flow out of her however spirit wanted it to.

As Dorothea entered the ballroom, she saw Dirk on the riser facing the group. It was merely ten past ten, which Dorothea considered practically early, but Dirk felt it was important to start at the scheduled time. So if she wasn't there yet, he would call them to their seats and tell a few jokes, usually about her being late, which was annoying. But at least, then, all she had to do was walk up to the riser and start talking.

"Good morning, everyone," she started out. "How are you this morning? Ready for a wonderful weekend?"

Nods and smiles, a few people clapped.

"Good, good. It's so good to see you all here today, and we're going to have a very special time together this weekend. We'll talk more about that in a bit."

Without deciding to, Dorothea changed the plan. She would give them the new stuff first.

"But before we do that, I'm going to start by telling you about the message I got this morning, when I was tuning in to universal energies."

Dorothea looked around as she spoke. Quite a few new people. Good. Some familiar faces, too, though she didn't recall many names. It wasn't her fault that she was bad with names, because she remembered their souls instead, which was obviously much more important. To compensate, she relied on affectionate nicknames, like "hon," a lot. Most people responded well to that.

"The non-human energies want me to share this message with you. It's very important. It's about why we're all here. The message is about transportation."

Somebody laughed. A new guy, about halfway back. Dorothea started to be bothered by it, but she quickly took a mental breath and let it go. He wasn't in tune with her beingness yet, that's all. It wasn't personal.

"Now, y'all know that we all need transportation. We need to be transported, right? Not our bodies, we're pretty good at managing that, aren't we? We get around pretty well. Y'all got here, didn't you? Well, this message was about that other kind of transport – bliss, ecstasy, and all that. Folks, we all need to have bliss in our lives. We need a lot of bliss.

"Let me give you an example. We transport ourselves just walking places, right? But how often, when we're walking around, getting from one place to another, do we say to ourselves, "I'm transporting"? Well we should. We should say it every time. Because if you don't know – if you aren't fully aware – that you're transporting, then you aren't really being a transporter. You're just going from place to place, without even knowing it. And if you aren't a transporter, then what are you? Well, then you'll find yourself being just a reporter. Just reporting on things, not allowing yourself to merge with them as they happen. See what I mean?"

Dorothea paused and beamed at the audience.

"Well that's it. That's what they told me to tell you. You got that? Well good, everyone. Now, I'll tell you what. Let's do a little transporting right this minute. Let's take a journey. Why don't you settle in and get comfortable and we'll get started on the first exercise. Just one more thing I need to tell you before we begin. Listen up, now, this is important. When you begin to wonder where your life path is leading you, remember this." She paused and looked around the room, building the anticipation.

Then said slowly and with great feeling, "A journey of a thousand miles...begins by sitting down."

◊ ◊ ◊

Rennie stifled another laugh. So far he was not overly impressed with Dorothea Light. To be honest, she seemed a little flaky. Rennie did not need to spend his time with flaky. He had been around the real thing enough to know the difference. However, Rennie also knew that it he could still get something positive out of the workshop, something he might not expect. Even the not-so-great teachers had their moments when truth and meaning peeked through. Or at the very least, he could learn what not to do at his own seminars.

So when Dorothea began the intro to her guided meditation, he closed his eyes and followed along if he were listening to the wisest guru on the planet. Soft, trance-inducing music came through the speakers. Dorothea's voice was amplified above it so she could be heard clearly.

"Okay, now, everyone. You know you are perfectly safe here. You can relax your body completely." She began going through a physical and mental relaxation that Rennie knew was to allow them to let go and sink into a deeper state of awareness.

While he could hear Dorothea's words, at the same time Rennie was already deeply focused on his inner landscape. As an experienced meditator, it was easy for him to drop into this state of consciousness. He became much less aware of the world outside himself – even sometimes of his own body, if he was deep enough – and highly focused on this universe within. It was so natural for him to focus inward, he found it a little distracting to stay with Dorothea's words. But he reminded himself that he had come to this workshop to experience her particular teaching, so he would do his best to go with the program and see how it worked out.

"With your body relaxed, observe your thoughts and feelings, and see if you can sense a direction they're going. Up, down, to the side. It's even okay if there's no direction, or if they go all over the place. (Pause.) Now, just see if you can follow your mind, like having a dog on a leash pull you wherever it wants to go…"

Dog on a leash, thought Rennie. He'd never heard someone do an imagery like that before. He nearly laughed. He again reminded himself, *stay with it…*

His mind wanted to go down and to the right. He followed it…

"Keep going in that direction… it's taking you somewhere… (Pause.) Now look for a place … it could be someplace you recognize or someplace new to you…"

With his inner eye, Rennie looked. It was dark – nighttime. Small buildings. He was in a village …

"Explore your place. Is there anything in it? Is it nature? Something else? (Pause.) Any structures? (Pause.) Are there beings there? People or animals or any other kind of … other beings?"

There were small houses in Rennie's village. Almost like huts. The houses were white with plain square windows and thatched roofs. Fig trees. There were people here, he was aware of that. He also sensed they were asleep. Just outside the huts he glimpsed a larger building, bright blue. To the right of that, he saw smoke, went toward it...

"Continue your journey and see what happens... (Pause.) I'm going to leave you in your place now... keep exploring... (Pause.) Whatever happens, be open to it..."

Dorothea's voice trailed off, leaving just the soft music, but Rennie wasn't paying attention to outside sounds at all anymore. He was moving around his village. He was going toward the smoke.

He saw several people standing by a fire. Thin brown people in white clothes, some in turbans. Ah! India. But this was not somewhere he had been before; nothing he recognized. A man turned to him. This was a very old man, Rennie thought. He was the oldest looking person Rennie had ever seen, even in India, where you could be fooled because some people looked a lot older than they were and some a lot younger.

The man looked right at Rennie and seemed pleased. He made a welcoming gesture. The other three appeared younger. Two of them, an adolescent and a middle-aged man, stood on the other side of the fire, and the third, grandmotherly, was with the old man on the side nearer to Rennie.

Rennie went up close to them. The smoke was coming from both a small fire and from the pot hanging above it on a metal tripod. Black smoke came from the pot in a thin line straight upward into the sky, while grayer smoke from the fire danced around it. It was quite beautiful.

Now the old woman handed a wooden bowl to Rennie. He eagerly looked down, but it was empty. The middle-aged man lifted the lid off the pot and began stirring. The boy leaned over and peered in.

"Are you ready?" the woman asked Rennie. The middle-aged man put a cup into the pot. He came around the fire and held the cup over Rennie's bowl. Rennie thought it must be food of some kind, although the smell was wrong. Metallic. When the man turned the cup over, a thin stream that looked like molten gold poured into Rennie's bowl.

The old man had a faint smile and his eyes were bright. Rennie hoped he would say something.

"Is everyone ready?" It was Dorothea's voice instead, intruding itself out of nowhere into Rennie's inner journey.

No! He was not ready. He did not want to come back yet. He wanted to know more about what he'd seen, especially the gold, and these people. He felt there was something very important about the experience he was having, and he didn't know what it was yet. He needed to stay longer. He tried to tune back in on the scene but it was leaving him, he was losing focus...

"All right everybody, start to come back from wherever you are..."

Rennie was irritated at the interruption, and that emotion brought him fully back into his body and into the room. He lost connection with the scene entirely. He was very frustrated.

"Good, good, how's everyone doing, then? Don't answer me, we're going to do the next exercise right away, which is a journaling session. If you didn't bring a journal, don't worry, we have paper and pens and art materials around the room."

Rennie looked around and saw that most people were "back," and reaching around or into their bags for journals and pens. One woman sobbed loudly, and another woman, one of the staff, put an arm around her and began helping her over to the corner, dragging a pillow and blanket behind them. When they reached the corner, the crying woman sat on the pillow and the helper put the blanket around her while she cried. The helper handed her tissues one at a time.

Rennie was still frustrated, but he attempted to set the feeling aside while he did the journaling exercise. He had brought, as per instructions from the confirmation letter, a new blank notebook, a pen, and some colored pencils, all of which he pulled out of his messenger bag and placed next to him. The journal was a black composition book with unlined paper, so he could either write or draw.

"Okay, when you're ready, use any combination of words and pictures to say whatever you want about your inner journey. You can describe or make a drawing of what you saw to help you remember, or you can use words or images to express your feelings, or you can use the journaling to explore more about what you experienced."

Right, Rennie thought, and if she hadn't stopped them so soon, he would have actually experienced more of what he was experiencing while he was experiencing it, rather than have to imagine what might have happened next. He wondered if anyone else in the group felt the same way. He looked around but no one else seemed disgruntled.

So Rennie obediently sketched his images of the white huts and the fig trees, the smoke, and the people standing by the fire. He did another drawing of the woman holding out the bowl to him, and a close-up of the liquid gold pouring into it from the cup. Lying near him was a gold-inked marker, so he used it to add the real gold color. On the pages following the artwork, he wrote about what happened in as much detail as he could, ending with the remark, "ENDED TOO SOON! WANTED MORE!!!" which helped ease his frustration a bit, but not entirely.

As people finished journaling, they drifted out of the room a few at a time to go to lunch, after which they would regroup for another session in the afternoon. When Rennie looked up from his journal, he realized he was one of the last to leave.

Lunch was included in the workshop. It was in another meeting room on a different floor. After a stop at the bathroom, Rennie wandered around until he found the Potrero room, where workshop participants sat at six large circular tables covered with white tablecloths. The wait staff were serving salads to those present, and there was a lively level of conversation in the room.

Rennie first looked for the pretty girl from the registration desk, but her table was completely filled, as were most of the others. The one in the farthest back corner had only a couple of people at it. He sat down and introduced himself. Two large women who apparently knew each other were discussing a recent trip to New Mexico, where they had visited some of the Pueblos. They introduced themselves as Margaret and Marguerite. Rennie had been to New Mexico, although not for several years, so he peripherally included himself in the discussion with a comment or two, then focused on his Caesar salad.

He had taken only a couple of bites when Dorothea and a small entourage entered and looked around, just as Rennie had done a few minutes before. They were heading toward his table. The entourage consisted of Dirk and two other staff members who had been introduced early in the workshop. Foxton, a tall man with a dark mustache, and Genevieve, a sweet looking blond, both in their forties.

When Dorothea placed herself next to Rennie, with the other three arrayed next to her, the two women sitting across from Rennie simpered, smiled, resettled and fluffed themselves like a couple of chickens when the rooster enters the henhouse.

Dorothea gave a big smile. "Well hello, hon," she said in their general direction. "How's the workshop going for you so far?"

While the two women related how much they had gotten out of the morning, the three remaining chairs at their table were quickly filled by people moving from nearby seats, bringing their salads and iced teas with them. They were apparently the fastest to move, because Rennie noticed a few others halfway out of their chairs scowling and sitting back down.

Salads were quickly supplied to the four newcomers and,

when Margaret and Marguerite had each finished describing their inner journeys in what Rennie thought was excruciating detail, Dorothea turned to him and put out her hand.

"Hello, I'm Thea. Have we met before?" Dorothea said.

"I don't believe so," Rennie answered politely. "This is the first time I've been to one of your workshops. I've read your books though. My name's Rennie Morrow."

"Oh that's so sweet of you!" Dorothea said, as if he had been doing her a personal favor to read her books. "I'm so glad you could make it. Do you live nearby? Are you a therapist?"

Rennie told her briefly where he lived and what he did for a living. She drew him out with more questions, and seemed particularly interested in the meditation teachers and gurus he had studied with.

"Your trips to India sound wonderful," Dorothea said. But when she turned to Dirk that was not what she mentioned. "Dirk, honey, this is Rennie. His company imports and distributes incense. Isn't that interesting?"

Dirk had been chuckling with Foxton and Genevieve and now turned to Dorothea.

"Incense," he said. "Is that right?" He looked at Rennie. "Never thought about it, but I guess someone has to do it. Is that a good business?"

"We do all right," Rennie said. "I've built it up over the years, and we're ahead of the competition. Do a lot now online."

He thought it was odd that their conversation had turned to his business prospects, but perhaps they were just being polite and inclusive by focusing the conversation on something important to him. Or maybe they were assessing his likelihood to attend more workshops.

Rennie changed the subject. "Margaret here was just telling me you live in Santa Fe. Is that by way of Texas?" he said to Thea.

Dirk turned and resumed his former conversation.

"Oh, no, honey. I grew up in Florida. People think everyone

living in New Mexico with a drawl must be from Texas, but we native Floridians have one too. It's not the same accent, but most people can't tell the difference. I've never lived in Texas."

She wrinkled her nose, making Rennie wonder what she thought might be wrong with Texas.

The salad plates had been picked up and a pasta dish with vegetables in a tomato cream sauce was set down in its place. It tasted like the food in nearly every other hotel workshop he had been to. What a shame to eat food this mediocre in the middle of San Francisco, where there were so many great restaurants. He supposed it was worth eating schlock to get a closer look at Dorothea, her staff, and other workshop participants before deciding if he wanted to do more with this group.

Dorothea now focused on the three newcomers who had rushed to the table when she sat down. Their previous seats were now the only ones left for the stragglers who'd come in late, forcing the wait staff to lay out new sets of clean silver, folded napkins, and glasses of iced tea.

Rennie listened to more endless stories about people's journeys that morning, and what they'd been doing since they'd last seen Dorothea. He focused on the way Dorothea honed in on each as he or she was talking, and how they seemed to grow and shine as they spoke to her. At the same time, they competed for her attention and praise, which she doled out generously, seeming to draw from it herself in the process.

Rennie had seen this before with other "teachers" but Dorothea performed better than most. It was a closed system – the participants fed off of her attention and she fed off of their adoration. He had felt it from her when they spoke. She had appeared very interested and impressed by his travels to India and his meditation practice. He'd felt appreciated, and better about himself than he normally did. He wasn't sure if that was a good thing or not.

◊ ◊ ◊

The afternoon session, and Sunday morning's, followed the same pattern. Dorothea gave a lecture, then led them on a new guided journey with music. Rennie had two quite strong experiences that brought up feelings he'd been edging toward but skirting in his meditation practice.

The last session was Sunday afternoon: a closing ritual, and another less-than-inspiring example of Dorothea's messages from the spirit world. The high point was getting Lark's phone number and a date for the following week. Between that and his meditations, the weekend had been worth it.

His main disappointment was not getting to re-experience the village in India with the fire, the people in white, and the molten gold. He was left with a sense of both importance and incompleteness from that vision. But he couldn't force it to come back and give him more information. He knew if it were meaningful, eventually, he would find that out.

12
Marin

*F*our days after the fiasco at Eighth, Michaela still didn't
know what to do with herself. She was bummed out from
the experience, horribly upset not to have the job, and couldn't
seem to get past it. The worst was that they really liked her
work, and still wouldn't hire her. And for the most disturbing
reason she'd ever heard.

Not spiritual enough. She had never even cared about
being spiritual before, and didn't plan to start now. Trying to
meditate was a waste of time. It had made her feel worse. So
there was no reason the Eighth owners' accusation should
bother her. Yet it did.

She still didn't care about becoming spiritual, but she was
desperate to feel better. She tried distracting herself with all
the usual means. She went to the gym every day to feel good
about her will power, to keep her body in shape, and to increase
her endorphins. She met girlfriends for drinks and flirted with
guys she met. She ate at good restaurants. She saw a movie.
She shopped for shoes at Nordstrom and bought two pair. But
she didn't really enjoy any of it, and it didn't change her
underlying mood.

She could hop on a plane somewhere – Vegas, maybe.

That was always fun. She sat in the tomato red chair (she had forgiven it for being in the wrong place at the wrong time) and searched for flights on her laptop. But after a few minutes, she stopped. She didn't have interest enough make the trip: reservations, pack, get to the airport. She couldn't be bothered. Doing anything.

She knew Roxanne was flipping out. Michaela had texted on the way home, "MTG TOTL DSASTR." Ever since, Roxanne had texted, called, and emailed her with increasingly frantic messages that Michaela ignored. Roxanne would think she'd lost her edge, not able to score the job. She'd want to know why, and Michaela didn't want to tell her.

Michaela herself wondered if she'd lost her edge. She'd certainly lost something. She hadn't felt normal for a long time. Not since the radish – followed by the bookstore and that guy Rennie, and then her disastrous meditation attempt. She squirmed thinking of it. And then, worst of all, those awful restaurant owners. Angelo and JozEF. What complete assholes.

The only decent thing that had occurred all month was meeting the monks. They were so nice, and really seemed to want to help her. What was it that one had said she should get? A prayer something. She had made a mental picture of their yellow car as a mnemonic note. Oh yeah, a prayer wheel. Whatever that was.

Her computer was still sitting open on her lap, so she typed in "prayer wheel." Okay, lots of sites.

Click. Images. There they were. Prayer wheels large and small. Colored wood and metal. The hand-held ones looked like the reel end of a fishing rod, without the line, but with a little tail of chain or cord on the spinning part. It said that was to make it spin easier when you hold the stick and flick your wrist. Most had writing on them; must be ancient Tibetan.

Click. Really expensive antique prayer wheels for sale.

Click. They were said to have the mantra "Om Mani Padme Hum" written on the outside. She remembered the monk saying that phrase to her. Padme, she had thought, like in Star Wars. She read that spinning the wheel is like reciting the prayer. Either gets rid of bad karma and brings good karma.

Maybe that's what was wrong with her. Bad karma had been piling up and needed to be dumped. Michaela pictured the three disposal bins outside her house: brown for trash, beige for recycling, green for yard waste. What color would a karma disposal bin be? Clear? She supposed the monks would have an answer.

Click. Okay, here we go. This was something she could use. Instructions on turning a hard drive into a prayer wheel. She could just download a picture of it to her computer as a screen saver, and let it spin around, getting rid of negative karma.

She not only downloaded the file, but she ordered an attractive hand held version for only forty dollars plus shipping.

Once it finished downloading, she opened the file and the thing started going around on her screen. There! She was more spiritual already. This was a lot easier than trying to meditate.

As Michaela sat, watching the Tibetan writing go around and around on the digitized wheel, her thoughts drifted. Suddenly she realized she was hungry. She looked at her watch. She had been sitting there for nearly an hour. How funny.

Funny, but nice. She actually felt a little bit better, less depressed. She got up, stretched, and went to the kitchen.

Halfway there, she turned and went back for computer. She would leave it open on the counter with the prayer wheel going, so she could watch it while she cooked. The phrase Om Mani Padme Hum was in her head. Fine, no problem. It didn't bother her, the way some bad song would. Not only that, the mantra was supposed to mean something good, something she wouldn't mind being on the receiving end of lately. Compassion. Yes, she could use some of that. That's what the monks had given her. She realized that there had been very little compassion in her life, either received or given. She wasn't sure what that meant, but for some reason it interested her.

Spin, spin, spin.

Om mani padme hum, om mani padme hum, om mani padme hum...

13
101 North to Petaluma

R ennie crossed the Golden Gate feeling relieved and looking forward to a nice, relaxing Sunday night. He called in an order to Mary's Pizza Shack in Petaluma, and picked the pie up on his way home. The smell in the car was so enticing, he ripped into the first warm, melty slice while still on the road.

Heaven.

Between bites, Rennie sang along with the radio. The pop melody of the song seemed at odds with its lyrics about following your loved one into death. He changed the station. Beatles, "When I'm Sixty-Four." Another pop melody, at odds with following your loved one into old age. He sighed and turned off the radio.

Rennie had not been overly impressed with the LightWorks Shamanic Meditation Workshop. It wasn't the worst workshop he had ever been to. In fact some of the inner work he did there had been fairly productive. Although Dorothea Light was a decent teacher, and had some novel ways of presenting her material, he wasn't sure he was completely comfortable with her as a person.

And while it was true he'd had good experiences in the meditations, they weren't that different than he would have had on his own at home. All in all, he was not blown away. This left him undecided about further work with Dorothea and her program.

Chewing a bite of crust, he turned the radio back on, this time to country. Ah, more like it. Brad Paisley checking a girl for ticks. Well, since he was not overly excited about LightWorks, he just wouldn't do anything about it for now. He would wait and see if the Universe gave him any signs on this one. He could still try some of the weekend's meditations on his own at home, with the tapes he bought before leaving the workshop. See if that helped him make a decision.

As he opened the front door, Rennie was greeted by his black and white cat, Philosopher. Phil complained loudly about Rennie's long absence while rubbing against his legs, then allowed Rennie to pick him up for exactly three seconds before squirming to get back down. After topping off Phil's water and food, Rennie pulled a bottle of Red Tail from the refrigerator and sat down to enjoy the remainder of his pizza.

So it was not until he had been home for a good half-hour that Rennie noticed the package. It was sitting with the rest of his mail, brought in and left on the kitchen counter by the girl who fed Phil when Rennie was away.

The package was small – just a foot or so long, three or four inches wide, and less than an inch high. It was completely covered in thin, shiny brown paper that had been wrapped or folded over itself several times, creating a soft bulk with a lot of paper edges, most of which had been taped down. The entire thing had also been tied with brown cord, knotted together in three or four places. It was a mess. So was the writing on the label – Rennie's name and address – with smudges and corrections, but no errors. And no return address.

Rennie held the peculiar package in his hands for a long time, turning it over and examining it. Phil leapt up and walked back and forth in front of Rennie, rubbing his head against the package. When Rennie put the object down on the counter,

Phil draped himself over it, purring. Rennie wondered if someone had mailed him a box of catnip.

Rennie pulled the package out from under the cat and put it to his nose. No, not catnip. Not any kind of herb. Not marijuana, thank goodness, as Rennie had quit getting high years ago and wouldn't have known what to do with that. Nor was it any type of incense he was familiar with. Now extremely curious, Rennie took a steak knife and began hacking away at the wrappings.

He got through the mass of cord, tape and paper, until only a flimsy cardboard box was left between Rennie and the contents. He pulled off the top, unwound yet another layer of wrapping – tissue paper – and finally reached the contents. It was a small cache, merely twelve sticks, of some type of incense.

With the wrappings off, Rennie could smell it better, and so could Phil. The cat pushed his face right up to the sticks. Rennie held them out, and the cat took several whiffs, then jumped high into the air, landed on the floor, and ran into the next room, where he sat down and began enthusiastically licking a front paw.

Rennie held the sticks up to his own nose and inhaled deeply. It was a pleasant odor, but unusual. He hadn't smelled anything quite like this before. He wondered what combination of herbs, oils, flowers and minerals had been used to create the resin on these sticks. They were clearly handmade. He knew, or knew of, many incense makers in India and other parts of the world, but this didn't look like the work of anyone he was familiar with. It was very strange. And with no return address, how did they expect him to order more if he wanted to carry it?

Rennie looked back through the paper, tape, string, tissue and cardboard packaging. In the bottom half of the box was a small square of paper with a handwritten note:

To mister R. Morrow, Petaluma, California, United States. Please enjoy agarbatti with our compliments. Yours sincerely, R.K. Ashvin and family, Sumana, India.

Rennie knew agarbatti simply meant incense sticks, so that gave no clue to what it was, or why someone would send it to him in such a way. In fact, he couldn't understand how it could have been sent to his house instead of his office. He had a business address for deliveries, and a post office box for his personal mail. The only mail he got at home was advertising. Never business correspondence, and certainly never samples.

He held the sticks to his nose again and took another big sniff. Usually he could tell most of what was in a new incense. There were hundreds of potential ingredients, but he could identify by smell all the common ones, and most of the rarer ones too. In fact, now he was sure he did recognize a few of the ingredients. The ubiquitous sandalwood, of course. Sambrani, an ingredient often burned in temples in India. Myrrh, camphor and juniper, he was pretty sure. But there were some other things – several of them. He had no idea what they could be.

He supposed he ought to burn some, but was not inclined to do so at this hour on a Sunday, especially after his full weekend. He wanted to take a shower, get into bed, read, and go to sleep. Besides, if he didn't know how to reach the makers, he couldn't order any, so what was the point? He rolled the sticks back up in the tissue paper and placed them, along with the square of paper, inside the box, which he then closed. He left the box on the counter, but threw the ripped, taped up paper and the string into his recycling can. He turned out the lights and left the room.

◊ ◊ ◊

That night Rennie dreamt of the old Indian man and the other people from his workshop vision. They were standing by the fire, huts and the blue building in the background. The man held out the wooden bowl, offering it to Rennie.

Rennie took the bowl, although he didn't know what he

was supposed to do with it. He looked down and saw liquid gold at the bottom. The golden glow reflected the moonlight, so bright in his eyes, he had to blink. He looked back up, and the man was gone.

When he woke up, he'd forgotten the dream. He didn't remember it until after breakfast, when he saw the paper from the incense wrapping in the trash. For no particular reason, he pulled the paper back out and stuck it in a drawer. He didn't think of either of them again – the paper or the dream – for some time.

14
Santa Fe

Dirk had trained himself to awaken earlier most days than he would have liked, in order to leave the house before Thea got up. Seven-thirty usually gave him time to throw on some clothes and take the Beemer into town for breakfast. After that, he'd do errands, make calls to the east coast, work on his laptop, or just hang out. This morning he was in one of his hangouts, a small café with Wi-Fi and great ham and cheese croissants. He was careful to keep the crumbs off his keyboard as he caught up on emails he had not already answered on his Blackberry.

If he didn't get out early, then once Thea was awake, he would rarely get any extended time to himself during the day. She would want him to do this or that task for her – drive her somewhere, find an item she'd lost, remember the name of someone they'd met for ten minutes two years ago. Or she'd have him read whatever she'd just read and thought he had to know, or something she'd just written. Or she'd want him to listen to her latest mental musing, or to some so-called message she'd just received from the spirit world.

Not that he doubted the validity of her messages – sometimes. Dirk was occasionally amazed by the accuracy of the information she received – or channeled – or whatever you want to call what she did.

Even little things. Like the time they were in the car going to a dinner party. When they were almost there, way out of town up some mountain road, Thea abruptly stated she was told they should bring flowers instead of the expensive bottle of wine in a gift bag laying on the back seat. She insisted Dirk turn around and go all the way back down the mountain, and stop at three different stores until she found flowers she liked. He was extremely annoyed, but knew there was just no arguing with her when she was following instructions from one of her messages. They found acceptable flowers, arrived forty minutes late and left the wine in the car. It turned out the guest for whom the party was being given had decided two days before that he should give up drinking, and the entire dinner was alcohol-free. The man was delighted when Dorothea reported that she had been told so by Spirit.

So Dirk's complaint was not about Thea's abilities, only about how much time it took – his time. He considered it his job to figure out how those abilities would provide them with income, and he needed the opportunity each day to focus in on it, not run around after Thea with a newspaper and slippers.

What was primarily on Dirk's mind these days was the *Ivy!* show. Besides being a cultural icon beloved by nearly all women and many gay men, Ivy was the country's primary maven and arbiter of all things related to self-improvement and personal transformation. Thea wanted to be on *Ivy!*, and Dirk wanted her to be on *Ivy!*.

Getting Thea on *Ivy!* was the golden ticket. It would sell the books and CDs, and get people to the workshops. And Dirk was nearer than ever to achieving this goal. He had hired Russell, a publicist who'd formerly worked for the show as a guest booker. Russell said Thea was a shoo-in, and that Ivy would love her.

It was just a matter of timing. Russell had talked to the

person now in his former job, and thought the organization would soon give Dirk and Thea a date for her appearance. It was never altogether out of Dirk's mind. Everyday he had the urge to call Russell and see how it was going, although he held back so he wouldn't be one of those overbearing, annoying clients. But Russell's services weren't cheap. It had been over a week since their last conversation, and if he didn't at least get an email in the next couple of days, he would call for an update.

Meanwhile, he was evaluating the success of the prior weekend in San Francisco, trying to figure out how the next couple of events were shaping up, and planning her newest book and media releases, another part of his role as promoter. Before he came along, Dorothea had only one book and had been dawdling along on her second for nearly two years. She hadn't done anything on audio or DVD. Now, thanks to him, they had a whole series of recorded stuff, and four books.

In terms of PR, he wasn't doing too badly. For each book, she'd done plenty of signings around the country, and on his own he'd managed to score some radio shows and a couple of local TV spots. Then he'd convinced Thea they should spend the money to hire Russell. If that worked out, and she was on *Ivy!* it would make the five-figure fee look like a bargain. Dirk would consider that his success as much as, if not more than, hers.

Dirk's phone buzzed in his pocket. He didn't have to be psychic to know it was probably Dorothea, and ignored the call. If he answered while he was still in the café, she'd want him to bring back a drink, probably one that would take him as long to order as it did to make. No, he would call her from the car, when he'd already be on his way home and it would be too late to get her something. Besides, Thea needed to cut the calories, if she wanted to look her best to the public, especially for television. So, really, he was doing her a favor and shouldn't feel bad. He made sure he had all his devices, and headed for the door.

15
Mill Valley

Michaela sat at her desk. She wanted to work, but was still not able to get going. She just didn't feel up to it. Except for the little lift she got whenever she saw the spinning image of her digitalized prayer wheel, Michaela wasn't doing well. She was not functioning up to par in either her work or her personal life. She didn't want to return calls. Some mockups she had promised were late. She was restless and unsure of herself.

Worst of all, she could not stop thinking about Eighth. She couldn't get over missing out on that job, and wondered if they had found a menu designer yet. She just hated the fact that the coolest place on the coast was going to open in a few weeks and she would not be a part of it. It also still bothered her – and she knew it shouldn't, because they were obnoxious and weird – that the two owners, Angelo and Jozef, had rejected her.

Because she wasn't spiritual enough. Because, as they put it, she wasn't spiritual at all.

But why should she care? She never felt spirituality was a quality she needed in her life. Did that mean there was something wrong with her? Obviously Angelo and Jozef thought there was. But until now, it had never been an issue for her. Nobody else she associated with cared much about that stuff either.

Well, there was that one guy, Ivan, who she'd gone out with a few times last year. He was a runner, and a health nut. He was also a bit new age-y, though she hadn't minded. He would go on about "cosmic energy" or "gaia consciousness." Michaela didn't understand most of it, so she'd either laugh it off not say anything. But then he stopped calling, which surprised her, since they'd had some good sex. When she ran into him a few weeks later at a restaurant, she asked if he wanted to get together.

He'd said, "You know, I'd like to, Michaela. You're fun to be with. But it was messing with my chakra balance to hang with you. I'm trying to stay at the heart level and above, you know, and you're more of a lower three kind of girl. Which is great, I love that about you. But it just isn't good for my development, you know?"

At the time, Michaela had blown it off. She'd thought, well, he really didn't make much sense; that crap he spewed would start to drive her crazy at some point anyway; and besides that, she was dating two other guys with a third in the wings, so why should she care if this one didn't work out? But now that she thought about it, wasn't he, too, putting her down for not being spiritually-minded? Implying that she, or at least her chakras (another incomprehensible concept) were too "low," and he wanted someone higher? Looking back, maybe he was.

And another friend – a restaurant manager named Abby, who she'd met through work – had several times told Michaela she was busy with events, "you wouldn't be interested in."

When Michaela asked for details, once Abby said she was going to "a retreat with a Shaman from Tuva who teaches throat singing. He's supposed to be pretty tapped-in," and another time, "Oh, just a lecture given by this Buddhist teacher whose book I liked."

Abby was right, it all sounded amazingly boring. Michaela

hadn't given it another thought either time, and had gone out for drinks with Roxanne instead.

So, apparently, there were these lectures and meetings and classes going on all around her, and Michaela hadn't noticed. And what about that guy, Rennie? The one she'd met at the bookstore. He had been going to some workshop, too. That store had displayed brochures for numerous events. In fact, hadn't she picked up a couple of them, as well as some free magazines, when she was there? Maybe she should see what workshops were available, and try one.

Michaela wasn't sure what had happened to that material, but she remembered tossing the incense back into the blue plastic bag with the books she'd bought, then dropping the bag on the couch. Everything was probably still in there. She checked the couch. It wasn't there, nor anywhere else in the living room. She didn't remember moving it, but started searching the house.

The longer she looked, the more she panicked, worried that it might be another disappearance. Then she remembered that Nelda, the house cleaner, had come since her botched meditation attempt. Nelda always moved whatever Michaela left lying around to the upper shelf of her coat closet. Michaela's tense hopefulness became relief as she peered over the coats to the shelf and, sure enough, there was the blue bag. Then, knowing how irrational it was, she reached her hand up and felt around the entire shelf, just in case the radish had somehow made its way up there too. But of course it hadn't.

As she expected – thank goodness – the bag still held two free magazines she had picked up at the store. Michaela carried them back to her office and sat at her desk. She flipped open one of the zines.

It was divided into categories, most of which didn't sound too weird, like Travel and Retreats, Business and Finance, Schools and Training. But there was also a category for Psychics and Readers, and one called Soul and Spirit. Michaela flipped to the section for Workshops.

What looked good? After seeing the options, Michaela revised the question to: What looked almost halfway not too weird? Not much.

Alchemy? They had to be kidding.

Change your brain waves? She liked hers the way they were already.

Learn Chakra massage? There it was again. She was afraid to find out what "lower three" really meant.

Become an Avatar? Did that mean ask James Cameron if she could be in the sequel?

Talk to Angels? Only if you don't expect them to talk back.

Wait! Here was something. An ad for that LightWorks thing, the one that guy – Rennie – had told her about. But the workshop was already past, in fact had happened just the previous weekend. But that was an idea – she could call Rennie. He'd probably have some thoughts, know of something she could try.

He'd given her his number. Michaela reached into the bag and found the brochure where Rennie had written his office number, just as she had remembered.

"Why wait?" she said aloud, and made the call. She expected his voicemail, or maybe a secretary, so was surprised when Rennie answered on the second ring. She wasn't quite prepared to talk to him.

"Oh, uh, hi. Hi, um, Rennie. This is Michaela Thomason. We met at Coffeeteria a couple of weeks ago. I don't know if you remember. Your appointment book was missing? And I talked to you about my, um, similar experience with a radish…?"

Feeling stupid, Michaela tapered off and waited for a reply.

"Oh, right," Rennie said. "Sure, I remember. Hi. How are you?"

"I'm good, thanks," she said quickly. "Well, actually, things have been a little weird since then. I mean weirder, even, than before. I'm not really sure what's going on. I mean, I'm fine, but…it's just, some things have happened that I'm trying to get my mind around – some more things, ha ha, besides even the radish – and I remembered about that workshop you told me you were going to, and I was wondering if you ever did go."

"Oh, right," he repeated. "That was last weekend. Yes, I did, as a matter of fact. It was pretty good. I might do another one. Haven't decided yet. Why? Are you thinking of trying it?"

"Maybe," Michaela said. "Well, I should probably do something. I'm, um, feeling like I need a little… oh, I don't know… something to make me be more, um, you know…"

"More conscious? Connected with your inner self or your higher power? Are you looking for healing? Expanded awareness? Soul expression?"

"Sort of, I guess. Some of that. I mean, I just want to be more…it's kind of weird to say, but more, um, you know." She half whispered it. "Spiritual."

"Oh," said Rennie. "I see. Well, there are many forms of spirituality. Did you have something in particular in mind?"

"Well, that's the trouble. I don't even know where to start. I was just reading this magazine, *InnerChange*, and there's so much *stuff* in there, and most of it sounds so weird, and I'm not sure what half the things are they're even talking about. But you seemed pretty up on this sort of, um, this kind of, you know, *thing*. So I thought I'd see if you had any suggestions for me."

"Oh," he said again. There was a long pause and Michaela braced for another rejection. "That's a pretty big request. I'd want to give it some thought."

"No, that's okay, then. Never mind, it's fine. I'm sure I can sort it out."

Michaela felt stupid. What was she thinking? She didn't even know this guy. Normally, if she called up a guy she'd just met, they were on the same wavelength – get together, have a meal, go to a movie, consider if they wanted to date again, have sex, or whatever. But this was just weird.

Rennie said, "No, wait. I'd actually be glad to talk to you. I just meant I couldn't do it right now, on the phone. In fact, I think we should get together and talk in person. That would give me a chance to think about it ahead of time, and get a better sense of what you're looking for."

"Uh, yeah, okay," Michaela answered. Was she mistaken, or did she feel a hint of interest from Rennie that was maybe for her, and not just her dilemma? That was okay though. She was open to something happening between them. She could eat two oysters from one shell, so to speak. Not that she cared much about eating *or* sex lately, but it was always a boost to think somebody might be interested.

They made a plan for Friday night. This was Tuesday. She offered to drive to Petaluma and meet him at his place, since he had a lot of books she could look at. She figured she'd hang out for a while, they'd talk, and if it wasn't too weird spending time with him, she'd offer to take him to dinner. She got the address and directions he thought might not show up on her GPS. When they hung up, Michaela actually felt better, even though she had no idea where it would lead. It was the first positive thing she'd done in a long time. At least she hoped it was positive.

Funny, though, she was also nervous. Well, whatever. This was only research, she reminded herself. She didn't have to change who she was, or do anything different, unless she really wanted to. And whether she wanted to remained to be seen.

16
Santa Fe

Dorothea had a problem. Actually she had several problems, but one in particular was bothering her at the moment. She was creating a guided meditation for her next CD, which Dirk said they had to release soon. All she had determined so far was that it would be about relationships. She'd had the brilliant idea to title it "The Ship of Relations." She'd do a whole metaphor on taking the relationship journey on the sea of … the sea of…well, some kind of sea. The Sea of Life, maybe, with sharks and octopuses ready to bring you down if you fall in. Something like that. She hadn't figured it all out yet, but she would. That part she was good at.

The problem was, she didn't know much about ships or boats or any other water doohickeys. At the beginning of the meditation, she wanted the listeners to imagine going to the shore, where their Ship would come in. But she didn't want to specify what kind of Ship. She wanted them to receive whatever water vessel appeared. Because that's what made the imagery work, when it was open-ended, so anything inside could emerge and reveal something.

But if she used the word "Ship," wouldn't that imply a big old giant cruise ship, or battleship, or slave ship (that was a good one for some of those relationships) or something else really huge? She didn't want that. To the listener, it ought to imply any kind of vessel their mind came up with. Maybe they would think of a big ship like that, but also, maybe, a rowboat, a sailboat, or a Viking vessel. Even a kayak or a Jet-ski. But she didn't think you'd refer to most of those as ships. Some of them were just boats. She wasn't sure a kayak or Jet-ski was even a boat.

But she couldn't very well say, "Ship-or-Boat of Relations." Or "Ship-or-Boat-or-Personal-Water-Vessel of Relations." That sounded stupid. Which meant her metaphor might not work. Also, she didn't know how to get them from the shore out to the ship, or boat, or whatever. If it was a cruise ship, for example, it couldn't just come up on the beach, now, could it? She was frustrated sorting it out, but the metaphor overall was too good to give up on. She needed help.

Dirk's help. This was just the sort of problem he was good at. He would give her what she needed, the information and support to figure it out. Either he'd know the answers already, or he would find out for her. But Dirk wasn't here. And she needed him *right now*. Usually, he was back by 11, and it here it was, practically 11:30. Well, okay, 11:12. She'd tried calling, but only got voicemail. She knew if he was on a business call, he wouldn't pick up. But that wasn't right. She needed him more than anyone else he could possibly be talking to. And she didn't know why he had to stay out so long. He could call from home just as easily.

This was happening more often. He woke up earlier then her, went out for breakfast, and began his workday. That was okay while she was still asleep. But recently he was coming back later and later. It was disastrous when she needed him and he wasn't around. But worse, this was part of a bigger problem: Dirk's failure to give her enough attention.

If the situation was merely annoying, she would be distressed, but she'd tolerate it. At this point, though, not only was she suffering personally, it actually limited her creative outpouring. Which meant all the people out there who depended on her work in the world were affected. Dorothea functioned best when she didn't have to worry about the mundane, and could stay as connected as possible with the higher planes, so she could bring that energy in for others.

Dirk knew all this. And he knew in order for her to do what she needed — and provide what people needed from her — it was his job to take care of the other stuff. All those distracting, boring activities like household chores and meals; phone calls and appointments. And he couldn't do it if he wasn't actually there, could he? His presence was imperative.

And besides which, she was hungry.

She couldn't work on this stupid meditation any more until she ate. In frustration, Dorothea realized she would either have to go back to bed or fix her own instant oatmeal. And even that wouldn't be the same without the fresh orange juice Dirk always squeezed for her. She opened the refrigerator. There were plenty of oranges. Perhaps she'd make the juice herself. But that would make her fingers sticky. So she shut the door, went back to her phone, and speed-dialed Dirk several more times. Finally, he picked up.

"Hi Thee, I'm a block away. Almost there. Up long?"

"*Yes*," she whined. "Over an hour. I'm trying to work, but I *can't*; I'm *hungry*. And I have to ask you about watercraft. You know, for the new CD. I had a brilliant idea but I can't get any further until I find out more about…well, you know…boat thingies."

"Okay babe, no worries, I'm coming right in. Hear the garage door?"

"Humph," Dorothea said, hanging up.

She decided not to confront Dirk now about his overall neglect. This morning, she needed his immediate help. But she would have him squeeze her an extra-large juice before she asked him about all the boaty-floaty stuff. Good thing there were a lot of oranges.

17
Petaluma

Rennie was flattered by Michaela's call. He thought about it on his way to the office the next day. She needed help connecting with her own spirituality, and she had reached out to him. Unknown to her, his greatest wish was to help people on their paths. So for her to call, especially now, was like the universe sending him a sign. Like that Buddhist saying, but reversed: "When the teacher is ready, the students will appear." Well, in this case, it was student, singular, but you have to start somewhere. He would have to decide if he should make a plan for the meeting, or just wait until she arrived and see where their conversation led.

Also, she was attractive. Not his usual type, but nice to look at. He would look through his library of books and audio CDs, see what might appeal to her. Maybe he'd try some meditation. And he'd have wine and snacks, in case they wanted to hang out afterwards.

The timing was good. He wasn't overloaded at work. His small staff kept on top of things, which left him plenty of time for other pursuits. Rennie knew he was lucky to have two such great employees. Noeletta had been with him for twelve years, while they grew from a simple business-to-business setup, first to a successful mail order business, and now to a significant web presence. She had helped him through each phase of this and, except for Rennie's personal touch with sellers and customers, and his ultra-talented nose, she could nearly run the business on her own. Noeletta was 50 and Rennie hoped she would never retire. Once his workshop career took off, he'd make her a full partner in the incense business. J.J. had joined them two years ago, and had worked out fine. The three of them got along well, and the work atmosphere was relaxed and pleasant.

The business was in a small, newish warehouse with office space halfway between downtown Petaluma and Highway 101. They had air conditioning for the days when there wasn't fog or a sea breeze, or when the fertilizer smell got a little too strong. The women could choose what music or talk radio to play in the office, and they could make their own hours. As long as the business was kept running smoothly, Rennie did not care how they accomplished it.

When he reached the office at ten, Noeletta was on her computer in the large room she shared with J.J., who was out running errands. Rennie stood behind J.J.'s empty chair, and Noeletta turned hers around to face him.

"So, boss, how was your weekend?" she asked.

"Okay," Rennie said. "You know. A workshop is a workshop is a workshop." He shrugged.

Noeletta chuckled. Rennie knew she had been down that road herself, years before. She'd done EST and Lifespring in their heydays, tried rebirthing, studied tarot and massage, joined trips to South America for shamanic journeying experiences, taken programs at Esalen and Omega and Kripalu. The whole trip. She, like Rennie, was still a long time meditator, but for the past ten years had more or less avoided the whole organized transformation thing.

"Yours?" Rennie asked.

"We're at the all-wedding, all-the-time stage." She shook

her head and raised her eyebrows. "Not how I would do it, obviously. But it's her wedding, not mine."

Noeletta's daughter was getting married in two weeks. Despite her alternative upbringing, or maybe because of it, Serena was quite a traditional young woman. She was working on her MBA at San Francisco State. Engaged to a young lawyer, she wanted a "normal" wedding with all the perks, "not some hippie party in the woods like you had, Mom."

Noeletta had no objection, especially since the couple were paying for most of it themselves. In fact, she found the whole extravaganza amusing, at least at first. But now the combined force of Serena and the wedding planner was finally getting to her, and she couldn't wait for it to be over.

"Good for my practice, at least."

He imagined the normally unflappable Noeletta meditating; her face red, and steam coming out of the top of her head. He'd felt that way himself sometimes.

"Lucky you. Would it be asking too much for you to pick something from their registry and send it for me? I'll write a check. We can do it right now."

She gave him their oversized business checkbook, and he scribbled out a check for $150 and handed it to her.

"I know just the thing," she said. "A burner. Goes with the three-foot paella pan someone sent already. Serena and Dom went to Spain last year and decided they want to have paella parties. Honestly, you could take a bath in this thing." She rolled her eyes.

"A giant burner," he chuckled. "Very appropriate. Thanks for handling it. I'll be in my office."

"Thanks, boss," Noeletta said.

He waved before disappearing into the next room and quietly closed the door.

Once alone, Rennie sat at his desk and turned on the computer. He had business calls to make, and orders to write up, but first he would take a few minutes to work on his secret project. Not that it was really a secret. He just hadn't told anyone about it yet.

Rennie was building a platform. He had been working on it for two months and two days, which was the exact amount of time since he first heard the term platform used in the sense that he was using it, to describe the type of thing he was building.

This kind of platform was not something he would be piling cartons of incense on to keep them from getting wet. It was not a political manifesto. It was not a bed, or a train station, or a stage. Well, maybe it was something like a stage – a metaphorical one. But Rennie, who often watched war programs on the History Channel, thought of it as being most like a military platform. It would be a launching point for him to get out in the world as a workshop leader and a teacher. And, in this, Rennie had a plan of attack.

Phase 1: To get his name out there, he was starting a website with a blog, and it would be just as cool, deep, intelligent and wise as any website and blog he had seen. He would write about the insights of his meditation practice and give tips to people who wanted to develop spiritually.

Phase 2: Through his business he had contacts with incense sellers, including bookstores and spiritual centers all over the U.S. He was going to ask those people to put him in touch with groups in their area where he could give lectures and mini-seminars. He didn't mind traveling around a bit and spending his own money to advertise these events in order to get known. Then, when he was ready to start doing real workshops, he would already have name recognition.

Phase 3: Well, he needed to think more about that. He supposed one part of it would be to eventually write books, but that seemed beyond him right now.

Rennie had the launch planned out and he knew it would be successful, except for one thing. It was the thing he'd been bothered about for so long now, the only aspect that had been holding him back. He still needed a unique approach to make him stand out from the crowd of meditation teachers and shamanic practitioners; the healers, life coaches, intuitives, empowerers, self-actualizers and communicators. Something that didn't involve tantra or hypnosis or chakra balancing, or even – especially – singing, chanting or public speaking.

In fact, the less speaking, the better. The way he knew best, and felt was most effective toward a deeper spirituality and more fulfilling life, was the inner path. That's what had always worked best for him and what he had learned from those teachers he respected most, all over the world. But still, he wanted to tell people about it, and be known for that, and in order to do that, he had to first get their attention.

He had to offer something extra, so his workshops would be special. He had pondered this over and over, for two months and two days. Longer, really, because before he even knew what a platform was, he knew he had to have that special something in order to stand out. Rennie needed a pinnacle for his platform. He needed a secret weapon.

◊ ◊ ◊

The next day, Rennie left work early to prep for Michaela's visit. He wanted to straighten up the house, pull out some books for her to look at, and have an hour to sit in meditation so he could be in a clear, centered frame of mind when she arrived.

There was a bit more cleaning up than he'd realized. He washed the dishes from breakfast, stored boxes of cereal and bottles of vitamins, wiped down counters, closed drawers and cabinets, and tossed a dish towel into the hamper. He cleaned the small bathroom, which wasn't bad because Lolita, the housecleaner, had been there only three days before.

Next, the bedroom. He could just shut the door to hide the unmade bed, and the few clothes and books scattered around.

But maybe he should straighten up. What if she asked to see it? Or what if…? Okay, he really didn't think so, but just in case. He folded and put away clean clothes and hid dirty ones, neatened the books into a pile with the most impressive sounding ones on top, pulled up and smoothed down the comforter, and plumped the pillows. He didn't change the sheets. That seemed entirely too optimistic, and they hadn't been on long, anyway.

That left only the living room. He refolded newspapers and put away DVDs, moved his iPod to the bedroom, and placed his laptop in its case. He just needed to straighten the sofa cushions and he'd be done. Lifting the second cushion, he felt something firm and covered in paper. That odd package from India had somehow wedged its way between the cushion and the back of the sofa. Probably Phil's doing.

Rennie re-examined the flimsy box in his hands. He'd given no thought to it since he last saw it, but now he took the incense sticks out and inhaled their unlit fragrance again. It was an interesting combination of scents, and he was curious how it would smell while burning. He was just about to meditate anyway, so why not try it?

Rennie wished he had a separate room just to meditate. Instead, he had set up a corner of the living room with a cushion and an altar. The altar was on a low, carved wooden table. It was covered with a white silk cloth, upon which he'd placed items symbolic of his spiritual life: Pictures of the teachers he was most attuned with; statues of Buddha, Kwan Yin, Saint Francis and Hanuman; a crow feather; a Zuni bear fetish; two kinds of beads – a rosary and a set of mala beads from India; a large piece of rose quartz; a section of rattlesnake skin; and, of course, an incense burner – an unusual one carved from bluish stone in the shape of a feather.

He started up a disposable lighter and brought the flame to the stick. When red showed beneath the flame, he blew it out, leaving just the burning ember. He set the end of the stick carefully into the hole of the blue stone feather. Then he sank down onto the meditation cushion. He took off his watch, glanced at it, and put it out of sight under the altar.

Adjusting his legs and torso in a half-lotus for maximum comfort and stability, he placed his hands in a cosmic mudra – his left hand over his right, with his thumbs touching to form an oval, and resting on his lap near his abdomen. This was his current favorite position.

Rennie closed his eyes. He had practiced many types of meditation over the years. Some he had learned from the teachers he'd sat with. Others he'd tried after reading about them. He'd done chakra meditation, breath meditation, and used numerous mantras. They all involved focusing the mind in some way, and then, when the mind wandered as it always did, bringing his focus back to the mantra, chant, breath, or whatever it was. A particular favorite was the Ham Sa (or So Ham, the same mantra with the syllables reversed). It meant "I am that" or "I am that I am." It was simple, and his mind seemed to rest in it more easily than some of the other mantras he'd used.

Sometimes he would sink immediately into a deep meditative state of one sort or another. More often, his thoughts would be active, his sensations or emotions would want his attention, and he had to go through all of that before his mind quieted. That was how he started off this time. He had barely begun So-Hamming when he heard the loud twittering of a bird. Then his knee itched. Phil was scratching, and Rennie wondered if it was time for another dose of flea control. Now Phil was moving around more than usual. It sounded like he was rubbing himself on the floor and purring.

Oh, right. Wandering mind.

So Ham, So Ham. There was a lot of saliva in his mouth. He swallowed. *So Ham.* That incense, that new incense. Right, Phil liked it. That's why he was rolling around. Maybe it really was made with catnip. Maybe they forgot to tell him in the

note, it was incense for cats. Pet stores, new market. *Ham Sa.*
Ham Sa. So Ham. It switched. Had it switched? *So Ham.* Really
didn't matter. I am That. That I am. *So Ham.* Then, there were
no more thoughts. There was no more Ham Sa or So Ham
either.

And then – but of course without him realizing it – there
was no more Rennie.

As if traveling a far, far distance, Rennie came back to
himself. For a very long time he remained completely still,
trying to recapture as much as he could of what he had just
experienced.

Yes, he had experienced something, although for what
seemed like forever – after all, he hadn't had a sense of time,
either – he had lost the awareness of being the one experiencing
anything. Now that he was more or less "back," his own
perspective was back too. And so naturally his mind was trying
to capture, define and explain to itself – himself – what had just
happened.

The most remarkable part was the very fact that, for all that
time, he had not been aware of being aware. He knew in theory
this was possible, but it certainly had never happened to him,
nor had he expected it to. He had not sat down that afternoon
thinking, "Oh, maybe today, I'll lose my sense of duality.
Maybe today, I'll become one with the universe."

Yes, that was what it was, wasn't it? His studies had told
him this was a state of what some called Samadhi. He knew

there were different types of Samadhi. Not that it mattered – nothing could take away from the actual experience, after all – but out of curiosity, he'd look it up later. For now, he wanted to keep as much of the memory and feeling of the state as he could. All he knew was that, for some time, he had not been himself going through something. He had just been the experience.

And having been there, it made him so very aware of the difference of that state from the ones he was usually in. Even deep in a meditation, or some other type of altered consciousness, Rennie was always aware of himself as the experiencer. But for a while there, he hadn't been. But he hadn't been nothing either. It was almost impossible to describe or explain, even to himself.

Now that he was back to self-awareness again, other sensations were coming back too. For one thing, the cat was purring so loudly, he didn't know how he could have missed hearing it all that time. Or had it even been a lot of time? He might have been sitting two minutes or two hours or two days. He leaned over to reach his watch – it was now about fifty minutes since he had started to meditate. The incense had burned all the way down and gone out. Not surprising, since thirty to forty-five minutes was normal for a stick that size, depending on how it was made.

Rennie unfolded his legs and stretched his limbs in all directions. The farther he got from what had happened, and the more he thought about it, the more astounding it was. Was it really possible that he had just known Samadhi? That would be an incredible and amazing achievement.

Well, no. Not an achievement. That sounded terrible, like he was grasping for it. It wasn't an accomplishment, either – that still sounded egotistical. Let's see, what would be an acceptable way to describe it. An attainment? Better. Realization? Well, that was more neutral, didn't make it sound so, well, materialistic.

Whatever word he used, the fact that it happened was

surprising. After all, he was not a monk spending hours, days, months, years in meditation and study. He was not even in the presence of one of the highly advanced teachers he had met over the years, who could sometimes raise your practice to a much higher level just by being in the same room.

No, he had just done what he usually did, the way he usually did it, for an hour a day, sometimes two, unless he was on a retreat or at an ashram where he could truly devote himself to his practice. He had never thought he was especially accomplished or advanced. And he hadn't done anything different or special this time. He really had no idea how this had occurred or why he had been so blessed. Samadhi, wow. Now, that really was something.

And what next? If he meditated tomorrow, would it happen again? That was an intriguing thought. If not, then what *would* happen?

He'd have to wait and see. Now, he had Michaela coming over. What was that Kornfield book title again? *After the Ecstasy, The Laundry*? Well, this hadn't been exactly ecstasy, and Michaela certainly wasn't laundry, but same general idea. Moments of enlightenment, and then you still have stuff to do. Not that having Michaela over was a chore. Too bad about the timing though, as he'd like to try meditating some more to see what happened. Or to at least read some of his source material to learn how his experience was described by the great spiritual masters.

But, in a way, wasn't it perfect that she was coming now? Here she was, seeking him out for spiritual guidance, and here he was, just having had attained – no, *realized* – a great spiritual truth. Wasn't that the universe telling him this was the right time, and he was on the right track? Rennie excitedly rubbed his hands together and jumped up, ready to go. Things were coming together. He knew he would be led to whatever was supposed to happen next.

18
Santa Fe

*I*t was a horrifying dream. Instead of laundry soap, she had poured red wine, right out of the bottle, onto the clothes. They weren't even her clothes; they were her brother's, or maybe his wife's. She couldn't remember what sort of wine it was. Maybe that nice Syrah they had a couple of nights ago – the bottle was the right shape. Whatever it was, the white laundry bloomed red as she poured, and a terrible feeling came over her when she realized what she was doing.

She had to pull it all out, and spray everything with stain remover. That would get rid of the red, but it was going to be a huge job. And as she pulled, she saw there were not only clothes in the load, but photographs and record albums – a lot of Beatles – and wool rugs, and she had to sort all that out too. And no one to help her, she had to do it all by herself. Oh, it was awful. She was so glad to wake up and realize it wasn't really happening.

But what did it mean? Not that her dreams always had meaning. Some of them were too mundane to be useful, and others were too obvious, like the ones about vampires. Clearly, they showed her fear of losing all her energy to her work, and to the many people she wanted to help. It was a warning not to let them drain her.

Maybe this dream was like that too, in a way. She was making an offering of good wine, doing something positive. But when she spilled it out, instead of being admired for what she gave them, their dirty laundry got in the way. Yes, that was probably it.

Well, once she was on *Ivy!*, she'd be even more admired. And by many more people. Maybe even by those who gave her credit the least – her family. What would her brothers say when they saw her on *Ivy!*? Even they would know it was a big deal, and that she had to be somebody important. Not that she cared what they thought, or that they even came into her mind much.

She rolled out of bed. She wasn't going to give her brothers and their, or anybody else's, dirty laundry another thought. She had work to do. She had finally figured out how to make the Relation Ship metaphor work in her guided meditation, and later today they were recording it for the new CD. That would be fun. She liked having Dirk and the engineers fussing around, while she stood ready to be recorded. Sometimes they even referred to her as "the talent."

She wanted to video the guided meditations instead of just making audio recordings. But Dirk said CDs were still useful to people, especially for the meditations, since listeners were supposed to close their eyes. But he *was* putting her talks on a DVD series. A woman named Lorna Beth, who came to many of Dorothea's workshops and was a big fan, offered to sew her some special outfits for the videos. They would be in different colors to match the topics.

Dorothea was in the bathroom applying moisturizer when the phone rang. She scowled. Dirk was not back yet from his morning ramble, and she was certainly not going to run and answer it. She recognized the ring as the less restricted of their two unpublished lines. It could easily be someone she didn't want to talk to, especially at this hour. She did not want to get snagged into some therapeutic situation before she had even properly got up, nor answer business questions, nor make arrangements about anything. Let them leave a message, and Dirk could deal with it later.

But when Dirk's outgoing message finished, and she heard the voice of the caller, she knew this was one he'd make her reply to herself.

"Dottie – I mean Dor-*thee*-a. Pick up the phone, girl. I know you're there. Probably not even out of the bed yet, heh heh. Okay, don't answer. I know it's early; just thought I'd catch you in, still, at this hour. Call me back! I'm not kidding, I need to talk to you. It's about Mama, remember her? And don't make that husband of yours call this time, either. You've got my number."

Dorothea placed her palms flat on the counter, arms straight, all her weight on them, feeling lightheaded as she stared at her blanched face in the mirror. Good heavens! Guy. Her eldest brother, whom she hadn't spoken with in two years, or seen in five. The brother she had the hardest time with. The one whose laundry she had just washed in wine.

19
Petaluma

Michaela drove slowly down the country lane, waiting for the GPS to announce the turnoff to Rennie's. She was supposed to take a private road to the left, at a small sign for Macaroon Farm, and just as she saw it, the Voice announced, "Arriving at destination." Which meant from here on, she was on her own. She turned into the road and followed it a mile and a half, continually taking the right-hand turns or forks at every juncture, as Rennie had told her to.

When she passed the final pasture and saw the cute cottage sitting among a small stand of trees, Michaela felt relieved. She pulled in behind the Prius in the driveway and turned her engine off. Then she just sat for a minute, not quite ready to go inside.

The last couple of days, she felt more lost and disoriented than ever. She found it hard to get anything done, didn't want to talk to people, barely ate. She even found herself crying sometimes, partly in frustration about her state of mind, and partly just feeling down, for no reason she could think of. She almost didn't come today, because expecting Rennie to help just seemed silly and pointless. But since she couldn't do anything useful or fun anymore, and had no other plans, she forced herself to get in the car and go.

So here she sat outside of Rennie's house, feeling more stupid and less worthy than she ever had in her life.

Michaela sighed. She picked up her purse, and left the car without even bothering to check herself in the mirror. She walked slowly up to Rennie's front door, not caring, as she normally would, about the details of the attractive little house and charming setting. She expected little from this meeting, but at least she could tell herself she'd tried.

Rennie answered soon after she knocked, friendlier and more animated than she remembered. He took her jacket, led her into the living room and offered her a seat on the couch while he went to get iced tea. A tuxedo cat came around the corner, rubbed Michaela's legs, and walked out. She didn't bother to pet it. Michaela looked around the room. There was a stack of books on the table and an altar in the corner. No TV. And surprise, surprise – the house smelled like incense. Ugh. Well, there were worse things a guy could be into than all this weird stuff. She'd dated enough to know.

"Here you go."

Rennie was back with two tall glasses of tea, which he set on the glass coffee table.

She mumbled thanks.

"The mint sprigs are from my herb garden," he said, stepping around the table to sit on the end side of the couch. He turned to face Michaela.

"So how've you been?" he asked. "Did you contact LightWorks?"

"Um, no. Thought I'd wait 'til we talked and then see how I was feeling about, um, everything."

Rennie nodded encouragingly and waited.

"Truth is, I feel like shit lately," she said. "I can hardly get myself to do anything."

"You do seem different from when we met."

"Different? Do I?"

Michaela had picked up her tea but set it back down without drinking.

"Different how?" she asked.

She leaned toward Rennie and stared intently, waiting for an answer.

He sat back, picked up his own glass, and took a long sip before answering, "How you look, for one thing."

"I look different?"

"Yes. But better, if you don't mind me saying so. Your hair is longer and less, um, styled, I guess."

She sighed, put a hand up to her hair and brought a lock around to look at.

"Cancelled the appointment," she muttered.

"And you're wearing less makeup."

She dropped the hair and put a finger to her cheek as if she was checking what was on there.

"Yeah. Too much trouble."

"Well, you don't need it. Again, hope you don't mind me commenting, but you asked."

"No, it's okay. Um, thanks, I guess. What else?"

"Well, it's not just the outer stuff, you seem more... hmm...I don't know how to put it, exactly. It's just a different feeling. Like you're less, mm, far away. You seem more ... accessible, maybe?"

"Hmph. Really? I just feel confused. About everything. Like, the way the world has always been one way, and then it suddenly changed, you know? And now I don't know what it is anymore. Or how I fit into it. Or what I'm supposed to be doing in it."

Michaela surprised herself with these words. But when she heard them, she realized it was precisely how she had been feeling.

"Hmm," Rennie said. "I see. Well that makes sense. You know, at times, those feelings are not necessarily bad to have."

Michaela looked up sharply, and Rennie added, "I mean I know they *feel* bad. What you're going through sounds awful. Not to take away from that. But in terms of your, um… well, didn't you say on the phone you were interested in your spiritual path?"

Michaela nodded and Rennie continued, "Well, in terms of that, it's not so terrible, and can even be positive in the end. Because sometimes we have to fall apart for a while, so we can get back together a little differently. If it feels like the way we've been in the world isn't working anymore. We want to change, but we can't just make that change happen on our own. So everything cracks apart, and you feel bad for a while, but then we get to restructure ourselves –some aspect of ourselves – in a new way."

He stopped and looked at her, apparently waiting for a response. Michaela thought he seemed pleased with his little speech.

"Um, okay," she said. "I never thought about it that way. I guess that makes some sense."

But it didn't make much sense to her, really. She didn't see how feeling awful could in any way be good. In fact, she didn't get it at all. Maybe all that incense sniffing and those workshops had unhinged Rennie a bit. He was probably a nut case. Maybe she shouldn't even be here. It was probably pointless and stupid. She was an idiot to think he could help her. Feeling worse than ever, Michaela sighed deeply and sank back into the sofa.

"Um, a bit of a hard concept to grasp, I guess," Rennie said. "Maybe we should just start with something basic."

Michaela didn't bother to answer. She sat on the couch, feeling just awful. Worse, even, than she'd felt the last few days, which was worse than the week before and the week before that. Ever since she had been rejected at Eighth, despite the kindness of the monks and the prayer wheel spinning away all the time on her computer, she had just been spiraling down and down.

Now she didn't think she could get any lower. Her chest felt heavy, made worse by the incense Rennie must have lit when he was up pouring their tea. Smoke permeated the room, and seemed to swirl and settle in Michaela's body like a swarm of buzzing bees. Tears leaked from her eyes. This completely embarrassed her, and she didn't want Rennie to see them. But she didn't even have the will to lift up her hand and wipe them away.

In fact, her eyes had closed, and she didn't want to open them. She wanted to hide in here, in the dark, and not see anybody or have anybody see her. Rennie, who surely must have noticed she was acting strangely, put his hand on her upper arm and patted. He must think he was being supportive, but it really pissed her off. Why couldn't he just leave her alone? Didn't he realize how terrible she felt, how it was all she could do to keep from exploding into a zillion fragments of Michaela-ized ions and disappearing?

The annoyance that started with his hand – which she shrugged away, though it was all she could do not to reach over, lift it off, and shove it back at him – was growing. First into mild anger, and then even more intense anger, and then she was filled with a rage so big she couldn't hold it. WHAT THE FUCK was going on with her? How had everything in her life turned to shit? God DAMN it. Goddamn God, for that matter, or whoever was in charge of making things go the way they were supposed to. She wanted to scream FUCK YOU to that God, or to the structure of existence, or to whatever was pulling the strings, but she didn't even believe in any of that.

All she knew was that everything had been just fine, just great, and now... now it WASN'T. And that wasn't her fault, damn it. She hadn't done anything wrong. It had just HAPPENED to her. It wasn't fair, it wasn't at all fair, and it totally SUCKED.

Rennie took that moment to try talking to her – was he stupid? – saying, "Whatever you're feeling, it's okay, just let yourself go with it. Keep your eyes closed and let the feelings come up and pass through you."

Hah! If she let these feelings come through, she might just reach over and strangle him with one hand, while flinging her glass across the room with the other – hopefully in the process drenching the source of that revolting smell she was being forced to inhale. At the same time, a part of her said, "Okay. I can do that. I'll let the damn feelings come through."

And she sat there feeling not only as angry inside as she had ever felt – absolutely torrid with rage – but at the same time entirely vulnerable and stupid.

Her hands gripped the sofa cushions on either side of her legs so hard she thought they might tear off. She shook her head back and forth and – what was that noise? – Oh god, she was moaning. She was moaning and muttering.

"No. No, no, no, no, no, no, no, no. It's not right. It's not fair. It's not fair. IT'S NOT FAIR. I DON'T WANT IT TO BE LIKE THIS. I DON'T WANT IT ANYMORE! GO AWAY GO AWAY GO AWAY!!!!!"

What the fuck? Michaela thought to herself. She didn't even know why she was saying those things. Of course, it *wasn't* fair for her not to get the Eighth job. It was *really* unfair! When she could do the best work for them by far, and they didn't want her for the most stupid reason imaginable. She *deserved* that job. She had earned it. She was the best, the most well-respected in her business. What was WRONG with those idiotic people – wrong with how the world worked – that she didn't get it. Things were FUCKED UP.

She now felt not only RAGING and VULNERABLE but also DISAPPOINTED. Hugely disappointed. Devastated. She had worked so hard, come so far, and then, at what should have been a culminating moment of her career, she had failed. When it was most important, when she was flying the highest, everything stopped working. She was like a bird that got hit by a plane. She had crashed to the ground and was entirely broken.

Every large and small bone in her body was smashed, every muscle and ligament bruised and destroyed. Every organ burst. She was dead. She was nothing. She would never be anything again. She didn't exist. Michaela, whoever or whatever that was, had been demolished.

And you know what? Fuck it. Good.

Because if she was nothing, than she didn't have to worry any more, did she? She didn't have to impress anyone – especially the idiotic fuckheads who had insulted her and turned her away. She didn't have to do a damn thing for the rest of eternity. She was going to sit here on Incense Guy's couch and never move again. Fine. Perfect. She felt the cat again, back for another rub. Well let him. She wasn't even angry anymore. 'Nothing' doesn't have to be angry. 'Nothing' can relax. Nothing doesn't have anything to prove, because who gives a flying fuck?

She *could* relax. Michaela actually felt herself smile. Maybe her first real smile in days. Maybe in her whole life. She felt tickled inside, and actually started to laugh. She realized her eyes were still closed. But she didn't want to open them yet, and she didn't care what Rennie thought, either. Let him think she was nutty, why should she mind? She laughed more, imagining Rennie watching her: at first, spitting mad, and then laughing like a loon. That thought made her laugh harder, and she heard Rennie chuckling too, and soon they were both giggling and howling together like a couple of four-year-olds. Michaela opened her eyes for a second, and he wasn't even looking at her; he was rolled up in a ball on his end of the sofa with his own eyes closed, just laughing away.

Eventually, down to just a chuckle here and there, each of them wiped their eyes. They still smiled but did not acknowledge each other. Both sipped their teas.

Michaela was astounded. She could not have possibly felt any more different right now than from when she had arrived at Rennie's. And she had no idea why. Instead of feeling leaden, she was quite light. She no longer felt completely hopeless, as she had just a short time ago, nor was she boiling with anger any more either. She just felt....fine. Good, in fact. Not insanely good, but definitely relaxed good.

She did still feel self-conscious that Rennie had seen her go through all of that. She glanced sideways to see if he was looking at her, but he wasn't. He was bent over, petting the cat, until it left him and came to her. She stroked the smooth fur while he strode back and forth under her hand. Michaela liked cats. She'd grown up with a grey tabby, to whom she had been very attached. She would have been even sadder when he died, but she was in college and busy, and so could easily distract herself to keep from feeling bad.

Maybe one of these days she'd bring home a kitten.

She looked up at Rennie, who was also watching the cat. He looked up and caught her glance, stayed there. "Hey," he said.

"Hey," she answered. "Weird, huh?"

"Yes and no," he said. He paused as if thinking of what to say. "Definitely not light conversation, though."

"You're right about that."

She felt more comfortable with Rennie, now that they were talking. He didn't seem ready to kick her out because of her bizarre behavior. She wanted to talk with him about what she'd felt and seen but didn't know how to bring it up. She knew she'd sound crazy.

But Rennie handed her a pad and pen and said, "Write it down." So Michaela wrote, and when Rennie read it, he seemed to think she'd done something great. And he seemed excited about it.

She had to admit, she still felt tons better than when she got there, and it was the only time over the last few weeks she could say that. Maybe there really was something to all this woo-woo crap. She'd have to think about that.

20
Santa Fe

When Dirk came home, he was surprised and somewhat annoyed to find Dorothea still in her bathrobe. She was stretched out on the sofa, one hand pressing an emerald green silk eye pillow across her face, and the other arm draped behind her head over the end of the sofa. He knew some drama was in the works, but decided not to ask what, even if that was just postponing the inevitable. "Thea, sweetie, we've got the taping this afternoon. Shouldn't you be dressed by now?"

"Cancel it," she said, nothing moving but her mouth.

"Cancel? Why? Do you have a headache?"

"I probably do have one, now that you mention it. I'm so upset I didn't even notice. But this is worse."

Uh oh. Worse how? Dirk winced as he tried to recall past situations that had caused her to get like this. There were so many. What would it be this time?

"Did they stop making one of those face creams you use?" he guessed. "Or ... what? A shampoo or something? Lipstick?"

"No." Now the draped hand waved as she spoke.

"Did you talk to Grass or Seabird at the office? Did they tell you something you didn't like? Is someone in the core group getting married, or pregnant, or something?"

"Nooo." Dorothea moved the eyeshade enough to open one eye at Dirk. "Why? *Is* someone getting married or pregnant? You never tell me anything."

"That's because it looks bad to people if you get upset about that sort of thing, or try to tell them what to do with their personal lives. It makes you look like some manipulative cult leader. But no, not that I know of, at the moment."

She uncovered both eyes, and sat up a tad. "Dirk, honey, I'm not telling people what to do. I'm just letting them know when I see them doing the wrong thing. You know it's only because I love all those people and want what's best for them. And since I can see the greater perspective of what they're doing, if I see it's a mistake, how can I not want to tell them who they should be with, or whatever? Shouldn't I inform them if I know which choice of action is going to make them happier? Besides, people always think they're in love. All it does is take away their focus. And having babies can be very distracting from one's spiritual path."

Dirk rolled his eyes. "Okay, okay, let's not go there. I shouldn't have mentioned it. Let's fix today's problem. Why do you want to cancel the taping?"

"Hear for yourself. It's still on there."

"What's on where?"

"The message. The 03 line. Listen to it."

Dirk walked back to the office, where a phone was blinking. He listened impassively to Guy's voice, then returned to Dorothea, still half sitting up on the sofa, the green silk shade now on her forehead.

"Did you call him back?" Dirk asked, already knowing the answer. "You need to call him back."

She sank back down and covered her eyes. "Noooo. I don't *want* to call him back, Dirky-doodle. Can't you do it? Puh-leeeeease?"

"He doesn't want me to call him, Thea. He wants you to call him. You know he won't talk to me, he'll only talk to you. And you also know he'll keep at it until you do. So just call him back, will you?"

"But can't we…"

"We're not changing the numbers again. I can't tell you what a hassle that was last time."

"Well, if I have to call him, then I won't be able to tape today. If I have it on my mind to do it after, I'll be totally distracted. And if I talk to him first, I'll be too upset. You know how he gets to me. And what horrible thing do you think he wants to tell me about Mama? He just wants me to feel bad. He's always been like that."

"Thea, come on. You're a big girl. You're a spiritual teacher, for god's sake. You can handle it. Just think about what you'd say to someone else in this situation, if they came to you for help. Besides, you can't get out of the taping. It'll cost thousands if we have to reschedule."

"What if that's what Guy wants? More money?"

"Well, if it comes to it, *then* you can put me on the phone. But he knows he'd have to talk to me about money, so I doubt that's why he called for you."

Dorothea rolled on her side and scrunched into a fetal ball, holding the pillow to her eyes.

"Oh, o-KAY. Bring me the phone. But first get me some hot tea, will you? Chamomile. And one of those chocolate thingies I like – you know, those new organic bars. And Click-ee. And a box of Kleenex, just in case."

Dirk set off to gather food and drink from the kitchen, dolphin from the bed, tissues, and the phone, then delivered them all to the coffee table by Dorothea, still immobile on the couch. He dropped into a nearby armchair and picked up a magazine.

Slowly, letting go of the pillow, but without opening her eyes, Dorothea sat up and went into a full lotus on the couch.

She breathed deeply. She sat like that for a few minutes, finally raised her arms to the sky, held them there for several seconds, lowered them. She opened her eyes, pulled the toy dolphin and the chocolate onto her lap, and picked up the phone.

She looked at the phone then back up at Dirk, and held it out to him.

"Dirk, honey, you know I don't know the number. Dial it for me, hon, won't you?"

Dirk rolled his eyes and took the phone, waited while Thea slowly blew on, then took a sip of, her tea. When her hands were finally free, he punched in the numbers, which he had already looked up, and shoved the phone into her lap. He could hear ringing on the other end as he rose from the chair and headed from the room, glancing back as he left.

Dorothea, eyes closed, was holding the handset slightly away from her ear with one hand, and making ritual-like gestures over it with the other. He wasn't sure if she was giving it a blessing or a curse.

"As usual," he muttered to himself.

21
101 South

"**O**kay."

Michaela, driving home from Rennie's, was startled to hear herself speak out loud.

"Okay. What now?"

It wasn't an anxiety-driven, freaking-out kind of "what now?" It was more of a relaxed, curious, friendly "what now?" As if the answer wasn't all that big a deal. And that made it more confusing. Because that question was a big deal, wasn't it?

After all, something had been making her crazy. She could see that now. She had lost it there, for a while, whatever "it" was. Her sanity, maybe? Her sense of things being normal and right. Whatever she had lost, it wasn't completely back now, either. She wasn't totally depressed, freaked out, or pissed off anymore. But she still didn't feel all together either. She was in some sort of limbo.

Her craziness was from the stress of losing her position at the top of her game. She'd worked hard to be part of the hottest new restaurants, and now was being shut out. And it wasn't fair, because this time she had been thrown into a new game, onto a new playing field. In this game, she was not competitive, had not even thought it worthy of attempting before. And here she was nothing; nobody. That had been pointed out to her quite plainly, and painfully.

She saw herself now at a juncture. This juncture was not like, for instance, approaching a crossroads. Michaela thought about this as she met an actual crossroads in the car, and turned left. No, it was more like dropping onto a point, with an array of vectors moving away from her like paths in different directions. On one path, she could see herself thinking and acting the same way she had before all the weird stuff started happening – the radish, the rejection, and now this incomprehensible experience at Rennie's. Sure, she had been confused, and her ego was bruised, but she could come back stronger then ever. Eighth wouldn't be the hot new thing forever.

Who even knew if their completely absurd restaurant would be popular? Maybe for a little while they'd be the It place. But more likely, the food wouldn't be that great, and at the end of the day, that's what mattered. They'd disappear off the map of Foodiedom, she thought, glancing down at the map on her GPS screen, and the Foodies would move on to the next big opening – one she *would* do the menu for – and Eighth would remain an overpriced tourist destination or a joke. Probably both. That would show them.

But here was another possibility. Now that she had started attempting to be, well, (and here she put air quotes in her thoughts) "spiritual" – didn't that mean she could go back there and try for the job again? She could read a few books really fast, go to a workshop or two, follow Rennie's instructions for meditation so she didn't get frustrated like she had that first time she tried it on her own. Wouldn't that qualify her by Asshole-Dum and Asshole-Dee's, i.e., Angelo and Jozef's, standards? They'd already said they liked her work, so maybe that was all it would take.

The problem was, in order to find out if that would work, she'd have to go back and subject herself to their scrutiny. And what if they again said no? What if they had already found someone else? What if they still thought she was too unspiritual? If she put herself out there and was further rejected, she didn't think she could stand it.

There was another possibility, she considered, pressing the garage door opener while turning into her driveway. She could drop out for a while. Out of her business, her normal life, whatever. Do something different. She didn't understand what she had gone through today at Rennie's, but it felt significant. Rennie said her experience had elements of shamanism, which he explained as a kind of healing in native societies. Maybe she was supposed to be a shaman. Perhaps she was meant to go find a tribe somewhere that needed one, and offer her services. She wondered if they posted on Craigslist.

She didn't know much about native tribes, but thought there were probably still some around, deep in rural Mexico, or the Amazon. But she hated being hot and sticky, and her Spanish wasn't exactly mucho bueno. That's if they even spoke Spanish. Some difficult, rare language, more likely, with sounds she wouldn't be able to pronounce.

No, it would have to be American Indians. Northwest and Southwest tribes didn't appeal to her because she felt their design elements had been overused. But there were some small, less famous tribes right here in California, judging by all the casinos. That was even better - close to civilization, in case she needed to shop for clothes or get a good meal. And if a casino tribe needed a new shaman, they could probably afford to pay her better.

Or maybe she should just keep getting advice from Rennie. He seemed to know a lot. Look what had happened to her already, just from spending part of an afternoon with him. She didn't know why she felt so much better now, but something about being at Rennie's had done it. She felt released from a spell. How did he do that? He must know some special techniques. She could ask him to show them to her. Rennie said he wanted to be a teacher, so he could practice on her. That would help him, and in exchange, she would learn from him and get his advice, which would help her.

In fact, he'd probably know exactly what she should do about Eighth. Maybe he could tell her just what to say to impress them. She could even go back there and take him with her, as a spiritual advisor. That would make her look good. She'd call Rennie tomorrow and ask him. Tonight, now that she finally felt better, she was going to have a nice dinner and get some work done.

Things were definitely looking up. After she called Rennie and officially started her spiritual quest, she'd decide whether to go back to Eighth or not. She didn't want to wait too long, but Rennie had said "the universe has its own timing," or something. That must mean you had to figure out when was the best time to get what you want. That would be a good first subject for Rennie to teach her about. She called in an order for linguini with clam sauce to be delivered, and took the bottle of Chardonnay out of the fridge. Finally, she was doing something positive again. Michaela had a good feeling. She just knew it. Now everything was going to be all right.

22
Petaluma

"**N**oeletta."

Rennie had been thinking over the possibilities in his office for the last hour and a half, and decided to give it a shot. He stuck his head out of his office.

"Got a minute?"

"Sure, boss."

She made a note on the invoice she was working on and followed Rennie back into his office. She sat across from him as he closed the door and returned to the desk, swiveling his Aeron around to face her.

"I'm not sure this is work-related," he started out, "but it might be."

She raised her eyebrows and held out her palms. "Let's hear it."

Not everything they talked about in the office concerned work, but they both knew it was unusual for him to ask her into his office to talk about something personal.

"In fact, that's what I want to know. What I want you to help me figure out, I mean. Because I had some confusing experiences related to this, um, this subject that I want to talk to you about. Confusing, but good – at least I think it's good

– and I'm trying to figure out if it's what I think it is, and I thought maybe you could help."

Noeletta nodded patiently, though Rennie thought he wasn't making much sense. He tried a more direct approach.

"Let me show you something. Then I'll explain."

He reached into his briefcase and pulled out the incense that he'd received at his house. Although the package was, of course, already open, Rennie had kept all the parts: string, outer paper with his home address and no return address, and cryptic note. Everything was there except the two sticks he had burned – one while he was meditating alone in his house, and the other when Michaela was visiting. He passed the whole thing to Noeletta, who took it without comment. She spent a few minutes examining the wrapping, reading the address and note, and looking at the sticks themselves. Finally, as Rennie had done when the package first arrived, and then again when he found it in the sofa cushions, she lifted the remaining sticks to her nose, closed her eyes, and inhaled deeply.

Rennie watched intently. He was dying to talk, but wanted Noeletta's reaction uncompromised by his own opinions. Her face went from concentration to puzzlement. She smelled the incense again.

"Weird, boss," she said. "What's in this? And where did it come from?"

"I know," Rennie said excitedly. "I mean, I don't know. But I do agree it's weird. I can tell what some of the ingredients are, but not all of them. And it came to my house, which doesn't make any sense either. I have no idea who this person is that sent it or how he got that address. Or how I'm supposed to order any more of it."

Noeletta sniffed the sticks a third time. "Are you sure you want to? I mean, yes, it's different, but maybe not in such a good way. I just don't know how commercial it is. How does it burn?"

"Okay. That's the funny part. I might just be making this

up, but some really strange things happened when I burned it. And not just once. And not just to me. But I don't know if it has anything to do with the incense, or if it's just a coincidence."

"Really? Well let's hear it."

"Okay. Well, first, I decided to try it out, and so I lit a stick and started sitting, just like I always do. And what happened was – and I know you won't take this the wrong way – I'm not trying to make myself special or anything, but – Noeletta, I know this sounds crazy, but I went somewhere in my meditation I never thought I would go. I mean, I know this doesn't mean I'm enlightened, but..."

"Come on, boss, just say it. Don't worry, I promise I won't kneel and kiss ring, no matter what state of consciousness you reached."

He chuckled. "Right. Okay. I really feel like I experienced Samadhi. And believe me, I've never had anything happen nearly that deep, or high, or whatever it is, before. I just disappeared. No separate consciousness."

"How long?"

"Maybe 45 minutes. Just the same amount of time it took the stick to burn."

"Interesting."

"Well, yes, but I didn't think about it then – you know, having to do with the incense or anything. I just figured it was an anomaly; maybe it would happen again, maybe not. Maybe it would change me in some way, or my practice would just be generally deeper, but I'd have to wait and see."

"That's reasonable."

"Right. But then something else happened." Rennie paused, not sure how to explain Michaela being at his house. He decided to take the straightforward approach.

"This woman had called me. I met her in San Rafael a couple of weeks ago. She started a conversation with me about disappearing objects because... well, it's complicated, but the upshot is, she's very um, unsophisticated. About spiritual matters, transformational stuff, you know. She's just getting into it. And she wanted some advice, so thought I might be able to suggest a few things. So she was coming over to get some books, talk a bit. It wasn't a date or anything, I don't think. I'm kinda sure about that. I mean, she seemed genuinely troubled and looking for answers."

Rennie thought, not for the first time, what a good listener Noeletta was. She was, or at least appeared to be, interested without judging. It made him appreciate her even more, and want to do something nice for her. Hmm, what would she like? Paid time off, most likely.

"So anyway," he continued, "She came into the living room, sat down, and I went to get some tea. While I was up, figured what the heck, I'd light a stick of this stuff and see what she thought of it. Not because I thought it would do anything special. I was just curious if she liked the smell. And I wanted to experience it again myself because, you know, being so out there in my meditation the first time, I didn't really notice the aroma. So it was just for a background scent.

"Then I sit down with her to start talking. But we never even get that far. She goes totally into process – you know what I mean – so deep into her own stuff that's all she can pay attention to. And I was wondering if maybe she was really mentally ill or something. I mean, the first time we met she seemed okay. Maybe a little ignorant, but nothing wrong with her. And this time, she seemed less artificial, like her defenses were down. So I thought, okay this is interesting. She's getting a bit more real. But then she starts going into this space, and I thought maybe she was less stable than I originally figured. Maybe really falling apart.

"But, you know, I've been in those places myself, and seen a lot of people go through that, though it's always been in retreats or workshops – I'm sure you have too."

Noeletta nodded.

"And so I just decided to treat her like she was going

through something and support her to do her inner work, you know?"

She continued to nod expectantly, probably wondering where this was going to end up, and where the incense came in.

"So she gets really mad; a lot of anger coming through, but she does great with it, just goes into it. And, you know, I'm sure she thought it was me making her mad. She had to, I mean, I was the only one there. But she did all right with that, too. Stayed internal, you know? Then, miraculously, she comes through it all and she's okay. Great, in fact. You could see; she was all relaxed after. But she told me that, too. She had what I guess I'd call a shamanic type of death-rebirth experience. But whatever you want to call it, she was like a different person after. And Noeletta, this is someone who I'm sure hasn't done a whit's worth of inner work in her entire life."

"Then what?" Noeletta asked, after Rennie had been silent for a few moments.

He said, "We both got hysterical laughing. And then she told me what she had gone through in her mind and body while all that was happening, and then about some stuff she'd been experiencing in her life. I didn't say much, gave her a couple of books to look at — basic stuff, you know. And then she left."

Rennie said he had then returned to the couch and just sat there for a long time, mystified by the fact that this woman had walked in entirely messed up, and had this huge breakthrough caused by nothing either of them did, then left in a much better place.

"That was when I thought of the incense," he said.

They sat in silence.

"So, boss," Noeletta finally said. "Are you saying you think it's the incense causing these intense experiences?"

He shrugged. "Don't know."

"Right. Well here's what I think. I think you need to try burning it again and see what happens. If it does what you're saying – which would make it a powerful activator of the psyche – that would be mighty incredible." Noeletta paused. "Dear god, it could be worth a fortune."

"Exactly! And I have no idea how to get more of it."

"Well, that's something J.J. and I can work on."

"Good. Great. I was hoping you'd say that."

"I have a thought," Noeletta said.

"Okay."

"We need another trial. Let me take one of these with me. I'll try it out someplace where we can get plenty of additional data."

Rennie hesitated. There were only a dozen sticks to begin with and he didn't want to give any more up. On the other hand, they really needed to try it out again, to see what, if anything, would happen. Or find out it was just some weird fluke and his previous experiences had nothing to do with the incense. But still, he would have preferred to do the testing himself.

"Trust me, boss, I mean padawan," Noeletta said. "I will test the midi-chlorians, and tell you if the force is strong in this one."

Rennie did trust Noeletta. She had never let him down.

"Okay," he said, "even though you're mixing up your Star Wars metaphors."

He handed her one of the potentially precious sticks. She took it immediately out of his office, tucked it into two layers of their best wrapping and an oversize plastic box, and hid it away in a file cabinet with her purse.

"More will be revealed. I'll let you know on Monday. Don't ask me anything until then."

23
Santa Fe

*T*hea took the phone back from Dirk. While it rang, she gestured a protection between the phone and herself. Although, in fact, it didn't ring at all. It was one of those cell services that let you replace the ring with music of your choice for your callers to hear while they wait. Guy had chosen "Jeremiah Was a Bullfrog," a song Thea hated. She made a face and held it away from her ear, waiting to see if Guy would pick up or if she'd have to leave a message. She didn't know which was worse. She'd have to talk to him some time. Might as well get it over with.

"Baby sister!" he boomed. "I finally gotcha! How's it hanging? You wastin' away again out in Kachinaville?"

"Hello, Guy," was all Dorothea could give him.

"Must'a been glad to hear from me, you called back so fast. You miss me much?"

"I wish I had time to miss anyone. The demands on me are as pressing as ever."

"Oh, I'm sure they are. But life's treating you okay? Things working out? Still get people to pay to hear you talk?"

"Dirk and I are fine. We're very involved in our work right

now, and I can only talk a few minutes. What did you want to tell me about our mother?"

"Oh, the Moms. She's fine. Don't have to worry about her – me and Kyle and the girls take good care of her. She mostly watches her shows and plays with the kids. I don't think she even worries about it anymore, how you never call or come see her or anything."

"Does she know Dirk and I help support her?"

"Oh, I'm sure we've mentioned it on occasion. Don't like to get her all upset, you know, with the details."

"You made it sound like something was wrong with her. Like there was something you needed to tell me about her."

"Oh, yeah, well, that was just to get your attention. Looks like it worked, too, heh heh. In fact, that was maybe the fastest you ever called me back. Dirk cracked the old whip, huh? Didn't want to hear from me every two hours for a week this time, did he?"

Dorothea was trying to stay calm and focused, but it was getting difficult. She held Click-ee up close to her face and concentrated on his round, black, non-judgmental eyes. Or technically, his eye, since the way they were set on either side of his head made it hard to see both at once. She kept him in front of her as she talked to Guy. Dirk had left the room; she knew it was just to seem like he was giving her privacy. He'd be lurking somewhere close enough to hear her side of the conversation.

With her palm over the phone, she made a kissy noise at Click-ee.

"So how's it going, your little workshop operation out there? Bringing in the big bucks?"

"Guy, if you want to talk about our business, then why did you ask for me? You know Dirk handles all that. If I were in charge of the business part of what we do, we'd never make any money at all. I'd work for free, or give it all away. You know I've always just wanted to be of service to the world."

"Yeah, right. 'The world, Chico, and everything in it.' Heh, heh."

"What do you mean?" Thea asked suspiciously.

"Just something from a movie. Never mind. Nope, don't need to talk to old Dirk, not yet anyway. Just makin' conversation. Actually, the reason I mentioned it's 'cause I'm getting into your line myself. Wrote a book, doing a little tour for it."

"What?" Dorothea said, dropping Click-ee into her lap. "What do you mean, 'my line'? What book? You don't write. I didn't even think you could read."

"Now, Dot... I mean, Dor'thea. That's not very nice and spir-tul of you, now is it? But don't worry, I'm not taking it personally. I've taken in a lot from watching you over the years. Actually read your books, you know. Learned something. Read some more. Long story short, I decided to write some of this up for folks like me, who wouldn't usually look at this stuff. And it's getting published by some big New York company, too."

Guy was practically crowing. The company he named made Dorothea feel nauseous. She had tried for years to get one of the major publishers to accept her first book, and the ordeal had made her miserable. She'd finally gotten a small niche press to take it, and they'd done a good job with that and her subsequent books, building their business at the same time that she had become more successful.

But she still felt the sting of rejection, as if the popular kids didn't think she was cool enough to hang out with. She couldn't imagine them wanting a book by her half-illiterate, football-obsessed brother. What could he possibly have to write about? Who would be interested? What universe had she fallen into?

When Dorothea didn't say anything, Guy went on.

"Yep, it's called, *The Regular Guy's Guide to Enlightenment*. I wanted to call it *The Redneck's Guide to Enlightenment* but they said the redneck thing had passed its peak. And they thought my other choice, *The Swinging Dick's Guide...,* made it sound like a sex book. So we went with *Regular Guy.*"

"Stop!" Dorothea burst out.

"What?"

"Stop! You can't do that! You can't write a book like that, it's ..." she almost said, it's not fair, but that didn't make sense. "It's bad for people. It's going to hurt them."

Guy snorted. "Only if they hurt themselves laughing. Nobody takes this shit seriously, do they? It's a hoot. You know, makes me out to be this ooh-la-la guru on a mountaintop, but it's supposed to be funny. It's all bullshit, natur'ly. It's not like I believe any of it. Nobody in their right mind really believes that crap, do they?"

"I... I..." Dorothea sputtered, unable to even form a thought, let alone put it into words. It was an unfamiliar and horribly unpleasant feeling. She'd have to remember what this felt like in order to address the topic in future workshops.

"Now don't get your panties in a twist. I know you let on it all means something, but whatever. Either way, seems like a good racket to me."

"DIRK," Dorothea yelled, holding the phone away from her as though it contained poison. "DIIIIIIRK!"

REPORT BY NOELETTA GROVES

Product: Stick incense from batch received at home of R. Morrow, sent from R.K. Ashvin, Sumana, India. Ingredients unknown. Sample #3 of 12.
Product was lit at approximately 5:15 pm on Friday, August 12.

Location: Belwood Community Church, Sonoma County, California.
Circumstances: Rehearsal for the wedding of Serena G. (daughter of tester) and fiancé Markus M.

Also present:
Reverend Deborah C.
Maid-of-honor: Chelsea R., plus four bridesmaids
Best man: Dan B., plus four groomsmen
Bride's father: Walt M.
Groom's mother: Ms. Naomi M.
Groom's father and stepmother: Mr. and Mrs. Marley M.
Flower girls: Cousins of bride and groom, both age 7
Wedding planner: Anastasia (goes by one name)
Pianist and vocalist
Observations: Prior to lighting of incense, mood among rehearsal participants was tense, due to several contributing factors:

1. Prior argument over dress of flower girl on groom side, whose mother did not like the style chosen by the bride and asked if her daughter could wear a white dress with trim and a hair ribbon in color to match bridesmaids (pale green). Bride, holding opinion that she was the only person in wedding party who should wear white, responded somewhat less than politely that having two flower girls was

less essential than having the mother "not give me any more shit about it."

2. Two groomsmen disappearing after arriving at church, reason or reasons unknown. Third groomsman dispatched to find them.

3. Wedding planner shouting continuously into air (presumably using earpiece) while talking to purveyor of cake, re: miscommunication as to agreed-upon date of delivery.

4. Ring-bearer (two year old male bulldog) chewing ring pillow into soggy clump of pale green velvet. Fortunately, ring safe with best man. Bride and wedding planner (interrupting phone use) explode simultaneously at owner of ring-bearer, i.e., groom. Wedding planner immediately back on phone for replacement. Groom taking ring-bearer outside, stating need to "be with someone sane for a change."

5. Singer and accompanist (piano) disagreeing at increasing volume over presumed "bad note" given singer by pianist, resulting in wedding planner interrupting pillow emergency call, in order to clarify instructions for provision of music, i.e., "shut up and play, you overpaid morons." Effectiveness of approach demonstrated by singer shoving wedding planner in chest and following accompanist out of the building.

6. Mother and step-mother of groom exchanging glares across row of chairs; one of those chairs containing father of groom as he observes progress of unidentified sporting event on his iPhone.

Upon reassembly of entire party (return of three groomsmen, singer and accompanist, groom and ring-bearer), and proceeding of rehearsal, tester removed incense, burner and lighter from bag, unwrapped incense and lit stick. By leaning under seats, tester was able to place burner on floor under chair, exactly two seats in from the aisle and two rows from the front, without being seen.

Initial reaction to incense took approximately 72 seconds, as tester noticed persons closest to ignition point (parents/stepparent of groom, across aisle from ignition point) begin sniffing and turning in their seats. In particular, mother and stepmother of groom each glare more intensely at the other, possibly presuming the source of the new odor.

As range of smoke widens, reaching additional persons, several reactions observed. Not all parties demonstrate awareness of smoke and odor. For instance, shortly after beginning music, singer places hand on shoulder of accompanist, closes eyes and raises face toward ceiling, while accompanist smiles. Both sway slightly in time to the music.

Wedding planner, now detached from phone, instructs rehearsal participants on timing and placement, then slowly wanders off to sit several rows behind tester and is heard to remark, "Isn't this lovely."

Bride, within point-five seconds of noticing smell, drops arm of father-of-bride and approaches tester at near maximum speed, given heel height. Bride observed to regress to age approximately 15 years. Bride suggests tester is "ruining my wedding. You know I don't want any of that weird stuff you do going on here."

Tester, in role as mother-of-bride, suggests to bride that since this is not actually the wedding, it is merely the wedding rehearsal, and as mother-of-bride she has not imposed a single request on bride except to choose her own dress, and the incense is not doing any damage to anyone, why doesn't she just let this go and enjoy the rehearsal?

Wedding planner: "You know, Serena, dear, it really is a lovely smell."

Bride: "It actually is rather nice. You know, it doesn't really bother me. Don't know why I was so fussy about it. In fact, I don't know why I was fussy about any of this. The important thing isn't the wedding, it's the marriage." Bride, smiling turns and walks back to father-of-bride, takes his arm and gives it a squeeze. "Come on Daddy, let's take a walk."

Rehearsal proceeds without further incident, with two exceptions:

7. stepmother-of-groom moves to sit by mother-of-groom, where both are observed whispering and giggling.

8. two groomsmen who disappeared earlier a) hold hands; b) become teary; c) are observed exchanging rings at end of ceremony rehearsal.

Tester observation (internal): Approximately 30 seconds after lighting, tester notices increased positive awareness of surroundings and associated sensations, i.e., church feels imbued with holiness; light through stained glass becomes brighter; music more lush and beautiful. Tester also observes feelings of love and compassion for all individuals present (including wedding planner and bulldog); feels completely satisfied with current moment, as if all things perfect and as they should be. Tester notes this response is consistent with descriptions of "peak experience" as per Maslow and others.

Tester observation (external): All participants in event appear to act more accepting toward one another and to the situation. As previously noted, former animosity of groom's mother and step-mother seem to become affinity. Wedding planner stops shouting instructions and lets events unfold as previously planned. Bride and groom exhibit exceptional affection toward each other in an appropriate manner (i.e., gazing into each other's eyes, etc). Groomsman and groomsman confess to mutual feelings. Father-of-bride turns off electronic device and smiles at everyone. Bulldog, after bearing pretend pillow and ring, falls asleep.

Summary: After lighting of incense, mood changed from tension and discord to benevolence and warmth. Remarks were made by several persons, including Reverend C., about sensing "the sacredness of marriage," despite this being just the rehearsal. Bride was heard to say, "We almost don't need the wedding anymore."

Follow-up: Tone of rehearsal carried over to evening's rehearsal dinner, and even to wedding day, where, despite normal amount of problems, all parties remained in calm, loving state. While only circumstantial evidence can be attributed to the incense being the cause of change of dynamics, it is remarkable that such a change occurred exactly when it did. Tester's belief is that the incense caused a "higher consciousness" in all parties that was mediated by the person's individual states as well as the situation all were involved in.

Signed, Noeletta Graves, tester.

24
Santa Fe

As he left the post office and popped the trunk to his Beemer, Dirk congratulated himself for keeping the old PO box after opening the Lightworks office downtown. Even if he never used it again, the box was worth the cost just to receive the bulky package he now held under his arm. It could never have gone to his home, and he didn't want to risk it arriving at the office, either, where someone might accidentally open it, or even just mention to Dorothea the fact that it existed.

He needed to be careful bringing it into the house, but he had a plan. Extracting a reusable canvas grocery bag from the trunk, he crammed the package into the bottom. On the way home, he would stop at Whole Foods and buy food to cover it. He'd leave the bag on the kitchen counter, confident that Dorothea would never go near it. As soon as she was taking a bath or engrossed in something equally time consuming, Dirk would unpack the groceries and sneak the bag back to his private home office.

His plan worked flawlessly. When he got reached the kitchen, Dorothea was, in fact, in the tub. He put away the bottles of Honest Tea, box of organic Gorilla Munch cereal, and package of cheddar flavored Pirates Booty, and started for the office, backtracking only to grab the Pirates Booty and one Green Energy tea and throw them back into the bag.

He locked his office and snipped off the end of the priority mail envelope. He pulled out the galley pages of a book manuscript. He'd correctly guessed that a friend of his, the leader of a series of men's workshops that Dirk had attended before he met Dorothea, would have a copy. The friend had skimmed the pages in order to create a blurb for the book, which he'd already written and emailed to the publisher. With no further need for the galleys, he was happy to send them on to Dirk.

To the friend, and to everyone else on the planet, this was simply another manuscript, and the book it represented would be just one more of the hundreds, maybe thousands, published in the self-help field that year – although Dirk suspected there would be few, if any, similar to this one.

To Dirk, however, it was a nuclear warhead, its trigger down the hall submerged in a tub of Tropical Kiss lemon-coconut scented bubbles, humming the theme from Star Wars.

Dirk sat behind his desk, tore open the bag of Pirates Booty, and popped a few in his mouth. With orange fingers, he turned over the first pages of the manuscript. Heart thumping, he began to read.

THE REGULAR GUY'S GUIDE TO ENLIGHTENMENT
BY GUY FIMPLE

Chapter 1

Regular Guy Enlightenment? Who Are We Kidding?

Hey, Guys, and welcome. Right off, let me say this. The unfamiliar object in your hands right now is not a book. Think of it as a Regular Guy hangout, a man-cave. Have a seat, right here on this leather recliner, or stretch on out over there on the couch. Relax. I, like you, am a Regular Guy. And also probably like you, for most of my life I had not given much thought – in fact, no thought whatsoever - to enlightenment.

So why think about it now? Honestly, Guys, I can't tell you. Why not ten years ago or next Thursday? But I can tell you what I was doing when I started thinking about it. I was watching a soccer game with some buddies.

We were having the usual soccer-watching discussion of, "Football by any other name isn't football." And I suddenly found myself lifted out of my body, and hovering over myself, up by the ceiling. I went through the roof, rising higher and higher. I was above the earth, racing around the planet. I saw and felt all the different games being played with balls and feet around the world. Suddenly, I was overcome, as all the names and forms of football swept over me all at once. Canadian Football, Australian Rules Football, Gridiron Football, American Football. Soccer, obviously. Even Rugby.

Then I went even further out, into the stars, and I saw the names and forms of every game for sport being played anywhere, ever. I even saw games that hadn't been played yet, or even invented. I got glimpses of sport on other planets. Then it was over. I came back to the living room, back into my body, and downed the rest of my Bud.

Guys! No big deal, right? Maybe you've been there. Add enough suds to enough televised competition and it's going to happen, right? But the experience got to me. I wanted more. I started experimenting with different combinations of brew and sports. I set up two, then three, then five screens: TVs, computers, even the camcorder playback of my kid playing basketball. I tried all different types and styles of beer, from all over the world. From imports to local microbrews. This went on for three months.

Guys, let me tell you, I was driven. I was committed. I was inspired. I was harassed night and day by an extremely irritated wife. But I was never able to repeat the experience I had during the soccer game. My quest wasn't working and it was taking all my free time. I was about to give up.

Finally one day, I stopped. I swallowed the tail end of a bottle of Ninkasi, turned off all the screens, and stood up. Without a plan, I headed for the back door and out into the yard. For no particular reason, I sat down under an orange tree. And Guys, you know what? I leaned against the tree and it dropped an orange on my gut.

And that's when I got it. I didn't need to fulfill my quest. I had something better. Here I'd spent three months staring at screens and drinking beer, trying to repeat one very special experience. And during that entire time, I had not appreciated that I'd been doing nothing but watching sports and drinking beer. Guys, I'd missed it! The best thing on the planet! While I was trying for something I thought I needed, I was ignoring the supreme goodness that I was actually getting.

And as I sat under that orange tree, it all came to me. I saw that we Regular Guys need enlightenment too, and that we can have it. We are not ignorant, sub-human morons. We are Guys, Guys! Regular Guys. We're no better or worse than any other variety of human. And we can be enlightened in our own, special, Regular Guy way without losing our Regular Guyness. Got that?

So that's what this book is about. Enlightening yourself without losing your Regular Guyness. Transcending it yet embracing it. Guys, if this sounds like something you want to do, then this not-a-book is the place for you. If not, put it down and go back to the couch. You don't need it. You don't need me.

And hey, that enlightenment thing? Truth is, you're already there. You just don't know it yet.

◊ ◊ ◊

Dirk leaned his plush executive chair back as far as it would go and turned his face to the ceiling. He hadn't known what to expect from Guy's book, but this was a surprise. Dirk thought that with enough promotion it might catch on as a humorous novelty item, the kind you pick up just for the title and get a few laughs out of. The subject matter was no threat to Dorothea's work, but that didn't mean she wouldn't see it as one. She'd be horrified and take it personally. She already did, just knowing it existed.

With a sigh, Dirk put the pages together and stuffed them back into the envelope. It would be safe in the back of his bottom desk drawer until he had time to read more. Right now, he had to get Dorothea to move a little faster. They still had taping to do.

25
Michaela

Michaela had no problem with the maroon robes. In fact she thought they were very nice, especially with the little touch of yellow peeking out at the shoulder. The matching maroon socks in brown clogs were a little clunky, but she liked having the brown prayer beads wrapped around her left wrist several times and resting on both sides of her silver watch. She was glad to be still wearing the Mini-Beluga with the diamonds, the one she got in Vegas. What startled her was reaching up and feeling her hairlessness; the unexpected unevenness of her shaven head. *I'm bald,* she thought. *Never expected that.*

She was surrounded by countless other maroon-wrapped, brown shod, bead-wristed, bald-headed persons, but none with a watch as nice as hers. *Should I feel guilty about it?* She tested out feeling guilty. Tried to summon the emotion. It didn't take. *No. I'm perfectly content to have on the nicest watch, and do not feel bad about it at all.*

All of them were walking together in the same direction. *How many?* Thousands, at least. Had to be. To the left, right, and front was a sea of maroon cloth. Chrome-domes of every shape and size, ears perched obediently on each side, bobbed ahead peacefully. She turned, looking behind her, where the story was the same, but with the addition of mouths, noses, eyes. The faces seemed kind and accepting. The face directly behind her smiled and moved its chin to indicate she should keep going forward. Michaela turned back around and faced the front, continuing to move with the group. *I wonder where we're going.*

The pack ahead was narrowing, and becoming a single file. The line stretched far away. Michaela took her place in line and followed the others. They had been walking at first on sand, but then it became dirt, and now ice. Their steps crunched loudly as they walked, but there were so many it became a white noise. The air smelled cold and salty. She stayed in line, following the maroon line ahead, sharp against all the ice. *I've been walking a long time.* She looked at her watch again, and saw it was 3:30. *But I don't know what time we started. Or if it's 3:30 in the morning or in the afternoon.* The sky was twilit, with streaks of red, and although it was not dark, she couldn't see the sun.

Far ahead, the maroon figures went over a rise, and then down a dip on the icy path, and she couldn't see what happened after that. She felt a sudden surge of excitement and fear mixed together. The closer she got to that place, the more anxious she became. *Something is going to happen to me.* But she didn't know what it was.

Sooner than expected, she neared the rise. She followed the others, her heart pounding and underarms becoming damp. Up and over each went, three ahead, now two, now one. She rose up on to the crest, and saw, just in front of her, the edge of the ice. Maroon-clad figures spread out five or six deep alongside it. And then one, or two, or several at a time, they were jumping off.

She realized now that they were all not just monks, as she had assumed, but penguins. Well, they were both, actually. Monks and penguins. In fact, there was no difference between the two. Monks were penguins and penguins monks. Now that she knew the secret, Michaela couldn't believe she had never noticed it before. *Why doesn't anyone talk about this?* It was so obvious. When she got home, she would paint a series of pictures showing this fact. Then she would write a book about it, with her paintings as illustrations. A lot of people would want to buy that book, so she'd have to be sure to print a lot of copies.

Still, Michaela was terrified of what was coming. As she came down from the rise, she had to choose: right, left, or straight ahead. She wanted to go right, but the ones behind her were all moving left and she was forced to go that way too. *This is scary. I don't want to jump off the ice. I can't see what's down there.* Those at the edge were going over, and they might be falling into nothingness or they might be plunging to their doom. Now she was being pushed ahead by the group as more and more came behind her, and everyone moved forward toward the edge. She heard her heart beating so loud and hard it was like a drum solo in her ears. She tried to stop, but couldn't. She was almost there.

The one immediately in front of her now stood at the end of the ice, and Michaela could tell he was trying to keep from going over. She couldn't help it, she was pushed from behind, and she bumped into him, and he took a step forward and was gone. Michaela tried to feel bad but was too terrified. At least now she would be able to see what was down there, what she would be going into. For a moment she stood right at the edge, and looked over, trying to brace herself for whatever it was.

All she could see were clouds, but they were not white, or even gray. These were candy-colored swirls of vapor and fluff, somewhere between cotton candy and those enormous lollypops made from twisted bands of brightly colored sugar wound into a giant spiral. It was fantastically beautiful, and for a moment her heart opened up like a song; like a summer day.

Then she received a gentle nudge from behind, and had no choice but to step off.

Falling through the air, through the colored swirls of light, she did not know how far down she would go, or what was at the bottom. *I might die. I'm probably about to die.* But she was not really scared any more. She didn't feel bad at all. The same words kept going through her mind, over and over, even though they did not make any sense.

So this is what it's like. All that time, and this is what it's like.

26
Petaluma

*R*ennie sat at his desk, twirled a pen absentmindedly, and stared with longing at his treasure trove – the nine slim sticks in their protective wrapping, resting serenely in their open box in front of him. They usually stayed in his safe, but he took them out at least once a day for a few minutes. It made him feel enlightened just to ponder their existence.

"You are amazing," he said out loud. "I have to have more of you."

Rennie glanced at the phone. He should call Michaela back, but first he had to decide. Should he set up an appointment with her? Or should he tell her he was too busy right now to help her find her way spiritually?

Rennie was flattered when Michaela asked him to work with her more formally, although he told her right off she had to stop referring to him as her "spiritual guide." That was the first thing she had to do – get the terms right. He informed her that her "guides" were the ones who aided her in this life as disembodied helpers from the other side. He was not dead yet, and hoped to retain that status for a good bit longer. He still had plenty he wanted to do over here. Especially now.

Which was why he possibly shouldn't take on Michaela as

a student. His primary focus was elsewhere. He was tremendously excited about the mysterious substance in front if him. It apparently held properties he had never encountered before in an olfactory product. He had never even heard of incense working like this. He needed to find whoever sent it to him. And soon. What if samples had also been given to other importers and distributors, his competitors? Rennie wanted exclusive rights to the product. It was crucial for his plans. He needed to work fast.

Noeletta and J.J. were already hot on the trail. They were using business connections in India to track down Mr. R.K. Ashvin in Sumana. But so far, no one they knew had even heard of the town of Sumana, and the name Ashvin was common all over the country. It was mostly used as a first name, but there were still places in India where people have only a single name. Often, when those persons went into a business or profession, particularly with westerners, they added initials in front, making the single name appear as a surname. That was likely the case here.

Mr. R.K. Ashvin was some fellow simply called Ashvin, living in a place so miniscule it was not even on the map. Perhaps he made up Sumana too. But if that were true, how would a person from such a rural background be able to not only create this incredibly sophisticated product, but to find Rennie at his home address in the U.S.? As well as whoever else he might have sent it to. None of it made any sense.

But Rennie had to make it make sense. This incredible find was all he could think about. He wanted to use it again in his practice and try it out on more people. Yet he was hesitant to burn any, in case he was never able to get more, even though that was unthinkable. But if it were the case, he'd want to use the sticks he had sparingly, and save them for times when they would be most useful for his own inner experiences and spiritual journey.

So this thing with Michaela right now... well it just wasn't where his mind was at. However, if he looked at the big picture – at what he intended to do once he'd secured more of the incense, and, hopefully, the exclusive rights to it – working with Michaela was a good idea. It would be his first inroad as a teacher – she'd be his first real student. It wouldn't matter if he charged her for his time or not. In fact he thought it would be better, more selfless, if he didn't. But it would be the first step toward his new work in the world, the work he really wanted to do. With this special incense in front of him, he knew he could be a teacher and workshop leader on a large scale. People would transform because of the incense – the incense and him. Their lives would change, and he would be a part of it. Whatever Eckhart Tolle and all those others do for people would pale in comparison.

Come to think of it, he could practice now by using the incense with Michaela. Sparingly, of course, a few puffs at a time, until he had more. It would be the ideal way to perfect his approach to combining the incense with his teaching. Then, when he got more, he'd be ready to go. He picked up the phone, then put it back down and went to the door of his office. With both hands holding the sides of the doorway, he leaned out.

"Noeletta," he said, for the fifth time that morning. "How's it going with India? Any progress?"

She looked up at him patiently. "Nothing yet, boss. But don't worry, we'll find him."

Rennie was confident that she would.

THE REGULAR GUY'S GUIDE TO ENLIGHTENMENT

Chapter 2

Ever hear about that toggle switch guys are supposed to have? You know the one I mean – it flips between "sports" and "sex." Either we're on one or we're on the other. The essentials, right? What Regular Guy would disagree? And yet, we all know there's more to life than just sports and sex. No, I'm serious. Even some damn important things. For starters, I'm thinking "food." Gotta love it, gotta have it, and not just to fuel the other two biggies. But let's go even beyond that. Some of you may be saying, "Guy. What the hell! You're forgetting beer." But no. I do not forget beer. Ever. For this conversation, however, let's just call beer a subcategory of food, and move on.

So now you have your three-way switch: sports, sex, food, I don't care what order you put them in. But then lurks the question: is there something beyond even those three most essential of life's components? And as soon as you ask the question, you know the answer. Yes, there is something more, something bigger. We all feel it. We know it's there, even if we mostly acknowledge it by shouting, "What the f—k is going on around here?"

I'm here to ask you that very question. What the f—k IS going on around here? I'm not here to answer. That's something each Regular Guy has to do for himself. Maybe there's nothing the f—k going on, who can really say for sure? But just to have something to talk about, let's just assume there is. Let's say, what if something IS the f—k going on. So what the f—k is it?

One place to start is with some other things the Regular Guy holds dear. You'll know them when you hear them. You'll nod in agreement. I'm talking about the three pillars (don't try to tell me there can't be toggle switches *and* pillars, this isn't English class) of family, country and God. That's right, you say. Here I was on the couch, and it was all sports, sex and food, and that seemed right. But how could I have forgotten family, country and God? And I say you didn't forget. Hear me out.

Because it's not just any family, country and God we're talking about, right? It's gotta be YOUR family, YOUR country, and YOUR God. Otherwise, why would you care? Do you go to work every day, bust your ass, and then come home and give your paycheck to the family down the street? Hell, no. Or wear a shirt with the French f—ing flag on it, instead of the good old Red, White and Blue? Or wake up early Sunday morning, shower, shave, and show up at somebody else's church? We've already established you don't even go to your own church if you can help it. (But that doesn't mean you don't think God "represents;" that God is "The Man," so to speak. Except we know he's not The Man, he's The God, but you know what I'm saying.)

So if it's YOUR family, YOUR country, and YOUR God, what's that but another way of saying that's all your TEAM? The ones you cheer for. The ones you care about. The ones you defend. Therefore, these ultra, major, Regular Guy biggies – those three pillars of family, country and God – are now incorporated right back into the toggle switch. And, guys, you see how they fit back in, don't you? What's that you say, Guys? You got it.

Sports.

Now here's where you gotta stick with me, guys. Here's where it gets interesting. Where some of you are going to throw down the book and say, "F—k you, Guy. I ain't goin' there with you." And that's okay. If it's time to throw down the book, then it's time. I can take it. The book can take it.

Of course some of you aren't actually reading the book. No. Some of you are having it read to you by your wife or girlfriend. Your wife or girlfriend who spotted the book when she was shopping at the mall, and went into the bookstore whether she needed to or not, because when she goes to the mall she has to go into EVERY FREAKIN' STORE. And she came home and pulled it out and said, "Honey, I got this book for you. I thought you might like it. It's about guys, and it looks sort of funny."

Which is a lie, of course. She doesn't think you'll like it, she thinks you should read it. She thinks it might actually help you get enlightened. And since she does yoga, and took a Kabbalah class because of Madonna, and spent forty bucks on *The Secret* and watched it twelve times, and SHE reads all those friggin' books about past lives, psychic pets, how to masturbate your soul, or whatever, she thinks you ought to be doing some Self improving too. And she's going to help get that going.

And you, of course, are letting her read it to you because 1) you're actually watching the game, even if the sound is down most of the time, unless it looks like your team is about to score, in which case you can just hit the volume with your hovering thumb, and 2) she made you a sandwich, and 3) obviously, it might help you get laid.

Anyway, besides all that, whether she's reading it to you or whether you're sitting in the bathroom reading it to yourself, what I got to say next is something you might decide you have a problem with. You might find it hard to swallow. But I ask you, Guys, hear me out. Even if it pisses you off, give it a chance to sink in and see if it makes sense. Here goes.

Remember how we just put family, country and God in the "sports" category? Well, don't worry. We're not taking them back out of there. No way. But we have to go back for a minute and look at the God part again. That's right. The Big G. Now, what are some of the qualities attributed to Big G? For one, he's Omnipresent – means Big G's everywhere, all the time. Eternal – mean's he's always been around, always will be. All-knowing – so he's got, not just the big picture, but the biggest picture, you know what I mean? Omnipotent – Big G's gonna do whatever Big G wants do to. And if there are any other Omnis out there, Big G is them too. Even the Omnis we never heard of, or thought of. Probably some Omnis we can't even imagine with our puny Regular Guy brains. Maybe your girlfriend or wife can't even imagine them.

The point is – if Big G's on your Team, and he's Omnipresent, then guess what? He's not JUST on your Team. He has to be a part of everybody else's Team, too. Even the Team that's your biggest rival.

Even the Team of your annoying co-worker. Even your mother-in-law's Team. Even the French Team. And if you remember, and if you didn't have the sound turned up when she was reading that part, their Team, like your Team, is who they're rooting for. That means that if you're rooting against those other teams, or the teams of anybody or any group you think you don't like, then you're rooting against Big G. No kidding. That's how it works, I just proved it. If you don't believe I proved it, here it is again:

1. Big G is on your Team
2. Big G is Omnipresent
3. Therefore, Big G has to be on everybody else's Team too
4. If you root against somebody else's Team, you're rooting against Big G

Get it?

And by the way, hey you wife or girlfriend who's reading this to your Regular Guy while he eats the sandwich and watches sports, guess where else the Omnipresent Big G is? Let's see if you read this sentence to him out loud: Omnipresent Big G is everywhere, therefore Big G is also someplace your Regular Guy always wants to get – under your clothes. Right in your very panties.

But this is one thing, enlightened or not, that your Regular Guy already knows.

27
Petaluma

Rennie's heart was beating like crazy as he gently nudged Phil out the front door, locked it, then went through the house turning off his phones and lowering the shades. A pounding heart was probably not a great way to start his meditation. But the stakes were incredibly high. Today's session had to be perfect. Everything that mattered to Rennie now depended on it.

Noeletta had not come anywhere close to locating the mysterious Mr. Ashvin. None of their contacts in India knew of any incense makers by that name, or had even heard of the town he was from. And Noeletta, who was nothing if not resourceful, had tried everyone she could think of. She'd even attempted subterfuge with the largest of their competitors – other incense importers who might have received the sticks just as Rennie had, possibly with more information. She'd called them pretending to be visiting the U.S. from India, and asked if her package had arrived. But no one at any of those businesses claimed to know what she was talking about. As far as she could discover, Rennie was the only one who had received a sample of the extraordinary incense. At least that was established.

But it wasn't enough; not nearly. The dilemma was on

Rennie's mind constantly. He needed more of that miraculous stuff, and soon. It was the key to his future.

Which is why Rennie was struggling with the decision to travel to India himself looking for Ashvin. He would go in a heartbeat if he thought he had a decent chance of finding the man. But what was the likelihood of success? India was an enormous country, and the town of Sumana wasn't on the map. How would he know where to start? If he even knew which state to look in, that would narrow it down a little.

Rennie had contacts in most parts of India. If he got close to the place, once he was over there, and started talking to local people, especially incense makers, he might have a chance to find the man. If someone didn't know Ashvin, they might have encountered his product, and Rennie could trace it back to him one person at a time. On the other hand, if he wasn't extremely lucky, the search could take months – maybe years – with no guarantee of success. And Rennie wasn't prepared to put in that kind of time.

Despite how negative it all seemed, Rennie still had hope, because he had thought of a plan. It was a crazy plan, by most standards, but Rennie had to try it. He kept thinking about that vision from the workshop, and the dream he had afterwards. That old man and those other people, with the liquid gold – that had taken place in India, he was sure of it. Could it be more than a coincidence that he had the first of those images, the one at the workshop, right before the incense package showed up? And the second one, in his dream, just before he found out what it could do? What if the old man was Ashvin, or someone who worked for him, and the gold pouring into his bowl represented the incense? What if Ashvin sent not only the package to his house, but was also sending these messages directly to his subconscious mind.

Part of Rennie believed it, at least wanted to. But he was too practical a person not to doubt himself at the same time. And to go all the way to India with only a vision of a hut, a few people and a banyan tree – how much help would that be? Even if they existed, he could still spend a lifetime looking and never find them. He needed more information to narrow down the search. But he wasn't getting it.

Then, yesterday, driving on 101 while obsessing for the billionth time on the problem, a large bug decided to sacrifice itself by smashing into his windshield. At least, he assumed it had been a bug; what he saw was a simply a bright green blob. Rennie had never squashed anything that particular shade of green before, and the color put him in mind of a flying beetle he had seen a few times in India. But only in one particular part of India.

And then he got it. There could be more clues. Ashvin could have sent him a more detailed message, he just hadn't received it all yet. Or Ashvin could have sent more messages since the first one. Rennie had been preoccupied – maybe he wasn't giving himself a chance to receive properly. Maybe all he needed to know was right there – out in the ethers, or in his own mind (he wasn't sure how these things worked) waiting for him to recognize and acknowledge it.

He knew what to do. He would try going back to the vision. But this time he'd have the incense to aid him. It could give him powers he never had before. He'd try to meld deeply into the scene and find out everything he could about the place. He'd look for details, specific buildings, trees or insects, maybe even something in writing. Or perhaps he could get the people in the scene to tell him where they were from or how to reach them. But even if he couldn't get that specific, he could find out at least enough to narrow the search. Then he'd go over there and see what he could do. It was certainly worth a try.

Rennie spoke aloud to the windshield, "Noble bug," he said, "Your sacrifice has not been in vain."

That was yesterday. Today, Rennie had cleared his schedule and was ready to see if he could pull a miracle out of his meditation. His super-charged, incense-assisted meditation.

The single precious stick he'd brought home from the office rested in the blue feather burner, ready to be lit.

He imagined touching the end with primal fire from his lighter, waving his hands to coax the smoke out of the end of the stick, and wafting it up into his nose, where it would morph into information-laden mental images that would tell him where to go in India to find Mr. R.K. Ashvin.

"Like a rabbit out of a hat," he muttered aloud.

Rennie went to the bathroom, emptied his bladder, and came back into the living room. He checked that his meditation cushion was in place, looked around the room one last time to see if he had missed taking care of anything before he started, and took a deep breath. He closed his eyes and said a silent prayer to the universe asking for help. Then he lit the stick and sat down to meditate.

Ahh, there it was. The somewhat unusual scent that he appreciated more each time he smelled it. Those Sticks of Destiny. Maybe he should call them that when he marketed them.

Rennie started out meditating the way he always did, which was to let go as much as possible of everything in his mind. He had been tempted to try holding the image of the earlier dream and vision, and he might still try that strategy later. But he decided against it to start with. He wanted to see what would happen if he was completely open, and not focused on anything in particular. Maybe the original image would come back with more information. Or maybe Ashvin, or the universe, would send him a different picture this time, or even a different type of message. Maybe even words. Rennie wanted to stay open to all possibilities.

Unfortunately, the one thing he was counting on didn't seem to be happening. He wasn't going very deep. In fact, he wasn't going anywhere. He seemed to be stuck on the last words that had come out of his mouth, that ridiculous comment about a rabbit out of a hat. It was a completely meaningless, irrelevant, and absurd thing to say, and now his mind was unable to let go of it.

He saw nothing but hats and rabbits, rabbits and hats. What began as a gloved hand pulling a large sleek white rabbit out of a traditional top hat became multiple bunnies of all colors and sizes climbing, jumping, flying out of assorted homburgs, berets, ski caps, trilbies and porkpies. A chinchilla from a Russian fur hat. A long-haired gray lop-ear out of a lavender bonnet. A jackrabbit out of a sombrero.

Rennie came back to his mantra, his breathing. More rabbits. He started to panic. This was going nowhere. He was wasting this session, wasting the incense. He noticed the panic, observed it, came back to his mantra again. Still more rabbits.

Another jackrabbit, this one from a Stetson. A jackrabbit wasn't really a rabbit, he mused, it was a hare. Now he saw one hare after another. A white hare out of an Eskimo hat. A black one from a stocking cap. Now a tawny one with black shoulders from a turban, and a second like that from a pointy white Gandhi hat. This was stupid, stupid, stupid. Rennie was trying hard not to judge his meditation, but was frustrated by not getting what he wanted.

At this point, he decided, the best use of the session would be to go directly to the former vision and see if he could get anything more from it. He took several deep, deep breaths to inhale as much of the transformative incense as he could. He said another prayer to the universe for guidance. Then he imagined walking again through the huts toward the blue building and the fig trees.

At first he did not see anyone. The place he had been before was empty. In the distance there were a few people bending over, perhaps doing some farming. It occurred to him that this was daytime, and before he'd been there at night. He decided to go toward the people and ask for Ashvin. The rabbits seemed to have carried over from before, and were hopping all over the place. Mostly, it was just those black-shouldered hares, all underfoot, and Rennie kept tripping over them. It slowed his movement toward the people, in fact as he walked toward them, the people got farther away instead of closer.

But then he realized he was almost there, and one person was standing up – and he did think – yes – it was the old man from the vision. Rennie was almost in speaking distance, he was about to ask if he was Ashvin and then…

CRASH!

The sound brought him out of the meditation and right back into his living room. For a couple of seconds Rennie didn't know what was going on. Then he realized the crash had come from outside. Phil must have knocked over a ceramic planter or statue.

Rennie put his head in his hand and moaned. He had failed. He had not gotten a single useful bit of information from this session, and had wasted one of the very few sticks of magical incense he had left. He glanced over to see what remained of the stick, but it was nearly burned to the end. He was too disappointed and frustrated to try again, so instead, he slid off the cushion and collapsed backwards onto the floor with his arm draped over his eyes in misery.

Why, oh why, did he have to want this so bad? He knew it was the desire that caused his unhappiness. Why couldn't he just be a good Buddhist, and let the patient attention to his thoughts in hour after hour of meditation wear away at his ego needs until he saw through the illusory world.

But this was his LIFE, dammit. He WANTED something out of it. Was that so wrong? Was it such a bad thing to take everything he was – this body, this soul, this… yes…this ego – and be passionate about creating something with it in the short time he had on earth? Rennie moaned again and flopped his hand on his face. That felt good. He did it again, harder. Slap. Harder. Slap. Again. He was startled and a bit embarrassed to find himself lying on the floor smacking himself on the face, but dammit, it just felt right. So he continued.

Now he felt like running his hands all over his face, so he did. He wanted to yank at his hair, so he did that too. With both hands, not pulling it out, just tugging at it enough to bring tears to his eyes. Damn hairs, damn hairs. Damn hairs was right! It was those damn hares in the meditation that had fucked everything up.

"Damn hares," he said out loud. "DAMN HARES," he yelled, jerking his whole head down toward his chest.

"HAAAARES" he screamed. "HAAAAAAAAAAAARES!!!!!"

Now he was beating his hands on the floor. Good thing for the rug. He went on and on until the energy died out of him.

"Aaaargh! Hares!" he said one last time, most of the power gone from the word and from him. He rested, feeling better, though a bit ridiculous after his outburst, but since there was no one around to see or hear him, he didn't really care. He rolled over on his side, in a fetal position. He was cold, but there was no blanket in reaching distance, so he pulled the meditation cushion over his feet, which helped only a little. He was sleepy. He could definitely nod off, if only he wasn't so cold.

So cold it was snowing. He was curled up in the snow. Rennie stuck out his tongue to catch some flakes. They swirled in front of him; now he was walking in it. Walking on a road, walking toward a sign, but he couldn't read it because of all the snow. There, now he could make it out. The sign was in Hindi. No, it was in Bengali or Urdu. Wait – there it was – English. It said...."Haryana."

"That's funny," Rennie thought in his sleep. "It doesn't snow in Haryana." Haryana was in India. A state in the northern plains. He had been there only once. Why would he go there now? India. He was supposed to find out something about India. It was important. But would he remember this when he woke up? He had to remember.

BAM! BAM! BAM!

Rennie again had his consciousness yanked back by a series

of explosions. No, not explosions. Someone was knocking. BAM! BAM! BAM! Pause. BAM! BAM! BAM! Pause.

That certainly wasn't Phil, he realized, now awake. He looked up. Noeletta was pounding on the window. He suddenly flashed on a series of thoughts – first, that there was something he was supposed to remember from the dream. Something important. Second, why was Noeletta there? And how long had she been standing at the window? What had she seen? It was possible he'd nodded off for only a second. Had she been there long enough to witness his self-attack, which must have looked much worse than it was? Maybe it scared her. She might be trying to save him from himself.

Rennie staggered to his feet, made his way to the window, and opened it.

"Uh, hi," he said. "What's up?"

"Hi boss," Noeletta said. "I'm really sorry to bother you, but it's important. Can I come in?"

"Sure, come on in," he said, without moving.

"Um, okay." She looked pointedly at the window, then back to him.

"Can I come in the door?" she asked.

"Oh! Oh, sure. Sorry. Come on around."

He made his way through the house to the door, and she did the same from outside. He opened it and she stepped inside. An angry black and white blur tore past her legs and disappeared into the house. They both stared after it.

"Sorry to bother you, boss," she repeated. "But I couldn't reach you by phone and I thought you'd want to know right away."

"What?" Rennie asked. "What is it?"

"I just got a call. From Ashvin. He's here, in the U.S."

"What? Really?"

"Yes, he's here, and he wants to see you. He was on his way, but I had to buy him a ticket. I knew you wouldn't mind. He flew to the States somehow, but he didn't quite make it to San Francisco. He arrives in about six hours."

"He's here? That's amazing."

"Yes, I know. Okay, that's it. I'll get going so you can get back to what you were, um, doing."

She was trying to avoid looking at his disheveled hair and twisted meditation clothes.

"Call me and I'll give you his flight info. One of us should go pick him up."

"Uh, yeah. Right. I'll go. Thanks, Noe."

He wanted to ask what she had seen before she knocked, but it was just too awkward.

"Okay then, bossman, I'm off," she said.

"Right."

She turned to leave.

"Noeletta, wait," Rennie called.

She turned back.

"Where was he? Where did Ashvin call you from?"

"Oh, that's funny. He was at the airport in Chicago. Oh geez, I can't think of the name. Senior moment. You know, duh, the big one, what's that called?"

"O'Hare?" Rennie asked, blinking.

"Of course! What's wrong with me? Ashvin was at O'Hare."

28
Marin
---

*M*ichaela had recovered her energy, all right. In fact, this was the peppiest she'd been in years. Maybe ever. She woke at five every morning, usually smack out of some bizarre dream that felt like it had gone on all night. Rennie wanted her to keep a dream journal, so she wrote down whatever she remembered. In a lot of them, she was falling or jumping, or opening a familiar door into a strange room, or driving down a familiar street but finding herself in places she'd never seen before.

Beyond writing them down, she gave little thought to the dreams. She planned to show Rennie the journal on their next scheduled appointment, and if anything about them was interesting, she assumed he'd let her know.

He also wanted her to meditate first thing every morning, but Michaela couldn't sit still so soon after she woke up. Instead, she'd go for a run, then complete whatever work she had; or else she'd do the work first and then go to the gym. She had always been prompt professionally, but now her turnaround was so quick, she often found herself with nothing to do, waiting for clients to get back to her with approvals or changes to the latest design. So she had started creating random projects in her spare time, just for something to keep her occupied.

In particular, she'd been designing clothes, which was entirely new. It started one day when she'd finished working on revising a menu design for a client. Wanting to continue drawing, she found herself sketching monks in their robes. This evolved into pictures of bald women in sarong-like dresses of maroon and yellow. Which further became simple wrap dresses in bold colors, patterned with triangles and ziz-zags. Every day for an hour or more she was driven to create designs. She'd work on them until the urge exhausted itself. Michaela kept all the drawings in a folder, though she had no idea what she'd ever do with them.

Also, nearly every day she fought the urge to drive down to Eighth and beg for the chance to do their menus. Roxanne, who seemed baffled and somewhat put off by Michaela's apparent lifestyle changes, but kept in regular contact anyway, had no idea what was going on with the mysterious restaurant. Nor, it seemed, did any one else in the business whom Michaela asked. She thought about it all the time – replayed in her head how the conversation could have gone if she'd known how to prepare ahead of time. She could have researched the kind of things they were into, learned the lingo, and presented herself perfectly. If only she'd known.

Well, at least she did have an excuse to go down there. She'd told that old monk she would come back in a month, and never did. Maybe she should go and have tea with him as he'd suggested. But then she'd probably see that Eighth was getting close to opening, and she'd feel worse than ever. Besides, the monks must have forgotten about her by now. She wondered if they were enjoying the yellow Maserati in the recent nice weather.

Michaela waited impatiently for her next session with Rennie, but the day before she was to see him, a woman called from his office to say he had to cancel. Some urgent business matter. It was hard for Michaela to imagine urgency in the field of incense sales, but whatever. In any case, she was on her own, desperate for a boost in her spirituality training.

If she couldn't see Rennie, Michaela had to do something with her energy and craving for movement. And right away, or she would surely go crazy. However much she wanted to, she really couldn't face going back to Eighth, at least not until she felt ready. And she couldn't spend a whole week waiting around for Rennie, and then not even get to see him. She had to make something happen on her own. She had to get more spiritual NOW. But how?

Then she remembered that training Rennie had gone to – some Lite Shaman or Shaman Light thing. She had been mortified when Rennie corrected her pronunciation. Of course it was not "charmin." What had she been thinking? She Googled various combinations of the words "shaman" and "light" but failed to find it. There were too many possibilities.

Then she remembered, the brochure was in her office, where she had started a file for this stuff. Retrieving it, she found the website easily enough. Now to find out where and when the next workshop was being held.

By now, Michaela was determined to go to a workshop immediately, so they'd better have something going on this weekend, it didn't matter where. She'd go to Canada or Colombia; Cleveland or Cuba. She'd be packed and out the door in twenty minutes. Nothing would stop her. She would do whatever it took get herself ready to face those Eighth idiots again, and conquer them. She would build her spiritual fitness the way she'd built her business, the way she'd built a fit body in the gym. This time, when she went back to Eighth, she'd be ready. This time, she would win.

29
Santa Fe

D orothea used every trick she knew to calm herself after Guy's phone call. When she hung up – without saying goodbye to Guy, come to think of it, but who cared – Dirk was nowhere around, and answered neither her hollering nor his cell phone. She was sure he had conveniently disappeared on purpose, just when she needed to tell him about this horrible development. In this awful state, she'd been forced to search room-to-room all by herself, looking for her Tiger Eye Mala Beads, her Holistic Silk Lavender Eye Mask, and her vial of Rescue Remedy. At least she had Click-ee. He had stayed with Dorothea during the whole excruciating conversation with Guy – what an awful person Guy was! – and she talked to the loving, accepting, furry creature as she looked around the house for the necessary items.

"Thinks he's so smart. 'Regular Guy's Guide,' huh? He should call it the Stupid Guy's Guide. The stupid guy's stupid guide to how-stupid-can-you-get? Stupid football. Stupid family."

She thought she'd seen the mala beads in her scarf drawer. Scarves flew in all directions as Dorothea searched for the desired strand. Not finding it, she tried the next drawer, piling twisted necklaces in all sizes and colors atop the dresser. She finally dug out the mala and held it up to the light to see the Tigers Eye stones better.

"Hmph," she said, looping it around her arm. She now headed for the unmade king-sized bed.

"You're smart, Click-ee. You don't have a brother, do you? You don't have to worry about your family embarrassing you and ruining your reputation. You don't have to deal with low-consciousness relatives, who Spirit must have put on the planet to challenge you to rise above their disgusting activities, like writing books that make fun of what you do, and trying to show you up by getting a better publisher than you have. It's really staggering what some people will do to make themselves look better than other people, Click-ee. It really is."

Pillows and comforters were tossed aside randomly. She leaned down to look under the bed, then behind the hand-carved mahogany headboard. She strode across the room and flung a pile of Dirk's folded underwear from the overstuffed gold-embroidered chair onto the floor.

"I just knew some day those people would do something like this. It's not enough they tortured me all through my childhood, with their FOOTBALL and their disgusting cans of cheap beer, and their nachos with fake cheese. No, now they've got to show up again after I thought I'd escaped... after I'd done all I could to bloom like a lotus blossom out of that murky swamp. Nobody appreciates how hard that was, Click-ee. I had to pull myself out of there like a ballerina by my own toe-shoe ribbons. And just when I'm feeling free of all that, just when I'm bearing the fruit of my work in the world, what happens but they rise up like GODZILLA and try to stomp all over my accomplishments."

Then she remembered that the eye mask was probably under the sofa and stormed from the bedroom. She went into her bathroom and opened a cabinet. A variety of holistic remedies and expired medications were pulled out and examined, then left strewn across the counter or where they'd fallen to the floor. She yanked open two adjacent drawers at the same time, and riffled through them in increasing frustration.

"What did I ever to do them to deserve this, Click-ee, I ask you? This bottle of Rescue Remedy is EMPTY. Where did Dirk put the new one, Click-ee? Do you know where it is? I need Dirk. I can't do this by myself. Where IS he?"

"I'm right here, Thea. My Blackberry rang and I took it outside. What's going on?"

Dorothea whipped around and glared at Dirk, standing in the bathroom door with the phone in his hand and a satisfied look on his face. His expression was incongruent with her highly upset state of mind, and that made her mad.

"You left me alone with HIM!" She said, pointing Click-ee's nose directly at Dirk.

"You're alone with Click-ee all the time, Thee. What's the problem?"

"Not HIM," she said, gesturing wildly with the dolphin, "HIM!" Click-ee was now used to indicate the direction of Dorothea's horribly disturbing conversation with her so-called brother. She did not want to even think his name, much less say it.

"You know how much he upsets me. You know I didn't want to talk to him. Well, let me tell you, Dirk, this was the worst ever. You aren't going to believe what he's doing. We have to stop him; maybe it's not too late. You have to get a court order, Dirk. Do it right now, or I don't think I can live…"

She tapered off, burrowing her head in Click-ee's nobly comforting back.

"Thea, Thea," Dirk said, coming over and putting his arms around her, which was awkward with the plush animal between them. He tried unsuccessfully to pry it from her arms, then gave up and cradled her as best he could. "It's okay. Don't worry about this. It's not going to affect anything."

"What? How do you know? You don't even know what he's done."

"You mean the 'Guy's Guide'?" he said.

Dorothea jerked her head up to look at Dirk. "How did you know about that? Were you on the extension?"

"No. I saw it in the publisher's catalogue. The book's being released this year, before the ABA convention. It's happening, babe. We can't stop it."

"Oh, nooooo," Dorothea moaned. She pushed past Dirk, carrying the beads, the empty bottle, and Click-ee, and headed for the sofa. "This is the worst thing that's ever happened to me. I don't know how I'm going to go on living after this. I'd kill myself right now if so many people weren't depending on me."

She flung herself on the sofa, pulled the eyeshade from underneath a cushion and placed it over her eyes. She set Click-ee on her chest over her heart. She then rested her left hand above her navel and fingered the beads, while her right waved the pill bottle in the direction of Dirk. When he didn't take it, she made a shaking gesture so he could hear there was nothing in it. Dirk removed the bottle from her hand, but made no move to go off to find the full one. Dorothea sensed him just standing there, and she pushed aside the shade enough to see him with one eye. He was watching her, and he was smiling.

"What? Is this funny to you?"

"Nope."

"What, then? What's the smile for? Did you hire a hit man?" Dorothea asked hopefully.

"Nope."

"Something good, though?" She sat up, the eyeshade and Click-ee falling into her lap. "What? What happened?"

"I think we got *Ivy!*" he said.

"Really? Oh, Dirk, really?"

He nodded. "Russell said they liked you. The producer he talked to saw the galleys for the book, and the demo tape. They want you to be part of the show they're doing on Spiritual Makeovers."

Dorothea sat up, her face lit like a kid at Christmas, with eyes shining and a happy expression. This was the side of Dorothea that Dirk loved most – the sweet, excited little girl. It was why he liked to surprise her with gifts and candy, so this part of her personality would emerge. He smiled back at her as she sat up and pulled him next to her on the couch.

"That's perfect!" she said. "That's what I do best, isn't it?"

"That's right."

"So it really doesn't matter about Guy," she shuddered, "You really think it isn't going to affect us?"

"Thea, nobody knows you're related. His last name is different. You don't even look alike."

"That's true," she said. "I hadn't thought about that."

"And even if it does come out that he's your brother, so what? People will just look at the two of you, and it will be obvious who the real teacher is. Nobody's going to take him seriously. He doesn't even want them to."

"And I'm going to be on *Ivy!*" she giggled.

"That's right. You're going to be on *Ivy!*. You're my girl."

She hugged him and gave a little squeal.

"But you've got to do one little thing for me now, Thea."

"Okay, Dirkie-doodle. I'll do one little bitty thing. What is it?"

"Let's get that taping done today, okay?"

"Okay, Dirkie. I can do it now. Don't worry. I'll be great."

"I know you will, honey," Dirk said, giving her a squeeze and then letting go. "So go get ready."

"I'm going. Have no fear, Dirkles," she said, heading back toward their bedroom. "I'll nail it. In fact, I'm going to kill them."

And Click-ee, one round, black eye staring up from the floor where he'd fallen, smiled in agreement.

30

San Francisco International Airport

*R*ennie stood at the bottom of the escalator near the baggage carousels, tapping his foot nervously, and holding up the large sign Noeletta had made for him. It spelled out "Mr. R.K. Ashvin," in block letters.

Friday evening was busy at SFO. If Ashvin had been coming straight from India into the international terminal, it would be less crowded this late in the day. But the domestic areas were packed with incoming business travelers returning to their homes and families, and weekend vacationers escaping theirs.

He examined each person as he or she came down the escalator and was revealed from the bottom up – shoes, legs, carry-on bag, torso, shoulders, and head. Which one was Ashvin? Would he look the way Rennie pictured him, like the old man in his dream and visions? In Rennie's mind, they were the same, although there was no particular reason to think that the visions had shown how he really looked. It was probably all metaphoric. For instance, Rennie had been offered liquid gold, not incense. It was just as unlikely that he had seen what the real Ashvin looked like. The way he appeared in the vision probably just represented some qualities Ashvin had, like wisdom or knowledge, instead of his actual form.

Knowing all of that, it still came as a shock when a person – one he'd dismissed just seconds ago based on his shoes – approached Rennie, pointed to the sign, and said, "Hello, hello. Aaaaah. You are here for me. Come this way."

Rennie stood staring, frozen in surprise. It wasn't just the shoes, though that would have been enough all by itself – reddish leather, wide-strapped sandals with what appeared to be elevated springs for heels. But everything else about him seemed wrong too. His pants looked like half of a cheap tuxedo – navy blue polyester with a band of satin down each leg. He wore a black bowling shirt with an orange, yellow and red flame design on the front and sleeves. Over his arm was what appeared to be a large gray hooded sweatshirt. His black hair, curled over his ears, was topped with a white cap with an extra large visor, the word "Ace" in large red block letters across the front. Between the visor and the huge, dark shades underneath, Rennie could see nothing of the top half of his face.

He wore a giant, stuffed, black backpack on his shoulders, and carried a sizable black nylon briefcase. Not to mention, he was quite tall and extremely thin.

But besides all that, this guy wasn't merely somewhat younger than Rennie had pictured. He was considerably younger. Rennie wondered if he was even out of his teens.

Without another word, the young man turned and strode off toward the nearest baggage claim. Rennie trailed after with his mouth open, still holding the sign at chest level. He took a couple of large strides to catch up, as the guy made his way toward the front of the still unmoving carousel.

"Wait," Rennie said. "You're Mr. Ashvin? Mr. R.K. Ashvin?"

"Yes, of course," the man said dismissively. "Now come with me, and you can get my bags. You are the chauffeur, yes? I will tell you what to look for and you will carry them for me."

His English was accented, but without hesitation. Rennie stared again, completely baffled. He had certainly not expected him to get off the plane in a dhoti and shawl, as the so-called Ashvin wore in the visions. In fact, he was quite sure he'd be wearing some manner of Western clothing, since most men, even in the smaller Indian towns, generally did. But this? He just didn't know what to make of this person's appearance and demeanor.

Rennie asked again. He had to be certain. "You are Mr. R.K. Ashvin, the incense maker? That's definitely who you are? Because I was expecting someone older. Also, I'm not a chauffeur. I'm Rennie Morrow, the business owner you sent the incense to."

"Eeeeee, ooooh, uuuuh." The brusque manner and confidence evaporated and was replaced by a squirming, embarrassed kid. "Well, yes, sort of. Ashvin is me, yes. Not R.K. Ashvin, however. I am his nephew, D.K. Ashvin. But you can call me Duke if you want to," he said hopefully.

"You – you aren't R.K. Ashvin," Rennie repeated slowly. An immense disappointment swept over him. He put his hand to his head as if he had a headache. "Is he coming?" Rennie asked without much hope.

"Eeeee, uuuuh, ummm…. No," the young man said finally, slumping as if air had gone out of him. "He sent me instead."

Rennie looked up. "He sent you? To talk to me about the incense?"

"Eeeee, errrrr, sort of." He looked uncomfortable. "I can explain to you in the car. No problem. I promise," the youth looked around and stood up straight again.

"The bags are coming off now," he said. "You are not the chauffeur? Where is the chauffeur? Who will carry the bags and drive us?" The arrogant persona had reemerged as he looked around, a head taller than most of the people nearby.

"I'm driving," Rennie said shortly. "And you can carry your own bags. I'll help, if you need it." Rennie wondered how many suitcases the kid could have. What was he, anyway, some North Indian drug dealer? Maybe he belonged to a street gang with a really weird dress code.

Rennie was devastated. He had been very much looking forward to meeting Ashvin; had thought of him as nearly a guru, with almost magical abilities. Anyone who could create something as powerful as those incense sticks had to have great spiritual knowledge and insight. Rennie had imagined spending time with him, asking questions and being given gifts of learning and wisdom. And that was even besides doing business together. He had ideas of the two of them becoming partners in some way. He wanted to negotiate exclusive rights to the product, and was prepared to make a generous offer to the man.

But he only had this boy. This absurdly dressed string bean of a youth, who had already displayed two completely different personalities, neither of which was very appealing. What was Rennie supposed to do with him? Had Ashvin sent him here as a test? Was Rennie expected to take the boy in as part of his payment to Ashvin, in exchange for getting more of the incense? He almost dreaded finding out.

"Look, there's one! Eeeee!" the boy was pointing and bouncing up and down on his bizarre springs.

"Well, go and get it, then," Rennie said, without looking up.

The boy bolted forward and pushed through his fellow passengers to lean over the side of the carousel. He couldn't seem to get hold of it, and was yanking and following his luggage around the moving metal plates, pushing past people as he went. Finally he gave a giant tug and pulled it free. Rennie expected him to turn and come back, but a moment later, he leaned over and pulled another piece off and set it down next to the first one. Still, the boy stood there.

Rennie could not see the suitcases through the other passengers, but he was baffled by the amount of luggage he seemed to have. Three bags? What had he done, gone and moved here? After grabbing yet a third case off the conveyer, he finally turned back toward Rennie, dragging all his stuff behind him. Rennie supposed he should go help, but had no inclination to do so, especially as the kid had seemed to expect someone to carry his bags for him. If he was going to be hanging around, even for a day or two, he'd need to know that Rennie was not some wealthy American nabob who provided servants for his guests. Especially the uninvited ones.

However as soon as the kid pulled free of the crowd and Rennie caught a glimpse of what he was half-carrying, half-hauling awkwardly behind him, he gasped and rushed over to the boy. Instead of suitcases, they were three of those enormous, clear plastic bags provided by the airline, the kind used to enclose things like child seats and other objects with loose parts – items that looked like they needed some containing to get through the baggage handling ordeal.

Encased in each bag was a large, flimsy cardboard box, held together with tape and string. The very same tape and string, Rennie noted excitedly, as had been wrapped around his mystery package containing the incense. His heart raced at the sight of the boxes, for he knew immediately that's what they were. Incense. Lots and lots of it. As he got closer, the scent wafting from the bags confirmed it. Ashvin had sent the boy, and he had sent the incense too. Rennie did not know what he was supposed to do with the first, but that was okay, because the incense was here and Rennie would do whatever he had to in order to keep it.

He quickly relieved the boy of one of the plastic-enclosed boxes, hoisted it up to face level and took a large sniff. It was definitely the right stuff. He reached as far as he could around the box, gave it a huge, extended hug, then put it down. He had a big, insuppressible grin on his face as he took the young man's free hand in his and pumped it up and down vigorously.

"Good work!" Rennie said. "You brought it!"

The boy was smiling now too, and looked quite relieved. Rennie clapped him on the shoulder, then reached his arm all the way around and turned it into a squeeze. The boy squirmed embarrassedly but smiled.

"What did you say your name was? Duke?" Rennie said. "Well, come on, Duke, let's get you a cart for all this stuff. Let's get it – and you – home. Are you hungry?"

Duke nodded vigorously and hoisted his two bags. Rennie took the other bag and the boy's briefcase.

"Okay, then, Duke, let's get something to eat. Do you like pizza? There's a great pizza place on the way home. Do you like movies? We can stop and rent some DVDs. I've got a sweet sound system. You look like you know electronics; you can tell me what you think. Come on, the car's this way. Are you a car guy? It's not a sports car or anything, just a Prius. Ever been to San Francisco before? No? To the U.S.? Well, we'll go into the city, drive around, see the ocean. Whatever you want. "

Rennie had never felt so pumped up, so excited, at any moment in his life. He continued his patter to young Duke all the way out to the car. Duke, the altitudinous youth in the weird clothes. Duke, Ashvin's bizarre emissary with the odd dual personality – arrogant hotshot and abashed youngster. Duke, the fulfiller of Rennie's dreams, and savior of his hopes for the future. Rennie had decided, at least for a couple of days, that he was going to take young Duke under his wing, and show him a really good time.

Chapter 3

Guys, we are a misunderstood subcategory of the male gender. Some would say we cannot even BE enlightened. Some would say that you sitting there reading this book, and even me lying here writing it, is a waste of time. They think we Regular Guys don't have it in us to rise off the sofa, or come down from our ATV, and do what it takes to become enlightened. I say, those "some" of which I speak do not know what a Regular Guy is capable of. I will show you that you already have it in you, no matter what your normal activities, to be enlightened just as you are, Regular Guyness and all.

Guys, you may not know this – and hell, you don't have to – but I'm going to tell you anyway. Throughout history, there's stuff people actually do to get enlightened. Yes, guys, and some of them you may even have heard of. Let's look at a few, just to see how they fit in with the normal Regular Guy range of activities.

Okay, guys, here's one you may have heard of. Yoga. Guys, you know this already: a Regular Guy is not a Yoga Guy. No matter how you look at it, there is nothing about yoga and Regular Guys that go together. Think about it – you've got your yoga mat – if you can even call them mats. They're more like giant fruit-rollups. Then you've got your yoga clothes: lightweight, skintight, stretchy – nice on the ladies. Nuff said. Then you've got your yoga instructors. Sure, plenty of them are males. I didn't say males don't do yoga. Just not Regular Guys. Regular Guydom and yoga are mutually exclusive. I mean Guys – why are we even discussing this?

But you know what? Let's be open-minded. Remember, Guys, no

matter how much we want to dislike Yoga Guys, we can't ignore that they've got Big G on their team too, right? So okay, let's say some Regular Guy wants to make an exception. Maybe, even though you're a Regular Guy in every other way, for some crazy reason, you want to try yoga as part of your path to enlightenment. I'm not saying that's impossible, I'm just saying I haven't seen it. But okay, you should do it.

However, keep this in mind. At that point, the very best I can offer is, you'd be a regular guy with an asterisk. You know, like when the baseball players went on strike, and you have to put an asterisk next to the record holders' names because the stats aren't for a whole season. Or you broke the record, but know everybody knows you were on steroids: asterisk. On the big Regular Guy list in the sky, it'll be Your Name*.

* yoga practitioner

Here's another one, Guys. Meditation. Guys, pay attention. There is a way you can do meditation and still be a Regular Guy. The trick is, you do it sitting in front of your computer screen. However your computer should be turned off, or at least in sleep mode, so the screen is dark. Here's how that works. The average Regular Guy's breakdown of computer time is something like this:

Work (25%). And by work, I include stuff at home you don't want to do either.

Looking stuff up on the internet (i.e., espn.com, etc) and buying stuff on the internet (15%).

Checking your spam (3%).

You know where you are the other 57% of the time online. It starts with a p and ends with an n, it's warm and slick, and I don't mean hot buttered popcorn. Let's say, just for argument sake, you reduce that non-popcorn time to 56%. Just take that 1% out of the total – say 15 or 20 minutes. You could even call it a break from not-eating-popcorn, so you'll enjoy your un-popcorn even more when you get back to it. And, Guys, here's what you do: You just sit there in front of the screen not doing anything. That's it. That's your regular guy meditation.

The next category leads logically from your non-popcorn, i.e. that other p-n, and brings us directly to Tantra. Stand back guys, this one's for grownups. You're probably thinking, "Oh yeah, Guy. I know about Tantra – Tantra's sex, that's what it is. That's how I want to get enlightened. Tell me all about that one, Guy."

But Guys! Wait! Be careful here. You are Ordinary Guys and you are used to ordinary sex. Okay, backtrack. I know, I know, "ordinary sex" is a contradiction. If it's sex we're talking about, how can we possibly describe it as ordinary? I mean, Guys, for pity sake. it's SEX. But, Guys, remember what we are. We're Regular Guys. The type of sex that is "ordinary" for Regular Guys is the variety that I have to refer to as NESEX. NESEX, you know – Not Enough Sex or Never Enough Sex. Sometimes No Effing Sex. So even if we get SOME, ordinarily, we are in the state of wanting some MORE.

(Now here comes a Regular Guy Enlightenment Alert. Remember that last statement, Guys: Even if you get SOME, you want some MORE. And not just sex. Keep it in mind. We're coming back to that one in Chapter 4.)

Which brings us to the trouble with Tantra. It may appear to be about sex. You may have heard it's about sex. But, Guys, don't be fooled. Real Tantra is not about sex. You will not solve your NESEX problem with Tantra. It's about getting enlightened, sure, but mostly you'd be doing a lot of practices that a Regular Guy would not especially want to do. Like a whole bunch of meditations that don't include any screens. Like chanting mantras other than the name of your favorite sports team. Like contemplating multi-limbed deities who are getting some when you're not. And a lot of other really boring stuff.

So then, sometimes, after years of your Tantra practice doing all that – then you maybe get some sex. Once you've proven you can do all the other stuff, that is. BUT, once you do get to have some, guess what? You are supposed to do it without desire. You are supposed to do it without lust. Guys! If you didn't have desire and lust, why would you want the sex? And if you didn't have desire and lust, well, here's a question for you. Would you still even be a Regular Guy?

And Guys, Guys, Guys. Here's the kicker. Or lack thereof. No orgasm. If you have an orgasm, you messed up. Not supposed to happen. In real Tantra, you came, you lame. You ooze, you lose. You spurt, you hurt. You come, you dumb. There's a flag on the play and you lose five yards. You can probably replay the down, but not right away.

No, Guys, no. You don't want real Tantra. What you're really after, as a Regular Guy, is to find one of those practices that *calls* itself Tantra, but isn't. Fake Tantra. There's a bunch of them. Find the one with the most sex. They're out there. Just do a web search or pick up one of those free alternative newspapers, and look for the words Tantra and Love. Like Lovefest, Cosmic Love, Love Journey. Unlimited Tantric Lovathon. Seriously guys. It's not enlightenment, but it will keep you busy in the meantime.

To sum it up guys, for now, don't worry about how a Regular Guy gets enlightened. For now, just do a little not-Tantra, consume a little not-popcorn. Maybe do some Regular Guy meditation, or even some asterisk Regular Guy yoga. Do it or don't do it, Guys, cause doing stuff isn't the path to enlightenment anyway. Be your Regular Guy self all the way. And lets see what happens next.

31
101 North to Petaluma

*R*ennie felt he should resist throwing all his questions at Duke right away. He was dying to find out all he could about Ashvin and, of course, the incense. But he didn't want to overwhelm the boy.

"So, Duke, will you be here long?"

"Eeee. Yes. You see, Mr. Morrow..."

"Rennie."

"Mr., uh, Rennie. You see, I am here just a short time. Uncle Ashvin gave me a letter for you and some instructions about the incense. When we finish our conversation about that, I can be on my way."

The incense. That was what he needed to know most. Instead he asked, "On your way? Where are you headed?"

"Oh, ahhhh, yes. I am on a quest, you see. To play poker. I am going to go to Las Vegas and I will play in a tournament there. A Texas Hold'em tournament."

Poker? Rennie thought. Seriously? At least that explained the dark glasses, the oversized "Ace" visor, and why the flames on Duke's bowling shirt were shaped like a spade. He'd probably bought them at online poker sites.

"So, what do you do, play online?"

"Oh, uhhhhh, yes. I have been playing, ahhhh, five years now. I qualified for tournaments before, but I wasn't old enough to go. And this year I turned 21, but father still didn't want me to come. But then Uncle Ashvin said to let me go so I could help him in his business."

"So Uncle, um, I mean, Mr. Ashvin said to come here? To me? How did he know who I was? Do you know why he sent the incense to me in the first place?"

Rennie couldn't help it, he was burning with questions, and Duke didn't seem to mind talking.

But he didn't answer. Instead, Duke started searching through his pants pockets, then in some of the many zippered compartments of his briefcase, which sat at his feet. All the while, little "eeee" and "uhhh" sounds emitted from his mouth like a tiny foghorn. Finally, he produced a rectangle of white paper and held it up to the car window, where it caught the small amount of light coming in from 19th Avenue.

"The Business Card Guru gave this to him."

Rennie glanced over and recognized the plain white cardstock with Rennie's name, business name, and home address on it. The reason it had his home instead of his business address was that it was not actually his business card. He didn't have any business cards on that trip to India. It was many years ago, and he was just getting started in import and sales. He had a company name, but no office at that time, and he didn't have cards either.

But he'd had some made. He'd made them because the Guru he wanted to see, the Guru of whom Duke was obviously speaking, would only allow people into his inner sanctuary if they presented him with their business card. If you didn't have one, you were instructed to go to the nearest town, find the printer, get some made up, and bring them back.

Rennie supposed the printer was the Guru's brother or cousin, but no matter. It didn't cost much and he could have them ready for you in two hours. At the printer's suggestion,

Rennie went to the café across the dusty street from the tiny print shop and had a cup of chai while he waited. He figured the café owner to be another relative. Clearly, it was a company town.

When the cards were ready, he got on the bicycle he'd borrowed from the ashram and began to peddle back. He had forgotten to bring a bag, and the printer didn't provide one, so he had to awkwardly carry the single long box with it's 500 cards inside while trying to grip the handlebars. Fortunately, it was not a long ride. Upon arriving back at the Ashram, Rennie returned the bicycle to its spot against the outside wall of the office, and went in to present his newly minted badge of identity, smelling sharply of fresh ink, to the Guru's people. This satisfied them and secured his admittance.

Once inside, it was a typical small sanctuary in all ways but one. A few dozen people, most in Indian dress but some wearing western clothing, sat in meditation or bent in prayer on overlapping rugs on the floor. A line of six or seven stood to form a center aisle leading up to the Guru at the head of the room. As one person would finish getting his advice or blessings from the Guru, they would turn and make their way around the edge of the room, passing the altars down both sides that were covered with candles, statues, and colorful cloths; and bowls of rice, fruit and flowers. The Guru would gesture, and whoever was at the front of the line would move up to take their turn. Those behind would step forward, and someone from the floor would stand up and go to the end of the line.

Behind the Guru's raised bench, where he sat cross-legged on a large cushion, was something Rennie had not seen at any other Ashram or temple. Giant heaps of business cards took up a large, otherwise empty floor. Almost all were white, with a few brightly colored cards scattered throughout like rubies or emeralds in a pile of snow. The colored ones must be from the few people who happened to have brought theirs from home,

Rennie thought. Most people probably ended up getting them from the printer in town, as he'd had to do.

Rennie took his place on the floor to wait his turn. He sat quietly in a half-lotus, but did not close his eyes. He watched the guru. As each person came up, the guru would accept their card and hold it, while he spent about ten minutes either in what appeared to be a blessing, or else just talking to them quietly. Then he would take both their hands in his, gently pull them forward, and kiss them on the forehead. As he let go, he'd dramatically throw both his hands into the air above his head and release the card, which would fly up and back behind him, and disappear into the vast sea of paper.

The last time Rennie had seen the card Duke was now holding, it had landed next to a speck of turquoise on the pile directly behind the guru. That was at least fifteen years ago. Acres and acres of nearly identical cards must have flown out of the guru's hands onto countless piles since then.

Rennie turned to Duke. "The Business Card Guru? How is that possible?"

"Eeeee, I don't know how he does it. It is a siddhi for sure. But everyone knows, if you want to find someone for any reason, you can go to the Business Card Guru and he will have the right person for you. A lot of people go to find a husband or a wife. Uncle needed an American who would be interested in buying his special new incense. He went to the Guru and told him what he needed. Uncle came back and told us how it works.

"The Guru listens. Then he gets up from his chair, and he goes back to stand among the many piles. He walks around for a few minutes and pushes some cards out of the way. Sometimes he goes deep into the stack, nearly to the bottom. Then he picks up a card, looks at it, and brings it back to the person with the request. It doesn't matter how long it's been since that card was put in the pile, the right one is always there, and he finds it and pulls it out. He gave your card to Uncle, and he said, 'This is the person you should send your incense to. He will recognize what it is and he will not cheat you.' Nobody knows how the Business Card Guru does these things, but he is always right."

"Incredible," Rennie said. He had heard similar stories about that Guru when he was there, but they were always third-hand from someone whose credibility he had no idea about. His own experience face-to-face with the Guru had actually been a good one, although no miracles had been performed. The Guru said Rennie was on the right path in all that he was doing, and should continue with his plans, and deepen his practice as much as he could. He gave him a new mantra to try. The advice was not remarkable, but after Rennie had been blessed, and kissed, and had his card tossed into the pile, he had walked away feeling elevated and very clear, and he noticed for the next couple of weeks that his meditation using that mantra had been especially fruitful.

"Can I see that?" Rennie asked, and Duke handed him the card. Rennie looked at it as best he could while glancing back and forth at the road, then returned it to Duke.

"That's the one I gave him," he said. "See that smudge in the bottom left corner? I dropped the card while I was waiting in line, and got some dirt on it when I picked it up. The box of cards was on the floor where I had been sitting and I didn't want to go back for a clean one, so I wouldn't lose my place in line. That really is the card I gave him. I'd never have believed it." Rennie repeated, shaking his head.

Duke put the card back into his briefcase. He didn't seem to think it at all surprising that the Guru had managed to find and identify one particular card given to him years ago by someone he didn't know, out of the many piles of thousands just like it. Duke appeared far more impressed by the sight of the Golden Gate Bridge, and the lights of San Francisco as he looked back over his shoulder, his mouth open and his eyes wide.

Rennie wanted so badly to ask about the incense, but he made himself be patient. He would read the letter from Ashvin first, then ask Duke whatever questions he still had after that. He hoped the letter would explain how it was made and what Ashvin knew about its properties. However the main thing was to acquire it – this batch for starters – and then develop a permanent, exclusive arrangement with Ashvin. It was all Rennie could do not to pull the car over and read the letter from Ashvin right then.

One benefit from years of meditating was that he knew how to wait. Now, though, with all that incredible incense stashed in his car, he was closer than ever to his goal – his dream of doing powerful work with people and being recognized for it. And the closer he got to the goal, the more difficult it was not to be there yet. *But soon* he thought, his whole being vibrating with excitement and anticipation. I just need to take one step after another and it will happen.

In the meantime, he'd distract himself with finding out more about Duke. He turned to the young man and asked about his poker playing, his trip to Las Vegas, and the tournament he was in. But Rennie barely heard the answers. He might be able to control his words, but he couldn't keep his thoughts from bounding ahead to anticipate the future.

I'm going to get everything I was hoping for. This is really happening.

It was almost more thrilling than he could stand.

32
Near Boulder, Colorado

L uckily, Michaela did not have to go as far as Colombia, Cuba, Canada, or even Cleveland to take a workshop. She only had to hop on a late morning Frontier flight to Denver. When she'd learned the Shamanic Light Training was in Colorado that weekend, Michaela decided she could credit her intuition for honing in on the "C" places. Also, she discovered they only had these events once a month, so the fact that one was available at the time she needed it was evidence of support from the universe. Michaela was glad to be feeling clued in on some of these important concepts of her new spiritual path. She noted them in her journal while she was on the plane, and thought Rennie would be pleased.

From the Denver airport, she rented a car and headed north to Boulder. The person at the LightWorks Shamanic Training office, to whom she'd given her credit card on the phone, had told her the address, which she entered into her portable GPS. Seventy minutes later Michaela was pulling up to a small retreat center outside of town. She was pleased with how smoothly all of this was going. More evidence that the powers-that-be wanted her to be here. The only downside was that she'd have to share a room, as no singles had been available.

But the woman on the phone had assured her that the rooms were reasonably large, and that her roommate, who the woman knew from past retreats, was an agreeable person.

When Michaela opened the door to her room, no one was there. Michaela found a note from her roommate, saying she had saved the double bed for Michaela, and taken the single for herself, and that she'd gone for a walk and would be back soon. Signed, "Robin." The top two drawers of the dresser had been set slightly open so she could see they were unused. Although there was no closet, a couple of hooks on the wall had empty hangers. Overall, the room was comfortable. Not luxurious, but not Spartan either. Two photos of mountains hung on the walls. Through the single, large, peach-curtained window, was a view of the real ones, with Boulder's well-known Flatirons formation figuring prominently. Michaela put away her clothes and toiletries and sat on her bed to plan her next move.

There was a small desk, upon which Robin had apparently made an altar by laying out a lavender silk scarf, a couple of small statues, a double-sided silver frame, a feather and a large green stone. The frame held, on one side, a man's portrait, and on the other, a picture of a woman rock climbing in bright sunshine, smiling and shading her eyes.

Not knowing the protocol for such situations, Michaela wondered if she ought to put out some of her own things in a similar fashion, or maybe even add to the display Robin had started. She thought about what she'd brought with her that might be suitable for an altar, but she didn't really have anything. She did carry a picture in her wallet of herself and Roxanne sitting by a fountain and laughing. However, they had been drunk, and looked it. Michaela was holding her silver Jimmy Choo sandals over her head and had one leg in the air, and Roxanne had been tilting dangerously back toward the water, like she was about to fall in. In fact, she *had* fallen in, just after the picture was taken, and both she and Michaela had laughed their asses off. Which was why Michaela carried the picture with her. Every time she looked at it, it made her laugh.

But even Michaela knew it was not suitably spiritual for an altar. She supposed she could go outside and find a rock of her own; maybe even an attractive, moss-covered stick or some other appropriately shamanic – she knew how to use that term now – item. Then she remembered the portable, professional-quality art kit and small pad of heavy drawing paper she had brought with her. The kit contained both watercolors and colored pencils in a reasonably large range of colors.

She pulled the kit and paper out of the top dresser drawer, where she'd stashed them next to her panties and bras. She placed the pad on her lap on the bed, arrayed the recently sharpened pencils next to her, and started to draw. Within about ten minutes she had produced a twelve-inch high figure of one of her Maserati-driving monk friends, as she thought of them, standing in his Tibetan robes. Using the scissors from the kit, she cut him out. Then she used some extra paper she'd left around the bottom of the figure and folded it cleverly behind him, to make him stand up on the desk overlooking Robin's altar.

After that, she did another one, this time a woman wearing one of the zig-zag wrap dress designs that Michaela had been coming up with lately. The figure stood with one hand held out, palm upward, a flame rising from it. With her other hand, she held up a small mirror, which was turned not inward to look at herself, but outward toward the world.

As usual when she made these drawings, Michaela wasn't sure why she was doing them, or what they meant. But she went ahead and cut out the second figure and stood it up next to the monk on the desk. Michaela sat back down and gazed with satisfaction at her creations. Then she put away her art supplies and decided to follow Robin's lead and go for a walk. Dinner was in less than an hour, and after that they would go to the first session of the workshop.

Michaela was surprised to find herself feeling excited. She did not know what to expect, but it didn't matter. Now that she was here, she was up for anything. Whatever happened, she felt ready, even eager, to get going. Humming, she adjusted her paper figures a little on the desk, put her room key in the pocket of her jacket, and let herself out into the bright Colorado sunshine.

◊ ◊ ◊

When she returned to the room thirty minutes later, Michaela saw through the window that Robin was back. Entering the room, she started to introduce herself, but Robin cut her off.

"Are those your paper dolls?" Robin asked, gesturing at the desk. "They're so cool. I can't stop looking at them."

"Paper dolls? Oh, you mean my drawings. I guess you could call them that. I did them before I went out."

"You made them yourself? Awesome. You're really talented."

"Um, thanks. And thanks for leaving me the bigger bed."

"It's cool. I'm easy about stuff like that. Is this your first time at a Thea retreat?"

"Um, yeah." Michaela didn't tell her it was her first time at any retreat.

"Where are you from? And I guess I should ask your name. I'm Robin, from San Diego."

"Michaela Thomason. I live in Marin County. It's…"

"North of San Francisco. Yeah, I know. I lived in Marin for a while. Woodacre, actually. I was volunteering at Spirit Rock. Do you go there?"

"Um, not recently," Michaela half-lied. She'd seen an ad for programs at the Spirit Rock Meditation Center. She thought she might go at some point, but hadn't been motivated enough yet.

"I know it's a great vibe, but I wish Jack taught more. He's amazing. Don't you love his last book?"

Not having heard of Jack, Michaela simply nodded.

"Are you going to do more paper dolls?" Robin asked. "I mean, or whatever you call them. What do you call them?" Michaela was beginning to notice that Robin asked a lot of questions. She didn't mind, but thought it could get annoying if she kept on at this pace. However, Michaela was glad to talk about her artwork, so she explained as best she could about the inspiration for the paper figures. She didn't want to tell Robin she had invented these two "dolls" on the spur of the moment because she didn't have anything altar-y to contribute to the décor.

"I met that monk and some of his, um, friends, or, um, co-monks, I guess you'd call them, about a month ago. Then I just started drawing monk's robes, and that became these different dresses – I mean, women in dresses, I guess. First the dresses were kinda robe-like, and then they evolved. It's funny, because even though I'm an artist and all – I mean, that's what I do, I design menus professionally – I never drew anything like this before. But Rennie – he's my, um, spiritual teacher – he said I should start being guided by my intuition. So I just let myself draw every day, whenever I feel like it. And that's what's been coming out. I never stood them up like that before, though," Michaela admitted.

"So the monk is someone you know. And who's the Goddess? She looks like you. Is she you? What's the flame mean? And the mirror?"

Michaela was now definitely feeling this was too many questions, especially since she lacked suitable answers. She didn't know what made her want to draw the woman in the pose she was in, or add the fire and the mirror. In Michaela's mind, it was more about the clothes.

"You think it looks like me?" she asked. "I guess the hair is like mine. Longer, maybe. Brown eyes."

"She has your figure, too. I think it's definitely you, even if you didn't mean to. Don't you think?"

"I don't usually wear that color," Michaela said, with a self-conscious laugh. "Or throw flames either. I have been known to look in a mirror, though. But I don't know why I drew those."

"Maybe the workshop will help you figure out what it means." Robin was kneeling on the bed, and she jumped up and down a little. "Say, you wouldn't do one for me, would you? One that looks like me, I mean. You can pose it any way you want. Later, I mean, not now. But would you?"

"Um, sure, I guess. I mean, I'll try. I've never done one like that, um, to order, before."

"Cool! I'll be your first commission. Maybe we could trade for something. I could do some Reiki for you tomorrow if you want. How does that sound?"

Again, Michaela was in the dark. She heard the word, but it didn't mean anything to her.

"Okay," she said, wondering what she was getting into.

This spiritual stuff just got more and more complicated. At least Robin liked her artwork. That felt good. Maybe she wasn't completely in over her head, even if she wasn't yet ready to swim with the big boys. Or girls. But she would be. That's why she was here, wasn't it? To learn to swim with the spiritual sharks, like those carnivorous buttholes at Eighth. She just had to stick with it. Like Rennie said, just keep showing up.

They washed up and made their way out into the early dusk, the sun throwing red fire above the mountains. Robin kept up her stream of questions, and Michaela did her best to sound like she knew what she was talking about, meanwhile wondering what they would be doing during the weekend, and what Dorothea Light would be like.

Robin held open the door to the dining room, and Michaela entered the room half-full of people talking and laughing. Robin gestured at one of several rectangular tables of six, and they sat down. She introduced Michaela to the others at the table, and soon they were all chatting together, as they waited for the rest of the group to arrive and the food to be served.

This isn't so bad, Michaela thought. *It feels pretty good being here. I'm actually glad I came.* Just then, the door opened and a cluster of people came in. Michaela was sure that had to be Dorothea and her staff. Everyone looked at them, and several stood up for hugs.

"I ran into them earlier," Robin said. "I've already said hello."

Strangely, Michaela felt that she had said hello already too, even though she was sure she had never even met any of those people before. It was a peculiar sensation, one she wasn't sure she liked. Her sense of well being from a moment before was gone. But as soon as the incoming group had settled at one of the tables, the food was served. Michaela's table companions resumed their conversation, and she felt okay again.

Next she knew, Robin was telling the others at the table about her paper figures, and everyone said they wanted to see them, and asked would she make one for them. And Michaela said, of course she would. She would be happy to do it.

Hey, she thought, *I have something to contribute. Even if it's just a bunch of silly drawings and nothing very spiritual at all.*

Chapter 4

Now, guys. Do you remember back in Chapter 3, when we had that Regular Guy Enlightenment Alert? Don't remember? That's okay. I'm going to tell you again. The alert was this:

Even if you get SOME, you want some MORE.

If you recall, the subject was Tantra, and the alert was about sex. Okay, NOW you remember. I thought so. Anyway, I gave you a heads-up we'd be coming back to that phrase, because for us Regular Guys who think we might at some point like to be enlightened, it's a point we probably want to pay attention to. Because it not only refers to sex, it refers to everything.

What you've actually got there is a short form of something talked about by that famous guy Buddha. Yeah, I do mean the fat boy in robes who lived in India a few thousand years ago – what about it? Even Regular Guys like us have heard of Buddha. Now before you go getting all "I'm not a Buddhist, I'm a (fill-in-the-blank)" on me, hang on and hear me out on this one. One of the tricks we Regular Guys can use to get enlightened is to be open to help from any source. Maybe not follow it all. Maybe reject a lot of it. But at least listen to it.

It's like big time coaching. Just because a coach is working for a team other than yours, doesn't mean he isn't a good coach, right? I mean, if he wasn't, would he even be coaching in the pros, or the BCS, or what have you? Of course not. Likewise, in the spiritual wisdom department, don't you think it's a good idea to find out what the coaches of other teams have to say? Of course it is. Even if we're just spying so we can find out what they got in the playbook, it's good for something. So we don't have to be Buddhists to want to know what their head coach, Buddha himself, has to say about playing the game.

Now to get back to what he DID say, or, let's just call it the Regular Guy version of what he said. Here's the deal, Guys. You want stuff. We all do. Can you think of any time you did not want stuff? By stuff, I mean more than just stuff stuff. I mean anything. New golf clubs. An icy beer. An iPad. A slice of perfectly cooked prime rib. Obviously, sex, which we've mentioned before, and will of course continue to mention at every opportunity. A Lamborghini, a Labrador, a lake in Labrador, whatever.

Or the non-stuff stuff. You want time – just more of it so you can lay back and take it easy, 'cuz you work too hard. You want the women in your life to quit being so annoying (good luck with that one, bro). You want your hair not to fall out, goddammit. You want your teenager to listen to you once in a while. You want to feel someone gives a crap at work. You want YOU to give a crap at work, or wherever.

If those aren't your particular wants, then you know what yours are. But, Guys, you know you got 'em. Cause it's a human thing, and you ARE human (do not listen to any female who claims you're not). And there's nothing wrong with us for having the wants, cause that's part of who we are. I don't know if Buddha said that. Buddha might not have actually said that. But some other of them head coaches did, and we're spying on those playbooks too.

But even if it's not like we're bad Guys just because we want stuff, a lot of the time, it still causes us shit. Because a lot of the time, having the wants makes us unhappy. We think the reason we're unhappy is not getting the stuff we want. True enough. But – and Coach Buddha did say this one – so does GETTING what we f—ing want. You think I'm kidding, right? Well, think about it.

You know if you want something real bad – and you think you SHOULD get it, but you don't think you're GONNA get it – then you are not pleased about that. You are feeling the itch and can't scratch it. Or you feel stuck with something you DON'T want. That's not fun. That doesn't feel good. In fact, it totally sucks.

HOWEVER – pay attention here guys – a lot of the times when we do get what we want, we're STILL not happy. Because whatever we get that we want, it's not gonna be enough. It's not gonna do the trick. Maybe you don't believe me. Maybe you're saying, "Guy, it's not true. I got the new clubs and I didn't want new clubs anymore. I was happy."

Okay, that may be so. Sure, the sticks made you happy, for a while. But I say you might not be seeing the big picture here. I'll give you an example. Let's say you've been wanting those golf clubs for a while. You put in a lot of time researching online and in magazines, narrowing down to what sounds like the ideal set. Then you go out and handle them, try 'em out, and you figure they're exactly the ones you want. And then, at some point, you decide to make the purchase. You hand over your plastic, you wait a few weeks while they're fitted for you. Then they arrive. As soon as possible, you go and play with them. Now, just for argument's sake, cause it doesn't always work that way, let's say they're perfect – exactly what you hoped for. Completely satisfying in every way. Look good, feel good, and you got the best score of your life. Guy! Congratulations.

Now, picture this. Nineteenth hole. You hang around, down a few, shoot the shit, make sure you drop in a word now and then about sinking that long putt. Then you go home. You bring the sticks in, put them within visual range of the couch. For a few days, you're all, "Cool. I got 'em. Look at 'em standing around over there, all proud of their bad selves." Next time you take 'em out, maybe you don't bring them back inside. Or maybe you do. Whatever. But after awhile, even though you're still glad about having them, the clubs just don't have that glow anymore. After awhile, they aren't new. They're still cool, but now they're just something else that you own.

The point is, the clubs aren't doing that thing for you any more. So, Guys, what happens? Next thing you know, you find yourself on the couch thinking, "Damn. I sure would like one of those new sound systems for my car. I'd get the GPS and the

Satellite Radio all integrated, and a big old subwoofer." And there you are, off and running on the next want.

My point being, Guys, that no matter what you get, no matter how much you like it, you're never going to stop wanting something else. It's the ultimate mosquito bite. No matter how many times that itch gets scratched, it comes right back. You keep scratching that sucker, and you know you're gonna dig a hole in your skin, whether you mean to or not.

Another example, in case you still don't believe me. Let's say you got a girlfriend. If you don't have a girlfriend, pretend you do. If what you've got is a wife, just humor me here and pretend you don't. Just a girlfriend.

Okay, Guys, now let's say your girlfriend is really hot. Like, supermodel hot. Or if the supermodel type isn't your thing, then how about starlet hot? Doesn't even matter. Just whatever's your version of a way good looking female. That's her – your girlfriend. Oh, and by the way, she puts out. Whatever you want, whenever you want it. I'm not kidding. This is a fantasy, remember. We can set it up however we want. However, Guys, there's one more thing. We also set it up that you can only keep it going as long as you don't step out on her. She's your own personal hot-as-shit supermodel, or starlet, or whoever, but only provided you don't wander off and do the deed with somebody else.

Okay, now, Guys. Let's say you're out with just us Guys one night, and lo! The room is filled with hotties. What does that mean for you? Right, it probably means you're in LA or Miami or Rio, but that's beside the point. Fantasy, Guys. Go with it.

But what else it means for you is that you see hotties, you want hotties. No matter how hot your hottie at home is. Even if she's a 10, and all the new hotties are only an eight-and-a-half, guess what? You still want the strange. You want it a lot. You may be a well-behaved Guy and not go after it, but you most definitely do want it.

The point here, Guys, is that no matter how attractive a female you got at home waiting for you, you're still going to wish you could have some of that other. Wait – I mean ALL of that other. I'm sorry, guys. I wish it wasn't true. We all wish it wasn't true, cause it makes things f—ing complicated.

But, Guys, let's face it. That's just the way it is. We're Guys. We're exactly like some wild stallion, when that cute little pinto mare just isn't going to be enough for us. We also want that bay with the long mane. And the palomino with the big eyes. And the sorrel that swishes her tail like that. Basically guys, we want the whole f—ing herd.

My point, let me remind you, being this: Even if you get SOME, you want some MORE. Buddha called that play big time, and he was right about it big time too.

And now, you may well ask, how does knowing that play lead to us Regular Guys being enlightened? Well, guys, I'll tell you. It's not complicated. In fact, you may find it hard to believe.

But the way it works is, just knowing that truth, and being aware of it, is a huge step on that road. You just gotta know that's how it is, and when it happens, you notice the sucker. You say, hey, there's that giant elephant in my tiny male pea brain of a living room. And you think – Yo! Guy (meaning me)! There it is, just like you said.

'Cuz, Guys. Life's gonna call that play sometimes – a lot of times – and if you know that's what's coming at you, then you can block it. You can say to yourself, "Self. I am not happy. I want things to be different. But Self! I'm always going to want *something* to be different! It's not the fault of the thing I want and don't have, or the thing I have and don't want. It's the fault of my humanness, which means it is the fault of nothing and nobody."

And then, Guys. Then. You're doing it. You're paying attention. You're experiencing some waking up. Every time you recognize how things are, it's a First Down on the road to enlightenment. You're a few yards less at the mercy of what's out there, and a few yards more your own Guy. That's getting enlightened. Guy! Take a time out. You earned it.

33
Petaluma

D uke could eat a lot of pizza. Rennie had called ahead, so their vegetarian combos were ready to pick up when they hit Petaluma. Good thing he'd ordered two larges. He almost got less, since he could only eat a medium by himself, but another glance at Duke's long, skinny frame and he decided to up the quantity. Rennie parked in front and ran in for the pizzas. Soon he and Duke were back on the road headed home. However, once Duke caught the aroma, it was all over. His eyes and nostrils popped open, and Rennie could practically hear him drool.

"You don't have to wait 'til we get home. Just eat over the box so you don't spill crumbs," Rennie said. Before Rennie finished the sentence, Duke had yanked the top pizza box over the seat and opened it on his lap.

"Mmmmph," Duke remarked, as half a huge wedge disappeared into his mouth. Olive and garlic pieces tumbled off the slice and back into the box like passengers off the upended Titanic.

"Eh uh ee ery uch ee ah ah ay," he said, sucking up the rest of the slice. After swallowing, Duke tried again.

"I did not eat very much for a long time all day," he

explained, prying loose his next victim, as it struggled futilely
to hang on to the rest of the pie with arms of stringy cheese.

"Just one very little banana and a McDonald's French fries
– small size – and three packs of pretzels. Eeeh, yes, and a half
a graham cracker and five goldfish I received from a small boy
on the airplane."

Rennie reached into the box for a slightly blackened section
of green pepper and ate it, as Duke shoved down his second
slice and went for a third. Slipping with a sigh across the paper
underneath it, the pizza stopped struggling and accepted its
fate. The slice quickly reached Duke's mouth and disappeared
into the void.

"Ish ery ood eetsuh," Duke added, nodding vigorously. He
politely, but with obvious remorse, closed the box and set it
gently back onto the seat behind him.

Rennie was as hungry for information as Duke was for
food. But still, he waited to ask about the letter. When they
reached the house, Duke went to wash up, while Rennie placed
the pizza boxes on the table, poured two iced teas with sprigs of
fresh mint, and put out a stack of napkins and a couple of
plates. Fortunately, it did not take long for them to finish the
food. Rennie barely noticed eating three slices – his teachers
would have scolded him for being so unconscious of his actions
– and Duke easily downed the remainder of the two pies,
slumping over and looking a little sad as he swallowed his final
bite.

Rennie cleared the boxes and plates, and brought out a
mostly full package of Newman-O cookies, which he set
directly in front of Duke. The boy perked right up and escorted
three of them into his mouth, followed by a swig of tea.

"So," Rennie started. He could wait no longer. "Did you
say you have a letter for me from your uncle?"

Duke nodded, his mouth full of cookies, and pointed
toward his briefcase by the door. After popping another
Newman-O in his mouth, he stood up and retrieved the case,

sat back down with it on his lap, and produced a white envelope from one of the compartments.

"Here it is," he said, as soon as his mouth was unoccupied. Rennie leaned over and took the envelope, which was closed but unsealed. He pulled out the single sheet and began to read, as Duke returned his concentration to the cookies.

Sumana, India

To My Dear Mr. Rennie Morrow, sir:

I am R.K. Ashvin. I enclose my business card.

Rennie looked back into the envelope and there was Ashvin's card, printed in the same basic black-on-white style as the one Rennie had bicycled into town to get printed for the Guru all those years ago.

I hope you know me from receiving earlier package sent to you. As nephew Duke to explain, Baba Card-ji say you are man I go to for business with incense. I send you sample first so you can know all about incense. I send Duke now with hope you will want incense and know how best to do with it.

So far so good. Rennie kept going. His heart leapt when he read that Ashvin was offering him all the incense he had made so far. Even better, Ashvin said future quantity would also be limited, however he would sell Rennie whatever he made. Of course, if Rennie wasn't interested, Duke had instructions to contact other distributors.

Baba Card-ji tell me you are a good man and buyer of incense. Nephew Duke has permission to accept fair price. Send money to Banking Account of R.K. Ashvin, bank name and numbers at end of letter. Two percent of total, you will please give cash to nephew Duke. Ninety-eight percent to send to R.K. Ashvin

Banking Account. I thank you very much with all my heart and look to see you when next we are together in thought. Probably you know what this mean thank you to incense.

That last sentence was not very clear, but Rennie strongly felt – with much excitement – that Ashvin may have been referring to the visions and dreams he'd been having. Rennie was now completely convinced that he had "received" information about Ashvin and the incense, whether Ashvin was sending it intentionally or not. He was getting knowledge that he needed in a non-ordinary way – you could say psychically, although Rennie had never thought of himself as psychic. There were past occasions when he had felt strong intuitions that proved true, as well as some amazing synchronicities. But the messages he "got" from Ashvin were more powerful than anything he'd experienced. And Ashvin was giving the incense credit. This had extraordinary implications.

Rennie's only letdown was that Ashvin had not said anything about which ingredients or preparation gave the incense its special qualities. Rennie was intensely curious. Of course, if he were Ashvin, he wouldn't have revealed his secrets either. He could ask Duke, but most likely, if the boy did know anything, Ashvin would have told him not to discuss it. It was still worth a try, and before Duke went on his merry way to Vegas, Rennie would try to get something out of him.

Meanwhile, he told Duke that yes, he did most definitely want to purchase the cartons of incense, and that they could discuss the specific financial and other arrangements in the morning. Duke nodded, but Rennie wasn't sure how much attention he was paying, as he was completely absorbed with consuming what was left of the cookies and staring intently at the fruit bowl on the counter.

Rennie proceeded to gather towels, sheets, blankets and pillows, and threw them on a chair in the living room. He pulled out and made the sofa bed. It was going to be a little short for the lanky young man, but Rennie thought if he slept at an angle, his feet would only hang over the end a little bit. That was, if he decided to go to bed at all. It looked like he might just stay up all night eating. The Newman-O package now held only the ghost of cookies past, and Rennie sat down to watch as Duke buried his teeth deeply into an apple, and then his head deeply into the refrigerator.

Rennie was satisfied to watch Duke make his way through whatever he could find to eat. It seemed perfectly appropriate to have Duke eeeing and ahhing his way about the kitchen, just as happy as he could be; an outer reflection of the inner contentment that Rennie himself was feeling.

34
Near Boulder

"**W**ords are symbols, and symbols have power," Dorothea told the gathered group.

About twenty minutes after eating their peach pie and sipping their coffee, Michaela, Robin, and the rest of the thirty or so people attending the workshop had made their way from the dining area to the nearby meeting room for the evening session. It was a large, airy room, with the long wall on the far side made up of sliding glass doors leading to a large deck, and, past that, out to the nearby creek and cottonwood trees.

The room was set up with three rows of those funny looking floor cushions that you can lean back on, like chairs without legs – Michaela overheard someone call them "backjacks" – and behind them, five or six real chairs for those who preferred to be above floor level. The seats were arranged in a semi-circle facing a dark gray armchair. Next to the armchair was a small, round table holding a vase of purple freesias and a glass of water.

Following Dirk's short welcome, which included introducing the three people on the support staff, Dorothea came in, arranged herself in the armchair, and immediately began addressing them.

"When you say words out loud, that creates vibrational energy. It's the power of sound. Sound is more powerful than the physical. It's how they built the pyramids, you know, back in ancient Egypt. The scientists, the historians, Egyptologists, anybody – they can't figure out how the pyramids were built. But some of us know. I know. I've been shown. It's true. Sound waves moved those blocks. Science doesn't know it yet, but they will, someday. It wasn't all those Egyptian slaves with ropes and pulleys. It was vibrations, sounds. We've lost that knowledge, but it will come back some day. Just like Atlantis, and all the knowledge they had there. That's coming back too."

She paused and sipped her water, looking around at her audience.

"When you use mantras, that's the power of sound vibration changing the energy around you. Every repetition of the mantra is like another little stone in the pool. All the ripples start moving each other in different patterns, and the patterns spread out and out and out, and interact with other patterns, other energies. Not entirely like a pool, because that's just a flat surface. But think of it rippling out in all directions at once. In all dimensions.

"You can use any word as a mantra, you know. It doesn't have to be some old musty thing from India that sounds funny. Those Sanskrit words have been around a long time, and they like to tell you they're the best ones. And they do work. But guess what? You can use good old American English words, too. We'll try that later this evening. We'll take some plain old word and make it into a mantra, and you'll feel the energy move."

She turned to a woman in the front row. "But don't worry, honey," she said. "You look worried. You look like this," Dorothea pushed out her lips and squinted her eyes. There was laughter from the group. The woman smiled but squirmed. Michaela was glad she was in the back. She wouldn't want to be singled out like that.

"I said we'd try using some plain old word, but really, you know, I'm not going to pick any old dumb, stupid word. I'll give you all a good word." More laughter. She looked back at the woman. "You know Dorothea will give you a word y'all like, right?"

The woman nodded, chuckling with the group. Dorothea's face went back to normal.

"Okay. So nobody worry. So, I was saying… Energy from words. Even if you just think them. You don't even have to say them out loud. You can say the mantra to yourself in your head, and it will still send out vibrations."

Dorothea paused again for a sip. Michaela glanced at the other people in the room. Rennie had said his workshop at the hotel in San Francisco had about 60 people in it. This one was smaller, maybe because this retreat was more expensive. She had a feeling it was also supposed to be more advanced than the introductory weekend Rennie went to. The registrar on the phone had asked if Michaela had ever been to one of their workshops before. When she said no, the woman asked her to stay on hold for just a minute, then came back to say it was fine to register. So she did. But Michaela wondered if Dorothea or Dirk would think the woman had made a mistake allowing her in.

Dorothea continued. "Just like, 'In the beginning was the Word,' you know. You heard that before, right? But if it was the beginning, whatever was there wasn't *us* yet in this human form, and so there weren't any mouths or voices either. But there was energy and thought. So that means we can use new words and make them create vibrations for us.

"We can follow in God's footsteps. Or whatever your name for God is. I like to say, the Great Everything. We can follow the footsteps of the Great Everything with our words, and our vibrations. The Great Everything had to make them up, without a mouth, or without anything like a mouth. Not even sign language. Not even any kind of body. And we can do that too.

Except we have a choice. We can use our mouths or not. If we don't want to use our mouths, we can use just our thoughts, like the Great Everything did, in the beginning."

Dorothea paused for a moment, and Michaela imagined Dorothea creating vibrations even as she sat there. If anyone could create vibrations, it was probably Dorothea. Michaela could almost see patterns of energy swirling around Dorothea right now. They were like spirals of breeze lifting leaves in the fall, or the darkening clouds that would become a storm. She wanted to draw those images.

Dorothea said, "Then there's the written word. That has its own kind of power. That kind of power can be good or bad. Well, they can all be good or bad, negative or positive. Mantras can too. Any kind of thought, or vibration, or energy. Not the nature of vibration or energy itself; that's neutral. That's not ever good or bad. But how you use it can be. You can make good or bad karma. You can be glad or sorry."

She leaned forward and her eyes narrowed.

"Some people can be very sorry. They can choose to use the written word to make good people look bad. They can harm good people's reputations. Even their relatives. Especially their relatives. They can write books that will harm their relatives and they choose to do that even though their relatives are trying to make the world a better place, and trying to help people. That's the power of the word."

Michaela wasn't sure she understood most of what Dorothea was saying, even before she started this last part about the relatives. But now she felt really confused. She looked over at Robin, who was staring intently at Dorothea and didn't see Michaela. But Michaela noticed a few other people in the room glancing at each other with puzzled expressions, as if they didn't quite get what she was referring to either. Michaela turned back to Dorothea.

"But you can help. If you find out someone wrote something and published it, despite hurting their relative, you can say bad things about the person who wrote the book. Of course, you'd have to know his name, because his name might not be the same as his relative, and then maybe nobody would even know they were related. So I'm not going to tell you who he is now, but if it comes out that he's the brother, or some other relation, of someone who YOU KNOW is good, and who is a teacher to you, and who wants only what's best for you.... Well, you'll know what to do. I hope you'll know what to do. Then they really will be sorry."

Michaela saw Dorothea's gaze move to the far side of the room, so she turned that way herself and saw Dirk frantically shaking his head and moving his hand back and forth across his throat in a "cut" gesture. Dorothea looked annoyed and turned back to the group.

"Well, never mind about that. That's just theoretical. It doesn't mean anything. I was just making a point, in case... you know... in case something like that were to ever happen. Theoretically."

She swished her water glass without drinking, then put it down firmly and sat up straight. "So! Let's try one of those mantras. Let's try a new word, shall we, and we'll see what those vibrations are like – what the energy does.

"I want you to get comfortable now, and close your eyes. And take a few deep, deep, deep breaths. Breathe all the way to your fingers and your toes. Feel the breath heating up your little toesies, now. Feel it heating up your little feetsies. And you bigger guys with the big toesies and the big feetsies (giggle) feel all that heat all through them.

"Feel that warmth come all the way up your legs, everybody. Feel it come into your pelvis and then into your torso. Feel it move from your fingers into your hands into your arms and meet with the other warmth at base of your neck. Let it flow on up, and all into your head. And now let it swirl there. Swirl around in your head, and gather power. Okay, now, keep swirling. And either out loud or else picturing it in your mind,

I want you to let the power release by saying or thinking the word…," here she paused, then said loudly, "…ASCEND!"

She paused again, then repeated, "…ASCEND…. Ascend….ascend…keep going now…"

All around her Michaela could hear other participants' voices speaking or whispering "ascend" over and over. She didn't feel comfortable saying the word out loud, so she decided to repeat it only in her mind. Dorothea had said that was okay. At least she thought that's what Dorothea had said. She wasn't sure. She definitely heard Robin's voice saying the word. She snuck a quick glance out of one eye and saw a couple of others who were not moving their lips either, so Michaela thought it must be okay to keep it inside, and she continued "ascending" to herself in her head.

"Ascend…" pause, "ascend…" pause. She said it to herself over and over. She felt relieved. It was going okay. She was doing what she was supposed to be doing. However, she had to admit, she did not notice any energy moving around. Nothing whatsoever. Maybe she was doing something wrong, or maybe she was just too new at this to figure out how to tell what the vibrations were doing. *This is a bit worrisome*, she thought. *But I should just keep going.*

Then she found herself with a new, even worse, dilemma. On one unfortunate repetition, the assigned word "ascend" morphed into the similar sounding "ass end." And that one time was all it took to push ascend out the door, so that inside and outside of her head, all she could now hear was ASS END, ASS END, ASS END.

The images that went along with it flipped back and forth between the butt of a donkey swishing its tail, and her own rear resting on the backjack cushion. *Oh my god. This is terrible. The vibrations for "ass end" must be hugely different from those of "ascend." Someone's bound to notice.* Maybe everyone, but for sure Dorothea and the staff, whom she could hear walking around among them, would be able to tell.

Michaela was in a panic. She was completely screwing up! Surely, her mistake would ruin the experience for everyone. But as hard as she tried to get back to "ascend," she just couldn't make it work. *Should I stop doing this now, or to keep going and hope that this horrible mistake doesn't mess up the forces in the room? I've never done this before, so maybe I don't have much vibrational power anyway. Maybe I'm not screwing with the whole room's experience. I just don't want anyone to figure it out and know it's me. Especially Dorothea.*

Then a new, and even more awful, thought occurred to her. What if Dorothea *did* notice the bad, "ass end" energy moving around Michaela? And what if she got mad and kicked Michaela out of the group. Surely that would be the nail in the coffin of Michaela's attempts to become a more spiritual person. It would prove that she really didn't have it in her. Even though she had thought of the "C" name places before she knew the workshop was in Colorado. Even though the monks appeared to like her, and Rennie didn't seem to have any worries about her. Even though Robin had thought her paper doll was a Goddess, and that Michaela had unconsciously drawn it in her own image. Despite all that progress, Dorothea could easily look over at her, see the truth about Michaela, and banish her into a non-spiritual existence forever.

Michaela, who had now given up chanting anything in her head at all, felt incredibly frustrated and disappointed, and tears started to form in the corners of her eyes. Noticing she was crying made her want to cry even more. The tears escaped, and started running down her face. She cried silently for as long as she could, until finally a gasping sob escaped, then another one.

Within seconds, an arm was around her shoulders, squeezing gently. A woman's soft voice was talking in her ear, but she couldn't get what the woman was saying. She seemed to be trying to have Michaela get up.

This is worse than I thought. They're going to ask me to leave right now, *before the chanting is even done. This is the most horrible thing that could possibly happen. I never should have come here, it just proves I'm screwed up and now they all know it.*

She cried harder, allowing the woman to help her walk slowly away from the group. Michaela realized her eyes were still closed, so she opened them to see where they were going. It was a corner of the room. The woman helped her down onto the floor where another backjack was waiting for her. She recognized the woman as one of those who had come into the dining area with Dorothea; one of the workshop staff. Michaela had forgotten her name.

"Just let it out, just let it out," the woman way saying from her right side. "Stay with the feelings." Michaela closed her eyes again, and was immediately back in the horrible knowledge that she had been exposed. Now they knew she had been doing the assignment completely wrong and had ruined it for everyone. She had been identified and taken from the group so she could no longer infect them, and as soon as she stopped crying, she was certain they would tell her that she had screwed up too badly to stay. They would make her pack up her things and send her home.

This made Michaela cry more. A Kleenex was pushed into her hand and she wiped at the tears. She felt completely despondent, lost, and – she noticed for the first time – also afraid. In the main part of the room, most people were still chanting, but she also heard some other sounds. Somebody had started to laugh – *at me?* – and another person seemed to be mooing.

Okay, that's weird. The mooing pulled Michaela out of her crying spell. She opened her eyes and blew her nose. The assistant who had moved her out of the group was sitting next to her, looking at her calmly.

She's just waiting for me to pull it together enough to escort me out. They can't wait to get rid of me. Another tear leaked from her eye. *Well, if that's the way it is, then I'll just have to gather myself up and deal with it. I'm tough. I can handle it. I just have to collect my strength.*

Michaela straightened her back and took a deep breath. The chanting had stopped and most people were now meditating, still sitting in the original semicircles. However, in two other corners of the room, participants had been taken from the group and were sitting apart with a staff helper. Michaela thought the workshop leaders were being rather strict to kick out three people at the very first session. Of course, one was the woman who had been mooing, and she could certainly understand why that person had to go.

"Okay," Michaela said, "I can leave now."

"You want to go back to your seat now?" the woman said. "Do you want to share what's going on for you first?"

"Uh, no. I don't want to talk about it. I'll just get my stuff and leave." Then Michaela realized what the woman had said. "What do you mean, go back to my seat?" she asked suspiciously. "I have to leave the workshop, don't I?"

A different voice said, "Leave the workshop! Gracious me, no! You don't want to leave us so soon, now, do you, dear? We're just getting started!"

This voice came from her left. It was Dorothea! Dorothea herself had come over while Michaela was pulling herself together, and had joined her and the helper in their corner.

"Ella, dear, what did you say to Michaela to make her want to leave?"

"Nothing!" the woman quickly answered. "At least, I didn't mean to. I just asked her if she wanted to talk about what she was experiencing." Michaela thought she sounded a little desperate. It occurred to Michaela that Ella was probably worried about screwing up too, which was weirdly comforting. She also wondered how Dorothea knew her name.

"I don't want to leave," Michaela said. "I thought you pulled me out of the group for my mistake, and you were going to make me go home."

"Dear, dear, no, of course not. Where would you ever get that idea?" Dorothea was still looking at Ella as if she had somehow done something to cause it. Dirk brought over another backjack, then quickly left, and Dorothea lowered herself onto it, joining them on the floor.

"I'm sure you couldn't have done anything wrong," she said in a quieter voice. "We just like to make sure you're okay, and let you cry if you need to, or talk about what's going on with you. Do you want to talk about it?"

"Well, uh, I guess so. Maybe. No, not really. I mean, I do, but it's embarrassing."

They both said nothing but smiled encouragingly, so Michaela explained about *ascend* becoming *ass end*. Dorothea and Ella listened, nodding, and from time to time patting her hand or arm or knee. Somehow, without meaning to, Michaela found herself going on and on – saying how she was sure they would see she didn't belong, and how she ruined the experience for everyone, and that she had been rejected recently by important people for not being spiritual enough, and it was screwing up her whole life and making her miserable, and all she wanted was to have everything be normal again, but no matter what she did she couldn't get back to feeling like her old self.

By the end she was tearing up again, feeling more shame and fear than ever, but they were holding her and telling her to cry it all out, which she did. It reminded her a lot of how kind those monks in the car had been to her, and she realized that not everyone thought she was a fuck-up. Some people accepted her just as she was, even when she told them flat out what was wrong with her. They weren't going to kick her out. They were going to keep her there, despite ascend becoming ass end. In fact, they seemed to think it was funny.

By the next day, Michaela had let go of the awful feelings of not belonging, of screwing up and not being spiritual enough, and of the fear of being asked to leave. In fact, she was having a wonderful time and, by the end of the day, felt like the center of attention and star of the group. Everyone had flipped over her little paper figures. They all wanted one made of themselves, which she was happy to do. And then they offered to pay for them, which she refused.

The one odd moment had been when Robin brought the original figures from their room to show the group at breakfast on Saturday morning. Dorothea had exclaimed over them as much as anyone.

She said, "Michaela, these are wonderful. You obviously have a deep intuitive connection to spirit. Robin, that Goddess-looking one resembles me, doesn't it? It has to be me! And look at this dress she's wearing – I just love this dress."

And Robin, who had clearly told Michaela that first night that she thought the Goddess figure was Michaela herself, was now nodding in agreement with Dorothea.

"It really has your energy, Thea," she told her "It looks so much like you."

Michaela wondered about this. Had Robin changed her mind, or did she just not want to disagree with Dorothea?

Dorothea held the figure up to look at it more closely. "The eyes are the wrong color, though," Dorothea observed. "I'm sure you want to keep this one of me for your altar. But would you do a new one that I could keep? I'd love to have one. With my real eye color, of course."

"Yes, of course. I'd be honored to make you one. Let me see your eyes so I can get the color just right. And I'll do another dress, too, just for you. One that matches them."

"Oh, I just love that idea!" Dorothea said. "Thank you. You know, it's wonderful to have you here, Michaela. You add so much to the group energy. You are an amazing spirit." She gave Michaela a warm hug.

This is incredible, Michaela thought. *I can hardly believe it. They appreciate me. They think I'm worth something. I'm a part of things here. Even when I told Robin and some of the others about "ass end" they thought it was funny. It was funny. I haven't laughed that much since Roxanne fell in the fountain.*

◊ ◊ ◊

If anything, Sunday was even better. It started out a little shaky for Michaela, when they did an exercise in the morning session to find their helper animal spirit. Dorothea said everyone has at least one animal spirit. To find out what it was, she had them close their eyes and, in their minds, go to a place where the animal was supposed to appear. At first Michaela had her usual worry that she was doing it all wrong, and it wasn't working. She had to force herself to imagine walking down the path Dorothea described, into a meadow surrounded by trees. She followed the instructions as best she could, but it wasn't very vivid and she felt like she was making it all up.

No, she thought, *I'm going to get this one right. I'm sticking with it. I really want to know what animal helper I have. It better be a small, cute one that I'll look cool hanging around with. What would be the shamanic version of a teacup Chihuahua? Maybe a hummingbird, or a fox. Or – I know – an elegant wild cat, like a lynx or jaguar.*

But what sauntered out of the woods, once Michaela had finally managed to conjure up a small stand of trees, was not small, cute or elegant. No, what she got was large and ugly and ungainly.

What is that – a buffalo, or bison, or whatever you're supposed to call them? Goddamn it! Why does nothing go the way I plan it? At least that shows I probably didn't make this up, unless it came from some inner part that wants to sabotage myself.

She was learning about all these inner parts she supposedly had, and she wasn't sure she liked them all.

Shoo! Go back in the woods. You're too big and hairy. I want to start over. No, no, don't lie down! Ugh, you smell bad. Don't look at me like that. It snuffled, and then put its head down and started nibbling the grass. Michaela sighed. *Is nothing about this spiritual stuff easy?*

Having an enormous, cumbersome, hairy, vegetarian prey animal as her so-called spirit helper in the shamanic underworld was less than thrilling. After the exercise everyone had to "share" about their animals. She hated saying what hers was, but then Dorothea gave them a handout explaining the qualities of different helper animals. After reading its traits of strength, creativity, courage, knowledge, and survival, Michaela liked her buffalo a little more. And it was certainly better than what some people had, like a mole, or a frog. At least a buffalo was the sort of animal that seemed shamanic and native and all that. But she envied Robin her doe, which was pretty and graceful.

Their afternoon task, the final exercise of the workshop, was to go outside and wander around in the trees or prairie or by the creek. Then, using a "merging meditation" they had been working on during the weekend, each of them, on their own, was to connect with some object that felt meaningful. If it was portable, and if they wanted to, they could bring the object back to keep.

Based on her experience so far, Michaela was not optimistic, either that she could do the meditation properly, or that she would be able to connect with any object. Or else, with her luck, something even worse would happen. After the buffalo, she wouldn't be surprised if a piece of prairie dog poop started following her around calling out her name. And someone would see it, of course, and she'd be obliged to put her power poop in a bag and wear it around her neck the rest of the day.

So she was pleasantly surprised, after walking about ten minutes alongside the creek, to find a large, shiny, oval rock that appealed to her. Dorothea had said the object would affect them emotionally in some way, either good or bad, and this rock made Michaela feel – well she wasn't sure if it was an emotion, exactly – but a kind of satisfaction. So she picked it up, and found a smooth, dry spot to sit with her back against a small tree. She stretched her legs in front of her and set the rock on her right thigh. Then she attempted that merging thing with the rock.

"I'm part of the rock," she thought. "The rock is part of me. We're both molecules, and space. We both exist in consciousness."

Once again, despite trying to follow instructions, she didn't respond as she thought she was supposed to. Nothing remotely merge-like occurred. Although she did notice that the tips of her fingers felt very tingly. And she felt sexually tingly, too. Quite definitely sexually tingly. How weird.

After sitting and tingling for what seemed like the allotted time, while, she had to admit, thinking almost entirely about sex, Michaela stood up and headed back to the meeting room. She brought the rock. About half the people had returned and were doing the next part of the assignment – to remain in silence and either write, draw, or in some other way record their experience with the object. Michaela thought she'd try to write something, but the only words she got were, "get your rocks off," so she decided to switch to the medium she was more comfortable with.

She sat at a round table in the back of the room, a large sheet of white paper in front of her, and spread out an assortment of colored pencils. She placed the rock next to the paper and began to draw.

She sketched the rock. Boring. She made lines come out of it, which looked like a two-year-old's picture of the sun. Dumb. This wasn't working either. She wanted to follow the directions, but she just couldn't.

What she really felt was a need to draw more clothing. She started doing so, and found she couldn't stop. Dresses, fabric patterns, hats, jacket and pants combinations leaped from her pencils onto the paper. She just kept going, page after page.

"This is crazy," she muttered out loud. "I can't do anything right. I'm hopeless."

Dorothea must have overheard her, because she turned suddenly from talking to someone, and was instantly standing over Michaela looking down at the pages. Dorothea gasped, and Michaela cringed. There was no hiding now that she hadn't completed the assignment. This time she was sure she was about to be scolded and sent to the corner of the room, or told to start the whole task over.

Dorothea looked at the pages, moving them aside to see the ones underneath.

"I'm sorry," Michaela said. "I did bring back this rock I found. I was really trying to express the merging thing. I know what I'm doing is really superficial, but these outfits were in my head and they had to come out. But I can still try to do the rock."

"Superficial? Honey, I'd call them super wonderful. Michaela, dear, do you know why I have y'all do all these practices and exercises? It's to find your true self, and not hold back or block it, but express it. And part of that is freeing your creative spirit. From what you're doing here, I'd say that it's working. How long have you been designing clothes?"

"Um, a few weeks. I'm just playing around. It's all because of those monks I met. I started drawing their, um, outfits and it turned into these."

"Hmmm. I can see that influence in the clothes. They're spiritually-inspired but designer quality. You know who would be the perfect person to display their higher aspects? Me. I could never wear robes, of course. They're unflattering. But to have clothes made just for me, that were attractive and fashionable, but *based* on monastic wear...."

"But they aren't real clothes. I couldn't even make them. I don't sew."

"Of course you don't, Michaela. And neither do I. But there are people who do."

Dorothea leaned over and hugged Michaela. "Honey, you

and I are going to do wonderful things together! I just know it. I don't have time to talk now, but I'll be in touch with you soon. What do you think? Okay?"

Michaela beamed. She stood up and got a full hug from Dorothea.

"Of course," she said. And Michaela could not have been happier.

◊ ◊ ◊

On the plane home, she kept thinking about the weekend, especially that moment when Dorothea said she wanted to wear Michaela's clothes. And best of all, Dorothea had said she was intuitive and an advanced soul! She no longer felt deficient in her spirituality or in any other way. She felt like she belonged. She knew she had made an important connection, and wanted to stay in this feeling, this vibration, with these people forever. She wished the workshop never had to end.

Chapter 5

Guys. Wake up. I wanna talk about fishing.

"Guy!" you may reply, "That's great news. Because I, too, want to talk about fishing."

Of course you do. But are you not, at the same moment, wondering why, in a guide to enlightenment, we're going to talk about fishing?

Duh! Trick question. Of course you don't wonder that – not if you're a Regular Guy. To a Regular Guy, it's obvious why we're talking about fishing in a guide to enlightenment. If you're a Regular Guy, what you're wondering is – why haven't we been talking about fishing this entire time?

(The trick question is included in case any of your non-Regular Guy acquaintances picked this book up when you left it in your throne room. Or in case your wife, girlfriend, or any other female willing to bother, is still reading it to you. If it's the latter, congratulations. That means you are probably also still on the sofa with one or more games on, which means you are experiencing multiple realities, which could mean you're already on the way to becoming an enlightened Regular Guy. Unless, of course, it means you are on your way to Multiple Reality Disorder. Strike that. There is no such thing as multiple reality disorder. There is only multiple reality ORDER, and if you are experiencing that, you are probably enlightened already, and should celebrate by consuming beer. This paragraph has been brought to you by the beverage Beer. *BEER – Distracting Humanity from Enlightenment for Over 8,000 Years.*)

Now, back to fishing. Gentlemen (yes, Guys, that's you), if you want the short form – the really short form – of the entire Regular Guy's Guide to Enlightenment, it's this: Go Fish. Because if that was your only instruction, and you followed it, and you kept at it for, oh, a couple, five, ten thousand years, then Guy! I guarantee you will become an Enlightened Guy.

Because everything that life has, fishing has, only more concentrated. You want some examples? Okay. Example one. Let's start with the most basic way to fish. You go out on the dock, or in a rowboat. You got your hook, your bait. You drop your line over the side. Sit. Wait. Watch the water. And what's that? That's meditation, Guys! Anytime you go fishing, it's like free meditation. Like passing Go in Monopoly. You get credit just for showing up.

What happens next? Two things. One, you keep sitting there. Keep meditating, or you could even be contemplating – you know, thinking about stuff. Take your pick. Cause what else can you do? Fall asleep? If you fall asleep, you're not fishing. That's okay, though. When you wake up, you can start fishing again. So you sit, and your mind does its thing – that's the easy part. Boring, sure, but easy. Nobody's giving you shit about something, nothing's going wrong. Yet.

However, that's only part of it. The second part of what happens in fishing is the same exact kind of stuff that happens in real life, only without the complicated details.

Alert! We're going to try out some metaphors here, Guys. Metaphors. You know, I tell you about something that's supposed to be like something else, for the purpose of figuring shit out. I'll spell it out for you: we're comparing what happens in fishing to what happens in life. If this is too complicated for you, that's okay. No problem. Don't even read this next part. You can go back to your meditation in front of the turned-off computer screen and it will work just as well. May take a few extra lifetimes, but eventually, it will work.

But for the sake of something to talk about – regarding fishing, life, et cetera – the deal is this. "In fishing, as in life...," and now imagine the following:

You got your good weather sometimes, but also you got your

rain, or sometimes even a humongous f—ing storm. You catch a fish now and then. Or else you don't catch jack. Or maybe you get hold of the proverbial boot, or whatever the hell else is out there that gets caught on your line. Or maybe some day you hit the jackpot and there's a fish on your hook every damn time you throw it in the water.

The question is, when all this happens, the good and the bad, what goes on next? How do you react?

"Well, Guy," you say. "How do you think I react? I reel in a fish and I'm happy. It rains on me, and I'm damn miserable. I break my line on an old tire some bastard tossed out here, and I'm f—ing pissed off. What's your point, Guy?" you say.

Well, Guys, I'll tell you. It's more interesting than that. Let's look at the big picture. The really big picture. Let's say you do this for ten thousand years. Or ten thousand lifetimes. Every day for ten thousand years, or lifetimes, you go out fishing in your little boat. Maybe for some of those days, your wife gives you lunch to take out. Maybe for some of them, you've got a dog to keep you company on the dock or in the rowboat. So things change, but they also stay the same.

Now, over the entire ten thousand years, what would you expect? You'd expect just about every possible thing that could happen to happen, that's what. Beautiful sunny days when all you need to do is just sit there happy to be alive. Terrifying storms when your little boat tears into splinters and you're thrown into the water, petrified you're going to die. Now and then, say every few hundred years or so, a beautiful big fish jumps right into your boat. Somebody comes by in another boat and shoots at you. Lightning strikes your little boat.

Or worse. Lightning strikes your dog and you lose your buddy. An alligator eats your wife and you lose your sandwiches. You see countless falling stars (okay, sometimes you're fishing at night). A mermaid jumps in the boat and seduces you. Okay, even in ten thousand years, that's not very likely, but you paid attention to that one, didn't you? But whatever. My point is, Guys, you get every possible feeling, every possible experience, positive and negative – probably more negative than positive cause life can be like that – and some of them over and over again.

You lose your way. You lose your life. You lose your mind. You get insights. You realize you're a part of the whole big thing, and it's all a part of you. You realize you ARE everything. And you are nothing.

And, just an aside here, let me point out that this example applies for ALL kinds of fishing, not just the basic toss-your-line-over-the-side variety. Fly fishing where you gotta have the skills. Deep sea fishing with the big boys in the big boats. In fact you can have the fastest, coolest boat, the finest equipment, whatever, and it still applies. You go out there for ten thousand years, endless shit's gonna happen. Over and over again.

Now you may be going, "Guy, I don't get it. What is your point? So what? I go fishing. Shit happens. How does that help me be an enlightened Regular Guy?"

Well, I'll tell you. My point is that if every single damn thing that's possible is going to happen, if it's all part of your experience, then why are you making such a big damn deal about it? It all happens, it would happen to anybody who sat there that long, and so whose fault is that? Yours? Nope. God's? Nope. Surely not some guy on the shore. Is it the alligator's fault that after ten thousand lifetimes, you don't always get a sandwich? I mean, think about it, Guys. Why blame someone else when shit happens? Why even get upset, or feel pissed off, about the bad shit? It's not about you. You're just there, experiencing it. And then, when stuff goes your way, that's not about you either. So why wait for good stuff to make you feel like you're the Man?

The truth is, you ARE the Man, all the time, no matter what you're going through. When you get THAT into your beer-addled, sex-driven, sports-obsessed, Regular Guy noggin – when you REALLY get: 1) that shit happens, and 2) you're still and always the Man, no matter what – THEN, you're going to mellow out. THEN, you're going to not get so excited. You've reached the point where you know that basically, at the end of the day, whatever happens, it's all part of what IS. You might even find, eventually, that for a Regular Guy, you're pretty damn enlightened.

35
Petaluma

A fter getting the couch made up for Duke to sleep on, and assuring the boy he had access to both food and WiFi, Rennie said goodnight and went to his room. He and Duke had brought the three cartons of incense, still cased in airline-issued plastic, out of the car and into Rennie's bedroom, the only place he felt safe keeping them for the night. He planned to store the boxes in a cool, dry, locked storage area, but for now he wanted them all with him. Before getting in bed, Rennie cut the plastic, string, and paper off one of the boxes, opened it, and gazed in awe at all the sticks it contained. All the beautiful, wonderful, magical sticks that were about to change his life and give him everything he'd ever dreamed of.

He took a small handful out of the box, then closed it and pulled the plastic back in place. After laying the incense on the table next to his bed, he sat up against the pillows to meditate before going to sleep. Mentally reaching inward, Rennie connected with his enormous sense of excitement and satisfaction, mixed with an occasional uprising of utter panic. He allowed all the feelings to exist equally in his consciousness without attaching to them, kept his mind on his breathing, and let all else pass through. After a time, he noticed less emotion, and more a sense of connection with the One Mind. He continued to meditate until he felt sleepy.

Rennie then said a quick prayer of gratitude as he ended the meditation. He opened his eyes, turned off the light, adjusted the pillows to lie down, and then closed his eyes again for sleep, which came immediately.

When he wakened suddenly in the night, Rennie felt like he'd been blasted with psychic dynamite from the inside out. His mind swarmed with so many thoughts he couldn't think them all. He grabbed the pen and a half-empty notebook he kept by the bed. Within an hour, Rennie had filled every spare notebook page and was looking for more paper. He had to keep pouring out all that was in his head. He found a legal pad, and just kept writing. He considered switching to the computer, but was afraid that might interrupt the flow, so he just kept putting it all down on paper.

By the time he finished, his hand was cramped, and he'd had to shake it out several times. But he hardly noticed the pain. He was astonished. Out of nowhere, he had this masterpiece. Or at least the framework for it. A detailed outline for his book – all kinds of stuff he knew, but didn't even know he knew. Stuff he'd been trying to pull together but didn't know how to get into an organized format. But here it was, all laid out and ready to go. And he also had a plan for the workshops he'd give on the same material, using the incense that would allow people to really get all the ideas and experiences he was talking about.

He went back to the first page he had written and across the top were the words,

"Breaking Through to the Other Side of You – A Handbook for Getting Past the Fears, Needs and Self-Inflicted Limitations that Keep You from Getting Everything You Want In Life"

Wow! Not a bad title. It reminded him of that old Doors song, "Break on Through (to the Other Side)," and wondered if that was a problem. Probably not; it was okay if his title sounded a little familiar. Younger folks who didn't know the song wouldn't care, and older readers would probably appreciate the reference. The title could work as both a book and, slightly reworded, for the workshops he would give too.

After the outline, he had written out a one-paragraph description of each of the book's chapters. Following that he'd jotted down a plan for his two-day workshop. Then he had listed numerous ways to go about promotion and marketing.

"Free talks at bookstores and temples," he said out loud. "I light the incense, talk for a few minutes, then do a short meditation to give the incense time to work. I won't burn too much, so they get a taste without going too deep." He also thought of doing teleconferences, an interactive website, and more. But mainly, it would be the free talks that would give people the experience and draw them in.

"That ought to do it." He laid flat and stretched out his arms and legs.

It was starting to get light outside. While Rennie was thoroughly pleased and satisfied with what he'd accomplished, he was absolutely exhausted. He decided to crash for a few more hours, and expected Duke would sleep in as well. As Rennie drifted off, it occurred to him that it was probably no coincidence that this powerful outpouring of creative energy had come while thousands of sticks of incense were so near to his bed, their pungent odor completely filling the room.

Once again, it was the incense that had done it – allowed him to go measures beyond his normal capacities. The incense truly was miracle stuff. Not only that it existed, but that it had come to him. He would have to be absolutely sure he didn't abuse this incredible gift. If he was very conscious and very careful, there was a chance he could really help people. He could do some good in this world. That, Rennie knew, would be a miracle too.

36
Denver International Airport

"*I* told you, Thea, this is ridiculous," Dirk growled. "We should have driven home like we planned."

They were waiting in the airport security line – the very, very long airport security line.

"It would have been the same amount of time and a lot less hassle," Dirk continued.

Not to mention the cost of their last minute, full price tickets, but he preferred to avoid discussing money with Dorothea.

"Oh, la," she said. "This is fine. Just be at peace with wherever you are, Dirk, honey, you'll be much happier. Besides, I told you: I woke up just knowing we had to fly. You know what happens when I ignore my intuition. There's some reason for us to be here. Or to not be *there*."

Dirk had heard this argument many times, but still could think of no useful reply. He made an aggravated growl loud enough for her to hear, and turned back to face the front of the line.

Dorothea turned around, toward the people behind her. Five back in the line were Ella, Robin and three women who had attended the workshop, all of whom Dorothea knew quite well. She gave a little wave in their direction, and they all smiled and waved back. Dorothea then addressed the passengers waiting in line between her and their group, starting with the couple behind her.

"Oh, hello there," she said to the couple.

They looked at her.

"Um, hi," the man said. He was an average looking, overweight, balding fellow in his forties. His black polo shirt had a small picture of a tiger on the front pocket. His wife was a petite brunette about the same age, wearing crisp white pants and a navy blazer.

"Oh, good, you speak English," Dorothea said. "Did you have a nice weekend? I'm Dorothea Light, by the way. Lovely to meet you."

Dorothea held out her hand, forcing the man to put down his bag in order to shake it. His wife narrowed her eyes at Dorothea.

"Um, right. Bob Gray. And Naomi," he nodded toward his wife, who made no move to put down her own bags.

"Hello, Bob, Naomi," Dorothea said warmly. "Say, could I ask a favor of you? It would mean so much to me. You know, we had a workshop here in Colorado this weekend, and my husband Dirk – that's him in front of me – he wanted to drive home, but I was too tired after teaching all weekend to spend all those hours in the car. So he asked one of our students to drive the car back to Santa Fe, you see, so I could be on this plane with you good folks. Well, that's silly of me, isn't it? We're probably not on the same plane at all. I'll bet you're not going to Santa Fe, are you? You're probably going home to Cincinnati, right?"

"Dayton," Bob said. Naomi glared at him and kicked his left Nike.

"Ow," Bob said. The line moved up a few feet, and Dirk tugged on Dorothea's arm so she would keep up. She stepped backwards in his direction, followed by Bob and Naomi, the three people behind them, and then the small cluster from the workshop.

"Mmm hmmm," Dorothea nodded, "Well, that doesn't really matter, but what I was hoping is that you'd let my people there – yes, those right there – move up the line so they could stand here with me. Is that okay with you, Bob?"

Bob's head gave a couple of slow nods. He seemed confused.

"Well, that's just so nice of you Bob, Naomi. Thank you so very much. I'm sure you don't know it, but you are helping to make the world a better place."

Bob continued to nod and Naomi to glare, as Dorothea turned to the next person in line behind the couple, a sweet looking, roundish, gray haired woman.

"Hello there, I'm Dorothea Light of LightWorks Shamanic Training Seminars. And you are?"

The woman did not have a chance to answer before the short, scowling man in line behind her spoke up. "I can't listen to this crap anymore. For chrissake, just let 'em through," he said, gesturing to the group behind him. "And keep it movin', wouldja?"

Dirk gave a yank on Dorothea's arm to keep her up with the line. She allowed herself to be moved, still without looking at him.

"Thank you, sir. You must be from New York. Is this your first time out west?"

He ignored her, which was easy with five people pushing in front him. They joined Dorothea and Dirk. Soon the entire entourage had nearly reached the person who checks IDs and boarding passes.

"Robin, honey, you can take this through for me, can't you?" Dorothea said. She pointed to the red carry-on that she had been pushing along at her feet, "Dirk has too many things to carry already."

She then removed her jacket and handed it to Ella. "Ell, dear, I'm going to give you this. It's better if I don't carry it myself. I'll be busy sending out positive energy for all of us to get through security, and it distracts me if I have too many things to put on the belt. Careful of those note cards in the pocket, okay? Thanks, sweetie."

"Do you want me to hold your purse, Dorothea?" one of the other women volunteered.

"My purse? Goodness, no, dear," Dorothea gave a little laugh. "Of course I'll carry my own purse."

"Right. How crazy of me. What was I thinking?" The woman looked horrified and immediately started fishing in her bag for a stick of gum, which she put in her mouth.

Once safely through security and having reached the boarding area, the cluster of women fanned out around Dorothea, while Dirk disappeared into another section of seats. Dorothea used the time to tell them stories about some of her visits to foreign spiritual leaders, such as the Dalai Lama and various shamans in Brazil and Peru. From time to time one or more of the party went to fetch something at Dorothea's request: bottled water for the plane; a cup of peppermint tea with honey to sooth her voice after the workshop; and copies of *Us* and *Star* magazines. She needed those, she explained, in order to send positive energy to the subjects of all those negative articles.

On the plane, Dorothea and Dirk sat together, several rows in front of the five women. Once she'd had the flight attendants supply her with a blanket, two pillows and a cup of ice, Dorothea pulled out the paper image that Michaela had made for her. It really did look like Dorothea, and this time Michaela had got the eye color exactly right, even the little golden flecks.

"See this?" she said to Dirk.

"How could I miss them? They were all over the place on Saturday. Nice artwork though."

"But, Dirky, did you see what I'm wearing here?"

"Uh, okay. I hadn't really noticed. Is that one of your

dresses? You don't usually show that much cleavage." He chuckled.

"Nooo, it's not one of *my* dresses, Dirk. She designed it for me. For this paper me, anyway."

"Very nice. And probably the least expensive thing you've ever worn, too." Dirk laughed again.

"Thank you Dirk, that's exactly what I was thinking."

"What? What were you thinking?" Dirk said. He suddenly realized he was being set up for something, but he couldn't figure out what.

"That I should get Michaela's designs made into clothes, and it wouldn't really be that expensive. It would probably be less than store bought, in the long run. Lorna Beth will sew them for me. She offered to do it anyway, but she was going to use patterns that are like the outfits I usually wear to teach in. These are much better, and they'll be designed just for me. Of course, there are the fabrics, too. Those are an important part of the look, and they're really special. Did you notice she incorporates some of the same shapes I use in my teaching? And she'd never even heard me before this weekend. So I *would* have to get someone to make the fabrics. That might cost a little more..."

As Dorothea continued, Dirk sighed and leaned his head back on the airline seat. He reached up and pushed the flight attendant call button over his head. If he had to spend the entire trip listening to Dorothea talk about getting clothes designed for her, and fabrics made, it would surely go down better with an alcoholic beverage. Or two.

37
Petaluma

M ichaela was on her way over. She'd called Rennie and said she needed to see him. So even though it was Monday and he should be going to work, not to mention Duke was still camped out in the living room, Rennie thought he ought to give her the time. He felt responsible. He'd jump-started her on her path, and should help her as she continued to search for direction.

She'd given him no details, just said she went to a LightWorks Shamanic Meditation retreat over the weekend and needed to talk to him. Her voice sounded either excited or stressed, he wasn't sure which. So he told her to come on over, and they would talk.

"Duke!" Rennie yelled. The kid wore ear buds most of the time, plugged into either his laptop or his iPod, so he couldn't hear Rennie if he spoke normally. However, Rennie could hear Duke all the time. He talked, mumbled, "eeeeed" and "ahhhed" to himself constantly, and was always getting up and sitting back down, fetching food and consuming it loudly, or just moving around, even when he was supposedly sitting still.

"Duke! Can you get this stuff out of here?"

Duke pulled out one ear bud. "What?"

"Someone's coming over. We have to talk in the living room, alone. Can you get this bedding and your things out of here, and stay busy for an hour or two while I talk to her? It's private," he added, in case that wasn't clear.

"Of course, Rennie! No problem, no problem!" Duke jumped up and began yanking at the sheets, blankets and pillows, and dragging them to Rennie's bedroom. He then came back for his clothes, shoes, electronics, and backpack.

"Don't worry. Eeee! I can be very not in the way while you talk to your friend. I will be online, or watch TV shows. I love *Ivy!*" Duke said.

"I think *Ivy!*'s on later, in the afternoon," Rennie said, as he folded up the sofa bed, put the cushions back on, and threw a couple of pillows into the corners. "How about a walk? Get outside a little?"

"Hmmm. Maybe. Anyway, I will go into your room now. Don't worry, I will be so hidden and quiet, you will forget I am even in this house."

"Great," Rennie said, thinking how much he would like to forget that fact. He gave the bathroom a quick cleaning, and moved on to the kitchen. He was rinsing off the last of his and Duke's breakfast plates when he heard Michaela drive up. He watched her get out of the car, tuck her purse under one arm, a large brown artist's portfolio case under the other, and head for his front door. Rennie went to open it.

She was barely inside when she started talking.

"So I was at this workshop, and a ton of things happened. I met all these people and Dorothea Light seemed to really like me. She said nice things to me. We did a lot of exercises, and some of them worked. I got a power animal! Stuff like that."

He led her into the living room and sat on a chair while she threw herself onto the sofa and dropped her purse and case at her feet. She picked up one of the Indian print pillows and hugged it in her lap.

"So you probably know most of those practices we did,

but I wanted to ask you about what Dorothea says – that she blends meditation and shamanism in her teaching, because they're both powerful, but different, and if you put them together it works even better. Like, you can get transformation faster using both together. So I wanted to know what you think about that."

Rennie opened his mouth to answer, but Michaela did not give him a chance.

"But also, I'm really confused about what to do, because Dorothea called this morning, and she wants me to come to Santa Fe so I can instruct her seamstress, because she actually wants to wear the clothes I've been designing! Oh god, I haven't even told you about that yet, the clothes. It just started happening to me, like I can hardly control it. I brought some pictures to show you."

This time Rennie didn't try to talk. He'd just wait her out.

"But I don't know what to do! I don't know if I should go, even though it's really cool. I mean, I'm not *really* a dress designer. Really, what I am is a menu designer, and even though all this spiritual stuff is going okay, I'm still just incredibly bummed about the job I didn't get at Eighth. So maybe I should just focus on that instead of Dorothea and Santa Fe and the clothes. I thought you could help me figure it out, or maybe you could…" She stopped abruptly. "Who's that?"

Rennie turned to see Duke leaning on the doorway, fiddling with his shirt buttons and twitching his eyebrows. He had changed from the sweatpants and AC/DC tee shirt he had on earlier. Now he wore a pair of light blue tuxedo pants – how many of those did he have? – under a black, short sleeved, button-front shirt with a large squirrel embroidered on the pocket. The squirrel appeared to be leering and holding up two acorns.

"Duke, I thought you were…" Rennie started.

"Eeee, ahhh, so sorry to interrupt. I'm just on my way to the kitchen. I forgot to take a snack into the bedroom."

Duke had not long ago downed seven pancakes with two bananas sliced over them, five eggs, and a bowl of granola; plus several cups of tea and a large glass of apple juice. Rennie felt like he was feeding an entire basketball team. To be honest, he was tired of grocery shopping and cooking. He wanted to be hospitable, but wondered how much longer Duke planned to stay. Especially since he'd told Rennie his original plan was to leave right away. Maybe if Rennie cut back on the unlimited provisions, then Duke would decide it was time to move on. But not now. Now, he just needed to get him out of the way.

"Fine," Rennie said. "Help yourself. You know what we've got. Duke, this is Michaela. Michaela, meet Duke. He's the nephew of an incense maker in India."

"Eeeee. Hello, Michaela. It's very nice to meet you. Are you the girlfriend of Rennie?" Duke stepped over to shake her hand, then sat down on the sofa and stared at her. As he passed, Rennie read the back of his shirt. It said, "I've got the nuts."

Rennie's annoyance with Duke was aggravated by Michaela's surprised laugh.

"No, Duke, she's not my girlfriend. We don't know each other that well. It's more of a, uh, professional friendship."

"It is?" Michaela asked. "Professional? Well, whatever. Duke, what are you doing in Petaluma?"

"Aaaah, I help my uncle deliver incense to Rennie, and then I go to play in a poker tournament. In Las Vegas."

"Poker? No kidding," Michaela said.

"Isn't that coming up soon?" Rennie asked hopefully.

"Eeeeh, ahhh, somewhat soon," Duke said, looking away. "I uhhhh, I uhhhh…" he squirmed on the sofa and stared up at the ceiling.

"What is it, Duke?" Michaela asked. "Is something wrong?"

"You didn't miss it, did you? The tournament?" Rennie asked, half rising from the chair in alarm. What if Duke had made up the whole tournament story to sound cool? What if he was really planning to stay here and mooch until Rennie kicked him out, which he couldn't do without risking the displeasure of the senior Ashvin.

"Eeeee! No, no, certainly I did not miss it. Do not even speak such words! It is not for three more weeks until I have to be there. And I should go to Las Vegas now and play for practice, but…" Duke stared down at his feet and Rennie sank back into the chair, relieved but still concerned. Something wasn't right.

"What's wrong, Duke?" Michaela asked. "Is there a problem with you going to Las Vegas?"

Rennie looked at Michaela, surprised. This was a softer side he hadn't seen before.

Duke shook his head. He was obviously bothered, but didn't seem able to talk about it.

"Is it money?" Rennie asked. "You know, I have that cash your uncle said to give you. You can have it any time you want."

Duke shook his head no, and Michaela patted him on the arm. His eyes went to hers, and he seemed in pain.

"Eeeeeee," he sighed.

"Duke, honey, tell us what's the matter. You can trust us. We just want to help you, and whatever it is, it's probably not going to sound as bad as you think."

Rennie felt a mild déjà vu. He had heard nearly that exact phrasing before, and not too long ago. Then he realized that Michaela sounded just like Dorothea Light. Rennie had listened to Dorothea say pretty much the same thing to people a number of times during her workshop. One weekend, and Michaela was already mimicking Dorothea, right down to the "honey" and the phrasing. He wondered if she was aware of it.

Duke said, "I ahhhh, I ahhhh," then suddenly stood up. His other persona, the "Mister Cool" side Rennie had first seen at the airport, took over.

"Don't worry," Duke said. "All is under control. Everything is very, very good. You may now have your discussion."

He veered off into the kitchen, where Rennie and Michaela

listened to him humming and rummaging around for several minutes, before he headed back to the bedroom, carrying a tray loaded with snacks and drinks.

Both Rennie and Michaela watched silently until he passed. Rennie put his face in his hands. "He's driving me nuts. He's been here all weekend, and he's constantly eating, and he makes noise all the time. This house isn't very big, and I need my privacy and peace. But his uncle is an important purveyer and I can't ask him to leave."

"He's supposed to be going to Vegas? Is that poker thing for real?"

"I think so. He showed me how he won a seat through this online tournament, and it looked real enough. I've watched him play. He's incredible. Maybe a genius."

"So wouldn't you think he'd be dying to get over there? I wonder what's the problem?"

"At the airport, he told me he'd be leaving as soon as he dropped off the incense. But he hasn't mentioned it since. I don't know if it's too comfortable here, or he's scared, or what he's thinking." Rennie sighed. "Anyway, that's my problem, not yours. You came here to talk about what's going on with you. So tell me about how you're designing clothes."

"Oh my god, Rennie, you won't believe this whole thing. *I* can't believe it. It's, like, something comes over me, and I get going with this frenzied drawing, and all these pictures come out. It started with those funny robes that monks wear, and they just kept evolving. Look, I'll show you."

Michaela opened the portfolio, pulled out a stack of papers, and handed them to Rennie. He spent a few minutes going through them.

"Michaela, this is impressive. I don't know much about clothing design, but these are really beautiful. And unusual. I think they're very special."

Michaela flushed at the compliments. "I don't know. I

wasn't trying to do anything. It's just … it's almost like I didn't really do them. More like it happened *to* me, you know?"

He nodded, and said, "But you did do them. Can you acknowledge that? And someone wants to buy them, and wear them. That should be very validating."

"Well, she didn't say buy them. I don't know if she meant that. I don't think I could charge for them."

"Why not?"

"Because, it's like I told you. I'm not a clothing designer. I'm a menu designer – *that's* what I do. And I'm the best. Except for now, as you know, I can't get the job I want. The most important job in years. And it's still bothering me. No matter what I do, I can't get over it. So I thought, maybe now that I've tried a few things – you know, studied with you and gone to this workshop, and I'm reading and meditating – maybe I could go back there and talk to them again. That is, if the job hasn't gone to someone else already."

Michaela thought for a moment, then brightened. She said, "But if it hasn't, do you think a reference would help? Now that I have a teacher."

"You could try," he said. "It wouldn't be any trouble for me to give you one."

"Well, actually, I meant a recommendation from Dorothea," she said. "They've probably heard of her. Maybe they've even met her." Her expression dropped again. "It probably won't help, though. They must have someone else by now. They've got to be opening soon."

Michaela didn't notice Rennie bristle, then close his eyes and take a couple of deep breaths.

When he opened his eyes again, he said, "Michaela. Listen to me. You're making yourself crazy trying to figure it out. Sometimes it's impossible to *think* these things through. You just have to make a choice, and trust that it's the best one."

"You're right," she moaned. "I know that! But how do I choose?"

Rennie thought for a moment. He could try having her use the incense. But he didn't want to send it home with her. She could meditate with it here, a short one. It could be just the trick to help her move on in this matter. Also, that would give him another opportunity to see what the incense could do. But he didn't want to tell her about its qualities, because of her new relationship with Dorothea Light. Dorothea would understand the implications of the incense immediately. He wasn't ready to go public yet with the substance's power. He needed to keep it to himself until he moved forward with his teaching and workshops.

"Listen," he said. "I have an idea. Why don't you meditate for a while right now, and see what happens. You had a breakthrough here before, so maybe being here will help you go deep, and give you some resolution. I'll put on some music, light a little incense, just to make you comfortable. You want to try it?"

"Um, sure, I guess. Can't you just tell me what I should do? Go to Santa Fe or try back at Eighth?"

"No, Michaela, I can't. I don't know what you should do. But you do, somewhere inside. All the answers are inside of you, someplace. That I do know."

She sighed. "Then okay, I'll try it. But what about Duke? I'd feel stupid if he's in here watching me."

"I'll make sure he doesn't come in. I'll go talk to him. Okay? You want to do it?"

"Yeah, okay."

While Michaela went to the bathroom, Rennie spoke to Duke, who, after procuring another glass of lemonade, swore he would stay put in the bedroom.

As Michaela settled herself on the meditation cushion, Rennie hooked his iPod up to the stereo and lit a stick of the special incense. Soon smoke and soft, rhythmic music began to fill the room.

"Do you want me talk you through a relaxation, to help get you started?" Rennie asked.

"No, that's okay. I do them in my head now. Okay, here I go."

"Let me know if you need anything."

Michaela closed her eyes and began meditating. Rennie sat on the chair nearest Michaela, not staring at her, but keeping part of his awareness directed toward her. He found himself going into a semi-trance himself, eyes half open, curious to see what Michaela would get from her session.

◊ ◊ ◊

Michaela's awareness followed the music. It was busy, filled with many sounds, both electronic and tribal. The rhythms changed periodically, and tracks of several different vocals moved in, chanted for a while, and disappeared.

As she sat listening, focusing on the in and out of her breath, and inhaling the slightly nutty smell of that peculiar incense Rennie liked, Michaela began to feel short of breath. It was strange, because on one level, she knew that she was actually breathing just fine. Yet, on another, her strong and disturbing sense was of not getting enough oxygen. She forced herself to take several huge, long breaths, but it still wasn't enough, and she started wheezing. Her head hurt too. She found herself moving it around in circles with the music. She put a hand above each ear and squeezed hard, still struggling to take in more air.

She knew this was a strange way for her to meditate, but remembered that both Rennie and Dorothea said to always go with whatever was happening, and not to judge herself in any inner work – meditations, exercises, and the like. Now she noticed the voices in the music almost had meaning, like people talking far away. Their tone was disapproving.

As the pain continued, she was concerned that something

might be physically wrong with her. Why the shortness of breath and the headache? Was it an attack of some kind? An aneurism? What if she was about to die? Should she stop what she was doing and get Rennie to rush her to the hospital?

She wanted to tell him what was wrong, and ask him to take her to the emergency room, but she was certain he would just laugh at her. She knew he thought she was ridiculous. He judged her materialism, her lifestyle. He thought her work in the world was superficial – that she was superficial. He thought she would give up on this new spiritual journey just as soon as things started going her way again.

The pain in her head got worse, and she became really scared of dying, but all she could think was, "Screw you Rennie. I'm going to die right here because you won't take me to the hospital. I hope they charge you with murder, selfish bastard."

Part of her knew this wasn't logical, but she was also completely convinced it was true. She was squeezing and rolling her head and breathing harder than ever, and the voices in the music were so mean and awful, she just couldn't stand it another second. She bent over until her forehead was in front of her legs, and her elbows stuck out over the sides of her knees.

In that position, a wave of nausea swept through her, then left. She moaned uncontrollably, and twisted her body back and forth. She observed herself moan and twist like this for several minutes, aware of how strange it was, but unable to stop. She just had to keep doing it. She went faster and faster, certain that these were her last few minutes on earth. She was terrified, and the pain in her head was unbelievable. Finally she gave one last big twist, and felt herself nearly black out.

Suddenly, everything changed. The headache vanished, and she dropped her hands into her lap. She observed the new calmness and sat still a little while, then leaned back. She could breathe again, but still felt disturbed, scared. Something was wrong. She was alone. She wasn't supposed to be alone, but she was. Someone had left her, abandoned her. Her father!

Somehow she knew her father had taken her away from her screaming and crying mother, taken her far away by cart through the woods into a patch of scrub, and left her here.

Michaela had two equal realities going on at once. Her normal Michaela self knew that this particular experience had not ever happened. But there was also the equally real, completely convincing feeling that she was a small female child experiencing heart wrenching terror in another time, another place. Her heart pounded and tears leaked from her eyes. She felt sorry for that person – sorry for herself.

Then, still very sad but less afraid, her reality switched again, and she was yet another person, someone different from either Michaela or the small girl. She was a man now. Or was she a woman? No, she looked like a woman, dressed like a woman, but knew she was a man. She was alone again – or alone still – living by herself in a small shack, eating what she raised, hunted, or traded for. She (or was it "he"? No, "she" felt right) was a craftsperson who carved things out of wood. All kinds of things. Useful items like bowls, spoons and cups. Flutelike musical instruments. And wooden statues of people, and of their dogs and horses.

Neighbors traded for the wooden tools and statues. She knew they thought her eccentric but talented. Mostly it was the women who came to trade with her. The men stayed away, unless she was whittling their image. They laughed at her whenever she ventured out into the community, so she almost always stayed home, or in the woods. Her life was satisfying in some ways, but lonely.

Then, another change. She knew it was the end of her life, and she was flying over the trees near her shack. Not just flying – she was riding a bird – an enormous owl. Her lower legs hung down in front of the wings, and she held on to a silver chain around the bird's neck. She swayed back and forth as powerful muscles moved the great bird's wings up and down. The owl swooped and circled, then flew up high.

Riding the owl was amazing. Michaela felt incredibly free and joyous. She laughed. She wanted to stay there forever. The owl flew for a long time. Michaela thought they had circled the whole world. Then the bird swooped down into a flower-filled field and lowered her head to let her rider slide off.

"Goodbye for now, Michaela," the owl said. When she heard her name, Michaela knew she was just herself again. "Remember I'm always with you, whenever you need me."

"You are?" Michaela said. "How come you weren't here before now?"

"Because you're waking up," the owl answered. "I've been with you, but you didn't know it. Now that we've met, it will be easier for you to feel my presence."

"Are you an animal spirit helper, like the buffalo?"

The owl hooted gracefully. "No, nothing like that. I'm not personal to you at all. But I am Power." The owl stretched her wings and seemed to Michaela to double in size. She was enormous, intimidating, and incredibly beautiful. Michaela knew she was more than just an animal spirit. She was a mysterious, larger conscious force; Michaela wanted to say a Goddess, even. Michaela also knew the owl was about to leave, and she didn't want her to.

"Don't go!" Michaela said. The owl looked directly at her, waiting. Michaela tried to think what she could say to keep the owl with her a few more moments. "I have a question."

The owl didn't move, and Michaela remembered she really did have one. "I can't decide if I should go to Santa Fe, or back down to Eighth to try to get the job again. What should I do?"

Michaela thought the owl wasn't going to answer. With a smooth pump of wings, the bird lifted off, and started to fly away. Then her voice came clearly down from above, and Michaela heard the words: "Always go where you feel more love." And then the bird quickly became a tiny shadow in the distant blue sky, and was gone.

◊ ◊ ◊

After a few moments, Michaela opened her eyes. Rennie got up and turned off the music, then sat back down. Michaela realized she was lying on her side, though she didn't remember getting there. She sat up and took a sip from the glass of water Rennie handed her, and wiped her eyes with his proffered tissue.

Rennie waited eagerly to hear what had happened for Michaela. He could tell she was affected by whatever she'd just gone through, although he had no idea what it was. But Michaela was in no hurry to report. She sat quietly for some time, absorbed in her own thoughts or memories. Finally she turned to Rennie. But her words were not what he expected.

"Well," she said. "I got my answer."

Rennie waited expectantly.

She sat very still for a minute, as if wanting to be absolutely certain, then finally stated, "I'm going to Santa Fe."

Then she raised one arm toward the living room entrance, where Rennie was startled to see that Duke was once again leaning wide-eyed against the doorframe, sucking on a bright green popsicle. Michaela pointed straight at Duke.

"And he's going with me."

THE REGULAR GUY'S GUIDE TO ENLIGHTENMENT

Chapter 6

Guys, here's an interesting statistic. There is a 72% chance you flipped to this chapter first, before looking at anything else in the book. Maybe you aren't even planning to read the rest of the book. You may ask, "Guy! How can you possibly know such a thing? You are writing this before the book has been effin' published."

Well, let me answer your question with a question. How many of you only care about becoming an enlightened Regular Guy for one of two reasons? Either because you think, A) "Dude! If I'm enlightened, I get to live forever!" Or, B) "Dude! If I'm enlightened I'll finally understand women."

Get my point? I thought so.

Since this book doesn't have a chapter on immortality (seeing as how that's a topic I can't even pretend to know shit about), you came directly here, to this chapter on intra-species, that is, Regular Guy-Chick relations, to see what advice old Guy might have for you on comprehending and apprehending such females.

Well, Guys, this is it. I am about to reveal to you the result of my years of study, investigation, and meditation on this most primary and difficult of questions. I hope you are not disappointed. What I have determined in my quest to become an Enlightened Regular Guy – not that I'm there yet, you understand, since it is, after all, a lifelong quest – is the following:

The difference between your basic Regular Guy and your basic Woman can be summarized in one word. One small, deceptively simple, yet packed-with-all-the-concepts-of-universal-importance-to-gender-relations-throughout-time-and-space, word.

The word is:

SUBWOOFER

Yes, you read correctly. It is the subwoofer. No other single word, object or concept is a better example of the differences in worldview, thought process and value system between we who wear the Regular Guy uniform, and those playing for the ladies team.

You may be saying, "Guy! How can you reduce something as complicated and important as men and women to this one thing? Are you deluded?"

And I say, Guys! Think about it. I completely agree with you that the issue of Guy-woman relations is the ultimate conundrum. Nothing will cause you more hard work, pain, and agony. Yet, should you persist in the effort and finally have a breakthrough, it leads to great rewards and a place in heaven. Or at least, you know, the heavenly place between her legs.

But, Guys! If there is any *other* dilemma that can arguably rival that one in complication, difficulty, importance, and rewards, it is that of the investigation into, technical evaluation of, personal affinity for, and – ultimately and with the greatest satisfaction – acquisition of the perfect subwoofer.

Still not convinced? Then answer me this. How much energy have you, the average Regular Guy, put into subwoofer-related activities in your lifetime? How important is it to you, at every stage of your life, to find, acquire, and live with exactly the right subwoofer for that time and place of your life journey?

Were you not, as a tiny tot, initiated into the importance of subwoofers by your father as, in the sacred space of his living room or den, he set up his new and most revered sound system? Can you not hear him now, saying, "Come over here and stand next to me, Little Guy. Watch and listen. See this speaker, this one right here? This is it, Little Guy. The crowning glory of speakers. It is what makes the sound come alive. For this, Little Guy, is the subwoofer. Listen and remember."

And, as a teenager, with your first car. It may not have been the Ferrari you really wanted, but instead perhaps an older sedan or a dented pickup. But it was yours and you cherished it. And what more could you do to perfect the experience of cruising pointlessly, blasting tunes and imagining Jessica Simpson hitchhiking around the next bend, than adding a dose of ass-kicking bass?

Then, when buying your first real sound system as a young man, what happened? Despite having limited cash, you were willing, yea, eager, to eat naught but Pringles and drink the cheapest of beers for weeks, just to be able to lay down a couple hundred more on a better subwoofer.

And finally, as a mature, adult man, perhaps married and starting a family, or even still riding that "I won't grow up" wave as long as you could stretch it out, what did you do? Yes, Guy, I know. You got up in the night. You hid from your wife or girlfriend for hours at a time, night after night, sacrificing needed rest, just so that you could commune with your computer as you researched every tiny, incredibly important facet of the subwoofer universe. You left no webpage un-clicked, no online electronics store un-shopped. You wanted to surprise her with the perfect listening experience by providing the most ideal and perfect subwoofer possible.

And after you accomplished this feat – what then? After worshiping at that altar of information – the internet. And studying with the most learned of holy men – your high-end audio sales guys. And communing with your fellow supplicants and seekers on this holiest of quests via endless blogs and chatrooms. When you took the sum total of your accumulated knowledge and applied it, along with most of your disposable income, and brought home, for her listening pleasure, this most magnificent of audio components? What then?

Guy! You idiot! What do you think happened? She looked at you like you were a cross between some drooling, reptilian creature from another planet and King f-ing Kong about to grab her ankle and swing her 1500 feet off the ground.

I.e., right, Guy. She did not get it. Not in the least. And you, instead of being rewarded for the wonderful sacrifices you made, on behalf of her and the bond between you, to provide the most pleasurable and perfect sound system for your home and castle. You, sir, were mightily scorned.

For when it comes to females grokking subwoofer culture, there is only one thing to know, Guys. Such a beast does not exist. It is not on the radar screen. It is a phantom, a delusion, and a mistake. I'm sorry, guys, but when it comes to understanding women, the first and toughest lesson to let into your bony little head is this: They do not, never have, and never will, "get" the subwoofer. To them it is merely a useless box, which does not go with the décor and has no place in the home. It is worse than unappreciated. It is an intruder, a blight.

[As an aside, Guys, you may ask, "If subwoofers are missing from the female consciousness, what exists in its place? Surely there must be something of equal importance?" Well, Guys, there absolutely is. Research shows that, depending on the age and psychology of the female in question, it's one of two things: A) chocolate or B) a pony.]

I'm sorry Guys, but the truth is harsh. If you want to get an inkling of what it feels like to exist as a female, you have to take the subwoofer out of the equation. You have to imagine what it's like not to have one, or to even to want one. I know the very thought is painful for you. I know you may not be able to even try such a thing, with your puny, stubborn, yet – dare I say it – noble Regular Guy consciousness.

I understand. For some of you it will not be worth it. You will say Guy! I give up! I can live without understanding the alluring, yet ever-confounding female. What I cannot do is attempt, even for a short time, to remove subwoofer-ism from my state of awareness. Even if I get to put it back in a few minutes later. It's just too terrible to contemplate. And, Guys! Let me tell you something. No Regular Guy will ever fault you for that.

But! Guys! Imagine this. For those of you who can stand it. For those of you who are brave and willing. For those of you who are a bunch of dumbf—ks anyway and figure, "What the hell, Guy. What have I got to lose?" Guys! Letting go of subwoofer consciousness for a brief time and communing with the soul of your female partner can bring you to a state of awareness you would not otherwise know existed. It will give you insights in to the mind, heart, soul and body of Woman that you can get no other way. And it may also bring you bliss.

"Bliss?" you ask. "Guy, how could such a thing be true?"

Well it is true. Because, Guys, think of this. Her world, whether she likes it or not, whether she asked for it or not, whether she wants to kill you for it or not, now includes the new and perfect, absolutely magnificent subwoofer. The one that you just brought home. The one you have already paid for, including extra for the service plan, and spent hours hooking up to the stereo. The one now taking up space in her otherwise perfectly decorated living room.

The one that, when you turn it on, and play something loud, and deep, and undeniably sexy, she won't be able to resist. Guys! It will affect her. It will overcome her. She may not like it. She may not want it. She may not understand it. But she's going to feel it.

And Guy!, You. Yes – you. The one who said, "What the f—k, I'll try to see it her way," are going to feel it with her. You and she will commune in the deepest unseen, indefinable way possible. It will resonate in the furthest reaches of your inner self – not only your deepest being, your heart and soul, but most importantly, Guys, your *parts*. You, like she, will feel the subwoofer. You will absorb the subwoofer. In giving up an aspect of your Guy-ness to merge in the deepest possible way with your female companion, Guys, you will achieve the ultimate in Enlightenment.

Yes, Guys, you will know – finally, really and forever – you will truly and deeply, in the ground of your being, without restrictions, without thought, get it. You will get it all. Yes, Guys, yes.

You will BE the subwoofer.

38
Petaluma

"**O**nly, of course, if you want to," Michaela said to Duke. "And after Santa Fe, we'll go on to Vegas and get you all set up there, and ready for your poker tournament."

Duke gave a small smile and nodded as though this was what he had expected her to say, and disappeared back into the bedroom.

Unlike Duke, Rennie was surprised by Michaela's invitation, though he probably shouldn't have been, considering what happened whenever the special incense was involved. He and Michaela went into the kitchen, and Rennie fixed chai for the three of them while Michaela described what she had experienced in the meditation.

"Past lives, maybe," Rennie commented, as he and Michaela took their steaming cups to the kitchen table. Rennie left Duke's chai on the counter, where the smell was certain to draw him sooner rather than later.

"I thought of that!" Michaela said proudly. "What about the first part, when I had the headache and couldn't breathe? I really, really thought I was going to die."

Instead of answering, Rennie got up and walked over to the tall bookshelf in the living room. He went directly to one with a blue and silver cover, came back, and handed it to Michaela, *Psychology of the Future*.

"I wasn't going to suggest you read any Grof for a while, but you're making amazing progress. I think at this point it might make sense to you. Only thing is, you'll have to get your own copy. This one's signed."

Michaela flipped through the book and read a paragraph here and there. She didn't think she'd have time now for a book this size. But she'd try to read it later, when things slowed down a little.

"Can't you just tell me what it says?" she said.

"Well, from your description, it sounds like you might have encountered something from your birth. There are whole explanations in the book of the different things you can go through during the birth process, and what significance they have. But there's lot of other stuff too. To tell you the truth, I don't remember most of the details. I probably should read it again myself."

Rennie realized he certainly should read it again, considering that he was about to introduce people to his mind-expanding incense on a large scale. There was a lot of reading he should brush up on before he went public with the incense. Although how he was going to find time, when he had so much else to prepare, he didn't know.

"Cool," Michaela said. She handed him back the book, and he returned it to the shelf.

"So did the Owl tell you to take Duke to Santa Fe with you?" Rennie asked.

"No. I thought of that myself. Actually She didn't say to go to Santa Fe, exactly. She just told me to go where there was the most love. And I felt a lot of love with Dorothea's group, and no love at all, obviously, at Eighth. So it has to mean that. But right after she flew off, I heard a voice talking in my head. Not the Owl, a different voice. And it said, 'Duke needs love too.'

"So I thought, 'Well, then, Duke should come with me.'

Which is really perfect because we can stay for a couple of days, and then I'll take him to Las Vegas. I think he might be nervous about going alone."

Now that she mentioned it, Rennie thought so too.

"Well, that's more than generous of you."

Rennie almost reminded Michaela that Duke wasn't the easiest person to have around, but he didn't want her to change her mind. Otherwise, he might end up taking care of Duke a lot longer himself. Besides, he had mentioned the eating and the noise already, so Michaela had been warned.

And also, she'd been internally inspired to ask Duke to go with her, so she was being guided at a deeper level. Those kinds of things frequently turned out to surprise you, by leading to something unexpected and important. So Rennie trusted that all would work out the way it was supposed to, and he would try not to worry about either Michaela or Duke. It made him laugh, though, imagining Duke showing up at the LightWorks office, sniffing around for his next meal.

"What's funny?" Michaela asked, sipping her chai.

"Oh, it's nothing," Rennie said, changing the subject. "But can you tell me one more thing about your vision?" Michaela nodded. "What about the Owl? Was that an animal spirit helper, do you think?"

"No! I asked her and she said she wasn't 'personal,' whatever that's supposed to mean. And you know, come to think of it, she wasn't completely an owl, either. Her body was an owl, and she had wings and feathers and everything, except on the end of the wings were hands, and her face was a woman, not an owl face. Isn't that weird?"

"Sounds like a goddess of some kind. Did she say her name?"

"No. She hardly said anything," Michaela mused. "What kind of goddess do you think she was?"

"Don't know," Rennie said. "You should research. Either online, or get some books on mythology and see what you can find about Owl Goddesses or Bird Goddesses. I think there might have been something like that in ancient Egypt or very early Europe."

Now it was Michaela's turn to laugh.

"What?" Rennie said, smiling with her.

"Remember when we met? And I asked you about the radish? You told me to go look up radish in a dream or symbol book to see what it meant. And now you're telling me to look up the Owl Goddess. Are you sure you're a meditation teacher, not a college professor?"

Rennie blushed.

"Do I need to write a term paper?" she laughed, and Rennie was surprised for the second time that day to find Michaela more likeable than he'd thought.

Well, it was understandable. They were on some sort of a journey together. Both were breaking new ground in their lives. They were still smiling when Duke strolled into the kitchen to fetch his chai. Duke peered at them for several seconds before retrieving his cup.

"You are sure you not the girlfriend of Rennie?" he asked, looking over the rim while taking a large swallow.

Michaela and Rennie both shook their heads.

"No, Duke," Rennie said. "We're just friends."

"Okay, sure, Rennie," Duke said. "I believe you." He turned back to Michaela. "Is it time to leave now?" he asked. "I am all packed."

39
Marin to Albuquerque to Santa Fe

M ichaela knew Duke was disappointed that they didn't leave immediately, but she needed time to prepare. The soonest she could leave was the next day.

First, she went home and booked their flights. Then she called the LightWorks office to confirm her arrival. At the same time, she explained bringing Duke, whom she said was "a friend of a friend I'm helping out," and asked them to book a second hotel room, which she would pay for. And finally, she had to tie up some loose ends, both business and personal, in order to leave town. Oh, and pack. Rennie offered to bring Duke down to Michaela's house the next morning, and drive them both to the airport.

She also wanted to call Roxanne. They hadn't talked lately, and Michaela thought it was due to her new interests, which Roxanne didn't seem comfortable with. Michaela wasn't worried about it. There were times in the past when they weren't as close, for one reason or another – usually some guy – and yet their friendship had always bounced back. Michaela left a message saying she was off again, "on stuff you'd say was a waste of time, when I should be either making a bunch of money, or blowing it doing something decadent. But, hey, don't worry, Roxy, I really am having fun with this – just not in our usual way. Call when you get a chance."

She imagined Roxanne would think it plenty decadent if she knew Michaela was escorting a 21-year-old to Santa Fe and Vegas. That is, unless Roxanne actually met Duke. Michaela herself wasn't quite convinced she should be taking Duke for any reason. Rennie said he was a nuisance, and everything she'd witnessed so far supported that notion.

But she'd had a strong urge, both to offer to take him and to give him support. At least, it seemed right at the time, although the further she got from the moment, the more doubts she had. She hoped it wasn't a mistake, but she couldn't take it back now, so she pushed the thought aside and continued getting ready.

When she woke the next morning, she had forgotten her doubts. The fog was already burning off. Rennie was prompt, there was little traffic, and their goodbyes were short and cheerful. Michaela and Duke negotiated security successfully, despite a large, bored guard who seemed to enjoy having Duke go back and forth through the metal detector, each time to remove items from various parts of his person – a belt buckle shaped like a playing card, a long chain he wore around his neck, and a charm of some sort in his pocket.

After an early arrival, they followed signs past numerous food outlets and news stands toward the baggage area. The airport was color-themed in turquoise and pink, and every twenty feet or so was a store or vendor selling silver jewelry, kachinas, painted statues of howling coyotes, patterned ceramic vases, colorful woven purses, prints of Indians on horses, chili-themed novelty items, and on and on. Plus key chains, magnets, cups, posters and tee shirts with pictures of all of the above. New Mexico, thought Michaela, Land of Ten-thousand Southwestern-themed Gifts.

LightWorks was supposed to have someone meet them at baggage, and drive them to the Santa Fe hotel. From there, Michaela would be taken to the office to meet with Dorothea. When she and Duke reached the luggage carousel, she was surprised but glad to see their driver was Robin. She stood smiling and waving enthusiastically, wearing a colorful sundress. Her hair was up in a loose ponytail; a few blond strands curling around her mostly bare shoulders. Robin gave Michaela a big hug. Michaela turned to introduce Duke, but he had disappeared.

"He was just here," she muttered.

"Probably in the men's room," Robin said, "Let's see if your bags are coming. Who is this fellow you brought? Is he really from India? Is he your guru? You never mentioned you had a guru. Is he a new guru?"

"Um, nothing like that, no," Michaela had forgotten about Robin's penchant for annoying questions. "He's just a friend of a friend I'm helping out. I hardly even know him."

She turned to the carousel to watch for her suitcase as Robin continued to chatter and ask questions. Michaela gave the shortest answers she could manage, her mind elsewhere.

It was unlikely that Duke was in the men's room, since he'd just gone, right after they debarked the plane a few minutes ago. She supposed he could be anxious about his backpack, which he'd checked, and might have rushed around to the other side of the carousel where she couldn't see him. But when the pack came down shortly behind Michaela's suitcase, and it stayed on for two complete rounds, she finally yanked it off.

"Where the hell is he?" she said aloud.

Robin seized the subject. "Do you think he's okay? Do you think he went to get something to drink? Most people aren't used to how dry it is here. I'll bet that's what happened. But why do you think he didn't tell you? And don't you think he should have been back by now?"

"I'm going to look for him, Robin. Stay here with the bags."

Before Robin could answer, Michaela stomped off toward the escalator she'd come down earlier, trying to remember if Duke was with her when they passed the security point, or if he could possibly still be on the other side, where she would not be allowed to go look for him. She was beginning to worry. What if she couldn't find him? What if a guard or somebody thought he was a terrorist, and he'd been snatched for questioning? Would she be held responsible for him, even though he was an adult? Was he in the country legally?

She was flipping out. First she had to get a grip, and then she needed to find Duke and get out of there, so she could go do what she came for. She didn't want Dorothea to think she was unprofessional the very first day they worked together.

She checked all the little stores and kiosks. No Duke. What now? Should she go back to the baggage area? She passed a large display board, muttering to herself, when suddenly a hand reached out and grabbed her sleeve. She was yanked into a shadowed area behind the board. There, crouched in the semi-darkness, was Duke.

"Duke! What the hell's the matter with you? Do you think this is the time to play hide and seek? I was freaking out. Come on, I've got your pack. We've got to get going."

"Eeee, Michaela! Your friend is so, ahhh, so ahhh, beautiful."

"Is that what's going on? You ran away from Robin? Are you completely nuts?"

"Eeee, what do I do? I don't know what I should say to her."

Michaela sighed. She wanted to yell at Duke, but it wouldn't help. She closed her eyes and deliberately tried to calm down. After all, she wanted to help the boy. Here was an opportunity.

"Okay, Duke. Here's what you do. You shake her hand and say, 'Hi Robin, good to meet you.' She's a nice young woman; she won't hurt you. Now let's get out of here."

She shoved Duke out from his hiding space and pointed toward a pink and turquoise exit sign, beneath which stood

Robin and the bags. When he hesitated, she went first, pulling him along.

"Robin, this is Duke. Duke, Robin. Come on guys, let's go."

While Michaela picked up her suitcase and marched toward the door, Robin took Duke's outstretched hand in one of hers and smiled.

"Duke, I'm so glad to meet you. That's really cool about you coming here for the tournament and everything. I always wished I could play in one."

Duke beamed. He vigorously shook her hand up and down, and said, "HiRobinnicetomeetyou. Eeee! You, ahhh, you, ahhh, like to play poker?"

"Yes, I do play! My dad taught me. Come on, I'll tell you about it on the way. We better go."

Robin inclined her head toward Michaela, who was about to disappear out the door to the parking lot, even though she had no idea what make of car Robin drove or where to find it. Robin started after her at a jog.

Duke, his hand still tucked into Robin's, hoisted his pack onto one shoulder and followed closely behind.

◊ ◊ ◊

"What are you doing out here?" Michaela asked Robin, once they were on the highway. Michaela sat in the passenger seat, and Duke in the very center of the back seat. Atypically, he was neither hooked up to electronics nor fidgeting nonstop. Instead, he sat very still, his eyes fixed on Robin, closely attending to the conversation.

"I'm volunteering at LightWorks, since I'm free for the next few months. I asked Thea at the end of the retreat, and she said it was okay. So far, I'm mostly running errands and answering emails, but I think soon they'll let me take registrations and help out at a workshop. And I get to be around Thea some of the time, when she's there, and the other teachers too, and sometimes we all go to lunch together. I feel like I'm picking up a lot just being in the energy field. I'm sure it will accelerate my inner work. Don't you think?"

Michaela remembered Robin telling her about various volunteer situations she'd been in. Either Robin was completely giving and lived on little in order to help people, or she had a source of income that meant she didn't have to work. Either way, it was a good deal for LightWorks, which got the benefit of Robin's unpaid labor. She wondered if LightWorks would do anything for Robin in return, maybe give her a set of Dorothea's CDs and books, or at least a nice pink and turquoise Kachina for her altar.

Michaela herself was still unsure if she should charge for her work and her designs. Oddly, hearing that Robin was there entirely as a volunteer made Michaela think she should probably charge after all. Maybe not as much as for her menu work, but something. If Dorothea thought her designs were worth wearing, then they must have value.

On the ride to Santa Fe, Michaela was struck by the vast quantities of beige dirt studded with scrubby plants, and by the endless azure sky. Where they met was edged with darker mountain ranges, some close by and some distant. Nearly every man-made structure was a square-shaped, round-cornered adobe in beige, pink or pinky-beige. Just like the airport. You had to give folks out here credit – they certainly kept to the theme.

After checking in at their square-shaped, round cornered, pinkish-beige adobe hotel – actually very nice inside, with whitewashed walls, rough dark exposed beams in the corners and ceiling, and the ubiquitous southwestern art – she and Robin hopped right back into the car to go to LightWorks. And, counter to plan, Duke hopped right in with them.

"Um, Duke, are you sure you want to go? It'll be really boring for you. I'll be there for hours, and all we're doing is discussing clothes and making drawings," Michaela reminded him.

She really did not want him to tag along. She was sure he'd be a total nuisance, not only to her, but to Dorothea and everyone else at the office. They'd probably be annoyed if she brought him. But she didn't want to tell him he'd be in the way, and risk hurting his feelings. He was obviously more sensitive than he let on. She tried to entice him to stay put.

"Duke, here in the hotel, you know, you can watch TV, or go online. And you can order room service. It looked like a great menu."

That should do it. What young guy – or any guy – wouldn't rather eat and watch screens than be around a dress designer and her client?

"Eeee, no, I will go with you. I can help, maybe, in your work. Or help Robin, maybe?" He looked hopefully at Robin, who seemed not to notice. He then climbed into the back.

Well, obviously, in this case, a young guy obsessed with a pretty girl. As they started off again, Duke gazed at the back of Robin's head with the same intensity Michaela had seen him staring into Rennie's refrigerator the day before. Come to think of it, here it was 1:30 p.m., and he hadn't even mentioned lunch. The thought of room service didn't interest him.

Michaela shook her head, and hoped this development would not interfere with what she was there to do.

40
Santa Fe

Since Michaela arrived, Robin had been updating the LightWorks office by phone at regular intervals.

"I've got them in the car and we're leaving the airport."

"We're almost to the hotel."

"We left the hotel and we're on our way to the office."

So Michaela expected to walk in and get right to work with Dorothea when they arrived. She asked Robin if they could stop and grab something to eat on the way over, since she and Duke hadn't had lunch and she didn't know when she'd get another opportunity for a meal.

"Oh, don't worry about that," Robin assured her. "We ordered in, so we could all eat together. Do you like sushi?"

Michaela liked sushi fine, but was concerned about Duke. She was not worried he wouldn't like it, because he was free to go out and get something else. In fact, she hoped he didn't like it, because, for one thing, she wanted to get him out of the office before he could be too much of a nuisance. And worse, she'd seen his capacity for food. They'd probably ordered enough lunch for normal people. What if he scarfed up the whole spread?

She was trying to think of some way to discourage him, but before she could speak, Duke spoke.

"Eeee. Sushi? I have not eaten that but see pictures online. I like new food. I will try it."

Michaela stared out her side window and tapped her fingers on the armrest. What had she been thinking to come here? She didn't know anything about designing clothes. Dorothea Light was a famous author and teacher, and once they were in close contact for an extended period, she would see that Michaela had no idea what she was doing. And Michaela was still such a newbie on her spiritual path – Dorothea would certainly not want to be around her for very long.

And now she had burdened herself with the ridiculous Duke. Most likely, Dorothea, Dirk and everyone at their office would be laughing at her in private before the end of the week, just like those guys at Eighth probably were. And then she wouldn't have a reference from Dorothea to try and change their minds about her. Of course, by now it was probably too late, and whoever did their menus would replace Michaela as the coolest, most creative designer in the Western states, if not the entire U.S.

She put her hands up to her face and sighed deeply.

"Oh, I'm sorry Michaela – you *don't* like sushi? I should have ordered New Mexican. Would that have been better? I just thought you'd be having a lot of that while you're here, and I wanted to get you something different to start off. Or maybe Chinese – do you like Chinese? Of course with Chinese, it's hard to know which dishes people will eat, and then if they do like one, you wish you'd ordered three containers instead of two, because everyone eats the Hunan chicken when you ordered more of the beef with broccoli 'cause you thought it would go faster. Or vice versa.

"But with sushi, you can order a bunch of rolls and everyone seems to eat them – crab and shrimp and vegetarian. And then some salmon and yellowtail pieces, and stuff, for the ones who are really into the raw fish. And the wasabi's always a conversation starter – how hot it is, and who likes to use the most. But I should have asked you ahead of time. Do you want to get something else before we get there? We're almost there, actually, but there's a deli right down the street. Maybe I should have ordered deli. Do you like deli? How about for tomorrow?"

"Robin! Stop! I like sushi just fine. I'm just thinking about something else. Something…unrelated to lunch."

Robin looked skeptical.

"Really!" said Michaela.

Duke said, "Don't worry Robin. Eeee. Michaela is scared about a lot of things, but she does not have to be scared at all."

Duke produced from somewhere in his briefcase a stick of incense and handed it over the seat.

"She needs to use this when she goes to work, and then everything will be fine."

Michaela took the stick and looked back at Duke. What good did he think a stick of incense was going to do? Even Robin turned for as long a glance as she could spare away from the road. Duke wore a serene smile, and was clearly the only one of the three who was relaxed and comfortable.

"So don't worry, Robin," he said. "Michaela will like the sushi. And don't worry, Michaela. I will eat only the sushi expected for one person. Eeee. I think we will have fun together on this trip. I'm glad I came with you to this place, Santa Fe, Michaela. This is a good place for me."

And Duke settled against the center of the back seat and gazed around him, clearly curious about what would happen next.

41
Santa Fe

*R*obin parked the car in a small gravel lot off a side street. Michaela waited impatiently as Duke extracted himself slowly from the back. They followed Robin down a short path to a two-story – adobe, of course – structure set back from the street behind another building. A small courtyard flanked by two cement benches led to the front door. On the wall was a sign, "LightWorks Shamanic Meditation Retreats," and their logo: an outline drawing of a person standing with head and arms held upward in front of a blue sun with four rays, in red, white, black and yellow.

Robin opened the door for Michaela, but Duke reached past with a flourish to keep it open for Robin, who beamed at him before following Michaela inside.

Michaela found herself in a short hallway with red tiled floors. Glass doors stood left and right, and straight ahead was a stairway. The door to the right was plain, but the one on the left also had the LightWorks logo, so Michaela flung that one open and marched inside.

The large room was bright from sunlight coming in through several big windows. It held desks and tables, with the usual assortment of computers and other office machines. As

Michaela entered, the only two people in the room, both women, looked up from their desks. Neither was Dorothea. Each looked mid forties, pleasant looking but not pretty; one tall, thin, brown haired and doe-eyed, the other round, blond and smiley.

As Michaela and company entered, the two women rushed up, arms held wide in hug position.

"We're here!" said Robin. She introduced Michaela to Grass (the round one), who Robin said handled PR and marketing, but was really an animal intuitive, and Seabird (the tall one), bookkeeper and registrar, who was also a third-level Barayka instructor.

Michaela wasn't sure she'd heard either their names or occupations correctly, but she was not going to ask. After the obligatory hugs, they enthusiastically invited Michaela to come in and sit down. The one she thought was called Grass took her jacket, and the other, named Seabird if she heard correctly, insisted on finding a place for her large case.

"And this is Duke," Robin said, turning toward him. Both women's heads swiveled toward the young man.

"Oooh," said Seabird. "So *you're* Duke. You're here from India, right?"

"It's such an honor to meet you," Grass added. "How long have you been here? Are you on tour?"

Michaela did a double take. Who did they think he was, some rock star?

"Ahhh, just a few, ahhh, days," Duke replied. "I have been to, eeee, Chicago airport and San Francisco airport and city of Petaluma. Eeee. And also town of Mill Valley, but only to pick up Michaela. And today at Alba-quar-key airport and now in city of Santa Fe."

"Oooh, that's exciting," said Seabird.

Michaela wondered how anyone could possibly find Duke's brief travelogue exciting, but kept her thoughts to herself.

Seabird and Grass ignored Michaela as they homed in on

Duke. Grass was patting Michaela's jacket, which was still over her arm, and Seabird had set Michaela's case down randomly on an empty chair, as they showered Duke with questions.

"What part of India do you come from?"

"What's it like there?"

"Which festivals do you celebrate?"

"Do you know any gurus?"

"Eeee.....," Duke started, but before he could answer, Michaela interrupted.

"Um, excuse me? Should I be seeing Dorothea? I know she's waiting for me."

"Oh, she isn't here yet," Grass said, with a wave of her hand in Michaela's direction. "Duke, do you teach yoga?"

"She'll probably come soon, though," Seabird added. "We should have lunch while we're waiting. Thea won't mind. Duke, are you hungry?"

Michaela thought it odd that Dorothea wasn't present, since she had come as fast as she could at her request. Dorothea had said it was important not to wait a single minute longer than necessary to get started. Michaela supposed something urgent had come up. But perhaps Dorothea had changed her mind about the clothing. That would be disappointing, but also a relief. However Michaela still wanted to ask Dorothea if she could use her as a reference for Eighth, and it would help if they did this project together.

Robin showed Michaela and Duke to a long table toward the back of the room. It was laid out beautifully with their lunch – a large assortment of sushi. The food had been removed from a pile of take-out boxes that were now sitting by a trash basket, and placed artfully on two yellow platters. Next to the platters were blue ceramic plates, red paper napkins, and chopsticks – not the plain disposable wooden ones that came free from the restaurant, but pretty black and gold lacquered ones decorated with birds and flowers.

Grass finally crossed the room to hang Michaela's jacket in

a closet, although her case remained where it was. Seabird had disappeared around the corner, and returned with a tray of bottled beverages, which she set down at the end of the table.

"Duke, what would you like to drink? This one is iced chai, but we can make hot chai if you prefer, or some other kind of tea. Bottled green tea? Kambucha? Herba mate? Coffee?"

"Duke, you have to try the unagi," said Grass. "It's delicious. Do they eat eel in India?"

Duke stood over the sushi Grass was pointing to and licked his lips. He asked for a root beer, which the ladies were very sorry not to have but were ready to fetch for him at the store. When he saw they had diet colas, he accepted one of those instead.

Michaela went to the end of the table, took a bottle of mint flavored iced tea, and picked up a plate. Robin did the same.

Duke began telling them all about the very large eels in India, which he did indeed like to eat. When he stopped talking so as to taste, at Grass's insistence, a slice of pickled ginger ("Eeee!" was the response), Michaela spoke up again.

"So, uh, does Dorothea actually know I'm here?" she asked.

"Oh, yes," said Seabird, nodding. "We called to tell her you were on the way. She's very happy you're here. She does tend to be late. It's nothing personal. She's probably receiving a message from spirit or something. That's the usual reason."

"Oh," said Michaela. "Okay."

At least there was a reason. Probably Dorothea really did have important spiritual business to attend to, something Michaela wouldn't know about. Maybe it even had to do with their project, and Thea needed to get the information before they started.

Still, Michaela felt a little put out – Dorothea not here to greet her; the women fawning over Duke. It wasn't how she'd pictured it, and that annoyed her. Immediately, she felt bad about herself for having expectations, especially since it had just been explained to her that Dorothea may very well have important messages to receive.

Michaela needed to learn how to just "be" – that's what one of those tapes she was listening to had said. Be present in the moment, no matter what happened. She was not good at that; not at all. It was hard for her not to compare this to a work situation. She just knew if she conducted her business anything like LightWorks did, she would not be as successful as she was.

Duke, Michaela, Robin, Grass and Seabird had each selected several sushi pieces, added their pickled ginger, took drinks and napkins, and wasabi'd up their little bowls of soy sauce. Duke had looked at everyone's sushi quantities, and had taken no more than the rest of them. But then Seabird and Grass insisted he add more, and loaded up his plate. He looked with regret at the last five pieces on the platter, even though his plate was full.

The five of them had just settled into chairs around the office and started eating when the door burst open and Dirk stepped into the room.

All eyes turned to him, and Michaela searched for a safe place to rest her plate so she could stand up to greet him with the requisite hug. Duke raised his eyes, but continued the machine-like movement of food from the plate to his mouth.

"Don't get up," Dirk said to Michaela. But she already had, and met him halfway to the table.

"Michaela," he said, hugging her briefly, "Welcome."

"Hi Dirk," she said. "I made it. Ready to go to work."

"Good." He glanced around. "Where's Thea?"

Dirk walked over to the table and popped a salmon-covered end of rainbow roll into his mouth. Duke twitched.

"She's not here yet," said Seabird.

"We thought she was coming with you," said Grass.

"Nope. I left early and haven't seen her since." He turned to Michaela, who had sat back down and picked up her plate. "Good thing we're not paying you by the hour," he chuckled.

Michaela felt uncomfortable. While she hadn't been planning to charge by the hour, the thought had crossed her mind. But they had never discussed anything about money. She wondered how he expected they were paying her, if at all. She didn't want to bring it up in front of everyone, but thought perhaps she should decide what she was doing – charging or not charging, and how much to ask for – then discuss it privately with either Dirk or Dorothea.

As Dirk polished off the last of the sushi, a tiny "Eeee," could be heard from Duke, who was sitting behind the door, previously unnoticed by Dirk.

Dirk turned to him with a raised eyebrow. "And you are?" he asked.

"Oh, sorry," Robin said. "Dirk, this is Duke. Duke, Dirk. Hey that's funny."

Grass began chuckling, then quickly stopped when no one else laughed. Dirk nodded to Duke, and the young man raised both eyebrows in reply.

"Duke's traveling with me," Michaela explained. "He's here from India. A friend of a friend I'm helping out. I, um, called ahead to see if it was okay, so I thought you knew. He wanted to come with me this afternoon, but if he's in the way, he can go back to the hotel."

"No, no, that's perfectly all right. I'll be in my office. He won't bother me. I don't expect anyone to do much work around here today anyway."

He turned to Seabird. "Why isn't Thea here? Has Michaela been waiting long?"

"Only about 15 minutes," Seabird said, looking uncomfortable. "I don't know what happened to Dorothea. I called her to say they were on the way, and she said she was coming." In a smaller voice, she added, "Do you think maybe she was getting a message, like, you know, from … beyond?"

"Sure she was," Dirk said. "Call her again and tell her I said to get her butt down here now. Even if Michaela's not getting paid by the hour, you two are. And nothing's getting done with all this dressmaking and entertaining going on. Let's get on with it."

Just as Seabird reached for the phone, it rang and she answered it.

"Hello, you've reached the LightWorks office. How may I be of service?" She smiled broadly and, nodding, pointed vehemently to the phone.

"It's her!" she mouthed to the room.

"I was just picking up the phone to call you! Oh, you knew that ...of course. You want Michaela to come there? To your house?" Seabird looked at Dirk, who shrugged. "I'll ask Robin to drive her. Okay, I'll tell them. Bye Thea."

"I'll take her," said Dirk. He looked at Michaela, "Let's go."

"Um, what about Duke? Should we drop him at the hotel?" she asked.

Duke, Seabird, Grass and Robin all spoke at once.

"Eeee! I would like to be here," said Duke.

"We'll keep him with us," said Seabird.

"He can help me with stuff," said Robin.

"Let him stay and do things here," said Grass.

"All right, all right. I don't care what he does," said Dirk. "As long as somebody's here to answer emails and the phones. I'll be back later. This yours?" he looked at Michaela as he started to lift her bag,

"I almost forgot," Seabird said. "Thea wants you to hurry. She's just had a big inspiration."

Grass ran to get Michaela's jacket and reached her with it at the door. Michaela took it, and followed Dirk and her bag out into the courtyard with just a quick goodbye to the three women and Duke. She took Robin's cell number to reach her later.

As she left, Grass and Robin were leaning forward in their chairs as Duke stretched back in his, arms behind his head, chewing his last bite of fish and rice. They were back to asking

Duke questions. Seabird was opening a bakery box. Michaela remembered Grass mentioning brownies, and hoped they would save her one. Although with Duke around, that wasn't very likely.

42
Santa Fe

M ichaela buckled herself into Dirk's little Beemer. He started the car, but didn't drive off. Instead he turned toward her.

"Lets take a ride up the mountain and I'll show you my favorite view."

"You're kidding, right? You're taking me to your house. Dorothea's expecting me."

"She's expecting you, all right, but she won't be ready. You'll have to wait. Seriously. Might as well spend that time driving around with me."

Dorothea had implored her to hurry to Santa Fe, yet didn't seem in any rush to start on their project. Now Dirk wanted to show her the scenery.

Normally Michaela would be willing to do what the client wanted. But who was her client, Dirk or Dorothea? The uncertainty was uncomfortable and she nervously tapped her fingers on her thigh.

"I should probably just get over there, in case she's ready. At least I can start laying out the designs I brought while I wait."

"Your call." He shifted gears and pulled out into the street.

As they rode in silence, she imagined becoming friends

with Dirk and Dorothea. It would be cool to hang out with them, get to know them better as people. Maybe that evening, they'd go to dinner together. She pictured Dorothea saying what a good time she was having; how hard it is to relax when people always see her in her teacher role. But with Michaela it was different. With Michaela she could let her guard down and be her real self.

Occupied with her daydream, Michaela was surprised to find they'd pulled up to the attractive exterior of a large pinkish-beige adobe home. It sat among trees and shrubbery, affording privacy from other houses, which were not close by, but still in sight. It was no mansion but they were probably in one of the more prestigious areas outside the city.

Dirk parked his BMW next to a shiny new Lexus hybrid. He grabbed her case from the backseat. Michaela gathered her purse and jacket and followed him toward the door, inside a small adobe-framed entranceway decorated with large pots of colorful flowers and cacti.

He held the door while she stepped inside. The entrance foyer was cool and quiet, with a colorful rug over dark wood flooring. To the left were two doors, with an enormous gold Buddha in the corner, and on the opposite wall, a single long shelf held several different female statues or Goddess figures.

Past the entranceway was a large open area, with the dining room left and living room right. In the center, at waist level, was a large, flat, square display case, the type you'd see in a store with jewelry or other small objects. Inside the case, resting on a background of white velvet, were each of the books written by Dorothea Light, as well most of her CDs and two of the new DVDs. Colorful stones and crystals were arranged around the items.

"Oh look, it's my drawing," Michaela said. She was surprised and pleased to see that the little paper figure she had made of Dorothea was also on display.

"Wait, there's another one. Did you make a copy?" she asked Dirk.

Then she saw that there were numerous copies placed among the other items, and most were packaged with a cardboard label and plastic wrap.

"We used cardboard so they'd be a little heavier," Dirk said. "They're already selling well on the website. Cool, huh?"

"You're selling them?" Michaela couldn't decide if she was flattered that her little paper image was good enough for people to purchase, or annoyed that no one had asked her permission. Didn't she maintain the rights to her work? Or had she given them up when she made a gift of the figure to Dorothea?

"You know I…" she was about to bring up the question to Dirk in the least confrontive way she could, when….

CRASH!

An inhuman sounding shriek came from the back of the house, followed by Dorothea's voice. "Dirk! Are you here? Come help me!"

"I'd better check on her," Dirk said casually. He waved in the direction of the living room. "Have a seat."

As he strolled off, Michaela went into the living room, but she did not sit down. Instead, she went to the far wall to look at an arrangement of photographs. They were all of Dorothea, standing or sitting next to one or two other persons. Most of those Michaela did not know, but a few famous faces she couldn't help but recognize.

The Dalai Lama was one. Andrew Weil was another, because his bushy face had been a huge poster in the makeup department at Macy's. Most of the men and women with Dorothea were in western dress, but some wore indigenous outfits. Michaela assumed they were important figures from world cultures, probably religious ones. Dorothea had nearly the same expression and pose each time: wide smile, eyebrows slightly raised, and head tilted slightly to one side.

"Michaela, Michaela, you're here! Finally!"

The voice caused Michaela to turn away from the photographs and face the woman herself, posed in the very same stance.

"I was going crazy waiting. I can't imagine what took you so long. I thought you'd be here hours ago. But never mind, I forgive you, of course. That's just how I am, all forgiveness. I'll even forgive Suela for leaving that cord sticking out AGAIN. All I ask is that she tuck all the cords back after she vacuums, but she just can't seem to remember. I don't think that's too much to ask, do you? But never mind; I wanted to replace that old lamp anyway, even if it was expensive. But who has time to shop anymore? Not me. That's why I'm so glad you're here. This is better than shopping. I just get to ask for what I want and presto! You design it, and Lorna Beth will sew it for me. Perfect."

She finally paused, but Michaela didn't know which part to answer. After a beat too long, she finally blurted, "Um, hi, Dorothea. Where are we going to work?"

She felt dumb that it was all she could think of to say, but Dorothea didn't seem to notice, and went right on talking.

"Oh, the dining room table will be fine. I had Suela clear it and cover it with plastic. I see you found my personal little wall of fame. Most of these were taken at conferences where I was a speaker. I always make time to let people get their pictures taken with me. Even the non-famous ones. Though of course, I don't put those on the wall." She laughed. "Do you want me to tell you who everyone is?"

Dirk came up behind Dorothea and put his arm around her waist.

"No, Thea, she doesn't. She just wants to do what she came here to do. Sorry to leave you like that, Michaela," he said. "Would you like something to drink?"

"A glass of water would be great."

"Ooh, I'll have some of that pomegranate iced tea, Dirky Doodle. Bring Michaela one of those, too. She'll love it. Come on, honey," Dorothea took her arm. "Let's get started, it's getting late. I don't know why everything always takes so long. I feel like all I do is wait, wait, wait, while everyone scurries around trying to get their act together."

She turned toward the dining room and Michaela was pulled along beside her. She grabbed her case from where Dirk had left it next to the book display.

Focus, Michaela thought to herself. No matter how odd things seem, you just have one task to do here, and the rest is distraction. Besides, maybe this is normal for people whose main focus is their spiritual life. It made sense they would be a little unconventional.

She sat down and pulled out some drawings she had already begun working on. "Dorothea, take a look at these. I thought they'd be a good place to start."

"This is so exciting, Michaela. I can't wait to see what you created for me."

Dorothea pulled up the chair next to her and finally they were getting down to work. Michaela was relieved to fall at once into her professional persona. Dirk placed their drinks on the table, far enough away so they wouldn't be easily spilled. He'd brought Michaela both water and the pomegranate tea. Feeling more comfortable, she again flashed on the three of them going out later. Maybe it would happen. Perhaps even Duke and Robin could come; they would be entertaining. This trip would work out just fine.

"So, Thea, show me which ones you like," she said, self-consciously trying out the woman's nickname and feeling proud of herself. Soon the two women were so absorbed in discussing the designs that they didn't even notice when Dirk delivered a plate with two small brownies and disappeared.

43
Petaluma

O h joy! With Duke out of the house, Rennie was finally alone with the incense. While he yearned to keep it close at hand in his bedroom, it would be safer in storage until he was ready to use it in his workshops.

He had purchased extra-strength plastic freezer bags, oversized glass jars with screw lids, and cardboard cartons. He took batches of the loose sticks from Duke's shabby boxes and sealed them into the bags. Bags went into jars, each tightly shut. Jars were then packed up, four to a carton, with one left out for his personal use. He taped shut each carton, and with a green Sharpie, wrote "RENNIE PERSONAL" in large letters across the top.

Around nine p.m., Rennie packed the seven cartons into the Prius, and drove to his warehouse. As expected, no one was around. Within the warehouse was a locked cage where they kept the most expensive items in inventory, as well as a safe with all the office backup files on disk. Rennie moved all the contents out of one back corner of the cage and stacked the new cartons there. He covered them with a black blanket he had brought from home, and moved the old items back in front of the new ones.

After double-checking the lock, to which only he and Noeletta knew the combination, Rennie went home satisfied that his precious new product would remain preserved and undisturbed while he prepared for its debut on the world stage of transformational workshops.

The next day, he told Noeletta about the cartons and made her promise to keep them absolutely secret. He had a surprise for her, too. He wanted her to take over the day-to-day workings of the incense business. She would become a full partner, stepping into Rennie's role, and could hire another person to work with her and J.J.. Since Rennie had talked about this possibility before, just not saying when it would happen, she had already thought about it and had a plan. She would bring her husband, who had retired early from his job as a printer, on board as the third person, and they would run it together with J.J.

Driving home, Rennie felt a rush of freedom and excitement. He really was doing this! Making the change he had dreamed of for months, even years. He could now put his energy full time into becoming a spiritual teacher.

Between his freed up time, his enthusiasm for the new career, and the effects of the incense, changes came fast. After experimenting, Rennie found that burning a small amount of incense fueled his creativity, allowing him to spend four hours a day working on his book or devising marketing materials. The incense business had often used a young, enthusiastic designer, who was contacted to start on this new project. Rennie soon had him working up a logo and creating web and print ads, and a cover for the new book.

He also designed beautiful small boxes for the incense. Each box would hold just four sticks. Rennie planned to instruct people to burn it in small amounts, and only when they were ready to do inner work. He might even make them sign an agreement to use it that way, and not give or sell it to anyone who hadn't been to a workshop. That would be the most ethical way to distribute it, and, as a side benefit, add to the mystique and demand.

After researching his options, Rennie decided to publish the book himself. It could be released faster, and he had a ready-made, if small, distribution network through the incense sales, allowing it to begin reaching stores and individuals right away. If the book sold well, he might attract a publishing company, further increasing his markets when he was prepared for a larger audience. This was not only the best business decision, but the safest. If things took off, he would be ready to work with people in the way that would be best for them, and he would not be stretched too thin.

He continued to meditate, aided by the incense, two or three hours most afternoons. It never failed to bring remarkable results. The range of what he went through was amazing. Some of it was similar to meditation experiences he'd had over the years, or in workshops. Some was new. He reread spiritual texts from different teachers and faiths, and believed he was experiencing much of what they talked about. But he had other inner adventures too, that seemed to cut across the boundaries of time, space and individual consciousness.

Sometimes he seemed to be in the past. He was in different cultures, some primitive, some so advanced, he had to be visiting the future, because it was so unlike anything he'd ever seen.

Often, in these travels backward and forward, he felt dropped into scenes that he suspected were his own past lives. Other times, he was floating through and just watching, or peeking through someone else's consciousness and getting a taste of the world through their experience. Once he found himself viewing a display case with books and pictures of Dorothea Light, accompanied by a feeling of confusion. He had a quick flash of Michaela and wondered how she was doing, before a voice in his head said, "she's right where she needs to be."

Another time, he was carrying a baby, and felt he was his own mother holding himself as a newborn. The love he felt became overwhelming. Then, he was every mother that ever existed, and that all their love was one love: so enormous he was certain his heart would not survive the pleasure and pain of it all. He had similar experiences with other emotions, including rage so huge it felt the entire universe would explode if he let it.

He received secrets of plant life and animal life, and sometimes even felt the souls, if that's what you'd call it, of different types of inanimate matter, like minerals or water. The information often came with an all-encompassing sense of the spirit present of all matter, and the interconnectedness of every part of the whole.

The experiences were innumerable, yet somehow connected. Rennie took notes after each session, and used much of it as examples in his writing the next day. In addition, he noticed that frequently, even during non-meditation periods, he would feel calmer than usual, and less apt to be disturbed by life's little annoyances. He even noticed being less needy and anxious about making his dreams of being a teacher come into reality. He did still see himself in that role, but it was more like something he was naturally flowing toward, rather than something he felt pressured to make happen.

Rennie watched this transformation in himself with interest, and hoped it meant he was clearing some of his old patterns and becoming more spiritually mature. He had always been uncomfortably ambivalent about his ambition, and was happy to feel less driven about the whole thing. On the other hand, he was afraid to count on the changes, in case he was wrong. Maybe he was just unfocused from all the meditation and writing he was doing.

One other curious effect Rennie noticed was that, more and more, he caught glimpses of Ashvin, not only during meditations and dreams, but when he was involved in a random activity, like washing the car or serving kibble to Phil.

It was like looking through space, and seeing the "real" Ashvin as he went about his life in Sumana. Once Ashvin was eating a meal with a group of people. Another time, Rennie saw him instructing a man and woman in making incense. Often, he was working in a garden, tending plants. And on one occasion, Rennie felt Ashvin "look" up and stare at him before returning to the plants.

Rennie wished he could reach Ashvin by phone or email. He didn't know why that shouldn't be possible, although he and Noeletta had still not been successful. When he'd asked Duke, the boy just shrugged and put in his earbuds. In the meantime, Rennie sent the senior Ashvin a letter by post, asking questions and suggesting Rennie set up a cell phone for him, so they could have contact. Despite the lessening of his ambitions to be a famous and respected spiritual teacher, Rennie still worried that someone else would get hold of the incense and learn about its unique properties, and his plan would be compromised.

And despite Duke's story about the Business Card Guru, and its implication that he was meant to be the one to distribute the incense, he wished he felt more personally in control of the situation. In this instance, as in all others, he wanted to trust the universe completely. But he wasn't quite there yet. For now, mostly, he just wanted to cover his ass.

44
Santa Fe

"So you like the neckline from this one, but you want it the way this other one wraps around…"

"Right. And the length about here," Dorothea pointed to a spot below her knee. "But with the fabric as you drew it the first time. I want those exact shades of green."

"Okay. So, I'm going to rework it right now. Meanwhile, you can look over this batch that are a little different, and…."

Dorothea grabbed the stack of pages before Michaela could finish her sentence, and went to the far end of the table, where she spread them out.

"That's not me," she pointed at a design. "Not me. Not me. Maybe. Ooh, this one! Me, me, me!" She moved the page aside, looked at the next one, "Not me. Hmmm, this won't work but I like that pattern," and put it aside too. "Not me. Not me. Not me. I'm done! I need some more."

Michaela had barely started on the new sketch combining the elements Dorothea wanted into one outfit, and didn't have anything else to show her. She looked up to see Dorothea waiting expectantly.

"That's all I have so far. Why don't you let me finish this, and we'll see how you like it? Is there, um, something you can do in the meantime? Or else I can take this back to the hotel with me to work on, and bring it to you tomorrow."

"But Michaela, honey, Lorna Beth, who's going to make the dresses, is coming early tomorrow. I want to have at least four designs ready for her to start working on. You'll do that for me won't you?"

Michaela felt a rush of anxiety. Was Dorothea serious? Michaela expected to complete one, or maybe two, outfits over the course of two-and-a-half days work. Certainly not four overnight. Dorothea's plans were overly demanding, and highly unrealistic.

"I...I don't think...you know, I don't think that's very..."

"Michaela, honey, you're not saying you can't do it, are you?" Dorothea interrupted. "Because this could be a great learning opportunity for you. You have to visualize yourself completing the task. You simply have to see yourself as more capable, as more than you think you are. That's how you become the person you were meant to be – your highest self. It's not always going to be easy, you know."

What does that mean? Michaela thought. *Is Dorothea saying that if I think I can do the impossible, then I can do it? And that this is somehow related to my personal growth? That sounds crazy. I can't imagine how it could be true. But really, what do I know? She's the expert. She's probably done it lots of times. I should trust her, since she knows more than me. I'd better be sure I'm clear on the concept, though.*

"So, you're saying, if I just think I can have four outfits done by tomorrow, then I can?"

"You have to *know* you can. *I* know you can. *I* have faith in you. Now you have to show yourself that you deserve faith in yourself. This could turn out to be a real breakthrough for you, Michaela."

She felt hope, panic, and confusion all at once.

"Well, if I look at it that way.... I don't want to say I can't. Right?"

"That's exactly right, honey. Now let me show you this other one I like, and we can take it from there."

THE REGULAR GUY'S GUIDE TO ENLIGHTENMENT

Chapter 7

So, Guys. Maybe it's crossed your mind that there's an important subject we haven't covered yet in our quest for Regular Guy enlightenment. Yet it's a part of the very essence of our Regular Guy being. Something we participate in every day. Something vital to our existence. Without this basic aspect of life, you almost couldn't have Regular Guy-ness. And if this particular subject has crossed your mind, you're probably wondering, "Guy! How can a Regular Guy take part in this activity and still become Enlightened?"

What am I talking about, you ask? Guy! Think about it. What's something you do all day, every day; from the first hour you're awake and figure out you've got no clean underwear, or lift the orange juice carton to your mouth and realize it no longer contains liquid; until the end of the day when you get up from the couch to pee during a commercial and slam your toe into a misplaced chair leg on the way to the bathroom, then return only to accidentally sit on the cat who jumped into the warm spot as soon as you got up? Not to mention at least hourly, if not more often, in between. Whenever you're awake and sometimes even when you're dreaming.

Yes, Guys. You know what I mean. I'm talking about swearing. Cursing, cussing, profanity. Expletives, oaths, epithets. The F word. The C word. The S, A, B, D, and H words. A few more letters and we'll be sending out invites to the Regular Guy spelling bee. Plus you've got your compound phrases of F, C, S, A, B, D and H. As in, how inventive and elaborate can you get by combining those beauties with each other – while also including a few more almost-as-interesting words, such as any type of family member, animal, or human body part, not to mention "lick," "suck" and "kiss" – to come up with something truly and creatively expressive of yourself as an individual?

All of which, admit it, Guys, you greatly relish. As one Guy remarked to me recently, "Why do we cuss? Because it's fun."

Yet at the same time, you feel bad about it. Some part way deep inside of you, probably speaking in the voices of your mother and all your ex-girlfriends, says maybe you shouldn't cuss so much. Or at all. That there's something wrong with you for cussing. It's bad. It's negative. It's a plague on society, and so are you.

This, Guys, is our dilemma.

Because, face it, Guys. We don't want to stop cussing. Cussing is like checking out the chip aisle in the grocery store. You stand there knowing every single bag contains a truckload of trans fats, and will probably contribute to your early demise. But son-of-a-Barbecue, aren't there just a whole lot of great flavors to choose from?

You're probably thinking right now, "*Nacho Ranch*, Guy, you Salt-and-Vinegar sucker, when are you going to mother-Jalapeno tell us what the Honey-Dijon to do about this dilemma?" Well I say, fear not. For all you brave Sour-Cream-and-Green-Onion brothers, help is on the way. Once again, Guy has your answer.

You see, Guys, first of all, a curse word, no matter how despicable, is still a member of the word family. It may be the crazy uncle in the trench coat, or the cousin with a toothpick hanging out of his mouth, but it's still in the family. And, let's face it, Guys, a word is a word is a word. When you say, "Son of a f—ing whore," does that turn the flat tire you are referring to into the offspring of a prostitute? No, it does not. When you call a person an ass licker, does the phrase cause that individual to suddenly be in the position of placing their tongue upon another individual's rear extremity? Of course not.

Can you see my point? Why should saying those words be in any kind of conflict with becoming enlightened? Why should you, or anyone else be bothered or upset by them? You don't actually do anything to anybody. It's all hypothetical. So what's the harm?

HOWEVER – and Guys, notice this is a big HOWEVER – it works both ways. If you are going to de-problemize your own use of swear words with that approach, and fit cursing into the Big Picture of enlightenment, you also have accept the concept in reverse. Here's how that works.

It has to also be true that you don't give a Nacho-Cheese when the swearing party is SOMEONE ELSE aiming their grease covered word missiles directly at you. Can you remain perfectly calm and happy, knowing that when a fellow Guy, or anyone else, says, "Screw you," they are not and never will be performing such an act upon your person? Can you accept being the recipient of a phrase such as "Dickwad" without care, entirely aware that, in fact, you are personally neither a male genital part nor are you any sort of "wad"? Will you be unconcerned by any such verbal attacks in your direction, because, after all, you know these are simply words that do you no actual harm whatsoever?

Guys! If you have such a capability – if you really can do that – then, I assure you, you are nearly there. Enlightenment cannot be not far from your reach.

It's a great thing, Guys, this realization that whatever vulgarities you encounter, and by implication, any words at all – in fact, anyone else's feelings toward you – do you no actual damage. You can accept the other person just as they are – hatred toward you and all. Isn't that freeing? Because then you can love 'em all anyway. They can't disturb you. You don't give a flying Chili. And loving 'em all, yes, ALL, is a big part of enlightenment. Maybe the whole Spinach-and-Artichoke, Garlic-and-Chives, Roasted-Red-Pepper bowl of chips.

You are then in a position to enjoy expressing yourself in any way you want. You can snack upon the most exotic of crispy, oily, tasty fried potato snacks. Chipotle, Honey-Garlic, Vinegar, even Bacon-Cheddar flavors can all be yours, to lay on the sofa and enjoy with the game and your favorite beverage (i.e., beer) to your heart's fulfillment. And you will enjoy them and not suffer, because you know it's all good, Guy. It's ALL good.

45
Santa Fe

Michaela called Robin to pick her up. As she gathered up her drawings and supplies, Dirk and Dorothea each said goodbye and disappeared into other rooms. Michaela waited alone by the front door until Robin drove up, whereupon Duke hopped out of the front seat and into the back. Michaela threw her case, her purse, and herself in the car.

"How did it go?" Robin asked. "Wow, it's late. Aren't you tired? Did you eat? What was it like?"

Michaela decided she could answer only one Robin question per outburst.

"Okay, I guess. She's expecting me to do a lot more than I planned. I'll really have to push myself tonight to get it done, and I'm not even sure that will be enough."

"I know. The first couple of days I was here, Dirk was out of town, and I had to drive Dorothea around. She can drive, but didn't want to. Said she needed to meditate and that it hadn't worked out too well when she tried to do both at once. So she sat in the back and called out instructions, like I was a chauffer. We went from store to store, and she bought a lot of stuff. But she must not have found what she was looking for, because we went everywhere. I'd wait in the car and think, 'this has got to be the last one for sure.' But then she'd have me take her somewhere else. I was exhausted."

Michaela was not listening. Her mind was on the designs.

"Michaela? Did you hear me? So do you have to start working right away? Can you hang out and have a drink? Did you have dinner with Dirk and Dorothea? Did they take you out someplace cool?"

From the hope in Robin's voice, Michaela thought that she, too, must have fantasies about sitting in a restaurant laughing and talking with Dorothea and Dirk.

Michaela didn't tell them that dinner had been a tray of slightly wilted turkey sandwiches made by Suela earlier in the day, and a bag of Sun Chips.

"I'm going straight to my room and get going on these designs. If I'm lucky, I'll be able to sleep a few hours. Though probably not many."

She turned toward Duke in the back seat. "How was your afternoon?"

Duke smiled. "Eee, Michaela, it was good. Grass and Seabird and Robin and I walked all over downtown and met a lot of native Santa Fe people. Robin and I will go to a party at their house."

"It's a festival at one of the Pueblos," Robin explained. "Duke started talking with the vendors selling art in front of the Palace of the Governors. You won't believe what happened. It turned out Duke was carrying around a card for one of the artists, that he had brought with him from India."

"Yes," said Duke. "Business Card Guru give this to me before I leave. He did not say what to do with the card, so I just keep it in my pocket. I like that card. Very beautiful red paper with picture of black pot on it. When I see those pots just like it here in Santa Fe, I show card to one maker. She tell me who is the person that goes with that card. So I met him."

"Yeah," Robin said. "It turned out the artist's son had been to India a couple of years ago. We figured out he left the card with Business Card Guru, who gave it to Duke."

"But Duke wasn't even planning to come to Santa Fe," Michaela noted. "He was only supposed to be in San Francisco and Las Vegas."

On the plane to Santa Fe, she'd heard about this so-called Business Card Guru giving Rennie's card to Duke's uncle, but was skeptical. This new story didn't seem any more likely. Duke could have picked up the card somewhere in Santa Fe before they reached the Plaza.

"And Chicago!" Duke added. "And Petaluma!"

"Yes, yes, I know," said Michaela. "The grand tour. But not here; not New Mexico. He only came here because of me."

"Well, I can tell you, the whole thing was really exciting," said Robin. "This Business Card Guru sounds incredible. Grass and Seabird are already planning to go to India and meet him as soon as they can, and some of the artists from the Pueblo want to go too. Duke said they can all stay with his family."

"Wow," was all Michaela could come up with. She didn't want to deal with whether Duke's story might be true, and, if so, what that would mean. She had more than enough to think about already.

When they pulled up to the hotel, Robin expelled six or seven more questions exiting the car. Michaela, trying to be civil, said, "I'll call you tomorrow." Duke just smiled, and Robin finally waved, said, "See you in the morning," and drove off.

◊ ◊ ◊

Michaela headed inside, as Duke watched Robin's tail lights disappear into the darkness. Finally, he followed Michaela into the lobby and caught up with her just as the elevator opened.

"I'm not tired," he announced, as they got in and Michaela pushed their floor. It was nearly ten o'clock.

"Good," Michaela said. "Wish I could say the same."

"I will come with you to your room and help you."

"I don't need your help," she said abruptly. Then added, "I mean, thanks, Duke. But, you know, I work faster alone."

"I will come to your room and help you go faster," he said, following her off the elevator. "Just for one minute."

"One minute, then you leave."

Michaela slid her key card in, but instead of the little green light to enter, she got the red one showing she couldn't. Irritated, she tried the handle anyway, but of course it didn't open. She examined the card to be sure she was putting it in correctly, then pushed it in and out several more times, using different speeds and twists of the wrist. No green light.

"Shit!" she said. "I'm going to have to go back downstairs and get this damn thing re-magnetized." She started toward the elevator.

"I try first," Duke said, snatching the card out of her hand.

"Duke, it's not going to work. Just give it back and let me ..."

But Duke already had the door unlocked and was holding it open for Michaela. She stared at him as she walked past and into the room.

"I don't know what you did, but thanks."

"You are welcome. All kinds of cards always work for me. It is because they like me and want to do what I say."

"Ohh-kaay," Michaela said. Again, she did not have time to think about or respond either to Duke's actions or his words. She just had to get inside and do all this stupid work, when all she wanted was to take a shower, get comfy in the bed, and go to sleep.

Duke followed her inside. "Here is card key back," he said.

"Take this." She handed him her purse. "Just put it in the big side pocket."

She set her case on the bed, and began clearing the desk.

Why was she putting so much effort into this? The clothes designing had just been for herself, and she hadn't intended to do anything with it. It had simply happened to her, without any effort or intention on her part, but it had felt really good. She was expressing herself – without thinking about results or wanting anything from it – and greatly enjoyed that feeling.

Now she had to stay up all night, at someone else's whim. A rather demanding someone, to be honest. She now felt she had to please Dorothea and give her what she wanted. And it was supposedly in her own best interest. She didn't really see how this was helping her spiritually as Dorothea said. But maybe she just didn't understand yet.

Michaela sighed. She had said she'd do it, and would be disappointed in herself if she didn't come through. But she'd already sketched every style she could think of, and they had completed only one design Dorothea wanted. What else could she possibly create that Dorothea would like? And then she'd have to come up with another one, and yet another after that. It was impossible.

Well, she had to try. She spread out her pencils, placed several sheets of paper on the desk, and sat down. In no time, without even thinking about it, she was completely absorbed.

She was not aware that Duke had stayed in the room. She also hadn't noticed when, putting her room key in her purse, he found the stick of incense he'd given her earlier and pulled it out.

While she was preparing her workspace, Duke lit the stick and placed it so most of the length protruded over the edge of the glass-topped bedside table. He found a bible in the drawer and placed it atop the unlit end of the stick to hold it in place, then set a small metal trash can underneath the burning end as an ash catcher.

While Michaela sat at the table lost in concentration, occasionally holding up a page and saying, "hmm," or "wow," Duke lay stretched out on her bed, his eyes closed and a little smile on his face, eeeing and ahhing quietly to himself. Meanwhile, the incense burned away.

◊ ◊ ◊

When Michaela finally looked up, she was shocked to see that only an hour had passed. It was astonishing. Without much effort, she had drawn three fantastic new outfits, ones she felt Dorothea would love. But how had such a thing happened, and so fast? She hadn't even been trying. In fact, it was as if she had disappeared and it had simply happened. She was blown away. She was as surprised at the unexpectedness as much as when she first started sketching clothing designs a few short weeks ago.

She looked again at the clock to confirm it had only been an hour. Her gaze went from there to the thick bible. Underneath poked the remains of an incense stick, and a small pile of ashes. How strange. She was sure she hadn't lit any, nor even noticed it burning. Though now that she was aware of it, there was that smell, the same kind Rennie used. Then she saw Duke, sprawled out asleep on her bed.

Michaela shook her head, stepped over to the edge of the bed, and sat down beside him.

"Duke," she said softly. "Duke. Wake up. You have to go to your room now." Duke gave a low growling "eee" and rolled over, wrapping an arm around Michaela's waist.

"Robin," he said.

Michaela unwound his arm and gave his shoulder a shake.

"No, no. It's Michaela," she said. "Wake up now, Duke."

Duke sat straight up and was wide awake. "Eeee," he said. "Okay. The incense is finished. I go now. But I help you go faster, right?"

"Umm, right, Duke. Sure. Yes. I go … went … very fast. I'm all finished."

"Good." He smiled, hopped up, and was out the door before she could say another word.

◊ ◊ ◊

Michaela sighed deeply. She was exhausted but also strangely refreshed and satisfied. At last she could get ready for bed. All she wanted was unconsciousness. But when she finally settled under the covers, the day kept replaying itself. Waiting for Dorothea; the uncomfortable car ride with Dirk; everything she'd experienced at their house. Then Robin and Duke's story about the card; and this last hour in her room.

It was one of the most peculiar days of her life. The people she met through LightWorks, like the owners of Eighth, all seemed to live differently than anyone she'd met before. They were like a school of brightly colored fish in a vast ocean, shooting one direction, then the other, all turning together in a single motion, following some set of instructions outsiders couldn't sense. At least, she couldn't sense it.

She tried to imagine Seabird and Grass and Robin and Duke connecting with the Indians in the plaza, thanks to this supposed Business Card Guru. What was the likelihood that Duke had carried that card all the way from India? But if he had – and Michaela had to admit, she was more open-minded about such things than she used to be – then what the hell *was* that all about? Maybe she should go to India herself and meet that Guru. Maybe he'd take her card, and give it to someone who would one day mysteriously turn up at her door and present her missing radish.

Radish-red-on-white was the color combination of the final dress she designed for Dorothea. She just now made that connection. Or was it a connection? No, it had to be just a coincidence, and it was silly to think it was more.

But if she was honest with herself, she really did feel there was something more to what she was experiencing here. Something she couldn't comprehend. How else could she have just sat down and created three – she had to admit – brilliant designs, all in less than an hour?

And Duke was taking credit for some of that, too. He said he would help her go faster, and she had gone faster. He had stayed with her – lit the incense – fell asleep on the bed – the whole time she was working. What if he did have something to do with the intense creative burst she'd had? Incense…intense, she thought sleepily. Intense incense… suspense… compense.

In her dream it was Dirk. "I tried to give it to you," he said. "But you didn't want it."

He was pulling lettuce leaves out of a drawer. Wilted lettuce leaves, and handing them to Michaela. They were in the kitchen at his and Dorothea's house. But no, she thought, what he tried to give her was not want she wanted.

"This is all I have," he said. "She ate all the good ones."

Michaela took the pale, droopy leaves from him, but she didn't want them either.

"What would I need these for?" she thought. "Where can I even put them?"

She didn't like iceberg. She wondered if he had any frisee.

Then, the lettuce he was pulling out of the drawer became small rectangular cards. He looked at each one carefully and put it down.

"Not that one. Not that one."

Michaela watched the pile of cards grow on the counter.

"Ah! Here. This one."

He handed a card to Michaela. She looked at it. The Monopoly guy had grown wings and was flying the coop. She put the card in her purse. She hadn't played Monopoly in years, but supposed it could be useful. You never know when you might need to get out of jail.

"That's it. Gotta go," he said, and he was gone.

46
Santa Fe

R IIIIIINNNG
IIIIIINNNG

Michaela didn't know where that awful noise was coming from.

RIIIIINNNG

Must be the doorbell. She hoped someone would answer it. She was too busy… organizing rocks and shells, on the beach… on the beach…so how was there a doorbell?

RIIIIIINNNG

Finally, the persistent shriek pulled her toward consciousness, but it was another few seconds before she figured out that the bedside phone was ringing, and she would have to move if she was going to answer it.

RIIIIIINNNG
RIIIIIINNNG

"Oh for crap sake," she said into her pillow, rolling over to reach for the receiver. "What?" she yelled into it.

"Michaela? Is that you? Who is this? Did that incompetent operator send me to the wrong room, *again*?" The voice was female.

"What? Who are *you*? What time is it? It's … it's…."

Michaela looked at the clock, "Three-twenty," she said, "A-fucking-m. What the hell?"

"Is Michaela there? I wish to speak to Michaela."

She suddenly recognized the voice. "Dorothea? Is that you?"

"Is this Michaela? You know, someone just answered your phone and she was quite rude to me. I hope you'll speak with her."

"Uh, I…that was, um…. Oh, never mind. Wait! Why are you calling? Is everything all right?"

"Yes, of course everything's all right. Why wouldn't it be? You know, Michaela, you shouldn't just assume something's wrong. Because if you expect bad things to happen, they will. You should really look at that tendency in yourself, dear.

"In fact, I'm doing really great. I just woke up a few minutes ago. And, well, you know how creative that half-waking state can be. Or maybe you don't. Anyway, so, there I was, overflowing with creative energy, and I had some wonderful thoughts about the designs, and thought I better call you right away so you could incorporate them before you come over later. Now, do you have a pen? Because you'll want to take notes. I'll hold while you get one."

"But… but… I'm sleeping. I was asleep. I finished the designs hours ago."

"Oh, that's impossible. I saw how slowly you work. You don't have to be defensive, honey, I'm trying to help you out. Did you find your pen?"

"No, Dorothea, seriously. I'm all finished. I was asleep. *Deeply* asleep. Dreaming," she added.

"Of course you were," Dorothea said. Michaela could tell Dorothea didn't believe her.

"Well, just take down these notes anyway. You know. In case you're mistaken and you haven't really finished. I want you to be done in time to come right over in the morning,"

Dorothea said. "Well, later in the morning," she laughed. "I guess it's morning now, isn't it?"

What do I do? Michaela thought. *I can't believe I'm having this exchange in the middle of the night. What is wrong with this woman? I better figure out what to say or she'll never let me get back to sleep.*

Dorothy interrupted her thoughts. "Really, Michaela, this is very important. If I don't tell you what I'm thinking, it will just keep going around and around in my head, and I won't be able to get back to sleep. Now, are you ready?"

I could just hang up. Or I could put the phone down and cover it with a pillow. Oh, hell, I'll just let her tell me what she wants and get it over with. That's probably going to be the fastest way out of this.

Michaela sighed. "Okay, Dorothea, I'm listening."

For the next half-hour, she tried to be patient as Dorothea gave her tips and instruction on various design points. When they finally hung up, Dorothea seemed delighted to have transmitted all her valuable information, and declared that she knew she'd be able to pop back off to sleep, now that she'd passed it all on.

Michaela, however, was now wired, and certain that was going to be the end of her night's sleep. She groaned and lay down, pulling the covers over her head. She unplugged the phone line. No more calls. All she could do was lay there, wide awake, trying not to think about dresses, or Dorothea, or anything else related to this stupid trip.

Except for one thing. Now she was certain she did want to be paid for her time and her work. It had just turned into too much of a hassle, and really wasn't any fun. And she didn't see that she was getting any spiritual benefits either, no matter what Dorothea said. And most crucial, she wasn't convinced Dorothea would give her a recommendation for Eighth. Judging by some of her comments, she didn't actually seem to think much of Michaela's progress on her spiritual path after all.

So Michaela decided she would write an invoice before she went back over there. If they were going to treat her as an employee, at least she wanted to be compensated like one.

47
Santa Fe

"Oh my god. That was the most amazing sex I've ever had. What did you do to me?"

"I worship your body with my body. That is all. And I light the incense first, so our minds and bodies are one."

They lay on their sides, facing each other, pressed together. Robin snuggled more firmly against Duke, who wrapped his leg around hers. He stroked the back of her hair, and kissed her nose, her lips and her chin.

The heavy covers from the hotel bed had been pushed over the side, leaving just a sheet lightly covering them to the waist.

She giggled. "You want to do it again?"

"You can feel that I do, can't you?"

"Yes, I feel you. I feel all of you, inside and out."

She unwound her leg from underneath his, and twisted it over his hip. She slid her hand between them and grasped his cock, moving to where she could push it inside her.

"Oh, heaven," she gasped, bliss immediately overtaking her. "This is incredible." His hand slid down her spine, over her hip, and then back up to take her breast. They kissed and began moving together, Robin groaning against Duke's mouth.

She stopped kissing him long enough to say, "You are amazing."

Duke looked in her eyes and smiled, and drove himself deeper into her.

"Yes," she said. "More. I can't get enough of you, Duke. Don't ever stop. I love you, Duke. I love you."

◊ ◊ ◊

BAM BAM BAM

Now what? Michaela thought. *Another interruption? Am I never going to be allowed to finish my work? There are so many shells to count and organize. Millions and millions of them. How will I ever get the job done if they keep pulling me away?*

BAM

BAMBAMBAMBAMBAM

"Michaela! Michaela!"

"Ungh," she said out loud, waking herself up. She flung herself out of bed and staggered to the door. Without considering who might be out there, or that she was wearing only a pajama top and panties, Michaela opened it wide.

Robin and Duke smiled in at her. Robin had her fist raised, about to hit the door again. Duke held up a large container of coffee and a small white bag.

"This really isn't necessary," said Michaela, falling back into the room and slumping on the bed. "*So* not necessary," she muttered.

Robin and Duke stepped inside. Robin sat at the table where Michaela had been working the night before, and Duke stood behind her.

"Do you know your phone's not working?" Robin asked. "We couldn't reach you. And is your cell turned off? 'Cause it went straight to voice mail. We've been calling and calling."

Robin examined the bedside phone. "Oh, look, it's unplugged. Did you do that on purpose? Were you asleep? Do you know it's ten-thirty? You said you wanted to leave at ten, you know. Did you forget? I thought maybe you went out for breakfast, or had Dirk pick you up, but Duke said you were probably sleeping and we should wake you. At least we got you breakfast. Do you want it? Here."

Robin took the cup and bag from Duke and thrust it toward Michaela.

She sipped the coffee. It was just how she liked it, with a little half-and half and no sugar. She took several larger sips and stood up.

She should get ready. Dorothea said to come at eleven, and she wanted to be on time. She would be professional, even if they weren't.

"Give me a minute," she told them. "Give me fifteen, actually, and I'll meet you in the lobby."

◊ ◊ ◊

They were soon on their way. Michaela had rushed to get ready, but took an extra few minutes to handwrite an invoice on a sheet of business letterhead. It was now in her case, along with the new drawings. She hoped Dirk and Dorothea weren't surprised. But why should they be? They were surely planning to pay her something, even if no one had mentioned it yet. And how would they know what was an appropriate amount, if she didn't tell them? They might be worried about offering too much or too little. This would save everyone an awkward conversation.

"What are your plans today?" she asked Robin and Duke.

It was a relief to Michaela that she hadn't had to worry about keeping Duke busy. He was apparently doing just fine without Michaela. And it was nice that Robin didn't seem to mind him tagging along with her everywhere.

"Gee, we don't really know yet." Robin glanced over her shoulder at Duke. "Grass and Seabird have to work all day.

Duke wants to know more about Native Americans, so we might check out the Wheelwright Museum. But we'll stay close enough that you can call for a ride whenever you want.

"Well, here we are," Robin said, stopping the car in Dirk and Dorothea's driveway. "You're only ten minutes late. That's practically early on Dorothea time."

Michaela got out and Duke took her place in the front seat. With a wave from Robin, they were off. As they disappeared around the corner, Michaela thought she saw Duke kiss Robin on the cheek, but she must have been mistaken. He was probably leaning over to say something to her, and the turn sent him off balance.

The front door was already ajar, so Michaela knocked and then pushed.

"Hello?" she called out.

"That you, Michaela? Come on in," called a voice Michaela wasn't familiar with. She stepped inside and made her way toward its source, which turned out to be in the dining room. A tall, fleshy woman in a long, colorful dress, with a mass of wavy salt-and-pepper hair piled on her head stood by the table. She was examining yesterday's finished design, which Michaela had, at Dorothea's insistence, left sitting out on the table the day before.

"Hi, Michaela, dearie. I'm Lorna Beth."

She put out a long-fingered, multi-ringed hand, and Michaela leaned across the table to shake it.

"I'm the one s'posed to make these into something Dorothea can wear. But don't worry, darling, I can do it. That's my gift. I'll make you proud. Both of you. The only thing I'm wondering about is this fabric. Does it have to be this very one, or can we just go to the fabric store or online, and find something similar?"

Michaela placed her bags down and went around to stand next to Lorna Beth.

"Well, to me, the fabric is an essential element. Part of what makes it unique. I guess it's up to Dorothea to decide, but I think that's a lot of what she likes about my work."

"So she'll just have to get it made then. That oughta slow things down and cost her and Dirk a bit, but hey, they shouldn't mind. Especially since you and me're doing this as service, right? Can't beat those prices, heh, heh."

Michaela squirmed. "Uh, well, uh…actually…I…I'm not…uh. I mean, I wasn't thinking of it quite that way."

"Oh yeah, sweetie! Being in service – that's what it's all about. Just getting to support Thea. What an honor, right?"

"I guess," Michaela pictured the invoice in her case, and felt uncomfortable. She needed to change the subject. "Where is Dorothea? She said to be here by eleven. Is that what she told you?"

"I'm sure she'll be along. Probably lost in the ethers, communing with the ascended Masters, as she will do sometimes. She's not entirely of this world anymore, you know."

"No, I, uh, didn't know that."

"That's right, honey. You must be new. I've been studying with her nearly four years now. My husband doesn't get it, but he puts up with me following her around to workshops all the time. He even moved here to New Mexico with me, so I could be closer. Be more in service, you know. Of course, he doesn't have to work any more; he mostly just golfs. So he doesn't mind. He travels around quite a bit himself."

Michaela wasn't sure how much more she needed to hear about Lorna Beth's life and devotion to Dorothea. But now Lorna Beth had her rethinking the invoice. Wouldn't she be better off being "in service" too? That seemed a lot more spiritual. Maybe she should wait and see how today went. And what if Lorna Beth was right, and they weren't expecting to pay her? But Lorna Beth apparently had a well-off husband to support her. Michaela was a single woman, in business for herself. And she had never said she'd work for free.

In any case, she hoped Dorothea would show up soon so they could get going. This was supposed to be her last full day in Santa Fe and she wanted to make the most of it. And since Dorothea had been very clear about her coming at eleven, Michaela was hopeful that meant she'd want to get started right away, and would not keep them waiting.

She was also eager, if anxious, to show Dorothea the new designs. If Dorothea liked them, she could just go over the details with Lorna Beth and then she'd have done what she came here to do, and could leave feeling really good about the project. Maybe she wouldn't need to charge them for her time, after all.

And tonight, once they had successfully completed the project, maybe Dorothea and Dirk would want to have dinner with her. But if not, Michaela would go out anyway, and offer to take Robin and Duke. She hoped she might even have time for a little shopping first.

Eleven thirty. No Dorothea. Lorna Beth and Michaela had finished discussing yesterday's completed dress and had nothing else to do. Michaela wandered back to the photo gallery in the living room and examined every picture, even though she had looked at most of them yesterday. Eleven forty-two. She went back to the book display case, and again felt that nagging annoyance that they had used her artwork to make a product and sell it, without asking her permission or giving her credit.

Where was everyone? Not only was Dorothea late, but the house was quiet. No one seemed to be moving around in it anywhere. Even Dirk hadn't shown up.

Finally, frustrated and bored, she returned to the dining table, where Lorna Beth had pulled out one of the chairs and sat calmly knitting. It was just past noon.

Michaela said, "You know, Lorna Beth, I was planning to wait for Dorothea's okay, but we really could go ahead and look at the three new designs I finished last night. I mean, since we're just sitting here with nothing to do, we may as well work on them now. I'm nearly positive she's going to like them."

"Hmmm. I don't think so, honey. Thea would want us to wait for her."

"I'm sure she'd prefer that, but since she's not here, and since we don't know how long it will be 'til she *gets* here, maybe we should just go ahead anyway. And, I mean, wouldn't she want us to make the best use of the time? So we can all be finished faster?"

"Nope. No, dearie. She'd want us to wait."

"But don't you have other things to do today? We've been waiting over an hour."

"Oh, no, darling. This is nothing. I waited for her once from ten 'til after five. You just never know what spirit might need Dorothea to do, or how long it will take. That's why I brought this knitting. You should have brought something, too. You know, I might have a magazine in here," she said, waving at her knitting bag. "Want me to check?"

Michaela was so frustrated, she couldn't even answer Lorna Beth. She was starting to lose it. She'd had enough. She might have to call Robin, or a cab, or a UFO, or the National Guard – whatever it took to get her out of there and away from all this endless Thea-centricity. She just wanted to do her thing – finish what she had said she would do. Simply fulfill her commitment and leave.

"Well, look," Michaela said, trying to appear calm. "She could be hours yet and I can't wait that long. I have to leave Santa Fe tomorrow. So I'm going to go ahead and pull these out and tell you about them, and you can just sit there knitting. You can't help it if you hear what I say, and it won't be your fault if Dorothea isn't happy about it. Okay?"

"I guess I can't stop you, sweetie," Lorna Beth answered.

Michaela put her case on the table and opened it, pulled out the three new drawings and put them on the in a pile. She also took out the invoice and placed it under her purse on the floor.

Just then, there were sounds from the back of the house. A door, some footsteps, and, a few seconds later, a flush. Then more footsteps, this time moving toward them.

Both Michaela and Lorna Beth turned toward the sound. In a moment, Dorothea appeared. Her hair and makeup were done, and she wore a long, sweeping, silk dressing gown in a deep shade of royal blue.

"I made that for her," Lorna Beth whispered loudly to Michaela.

"Everyone's here. Good. Good," Dorothea said. "I just have a few more things to do and then I'll join you. Where's Dirk?"

"We haven't seen him, Thea," said Lorna Beth.

"Hmph," Dorothea said. "Michaela, could you be a dear and bring me some toast with butter and honey, and a glass of grapefruit juice? I'll be in my study. You can leave it on the table just outside the door."

"What?" said Michaela. Was Dorothea actually asking Michaela to serve her breakfast? She had to be kidding.

"Um, so, Thea, shouldn't we go ahead and get started? Don't you remember you said to come at eleven? Lorna Beth and I were both here on time waiting for you, and now it's after 12:30 and...."

Lorna Beth interrupted, "I'll get your toast and juice, Thea. me do it. I already know where everything is, and how you Just go on back to the study, and don't worry about us. right here waiting when you're ready. And actually, I e, but Michaela didn't get here until ten after."

d at Dorothea, who smiled back, then turned to

ela, if you're going to be late, then you can't who may get held up once in a while. ion, you know. Don't you remember we workshop?"

Michaela was too stunned to form a reply.

Dorothea said, "You know, Lorna Beth, never mind taking it to the study. Can you just bring my toast and juice to the table? I'll eat right here while we work. Michaela's right. We'll all be done sooner if we get started. And I am excited to see what else you've done, Michaela. How did it work using my ideas after we talked last night?"

Michaela hadn't made a single change after that ridiculous conversation, but fortunately, most of Dorothea's so-called inspirations were ideas Michaela had considered aloud, and Dorothea had seemed open to, the day before. What Dorothea thought were her own brilliant bits of insight were merely reflections of what she had heard. So, the fact was, most of them actually were incorporated into the new designs.

Since Michaela did not want to argue with Dorothea about whose ideas they were, she merely said, "I think you'll like how everything turned out."

She took the three pages and spread them out on the table, then moved aside so Dorothea could get a better view.

"Hmmm. Hmmm." Dorothea lifted and examined each page in turn. After several minutes, Lorna Beth came back in with breakfast on a tray and set it at the far end of the table. Dorothea put the last page down and looked at Michaela.

Michaela couldn't help but feel nervous waiting to hear what the other woman thought. It had been an amazing experience, the way the drawings just flowed from her subconscious. She really hoped Thea would like them.

"Michaela, these are just right. They are going to be perfect for me to wear for all my events, and for tapings and talk shows. I can just picture myself in them. Oh, my, I am so excited. You did a great job with these designs. Isn't it amazing what happens when you're inspired by spirit?"

Michaela felt a rush of happiness. Finally, she was appreciated! She felt she had been waiting forever to be acknowledged in this way. And spirit *had* worked through her.

Dorothea could tell, she had just said so! Michaela had suspected that might be what had happened, but didn't want to get her hopes up. But Dorothea had recognized it, and she should know. Now Michaela felt she really could ask Thea for that reference for Eighth. Her work was "inspired by spirit." That's all those guys needed to hear, she was sure. Now maybe she would get the job, if it wasn't too late.

Dorothea continued. "These three really are a leap beyond the one from yesterday. I do love that one too, of course. I still want it. But these three – incredible! It still just amazes me, even now, how connected I am. I just woke up in the middle of the night, tapped into that unlimited creative spirit, and it spoke to me, and this is what came out of it. Good thing I called you, Michaela. I have to thank you for taking notes on my flow of divine creativity, and then being able to render it so well on paper. And you know, I thought you weren't really paying attention on the phone last night."

Michaela's elation dropped to numb disbelief, then became utter horror and panic. She could not have imagined being made to feel worse than when she was rejected at Eighth, but somehow Dorothea had accomplished it.

For a moment, Michaela thought she was going to faint, or cry. Then she started to get mad. In fact, she was furious. This was the last straw. She had had it with these people and their so-called spirituality. Dorothea, Lorna Beth, and all her other weird-named, turquoise-wearing followers. Those horrible Eighth guys. Even Rennie. They were all delusional.

She took a deep breath and looked directly at Dorothea. She was going to set this crazy woman straight.

"Dorothea," she said, "Those were my ideas. I told them to you yesterday. You must have forgot, and thought you came up with them on your own. I didn't change or add a single thing after we talked last night. Those designs were done before you called. In fact, you're right, I was hardly even listening."

"OH!" said Dorothea, her mouth open.

"Thea," Lorna Beth started to say, "Of course she's lying about the…"

Dorothea whirled around. "SHUT UP, Lorna Beth." Now it was Lorna Beth's mouth hanging open, and after standing frozen for a moment, she ran from the room. A second later, she came back in, grabbed her knitting and bag, and left again, slamming the front door on the way out.

Dorothea turned back to Michaela, who was fuming silently, reviewing and adding up of all the injustices that had been done to her of late.

"Now Michaela, dear, I want you to sit down," Dorothea pulled out a chair, but Michaela stayed standing. "Here, honey, have some tea."

Dorothea reached for the mug Lorna Beth had prepared for her and set it in front of Michaela.

"Go on now. Let's both just sit here together, and discuss this calmly."

Dorothea swept her gown out of the way and sat. She patted the empty chair next to her.

"Come on, now. We'll figure this out. It's going to be okay."

Michaela was reluctant to sit. However, she should be reasonable. If Dorothea wanted to discuss it with her, and there was some way to salvage the situation positively, she wasn't going to be the one to prevent it. She slowly lowered herself into the chair.

And Dorothea immediately jumped out of hers.

"Oh, dear! I forgot something important. Now Michaela, honey, don't worry about a thing. You just stay right here. Drink some tea. I'll be back in the shake of a skunk's tail."

Michaela pushed the tea as far away from her as she could. She gathered all the drawings, straightened them into a pile, and set them far from the tea. And from Dorothea.

As Thea disappeared into the back of the house, Michaela heard the front door open and close. A few seconds later, Dirk appeared.

"What's going on?" he asked.

"What do you mean?" Michaela said.

"I saw Lorna Beth driving out of here like her ass was on fire. She rolled down the window and screamed something at me, but I couldn't make it out. What happened?"

"I don't think I can explain. Ask Thea. And, hey, as long as you're here, take this." Michaela stood up and handed him her invoice.

"What is it?" he asked, taking the sheet from her. He looked at it, then up at Michaela, then back down at the page.

"My fees. You'll see they're greatly reduced. I just charged you per design. My hourly rate would be much more."

"Invoice? Thea said this wasn't going to cost anything. Just the fabric. You and Lorna Beth were gifting your talents."

"No, we never discussed that. I'm sorry you made that assumption. But this is much less than my normal fee would be, so I guess you could say it's a partial gift."

"It wasn't an assumption, it's what Dorothea *told* me."

Michaela smiled. "Then I'm sorry she made that assumption, but as I said, she asked me to come, and she sent the ticket. A check will be fine."

Dorothea flew back into the room, straight past Dirk, and excitedly took Michaela by the elbow. She was carrying a large manila envelope.

"Here, Michaela, sit back down. I want to show you something. I have just the thing for you."

"Thea, I want to talk to you about this," Dirk said, waving the invoice, which Dorothea ignored.

"Not now, Dirk, honey. I realized I made a big mistake with Michaela and I need to make it right. I didn't make her feel appreciated for what she did, coming all the way here and using her talents to make these beautiful dresses for me. I don't know what I was thinking, but you know how I am about something like this. When I make a mistake, I fix it. I'm going to make this right."

"She doesn't want appreciation, Thea. She wants money."

"Oh, there's really no difference, Dirk. Everyone wants appreciation. Money is just a form it takes.

"Now, Michaela, I'm very sorry for the confusion about the designs. I know spirit works through you, too, even if you can't comprehend it as well as I can. So I understand you weren't completely lying about who had the ideas. And I also apologize for you having to wait. I know you must understand that I lose touch with this plane because I spend so much time on higher ones, but that doesn't make it any easier for everyone to have to put up with me. That's really hard for most people. I know that. Even Dirk. You wouldn't believe how frustrated he gets, and he's used to it."

Oh, she believed it. Dirk seemed about two beats away from his head exploding right now.

"So, I'm going to give you one of these." Dorothea reached into the envelope. "They usually only go to my most advanced students, at a special training we give only once a year." She pulled out a single sheet of paper. "You can come next time if you want. But you don't have to wait, you can have yours now."

She lay the sheet on the table. It was a diploma.

The paper was vellum-colored, and embossed with a half-inch border of gold. Near the top left corner was printed the LightWorks logo. Underneath it were the words:

```
  LightWorks Shamanic Meditation Retreats
      and Sha-Woman Dorothea Light
             Hereby recognize

                (Blank line)

For successfully and proficiently completing the
                  course

            "Accessing Spirit"
```

Below that were two more lines, one also blank but labeled "date," and the other with Dorothea's signature.

"Now, you see, Michaela, this line would normally have your name written in when we give you the diploma, and the date would be filled in too. Seabird does those because she has very good handwriting, and she uses one of those gold calligraphy pens, so it looks really pretty. But, since she's not here, and it wouldn't be as good if Dirk or me did it for you, you can just fill it in yourself when you get home. You're an artist, so you probably have good handwriting and a gold pen too. But I do have..." and here she reached back into the envelope, "this for you, too."

She pulled out an oversized gold star, about two inches across, and peeled off its paper backing. She affixed the star to the top right of the certificate.

"There! Isn't that attractive? I'm proud of you, Michaela. You've been learning so much."

"If she's learning all that much, shouldn't she be paying us, instead of the other way around?" said Dirk.

Michaela was astounded. This was how Dorothea saw fit to show her "appreciation?"

"You're giving me a gold star?" she asked Dorothea, just to be sure she wasn't missing something. "For real?"

"A gold star AND a diploma. Oh, and a coupon, too," she said, turning the envelope upside down so the remaining item, a slip of lime green paper, dropped onto the table.

Michaela couldn't help herself. She picked it up and read aloud.

"Thirty-percent off our featured item, online or in the bookstore. A Dorothea Light Authentic Paper Doll. Place this realistic Dorothea replica on your altar or by your bed for inspiration every time you look at it. New outfits coming soon."

Dirk said to Dorothea, "Did you know she was going to

charge us? How hard is it to sit around coloring pictures of dresses? Maybe we should open a kindergarten."

"Maybe you should," Michaela said, waving the certificate. "And then everybody can get a big gold star."

"No, no! Those don't go to everybody, Michaela," Dorothea said. "They're special. You have to demonstrate a certain level of spiritual growth."

"Thea!" Dirk barked. "Do you really think Michaela cares about your diploma? She doesn't want spiritual growth. She's obviously more about growing her bank account."

"That's not true!" Michaela said. "I DO want spiritual growth. I just don't see how I'm supposed to get it from waiting around all day. And by being disrespected," she pointed at the breakfast tray, "or by getting a stupid diploma," she shoved the paper at Dorothea, "and by being ripped off."

She waved the green coupon in the direction of Dirk. "This is illegal, you know. I didn't give you permission to reproduce and sell my artwork. It's plagiarism, or piracy, or something like that. Anyway, it's stealing."

"But, Michaela, we didn't steal the doll," said Dorothea, "You gave that to me, fair and square. Dirk and I thought you'd be happy to share it with all the other seekers in our little LightWorks community."

"I bet *he* didn't think that," Michaela said. "I bet he saw a new product to sell, and figured I was just another one of your little followers who would put up with anything you dished out. Well, sorry, but that's not me."

Michaela's hands shook as she opened her case and slid the drawings inside. She grabbed the certificate and the coupon and stuffed those in, too.

Dorothea looked horrified as Michaela packed up.

"But, you can't take those," she wailed. "Those are my dresses. My beautiful new outfits. I have to have them. Dirk, I have to have those drawings. Make her give them back. Give her a check or…or…whatever she wants."

"Oh for pity sake, Thea," Dirk said.

Michaela started toward the door.

"Dirk, I'm not kidding. If those drawings walk out the door, I...I...don't know what I'll do. My life will be ruined. I'll never get over it. It will all be your fault. Make them stop."

Michaela opened the front door. She had her cell phone out, and was dialing Robin.

"God damn it!" Dirk said. "Okay, okay."

He followed Michaela to the door. "Wait!"

Michaela ignored him.

"Okay, please, Michaela, just hold on a minute. I'm sorry, okay."

Michaela hung up her phone before Robin's started ringing. She turned to Dirk.

"What?" she asked him. She could hear Dorothea inside the house, moaning, "My beautiful new dresses. Save them, Dirk, save them."

"I'll give you a check right now. Just leave the drawings, will you?"

"No. I'm not going to do that."

"Please, Michaela. You can't imagine how unpleasant she gets when she's this worked up about something. My life will be hell from now until Christmas if she doesn't get those drawings back."

"Well, sorry, Dirkie-doodle, old pal, but you married her, not me."

"I'll give you cash, okay? Extra cash. Double. I'll make sure everyone knows you designed the outfits. She'll thank you in her next book. You'll get other clients; lots of them."

"Nope. Thanks, but no thanks. This isn't even my usual work. I started out doing it as pure creative release, and that's what I'm going back to. If my designs end up being made and worn, great. But that's not my part of it."

"Shit," Dirk said. "I'm really screwed here. What am I supposed to do now?"

"I'll tell you one thing you can do."

"What's that?"

"You can quit selling my doll, that's what. Or you'll hear from my lawyer."

48
Santa Fe

*R*obin lay on her stomach, arms and legs stretched out from her body in four equal quadrants. Duke lay atop her, his weight partially resting on his elbows, his forearms under Robin's upper arms, his legs between hers.

Robin, recovering from another astounding orgasm, felt each of Duke's slow, methodical strokes as a shuddering echo of that pleasure. He had come a few times already himself, and was in no hurry.

She had never experienced sex anything like this before. They had become Shiva and Shakti, Adam and Eve, Yin and Yang. She and he were the duality of the cosmos; drawn together, thrust apart, in endless repetitive delight. They had entered a universe of sexual consciousness, where your lover's skin and scent are as necessary as breathing. There was no time, and the place was irrelevant. It's just you and your other, two aspects of a single existence, playing with the rules of reality as your beings explore the nature of oneness and separateness.

It was the crack cocaine version of sex.

When her cell rang, Robin had only to stretch a little bit to reach it, tucked under a pillow for easy access. She glanced at the screen – Michaela. She raised her free hand for Duke to stop, and he paused as she wiggled backwards, to wedge him safely inside her while she handled this bit of business.

"Hello? Michaela, is that you? How is everything? Are you done now? Are you ready to be picked up? Uh huh. Uh huh. Oooh," she squeaked, as Duke slipped out of her. "No, that was nothing. Just a big…spider. We'll be there really soon." She closed the phone.

Duke had taken what was left of the stick of incense into the bathroom to flick the burning ember from its end into the sink. Without a word, they quickly got dressed, paused at the door for a short grope, and were soon on their way.

◊ ◊ ◊

Michaela was waiting by the curb half a house away from Dirk and Dorothea's driveway. Robin pulled up and they went through the now familiar ritual – Duke hopped out and squeezed into the back, and Michaela and her bags took over the front passenger seat.

"So how did it go? Was she happy? Did she love them? Did you do everything you needed to do? Are you all done now, or do you have to come back here again later?"

"No!" snapped Michaela.

She sighed. There was no need to take it out on Robin. "No," she said again, "I'm not going back. I'm all done in there." Forever, she thought.

"You don't sound very happy. What happened? Did Dorothea make you wait a long time?"

"Well, yes, for starters. But that's not all. It was a disaster."

"Why? What went wrong? Was it the dresses, or something else?"

"Look, Robin, I don't want to talk about it. Let's just say, I don't think I'll be attending any more LightWorks events in the future."

"Oh, what a shame," Robin said. "You seemed to get so much out of the last one."

It's true, Michaela thought, she *had* gotten a lot out of the workshop. Somehow, the experience in Colorado had really helped her. She truly believed, even now, that she had opened up spiritually and touched some deep places in herself, ones that she didn't know she had. And she'd connected deeply with some of the people there, too.

With all that had happened in Santa Fe the last couple of days, she had forgotten those things. Now, knowing Dorothea and Dirk better, she wondered how it had even been possible. Had she been fooling herself? Because certainly, being with them one-on-one, or one-on-two, had been a nightmare. She couldn't see having anything to do with those people ever again, personally or professionally.

"Eeee," said Duke. "It is like that in India too. There are some who are very good at being teachers but very bad at being people. Most people know: You can listen to those teachers and learn from them, but don't try to be close with them, or it will be a lot of trouble for you. But someone always doesn't realize this, and gets too close, and causes herself suffering."

"Wow, Duke," Robin sighed deeply. "That is so profound."

They were stopped at a red light. Robin turned around to look at Duke and forgot to turn back. The light became green.

"Robin!" said Michaela. Robin quickly brought her attention back to the road and touched the gas.

Michaela looked at Duke. He was staring at Robin like a dog waiting for his supper. Then she took a good look at Robin, who was blushing and smiling. She had the sensation of being outside of some private communication between the two of them.

"Hey," Michaela said, looking at Robin. "Is something going on with you two?"

Robin quickly glanced at Michaela, then at Duke, then back to the road. She didn't say anything.

Michaela twisted around to look straight at Duke, who was now staring back at her, a huge smile on his face.

"We are in love," he said.

Robin giggled. They were almost to the hotel.

"In love?" Michaela repeated. "You're in love?"

It seemed so unlikely to Michaela, she couldn't quite get a handle on it.

"Both of you? Robin, are *you* in love?"

"Well...yes."

This strange concept did its best to plant itself, and gradually began to grow, in Michaela's consciousness. A related idea emerged and she struggled to express it.

"Are you...?" she began, "Are you actually... ? Are you two...*fucking*?"

No answer. A few seconds later, Robin giggled again. Duke was still smiling broadly.

Michaela couldn't believe it. It was obvious Duke had a thing for Robin from when he first saw her at the airport. No surprise there – a young guy hot for a pretty girl. But she never expected it to be mutual. She'd imagined Robin was more or less babysitting Duke, partly as a favor to her and partly as "service" to Dorothea. She would never have dreamed the two of them might hook up. Though, really, Robin was only a couple of years older than Duke. And Robin, Seabird and Grass had been highly impressed with the fact that he was from India and knew a guru.

But to fall into bed, and say they were in love? That was just weird.

Well, whatever. They were both old enough to do what they wanted, and she wasn't personally responsible for either of them. She was merely doing Duke a favor to drag him along to Santa Fe and then get him settled in Vegas. And now that she was finished with the former, she would be able to take care of the latter, and after that she could go home.

"Okay, then. You're in love. That's great. I'm happy for you both. What about Las Vegas, Duke? Do you still want to go?"

"Eeee! I will go, yes, yes. I will play in the tournament, of course. This is very important to me."

"Okay, then, we're leaving in the morning, early. So get packed up tonight."

"Michaela, eeee, but you do not have tomorrow to take me to Las Vegas."

"I'm sorry Duke. I know you don't want to leave Robin right now, but I can't wait around here any longer. I need to get going because after I help you get set up, I have to go on home. As soon as possible."

"Ahhh. But no, Michaela. I mean, you don't have to take me any more in the plane. I will go with Robin. In this car."

Michaela was taken by surprise. "Oh, well then," she said. "Okay, whatever. That's great, actually."

She wasn't sure why, but Michaela was annoyed by the change of plans.

Robin said, "I used to live in Vegas, for awhile, with a Sufi group out in the suburbs, doing volunteer work. They're cool. We can stay with them for as long as we need."

"What about your commitment here, with LightWorks? Are you going to just leave?" Michaela asked. Although she couldn't see why anyone would want to stay.

"Oh, that's no problem. I was only here because I asked if I could come and help out, and Thea said I could. It's not like they asked me to be here, or even need me. I like to be able to follow whatever opportunity the universe throws my way. Now I know I was here for a reason. Not just to help out at LightWorks, but mainly so I could meet Duke. And now our separate adventures will continue together. It's completely cosmic."

As Robin talked, Duke nodded slowly in agreement.

"So what do you want to do now Michaela?" Robin asked. "It's a lot earlier in the day than you thought you'd be done, isn't it? Do you want me to take you someplace?"

Any desire she'd had for a bit of shopping followed by a nice dinner had evaporated. She was angry and disgusted by what had taken place with Dorothea and Dirk, and she found Robin and Duke's metaphysically-charged mating dance completely annoying.

"You know what, Robin? I think I'll just go home."

Robin started to protest.

"No, really," Michaela said. "It would make me so happy if you and Duke just go do your thing – I mean, do whatever you need to get ready for Vegas. That's going to be great for him – for both of you. I'm really glad you found each other and it's all working out so well. I can get myself to the airport. Really, I'm fine."

◊ ◊ ◊

She held herself together through the necessary goodbyes, changing her travel plans, packing up, and getting to the airport. She focused on each task: check in, security, find the gate, wait for the plane, board. Finally, she was flying toward San Francisco.

At last she could, fully and without distraction, contemplate how utterly fucked up her life was. She had now officially lost faith in all of it and everything. Every aspect was utterly meaningless – her work, other people, any sense of purpose. What was the point in any of them?

She couldn't imagine what she was going to do with herself now. She wished she could go back to how she was before she had started on this whole spiritual quest thing. She'd been oblivious, but happy. But that was impossible. She couldn't undo all she had been through, nor deny that she had changed. She was stuck with where, and who, she was now.

She could think of only two possible actions in this moment: close her eyes and try to disappear, or call over the flight attendant and order a scotch. Not in that order, she did both.

49
Highway 101,
South of San Francisco

*T*his is insane, Michaela thought. What am I doing?

She should have just gone home. A taxi, or even the airporter, would have been fine. She would be almost to the bridge by now, if the traffic on 19th wasn't too bad. But, no. Here she was in a rental car, her stuff in the back seat, driving in the opposite direction.

She should have gone home. So why hadn't she? And where was she headed instead?

L.A.? Big Sur, maybe, or Carmel, or Santa Barbara? None a bad choice. She could stay away, distract herself, not have to face her real life, or lack thereof. If she was in physical limbo, maybe she could stay in emotional limbo as well. Not that it was even working. The depression, disillusionment, uncertainty were all there, just below the surface. She was just hoping to ignore them as much as possible, and that task was easier if she didn't go home.

Well, now, there went the turn she would take to go over to Highway 5, the faster route to L.A.. Which meant if she kept going, she would probably go down the coast. But which charming, restful, coastal town she should make her way toward? And how far should she go before stopping tonight?

Michaela sighed. Stop lying to yourself, she thought. You know where you're going.

There was no fighting it. It was like passing a car wreck, and you just have to slow down and stare. But this time, she was not just the passing driver. The entire horrible wreck was her, too. And the bleeding, half-conscious person inside.

She knew where she was going, all right. She was headed back to the scene of the accident. She was going to stare right in the face of the whole bloody mess. She was going to Eighth.

50
Some U.S. City

Rennie lay on his bed in another moderately priced hotel room, in yet another identical metropolitan area. He should probably change his clothes. The comfortable gray sweat pants and the black tee shirt with SpongeBob in full lotus wasn't cool enough for the interview. For years he had yearned to be in one of the big alternative magazines: *Yoga Journal*, *Spirituality and Health*, and the like, and now he would be featured in all of them. But he couldn't remember which this particular reporter was from. He'd have to check his calendar before going out to meet her – he hoped it was a her.

His new career as a spiritual teacher had taken off so fast, it was as if he had lit the end of a rocket instead of a handful of incense sticks. He even visualized himself riding a roaring, fire-spewing cartoon rocket, the words ACME printed on the side, zooming circles around the planet. Maybe *that* image should go on a tee shirt.

Barely six months had passed since Rennie, in a two-week period of incense-powered frenzy, had written an entire book, come up with a workshop format, and made a plan to take his show on the road. The campaign had worked. A series of book signings and free mini-workshops drew attendance to his longer events. His name was getting out there, and his work was getting known.

Then came blast-off. A starlet attended his L.A. workshop, and it was mentioned on Perez Hilton and TMZ. Right after, he began getting thousands of YouTube hits. Then his book was picked up by a publisher, and now they wanted another one, not to mention DVDs, CDs and workbooks.

In fact, every day he now dealt with some urgent business question. Rennie had not expected this much pressure. He really should hire someone to handle all that – an agent or a manager – but finding one was another big task. It all seemed so extreme for a simple meditation teacher. And it would take time, so in the meanwhile, he had to do it all himself.

At least he never had to worry about whether participants would like the workshops. All he had to do was light the incense, and most people had amazing experiences of all varieties. Deep understandings. Powerful emotional breakthroughs. Insights. Synchronicities.

Therefore, nearly everyone who came to the freebees couldn't wait to sign up for more. And they were not disappointed. Those full-length events, also of course fueled by the incense, required of him only a small amount of teaching. Mostly he simply had them do some variety of meditation or other inner work, while he lit a few sticks. He did teach people how to support each other by sharing their experiences afterwards, and to listen without judgment, and without trying to "help" or advise each other. He knew from his own experience that the best way to support the inner journey was to let people figure it out for themselves.

Newcomers were startled and overwhelmed by the power of their consciousness and the transformations they went through. Experienced meditators discovered aspects of their practice they had previously only heard about or imagined. He was honored and amazed to witness so much positive change, let alone support people through it. That was the good part of what he was doing. That part fulfilled his greatest hopes.

In fact, as word got out, the smallish bookstores and yoga studios with whom he had arranged free book signings and sample workshops weren't big enough to hold the crowds. They were now renting larger meeting spaces and charging a small fee. Rennie had to find bigger venues for his full-length workshops, too, and in some cities he now scheduled two of them.

Even his incense business, now successfully run by Noeletta and her husband Walt, was going well. Wherever Rennie had an appearance, regular incense sales increased. Even though he wasn't selling the special stuff from Ashvin, people wanted to recreate the experience with Rennie as closely as possible, and since that always included incense, they usually bought some along with his book.

But there was one big problem, and oddly enough, the problem was built into the plan: Rennie was the only one who knew why people had such amazing meditations at his events. No one realized it was the properties of the incense, so all the credit was going to him. People thought he was giving them *shaktipat*, or some special teaching, and that was what was accelerating their transformation.

He was getting a word-of-mouth rep as a very special teacher. Google Alerts informed him that his name was appearing in numerous personal blogs. Someone started a Yahoo discussion group about him. The words "master" and "guru" had been floated. Rennie really wanted to enjoy the praise and attention, but the more there was, the more he felt like a liar and an impostor.

Oh, he very clearly told participants, and anyone else who asked, that their increased capacity for spiritual truth was *in no way* attributable to him. Without specifically mentioning the incense, he noted that their expectation of such experiences, plus their willingness to show up, and maybe, too, the speeding up of time and evolution, made it possible. He always put the praise back on something about *them*.

To be fair to himself, Rennie did feel he contributed to the success of his workshops by leading discussions, by guiding people through challenging aspects of what they encountered in their inner dimensions, and by helping them work through on their own the questions raised by their experiences. But he did not want people to think he was causing those experiences.

But despite all his efforts, most people still preferred to attribute their sudden, powerful awakenings to something outside of themselves. And the obvious choice was the person who wrote the book and was now speaking at the front of the room. So, whether he liked it or not, Rennie got the credit. And he was shocked to find that, despite his daydreams and expectations, he did not like the attention as much as he expected. In fact, he felt terrible about it.

This dilemma was on his mind constantly. He didn't know what to do. If he told people about the exceptional properties of the incense, there was the possibility – indeed, the likelihood – that it would become widely used, and then misused. People would burn it indiscriminately. They would light it at parties and clubs. It would make its way into the schools. Unsavory people would hoard the sticks so they became scarce, and then charge large amounts of money for them. Basically, it would be treated as a drug. And then, it would probably become illegal.

On the other hand, if Rennie did not reveal that it was the incense responsible for their spiritual openings, people would continue to credit him. And that would make him the worst of frauds. Obviously, he was in no way a master or guru. But to say so only made his self-appointed "followers" praise him more.

"Rennie is so humble. Rennie is so self-effacing. You can really trust him."

He was freaking out.

In fact, he was worried about this interview. In a short

time, he would have to go down to the lobby and, once again, answer questions about why people who came to his workshops, or meditated with him, or sometimes merely sat in the same room with him, were suddenly capable of having such profound inner transformation. And Rennie would need to give them an answer. Either he would have to explain about the incense, or else he would have to lie. He didn't know what to do, and the last few days he found himself thinking about it constantly. Well, almost constantly.

To be honest, he had a second, smaller, but still worrisome problem, an example of which had reluctantly departed his room a few minutes ago. Suddenly, women were making themselves very available to him. Attractive women. The kind he had gone after, with only occasional success, when he was merely an incense salesman, traveling seeker, and workshop participant. Now it was different. Now, as a teacher, he was suddenly catnip.

At first, this was great. He was very selective, and also, he told himself, ethical, so it wasn't like he slept with just anyone. But there were so many women to choose from. If he was attracted to someone, and it felt right, he would subtly let her know that he was interested – maybe with an extra question or joke while signing her book. Or a hint of a smile just for her. Somehow, any others hanging around would sense what was going on, and disappear at the end of the hour. That left just the one lovely waiting around for him, pretending to browse titles nearby, or flipping through the pages of her freshly signed book while waiting for him to say "goodbye" and "thank you" to the owners of the bookstore or yoga center.

They would go for tea, or a walk. They would usually hit it off, because A) she was already after him, and B) Rennie was a basically good guy who was interested in people, and could focus that interest on her in particular.

That's all he had to do. She would wait for the right moment to kiss him. She would want to cook for him, or offer to take him to a special grove of trees, or to a lake, or the ocean. But he wouldn't have the time, since he was just in town for a couple of days. So she would come back to the hotel, spend the night, and leave the next morning, with promises to get together next time, or maybe she would offer to meet him on the road somewhere.

To his surprise, Rennie actually found this pattern of serial hookups was becoming a big problem. He liked the attention, and had no complaints about the sex. But the superficiality was getting to him. He felt a strong need to be with one special person. He wanted a deep connection, a real relationship. And he wanted to feel rooted. This moving from person to person, place to place, made him feel lonely and lost.

Rennie sighed. He knew the real reasons he wasn't happy. The cause of his suffering was described in every manner of spiritual literature known to man, and in some psychologies as well. He'd wanted something and he got it. So far, so good. That is, until he found he had merely exchanged one set of problems for another. He had achieved his greatest desire, only to find it didn't satisfy him.

Of *course* that's what would happen. Wasn't it obvious? And he knew the solution, too. The only real answer was to continue his own practice as he had always done. But that was also difficult while he was on the road.

"Screw me," he said out loud, feeling very sorry for himself. No, he berated himself, screw that. He could do better. He had an hour before he had to go out to meet the reporter. He would meditate right now.

With a freshly lit stick of incense in the burner, Rennie got himself comfortably lotused-up, and closed his eyes. He took some deep breaths and directed his attention within. Before long he was off. It was that simple. Rennie didn't know he was about to have an inner experience that would be his most profound and life-changing yet.

IVY: Welcome, everyone. How are you? It's Tuesday, the second day of our very special week of Spiritual Makeovers. We have some wonderful guests today. I can't wait for you to meet them.

We're also going to talk to some of you in our audience. We want to hear about your own spiritual makeovers, before and after. No only that, we have folks Skyping in from home with questions. They'll tell us about what they need for their own spiritual makeovers. And you never know, but we might just have a surprise for some of our guests today too.

So let's get started right now. To those of you who don't know her, I'd like to introduce Dorothea Light. Welcome, Dorothea. I'm so glad you could come on the show.

(Audience applauds.)

DOROTHEA LIGHT: Well, it's just my absolute pleasure, Ivy. I couldn't be happier to be here, and to work with folks in your audience. I'm always so thrilled to help people get to a new level on their spiritual path.

IVY: This is your first time on the show with us. I know you must have a busy schedule, so thank you for being here. And before we go on, I have to comment on that dress you're wearing. I just love it. The style reminds me of a monastic robe, but the colors and patterns of the fabric are so vibrant.

DL: Thank you so very much, Ivy! In fact, this outfit came about due to a spiritual makeover of one of my students. After working with me, she got in touch with her creativity for the first time. She was so inspired by my work that she designed this little dress for me, with no artistic background whatsoever, after just a single weekend workshop.

IVY: Is that right? How amazing!

DL: Yes, isn't it? We were going to develop a whole line of clothing together, but unfortunately she decided to go off on her own. I'm afraid I'm not even getting credit for the inspiration. But that's really okay. I do my part to awaken my students, and whatever happens after that, well, I'm just happy to see them go on in whichever direction their paths take them. I was lucky to get this one dress made, though. Another student of mine was kind enough to sew it.

IVY: Well, it does look wonderful on you. Now, those of you in the audience who are hearing about Dorothea's work for the first time, let me introduce you. Dorothea Light is a spiritual teacher, the founding director of LightWorks Shamanic Meditation Retreats, and the author of four books. Her most recent is *Living Lightly.*

(BREAKAWAY TO BOOK COVER)

She's also written *The Light Way of Life, The Light Way to Happiness,* and *Love and Light.* She has numerous CDs, and, Dorothea, I hear a DVD series is coming out soon, too, is that right?

DL: Yes, Ivy, it certainly is. It's called the LightStyle series. The first two DVDs are ready now, *The Meditation LightStyle,* and *The Shamanic LightStyle.* I'm very excited about the DVDs because I think it's an absolute truth that when you actually see someone, instead of just hearing their voice on a CD, you just take them so very much deeper into your psyche. So with the DVDs, it's a way for people who haven't met me to absorb who I really am, and make that a part of who they are too.

IVY: I'm not sure I follow that. Isn't the purpose of awakening for each person to become more of who THEY really are?

DL: Well, of course, Ivy. That's so very much the most important thing about this type of work. To become more of who you really are.

IVY: So how does it help if they... what was it you said, absorb who YOU really are? How does that help them become who THEY really are? Can you explain that to us?

DL: Well, Ivy, you see everyone starts out in this life at a very unique individual place. They come into the planet with different amounts of spiritual expertise or understanding. A few come in with a lot, some with less, and most people with scarcely a whit. You can think of it as a pyramid, with many people at the bottom who don't have a clue. Those folks mostly aren't even interested in seeing their lives as a spiritual path.

Then a lot fewer of them – but still many, many people – are starting to wake up to who they are as spiritual beings, as individual souls. But they still don't have much experience with the path, compared to the ones higher up. So at any point in the pyramid, the more spiritual understanding you have, the fewer number of people are at that level. So naturally, closest to the top, you have just a very few of us, like you and me, who really know who they are in the big picture, and are completely awake to their path. And quite a few of us very near the top end up as teachers in some way to the ones from about the middle on up.

IVY: I have to say, Dorothea, your analogy using the pyramid to rank people's progress as souls makes me very uncomfortable. I don't like the image of people being higher or lower than each other. That doesn't feel like a particularly enlightened way to look at people, with a few at the very top, above everyone else. But go ahead and finish your explanation. I'd like to hear the rest of it.

DL: Oh, please just call me Thea, Ivy.

IVY: Okay, Thea, so tell us, what does the pyramid you're describing have to do with becoming who you really are?

DL: Well, one way for people to wake up to who they are spiritually is to have direct contact with someone who's already there. It's similar to what they call *shaktipat* in the Hindu tradition, but this is the modern version, for how people are now, you know, growing up with television and video games.

You see, with all that electronic sophistication we all have, well, you know, just getting a pat on the head or being handed a flower, the way the gurus used to do, that wouldn't work very well anymore. People today need more action. We're used to a much faster pace. It's evolution. Anyway, before you wake someone up, you have to first, you know, get their attention. So going to a mountaintop, or an ashram in India, not only isn't necessary any more, it's counterproductive. The highest, most enlightened souls make sure they have electronic media. Or, think of all those native tribes around the world that had shamans. It used to be there was a single shaman in an entire tribe of people. He had to walk all the time just to reach everybody, or they had to come to him. Believe me, that shaman wishes he would have had YouTube! So the point is, it used to be much harder for a whole bunch of people in the middle of the pyramid to get to experience what it was like for the few at the top of the pyramid. And the ones at the top, they don't really want to have to reach too far down into the pyramid either. But all the ones below who don't have direct contact with the ones at the top can get their teachings through all the electronic media today. Your use of Skype is a great example.

That's why people are waking up faster and in greater numbers now. Because first they had audio, and then video, and now teleclasses and online workshops to get that direct contact with their teachers. That's how it is with my DVDs. Just by my being, I demonstrate to people how awake I am, and they absorb that by watching over and over again. Most will probably want to buy the whole series of ten. And hopefully by the end of them, they'll be much more of who they really are, because they'll have absorbed my teaching through my essence on the DVD.

IVY: So are you saying that just being around you, or watching your DVDs, makes people more spiritual, and that makes them more who they really are?

DL: That's right, Ivy, exactly.

IVY: And you're sure about this? Because, I have to tell you, it sounds like you're comparing yourself to a guru, or a major spiritual leader – someone who is, you know, very far on the path. Is that what you mean?

DL: Oh, yes, Ivy. You know a lot of those gurus aren't that great, really. A lot of them do the weirdest things. You wouldn't believe it. Some of them even tie sticks to their penises, and then carry around a person with the stick. I saw that in a documentary, can you believe it? I just don't get what's spiritual about that at all, do you? I think it's just silly.

IVY: Well, okay. (Pause) I'm not really sure how to respond to that. But why don't we move on. Thea, we have some film clips coming up later in the show, and we also want to have you take questions from some of the audience. But before we get to that segment I'd like to give our audience a chance to know you a little better personally. To hear some of your story. Can you tell us a little about your early years, growing up?

DL: Of course, Ivy. I see you have my first and second books, *Living in Light* and *Lighter than Light*. I've written most of my personal story there. You know, it was so difficult being a healer as a child. I suffered so much as a young person, trying to express myself around others and not getting any credit for it. It wasn't the kind of abuse you often hear about. Not physical or sexual abuse, like so many poor souls. But it was still quite traumatic, you know. It is so very difficult to be misunderstood, especially for a child.

IVY: Well, I can relate to some of that. Every child wants to be appreciated and loved. However we'd like to hear more about what, specifically, was it like in your family growing up? I think you briefly mention in the first book that you have two older brothers, but you don't speak about your family after that, except in the general sense that they couldn't understand you, didn't accept your psychic and healing gifts, which was difficult for you. So are you close to your family now?

DL: Well, I don't think about them very much now. You know, we've gone our separate ways, very much so, Ivy. I mean, we're not out of touch or anything like that. We do talk whenever we get a chance. I've certainly forgiven my family for their lack of support for me in my developing years. I did, of course, find my way to truth and healing despite everything, you know.

IVY: So, then, you must be aware, Thea, that one of your brothers has written a book – actually it's now a bestselling book – called *The Regular Guy's Guide to Enlightenment*.

BREAKAWAY TO BOOK COVER

DL: Oh! I...no, not really. Well, yes, but, I mean, I didn't think anyone would connect. But...how did you know? We're really very different, in our...in our last names, so I didn't... I mean, you know, we have different ones, so it's not like we're really related or anything. I mean, yes, of course we are, but not in our work, you know. We're not like brother and sister in that sense.

IVY: Well, how did you like this book, then, written by your brother, Guy Fimple? I understand he's reaching a lot of people with it. They really seem to enjoy his down to earth style.

DL: Oh, Ivy! But that book is a joke. It's a travesty. You have to understand. Everyone in my growing up family was a...a... Neanderthal. My brother – both my brothers – they're completely unenlightened when it comes to anything about higher consciousness. Except for when Mama made them go to church once in a while, I don't think they even knew the word spiritual. I can't even say they're even as far up as the middle of the pyramid. They have never understood anything deeper than a wad of spit on the sidewalk.

IVY: Really, Thea? Those are very strong statements. How do you...

DL: (interrupting) They just made all kinds of fun of me about my abilities growing up and they don't understand anything. So whatever Guy wrote in that stupid little book is just to get back at me for being a successful healer and teacher and so well known in my field.

IVY: Yes, but Dorothea, how do you know Guy hasn't learned and changed in all these years? People do start to wake up at different times in their lives. You should know that more than anyone.

DL: Not Guy. He's only as awake as a snake in grass, lying there waiting to bite. He's still trying to belittle me. It's so unfair. I don't know why he would pick on me like this. I wasn't planning to say anything bad about him in public, but now that people know he's my brother, I have to be honest. I have to stand in the light of truth about this.

IVY: So you're saying that Guy isn't really interested in spirituality, he just wanted to make you look bad?

DL: Yes, Ivy, that's absolutely what I'm saying. Thank you for understanding.

IVY: Well, I find that very interesting, Thea. By the way, have you read any part of the book yourself?

DL: No, no, of course not, Ivy. It's important for me to stay focused at all times on the positive. I wouldn't want to read it and have to think badly of my brother. I still send him nothing but love and forgiveness, no matter how mean he is, or how bad he's treated me by writing this.

IVY: Well, Thea, I'd like to read you part of the forward that Guy wrote. I don't think it's quite what you're expecting, and I'd like to share it with our audience.

DL: Ivy! Wait! I'm getting a bad feeling about this. I'm feeling, I'm getting... Yes! It's a message for you from Spirit. (Pause.) Yes. Yes. Okay. Ivy, here's the message. It would not be a wise choice at this time for you to read from this...this...book. The message is ... wait... yes...Spirit strongly recommends that you move on. There are audience members and people at home with a great need to speak with me today. Reading this would not serve the highest good.

IVY: Oh, is that what Spirit said?

DL: Yes. Yes it is, Ivy. It would be a very negative choice for you to read that, um, material today on the air.

IVY: Okay. Well thank you Dorothea. Thank you for delivering that message. However this is my show, and what my own instincts are telling me – and I trust them completely – is that reading this forward from *The Regular Guy's Guide to*

Enlightenment, written by your brother Guy Fimple, is exactly the right thing for me to do. Right now.

DL: But...

IVY: Okay, folks, this is from the last paragraph of the forward. (Reading) "And finally, I gotta thank my one and only sister. Now, Guys! I'm not going to say her name because I don't want all you regular guys going to her and saying, 'Babe! You helped out old Guy. What can you do for me?' That, and I don't want to blow her cover. That might make people tell her, 'Babe! How could someone as together as you be related to a dumbass regular guy like Guy?' I wouldn't do that to ya, Sis. But I gotta say something here. I gotta say to you: Sis! Thanks, girl! You inspired me. You're the real thing. You made a slugmuffin regular Guy like me think that maybe there might be something more than just football, beer and the sofa. Not better than football, beer, and the sofa. Just a more enlightened way to be, while I'm doing football, beer and the sofa. So, Sis, just know that in my book, no matter how you see it, to me you're the Regular Guy of spiritual teachers. And that's the highest compliment I got."

(Audience applauds.)

IVY: So, Dorothea, what do you think? Does that surprise you?

DL: Ahhh... Well... well... Ivy. I, ahhh...

IVY: We'd really love to know your reaction to the passage I just read. How does that strike you?

DL: Well, Ivy, actually, I...I'm surprised you fell for it.

IVY: What do you mean?

DL: It's obviously a trick. He's trying to make me look bad. I'm surprised you don't see it.

IVY: I don't see that at all. Guy has nothing but praise for you, but even so, he's deliberately not identifying you so you don't have to be concerned about the association. If we hadn't outed him as your brother, it's very likely no one would have made the connection between you.

(To audience) Well, folks, since we did make the connection between them, we had what we thought was a great surprise for Dorothea. We thought she'd be pleased to get to spend time with her brother. Now it appears we may have been wrong about that, but we know you're going to enjoy meeting him. So, audience, when we get back, we'll be joined by Guy Fimple, author of *The Regular Guy's Guide to Enlightenment*. And he and Dorothea Light can answer your questions together, and we'll talk with some of you at home about your recent spiritual makeovers, and how Dorothea's and Guy's books have helped with that.

DL: Gaaaahhhh.

(Audience applauds.)

END OF SEGMENT

51
Santa Cruz Mountains

*T*hwwwp ( )Thwwwp ( ) Thwwwp ( ).

The broom swept over the sage-green tiles in even strokes, picking up whatever dust and particles had arrived since yesterday when she'd performed the identical task, always starting in the northeast corner and working her way across the room toward the door.

Michaela was getting better. Thwwwp ( ).

Not better at sweeping. At sweeping, she was about the same. But her attention was improving. The monks were teaching her how to begin to still the mind. Do just one thing at a time, they said. When you sweep, sweep. When you chew, chew. When you walk, walk. When you notice your thoughts have moved elsewhere, gently return the mind to what you are doing.

Thwwwp ( )Thwwwp ( ) Thwwwp ( ).

It had taken awhile, but she'd noticed the practice getting easier. She found she was a lot calmer then when she had arrived three months ago, and she was grateful.

Three months ago, she was a basket case. Especially that first night.

◊ ◊ ◊

Driving from the airport, with no plan or reason, barely a thought about what she was doing or what she expected to accomplish; Michaela had made it as far as the stretch of road where she knew the unmarked drive led to Eighth. But she couldn't find the turn. Cruising back and forth, back and forth, past the same stupid, unhelpful landmarks for nearly an hour, she became more and more frantic with each pass.

How was anyone supposed get to this place? Couldn't those self-satisfied fuckers have put up a sign? Or was their oh-so-spiritual clientele supposed to be so highly attuned, or psychic, or whatever, that they could sense it without using their eyes. Or maybe people were expected to simply teleport in – no need for a car at all. The perfect green solution.

Michaela screeched to a stop on the side of the road, turned off the car, and yanked up the parking brake.

"AHHHHHHHHH! *GOD!* DAMN DAMN DAMN!" She pounded the steering wheel with her palms, and jumped up and down in the seat. She slammed her left arm against the door until it hurt. She nearly opened the door, ready to fling herself out of the car and go up and down the road on foot looking for the entrance. But that would be stupid. The stretch was at least a mile. Plus it was now very dark.

She had to do something. She was not giving up.

But what were the options? Drive back and forth on this road all night, until she ran out of gas? Leave now, sleep at a motel somewhere, then come back tomorrow in daylight? Go home, and try, try again to forget all about this place? So far, all her efforts to forget or ignore Eighth had been a pitiful failure.

Of course, if she did leave now, she could still imagine other, darker options. She could return as a customer, release a box of roaches, and call the health department. Or she could disguise herself, apply as a dishwasher, and then "accidentally" leave the burners on when she left one night, lighting a cigarette on the way out. Ooops. Either scenario was satisfying. But not satisfying enough.

Now, being this close, she did not want to leave. She would simply find a safe place to pull the car as far off the road as possible, and wait there until dawn. Maybe she'd get a little sleep. Then, in daylight, she'd be able to see the turn, go in, and … do what? She had no clue. The plan was terrible, but Michaela wasn't acting on reason. She was being compelled by something much deeper – and much more desperate. She started the car and prepared to ease back onto the road to find the best spot to park for the night.

But before she could move, lights in her rear-view mirror showed an oncoming car. She waited for it to pass. And waited. It was taking forever. The car must have been going ten miles an hour. Well, she thought, that's just perfect. Not another car on the road for the past fifteen minutes, but when she decides to pull out, here comes the slowest driver in the world. Michaela sighed impatiently and tapped her fingernails on the steering wheel.

When it finally rolled by, she stared hard at the vehicle, curious to see what sort of idiot was driving, and to give him a long, sneering glare, even if he couldn't see her. Instead, she was startled to recognize the car. It was the yellow Maserati belonging to the monks from Eighth. And, sure enough, the vehicle was filled to bursting with animated, laughing, maroon-robed Tibetans.

"I'll be damned," she said loudly.

As soon as the monk-mobile had passed, she pulled back onto the road behind it. The car went a few hundred feet and suddenly lurched hard to the right, disappearing into the trees. Even after seeing where it went, she almost missed the spot. But she blindly threw her rental into the darkness where the yellow car seemed to have vanished, and found herself on the gravel drive, which she recognized from her previous visit.

Following the monks to the parking area, she stopped and

turned off the ignition, then hesitated before getting out. Her anger had wilted, and she felt weird and uncomfortable. Surely they would want to know what she was doing here. She had no good explanation, especially at this hour. Any excuse would sound strange at best, maybe even crazy. They would probably tell her to leave immediately.

Well, screw it. She couldn't do anything about that now. She stepped out of her car into the night and took a deep breath of cool, tree-scented air. At once, Michaela was surrounded. She wasn't sure it was the exact same set of monks as before, but she did recognize a couple of them – the driver, whose name she couldn't remember, and Sangmu, who had brought her tea last time. But every one of the six seemed to know who Michaela was. And also seemed, to her shock, completely delighted to see her.

"You came back!" said the driver, who looked young, about Duke's age. "Do you remember me? I'm Darjay."

"And me? Karma?" asked a woman.

They patted her on the arms and smiled broadly. She felt like a long lost pet that had returned to its adoring owners.

"Come inside, dear one," said the oldest monk, whom she recognized. His name suddenly came to her, though she didn't even know she knew it.

"Gyaltso," she said.

"Yes," he answered. "You have come to stay with us, I believe. Let's go inside the monastery, and we will show you where you can sleep."

"I've come to stay?" Michaela asked. "Really?" She wondered why this idea didn't seem completely unthinkable.

"Yes, if you wish. You may live here, and work and study with us. Stay for as long as you'd like."

Michaela closed her eyes and considered the possibility. She had expected to be questioned, judged and sent away. Instead, she was being welcomed. She remembered from last time the strong sense of safety she had from the monks, and the feeling that these were truly warm, caring people. And they really did seem to want her to stay.

Why? Did they need her for something? Was their mission helping lost souls like herself? Whatever their motive, and despite feeling that it was crazy for her to stay, once Michaela let the possibility sink in, she suddenly felt better than she had in months. A sense of calm swept through her. She felt at peace for the first time since…well, maybe for the first time in her life.

All the things she should be worried about didn't seem to matter very much. They passed through her mind as almost a reflex. What would become of her life, her work, her home? Could she tolerate being here, right next to Eighth, when she wasn't a part of it? What would she actually do all day, just hang out with the monks?

The deep calmness allowed her to pay little attention to these fears. She sensed it would all work out, even if she had no idea how. She simply felt that if she stayed with the monks, everything would be okay. This could possibly be the only place in the universe where she wouldn't feel disturbed. She knew she needed to stay.

"Yes," she said. "Just tell me what I need to do."

"Ah!" laughed Gyaltso. "You need to follow us inside and let us find a place for you to sleep. And feed you, maybe. Are you hungry?"

Michaela nodded yes, and she and the monks moved off as a group, toward the large building she had seen before; the one with all the balconies and flags. That meant they would pass the restaurant, and Michaela was afraid to see it completed and nearly, if not already, open. She almost closed her eyes.

But as they got closer, Michaela was surprised to see that little had changed since her last visit. The building not only looked unfinished but, if anything, it seemed more torn apart. The ground was still just piles of dirt; no landscaping whatsoever. The front entrance had been completed, but the rear half of the back end looked like it had been demolished and only partially rebuilt. What was going on? She certainly would have known about an earthquake in the area, especially one big enough to destroy part of a building. She turned to Darjay, walking beside her, and pointed at the restaurant.

"Why isn't it done yet? Did something happen?"

Darjay gave a small shake of his head. "Very sad story," he said. "We monks did what we could, but the difficulties were too great. We are lucky it doesn't affect the monastery and the stupa. They are protected for us, and we will be allowed to stay here no matter what happens with the restaurant and its people."

That wasn't really enough of an explanation for Michaela, but she sensed it was not the right time for more questions. Still, she was shocked to realize that during all this time, while she had been obsessed and freaking out about the place, they were having problems of their own. Rather severe problems, from the looks of things.

Once they reached the monastery building and went inside, Michaela was shown to a small private room with a single bed, a small, plain desk with a lamp and an ergonomically correct chair, and a set of three shelves reaching her knees, with three hooks on the wall above them. On one wall was a painting on cloth that Michaela knew from her art studies was a tongha, and a good quality one from the looks of it. She knew it was a form of religious art, but did not understand the meaning of its geometrical shapes and colors.

After they showed her the sleeping space, she followed Karma to a room with tables and chairs, which must be where the monks ate. As she sat at a corner of one table, Sangmu brought her a bowl of vegetable soup, some fresh, crusty bread and butter, and a cup of tea. Michaela hadn't realized she was hungry, but as she ate, she not only felt nourished, but thought it was the best, most satisfying meal she had ever eaten. Karma sat silently across from her as she ate. If she hadn't been there,

Michaela would probably have started crying. A single tear did slip out, and Michaela quickly wiped it with her napkin.

When she returned to the room, Michaela found that someone had brought up her suitcase and other belongings from the car, but she noticed they had not left the keys. She wondered if they thought she was drunk, or too messed up to drive, but decided she didn't really mind. She wanted to hold on to this new feeling of being safe and cared for. She wouldn't think about whether she would stay or for how long, and if she did stay, what to do about her so-called "real life."

Right now she was perfectly happy not to have a real life. In fact, maybe she would never go back to it again.

◊ ◊ ◊

Michaela sighed as she realized that, for the last several minutes, her mind had strayed far from the act of sweeping. She was briefly disappointed with herself, but then simply let it go. The monks always said that opportunities to attend to the present moment would never stop offering themselves. And if she had a few instances now and then when she managed to stay in that moment, then she was doing just fine. The increasing sense of overall peace she felt was evidence that they were right.

And right here and now, there were some sage-green tiles still to be swept. Right here and now, in this moment, she was sweeping.

Thwwwp ( )Thwwwp ( ) Thwwwp ( ).

COVER STORY: OM! MAGAZINE

The Meteoric Rise, Amazing Revelation, and Surprising Retirement of Meditation Teacher Rennie Morrow: An Exclusive Interview
by Maija Trueheart

When Rennie Morrow joined me at the small café table, I had no idea the hugely popular meditation teacher and former incense distributer was about to radically alter my plans for this interview. Wearing brown hemp carpenter jeans and a white Super Buddha tee shirt, Rennie had an aura of quiet intensity that supported recent rumors of his advanced state of spiritual awareness. Yet he also seemed altogether relaxed and approachable; someone comfortable with the goings-on in this world, even if he was able to transcend his attachment to it, and help others to do the same.

I was prepared to ask him about his personal practice, his teaching, and the fact that so many people reported having remarkable breakthroughs from his workshops. But Rennie came to the table with something else on his mind. And as soon as we'd ordered tea, he revealed it.

RL: It's a great synchronicity for me that you're here at this moment, Maija. I've just had an inner experience that's led me to a crucial decision, and I want to let people know about it.

OM! I'm always honored to be part of someone else's synchronicity, Rennie. Tell me everything. What was the experience like?

RL: I'll get to that, Maija. But let me first tell you the decision it led me to.

OM! Of course! Please go on.

RL: Well, Maija, I'm quitting the road. No more public events, no more workshops. I'll fulfill the commitments I already have, but I won't be scheduling anything new.

OM! That *is* a big change! Especially since you've really just started. Six months isn't a very long time to give your work a chance to develop. Is anything wrong?

RL: No, Maija. Everything's great. The people in the workshops are just wonderful. I'm impressed and moved by their transformation and courage, their inner wisdom. I'll miss that, although I plan to continue working with people in a different way. But letting go of teaching at this level – when I thought this was what I wanted, was what I was supposed to do – that's huge for me.

OM! So why stop? And to do what instead? Go back to selling incense?

RL: (chuckling) No, it's safe to say *that* part of my life is over. It's like this: I've been a seeker and a meditator for a long time. I mention that in the book, but I don't go into detail. And I feel I have a deep practice. I mean, it's hard to be sure, because you might think you're progressing, but how much is just your ego, wanting that to be true? It's the "attachment to getting somewhere" problem. And, ultimately, that doesn't matter. You just keep doing what you do, and follow where it leads you.

Then, about six months ago – just before I wrote the book and started on the road – I had a major upgrade in my inner journey. You might call it an enhancement. It came from an unexpected source.

OM! What was that source?

RL: I'm getting to that, I promise.

OM! Okay, we'll come back to your "unexpected source." So your practice became deeper and...

RL: Yes. Everything happened at once – my inner work and my outer work – it all just snowballed. Suddenly, I saw a way to do what I always thought I should be doing: Going out to share with folks and help them on their journey. The way to do that dropped in on me, all at once, ready to step into. So I did. I was shown a plan about how to do that and I followed it.

Yet at the same time, I was going deeper and deeper in my practice. Getting clearer and more unattached. So this huge rift was growing between my inner and outer life. I had the opportunity to fulfill my lifelong desires. And yet...and yet... at the same time, I wanted more and more to be free of those desires, and my attachments to them.

OM! Sounds like you had very conflicted feelings.

RL: Exactly, Maija! That's been the whole problem. To paraphrase Joseph Campbell, I've been climbing the wrong ladder. But what's cool is that it was the very tool I'm using with others that allowed me to see this for myself. I mean, normally, it would take many years, probably even lifetimes, to move that quickly through manifesting your desires and then realizing their ultimate emptiness. My attachment to the whole trip should have kept me going indefinitely. But suddenly – just now – today – before I came here – I woke up to it. And I'm in shock about the revelation.

OM! So the synchronicity is that it happened now? Right before the interview?

RL: Yes. Hope it makes the article more interesting than if I'm just another teacher, doing what we all do.

OM! Well, yes, Rennie, but the whole point is, you're not just another teacher. There seems to be something special about your being-ness, or your presence. No disrespect, but what you teach isn't that different from many others. Yet the effect on people's practice is reported to be very powerful. I'm very much looking forward to joining you this evening myself.

RL: Thank you, Maija. But the specialness isn't me. And you're right about what I say not being that different. After all, there is just one Truth right? And we're all looking for a way to understand that truth, or some aspect of it, and to explain it to ourselves and to others.

The important part of my workshops – well, as I said, it isn't me. It's this tool I was given, to use with others, but it was a gift to me too. I'm trying to find the best way to share it with people.

OM! So, is that the unexpected source? Now will you tell us what that tool is?

RL: Yes, Maija. It's the secret to everything.

[Here Rennie paused, smiled, and stirred a little honey into his tea, which had been sitting untouched since the waitress set it in front of him.]

RL: So here's what happened. About six months ago, a mysterious package arrived in the mail...

52
Santa Cruz Mountains

*E*very day for the first week, Michaela asked the monks what had gone wrong at Eighth. Whenever she brought it up, they would shrug, smile, and change the subject. Finally, she gave up.

Each day she made her way over to the abandoned restaurant building and stared at it, trying to imagine what could have happened. But there was no way for her to find out. Either none of the monks knew, or they didn't want to talk about it.

They were forthcoming enough in all other ways. They would talk to her about where to find the laundry soap, or the weather, or why her life sucked. They helped her return the rental car to the airport and get things she needed from her home, both of which someone had simply gone and done for her. They patiently explained to Michaela whatever she wanted to know about their ceremonies and rituals.

When she asked Gyaltso what was expected of her at the monastery, he said that she was free to spend her time however she wanted. She could join them for meditation, rituals, meals, chores, and errands. Or not, as she wished. If she wanted, they could give her some tasks to do. So gradually, she'd taken on some responsibilities: sweeping the sage-tiled entrance hall, working in the large garden, and helping prep for dinner by chopping the same vegetables she'd tended to earlier.

The monks were also attentive to her questions about their practice, and tolerant of her frustrated complaints about her failures with it. She was not much better at sitting meditation now than when she started, but at least she could stay with it a little longer. It helped to learn that being unable to control her thoughts and feelings was normal for beginners, and didn't mean she was doing something wrong. But still, she struggled with all the crap her mind and emotions seemed to generate. It made her feel crazy. She always wanted to get up and bolt.

Walking meditation was easier for her. After lunch on the second day of her stay, a friendly monk named Nima had asked her if she wanted to go for a walk, and took her on a path through the woods. It quickly steepened as they made their way up the side of the mountain. After ten minutes, they came out of the trees into a clearing, where a large, square, white structure sat facing out over a hillside toward a valley. It was the width of a one-room house, and the height of about four or five stories, depending on how much of it you counted.

The main building was in three levels. At the bottom it was a square going up about ten feet, but without any doors. Above that was a series of steps like a section of pyramid. That part was also about ten feet high, but not as wide, so it sat atop the lower section like a tiered cake. The third level was a huge round dome. And above the dome, a fat conical gold spire rose high in the air.

Statues and objects, colorful painted icons and symbols, and other oddly shaped forms adorned the building, some in their own cutout sections. Prayer flags ran at the corners from the top of the dome to the bottom of the square. The entire building was surrounded by a wide walkway made of sand-colored bricks. Altogether, it was one of the strangest structures Michaela had ever seen, and she had no idea what it was.

Nima stopped at the edge of the clearing and they just stood and looked at it for several minutes without talking. Michaela found the building dramatically beautiful, if you liked that sort of thing. Whatever "sort of thing" it was.

"Okay, I give up," Michaela finally said. "What is it?"

"Stupa," Nima said. "It's the main reason we're here."

At first, Michaela bristled. What was stupid about her not identifying a big, weird, doorless piece of architecture she had never seen before? But since it was uncharacteristic of Nima, or any one of the monks, to be rude, maybe she hadn't heard correctly. She turned to look directly at him when she asked again.

"*What's* the main reason we're here?"

"This. The stupa. Our sect built it, we care for it, we hold ceremonies here. It's open to the public most of the time. You can't tell from this angle, but there's a trail leading to a driveway off the main road. And ample free parking."

"Oh," Michaela said, relaxing a bit. Even though he hadn't called her stupid, she did feel a little ignorant. She'd never heard of a stupa. "What's it for?"

"Look here," Nima said, and walked around to the other side of the building. "This will explain."

He waved Michaela toward two large signs enclosed in plastic and covered, like a bus stop. Near the signs were two benches facing the structure, and a third bench looking the other way, out over the valley. She went closer to read the displays. The first one had a definition, description, and history of stupas, explained their complicated structure and symbolism, and showed pictures of stupas around the world. A second enclosure pictured and described the phases of this one as it was being built, and told you how to "use" the stupa by saying prayers while walking around the outside. Also, there was a request for donations, which you could put through a slot into a large, locked plastic case.

"You see, it is the body of the Buddha, but also the mind of the Buddha. And most important, you can walk around it like this."

Nima began walking on the bricked path, with the building on his right, "And it will help clear your karma and bring you closer to enlightenment."

Michaela followed Nima, walking at the same deliberate pace a few steps behind him. He began chanting, and Michaela recognized it as one of the mantras she had read on the sign. When they walked past the sign again, she read the words so she could see how the unfamiliar sounds were written. After awhile, the short, repetitive phrase became familiar, and Michaela started to mumble it too.

For the next thirty minutes the two of them walked around and around the building. At some point after that, Nima silently slipped away, down the path to the monastery. Michaela decided to stay a little longer since the warming sun and pine scented air were lifting her spirits. She decided she liked the stupa, whatever it was.

◊ ◊ ◊

Unfortunately, her spirits didn't stay lifted. Over the next two months at the monastery, she was relieved not to have the pressures of her life, and of deciding what to do with it, but she still felt bad nearly all the time. She thought it was from being so close to Eighth. Despite her daily meditation practice, she woke up each morning feeling something was wrong. She just couldn't stop thinking about the restaurant and her failure. The abandoned building so close by was like a ghost. She found herself replaying over and over again the meeting with Josef and Angelo, and it still upset her.

If only she could have a do-over of that conversation now, when she was so much better prepared for it. She knew it was crazy to keep trying to prove that she was worthy of something that didn't even exist anymore. She should have felt vindicated that they failed so completely and abandoned the project. But somehow, the fact that it was gone forever, and with it, any chance for her redemption, made her feel worse.

She knew she had to stop thinking this way. She desperately wanted to feel better. Each day, after going outside and staring at Eighth, she would head back past the monastery and take the path up to the stupa. There, she would circumambulate and chant as long as she needed to. She tried to give full attention to the mantra while she walked, as she knew she was supposed to. Despite her efforts, she still carried her obsession around and around the building with her.

But something was happening. Each day, when she got to the stupa, she would be upset, and start out swinging her fists, growling the mantra, and stomping angrily along the path. And then she would start having other thoughts and feelings. Each time it was different. Sometimes she'd remember an event from her childhood. Or she'd feel like she was fighting in an epic battle. Or she'd get an image of riding on the owl spirit again. Or she'd feel lost and sad. Then, things would shift again, and then again, until the negative feelings and energy worked their way out of her system. Gradually her step would lighten, and she'd feel better.

Then, after she calmed down, she'd finally stop walking for the day. But she'd hang around the stupa for a long time after. It felt good there. She would pull weeds out of the bricks, or pick stray leaves and pine needles from the statues, or just sit on the bench looking over the valley, watching the birds fly from tree to tree and the sun move across the sky. Occasionally one of the monks or a passing civilian or two would visit the stupa, and do their thing while she did hers. But usually she was alone.

◊ ◊ ◊

She had been at the monastery about three months when, one day, walking her circles as usual, it suddenly dawned on

Michaela that she hadn't gone over to stare at Eighth before coming up the path. In fact, she hadn't done so for several days. She had, without planning it, come straight to the stupa and begun walking. And come to think of it, she hadn't been angry or obsessing for quite a few days either. She'd simply chanted and walked, while inhaling the mountain air and listening to the birds and squirrels.

How strange. She tested herself to see if it was an accidental oversight, or if she really did feel different. First, she deliberately pictured the restaurant. No reaction. Then she visualized Angelo and Josef, their interrogation and her answers. She replayed the entire experience without getting excited or pissed off or mortified.

Good gracious, was it possible? She actually seemed to be over it. Michaela couldn't believe she had really changed. She kept trying to find a reaction as she circumambulated the stupa, looking for anything that might bring up the bad feelings again.

Nope, nope, nope. When she finally accepted the truth that it no longer bothered her, she was actually giddy, as if she'd been drinking champagne. She laughed with pleasure. Well, this was certainly remarkable. She continued around the stupa, laughter and wonder still alternating with the mantra.

Until – WHACK! She turned a corner, and smacked face-first into another person.

"Hey!" Michaela exclaimed, interrupted mid-giggle. Normally, she'd get mad at this person for facing the wrong direction, since anyone circumambulating properly, such as herself, would come blindly around the corner and hit him. But today she forgave him. He was obviously just ignorant.

She glanced up. The man was wearing a coat and tie, which made him seem particularly out of place. She nodded a greeting, then started to go around him. But as she passed, he placed a hand on her arm, then quickly let go. He seemed nervous.

"I'm so sorry," he said. "You are Michaela, aren't you? They told me you might be here."

She stopped in mid-stride, confused. Who could possibly be looking for her? She had told only a few people that she was on sabbatical, but not where she was. She didn't want anyone to find her. So who was this person? He seemed familiar. She took in the man's elegant clothes, his combed back blond hair and deep blue eyes, and had an unnerving jolt of recognition.

Michaela was suddenly light-headed. Her legs started folding, and she grabbed the corner of the building for support. It was impossible! The man standing in front of her had manifested right out of her very thoughts. It was one of *them*, in real life. He had, for months, haunted her worst daydreams, and more than a few nightmares: *Angelo*, visionary businessman and co-owner of Eighth.

◊ ◊ ◊

Michaela must have blacked out. She came to, sitting on the ground, leaning against the side of the stupa. Her heart was racing. Then she remembered what had caused her distress, and looked up to see Angelo kneeling next to her, looking distraught.

"Michaela? Michaela, my dear, are you all right? I'm sorry I startled you."

He lifted her left hand and patted it.

Great, she thought, *now* he wants to comfort me. And what else did he want? What could he possibly be doing there, and why was he looking for her? Eighth wasn't opening, and even if it were, didn't he remember she hadn't been good enough for it? He wanted nothing to do with her before, so what did he want now?

And how bizarre was it that only minutes before she had realized that, after going crazy about it for all this time, she finally no longer cared? And that she had been giddy about that very fact when she literally ran into him.

It was incredibly bizarre. So bizarre, in fact, that she started laughing again. The fact that he was actually right there in front of her – well, next to her, on the ground – felt like a joke or a cartoon. Everything about it struck her as ridiculous. The restaurant that served "all sentient beings"? The self-sacrificing seafood? The blessing of the plumbing? How could she have taken any of it seriously? Before Michaela knew it, she was laughing hysterically and couldn't stop.

Angelo didn't seem to know if he should try to help her, or to laugh along with her. Finally, he let go and gave a tentative chuckle, and then laughed harder. Still holding her hand, he collapsed onto the ground.

As the laughter subsided, Michaela looked up at Angelo. He seemed concerned, but now he was also smiling.

"So, Michaela, my dear, do I get to know what is so funny?"

"I'm afraid not. I couldn't explain it, or at least not now. It would take too long. Do you want to go sit on that bench? My butt hurts."

That made them laugh again. Angelo got to his feet and helped Michaela stand up. Although she was fine, he seemed to really want to help her. So she let him hang on to her hand while putting his other arm behind her back, and they made their way to Michaela's favorite bench, the one that looked down over the valley.

At first, neither said anything. They both began talking at the same time, then stopped.

Finally, Michaela said, "I guess I should ask what you're doing here. But what I really want to know, and can't get anyone around here to tell me is, what the hell happened over at Eighth? I mean it's worse than abandoned. It looks like you started building it in reverse."

"Ahhh," Angelo sighed deeply. "It's terrible. Everything fell apart. Not the building. You're right about that – the building really was being disassembled. But what fell apart was trust, and partnership, and friendship. I hate to say this, but, Jozef and I, we wanted to put everything good and positive that we had into that project, and instead we lost our souls. Or at least misplaced them."

"Wow," Michaela said. "That's very poetic. Very sad. But could you tell me what actually happened?

"Mmm. Yes, of course. Well, as you know, everything about Eighth was to have a spiritual intent. It was to be built with the same type of consciousness with which this stupa was created. The monks even placed relics from many faiths and practices into the restaurant floors and walls. But they couldn't build everything. It was too big a project. So we hired a contractor. One who promised he would follow our wishes, and was paid well to do so."

Angelo stretched out his legs in front of him, and his arms above his head, and took a long breath. Then he reached down and picked up an oval-shaped stone from the ground and held it in his lap. He looked at Michaela.

"I don't know how well you remember coming to see us, but soon after we discovered that the contractor had been lying to us. He had not ensured that each of the sub-contractors and their workers were blessed, as they were supposed to be. He did not use the materials we requested and paid for – the very expensive ones we thought were being imported from small manufacturers whose operations are entirely conscious and green. Instead, he bought everything from large distributors and pocketed the difference. When we found out, we fired him, of course. But it was too late. Much of the building had been made without the spiritual vibrations built into it, the way we wanted it."

Michaela didn't say anything but watched his face as he relived this painful realization. It amazed her that he could possibly think she wouldn't remember them very well. She recalled every excruciating minute of her first visit to Eighth. But this wasn't the time to bring it up.

"Wow, that's rough," she said. "So what did you do?"

"Well, that's where Jozef and I started to disagree. He wanted to fix what had been done wrong, and start completely over. He said we would not be true to our vision if we didn't do exactly what we had intended, and that we would be opening the restaurant under false pretenses. He said it would affect his cooking, that nothing would ever taste as good as it could, or be as spiritually nourishing for guests."

"And you saw it differently."

Angelo looked down at the stone in his lap, passing it from hand to hand.

"Well, yes. I could see his point, of course. It was a huge disappointment to me as well. I actually broke down and cried. We really had tried initially to think of everything we could do to make it all perfect. And we were so close to having what we wanted.

"At first I agreed with Jozef that we should start all over. But when I realized how great the delay and what the cost would be to rebuild, I didn't see how it was possible. We didn't have the resources. We'd never be able to finish. We'd end up with nothing. So the choice was, either complete the restaurant and open it on schedule, but have it be less than we'd hoped for, or else not to have it at all."

Angelo tossed the rock into the air a few inches and caught it. Michaela was surprised to find herself feeling rather sorry for him.

"I didn't know what to do. I thought about it and thought about it, and couldn't figure out a solution. So, finally, I went to Gyaltso with the dilemma. He'd helped me solve problems before, during the planning stages, like how we could incorporate the sand painting, and I thought, well, he's a highly experienced monk. Maybe he has a lot of insight. And he did."

"What did he say?"

"He said it was unfortunate that the contractor hadn't done what we asked, but that it really didn't matter. First of all, the relics and prayers were in place and nothing could take that away. But more important, if this was the way the building was made, then it was what it was. Nothing that exists in form is any better or any worse than anything else. The consciousness of the building and what we were trying to do here wasn't lessened because some of the materials and workmen didn't fit an arbitrary standard we had for spirituality. Basically, I think he was trying to tell me – in a nice way – that we were full of shit."

Michaela started laughing again. And, again, Angelo seemed unable to stop himself from joining her.

Michaela shook her head.

"Now I can tell you," she said. "That is exactly what was so funny to me before. Realizing that you were full of shit. Especially about me, because for a really long time, I thought you were right and there was something wrong with me. But what's blowing my mind is that I just figured all that out about two minutes before you showed up."

Angelo first looked hurt, then angry. He sat stiffly silent for bit. Finally, he gave a wry smile.

"So you think so too, eh? Are you sure it's not a conspiracy? How long have you been studying here? What else have you learned from Gyaltso?"

"I'm not exactly studying. I'm not sure what I'm doing. And I've never spoken with Gyaltso or anyone else here about you, though Buddha knows I've tried. But tell me the rest of the story. If it was fine to keep the building as it was, why did you tear it down?"

Another big sigh. "Jozef didn't agree. In fact, he didn't budge in his views at all. He had always wanted the perfect environment to pursue his calling and he wasn't going to 'downgrade,' as he put it. Not one bit. When I suggested keeping what we had and moving on, he accused me of being uncaring and only concerned with money. Then he said I was so unenlightened, he didn't know how he could continue to be my partner. But finally, he calmed down and seemed more reasonable. So I asked him to think about it for a few days while I went on a business trip, and he said he would."

"I'm guessing that didn't happen," Michaela said.

"Right."

Angelo took the rock in his right hand, leaned back his arm, and threw it as far as he could. They both watched it fly out over the valley until they couldn't see it any more.

"While I was gone, he drove a truck out to where immigrant day laborers wait for work. He brought a pile of tee shirts with a picture of the Lady of Guadalupe, and asked, 'Who wants one?' He figured the ones who got the most excited about the shirt must have some kind of faith, so he loaded them into the truck. Each guy got a shirt and a couple of days pay for coming out here and pulling apart the building. By the time I got back, it was just like it is now. I said if he didn't stop, I'd call the police. We had a big fight, and Jozef left; said he was done with me and I could have what was left of the project. But with no chef and not enough money to rebuild, there wasn't any more project."

Angelo gave Michaela a small, sad smile. He seemed very different now. Even though he had been the slightly nicer of the two partners when they interviewed her, he had still been arrogant and judgmental. But now he seemed thoughtful, and much more humble.

Michaela felt chilly, and realized it was late in the afternoon. She should get back soon. But she still hadn't discovered why Angelo had come here looking for her. What could he possibly want? She wasn't leaving until she heard everything.

She wrapped her arms around herself to stay warm.

"Here, take this," Angelo said. He took off his jacket and put it on her shoulders. Michaela decided not to argue.

"Thanks," she said. "So what did you do then?"

"Took time off. Climbed a mountain. Spent a month in the jungle with a very powerful shaman."

Maybe he hadn't changed that much after all.

"I was looking for insight. I knew I couldn't ignore the situation here. I had to come back and do something, so that Gyaltso and the other monks wouldn't have to look at a half-finished building every day. But while I was gone, somehow the word got out about Jozef leaving. And other chefs started contacting me. A few of them were very excited about getting involved in the culinary vision we were trying to create, and some of those were very talented. That's when I knew it would be possible to open without Jozef. But I still didn't have the money to finish. I tried everything, everyone I could think of. But they all thought it too risky."

Michaela wondered if he was there because she knew people in the restaurant industry. Perhaps he hoped she could find him another investor.

"I was ready to give up. In fact, I called Sotheby's about listing the land – just the part with the restaurant, not the monastery or the stupa. And while I was on hold, another call came in. It was the last thing I expected – someone who wanted in on the project. He – they – were ready to put up whatever was needed for the start up. But there were two stipulations. And they were rather strange."

Angelo paused and bit his lip. Despite the ease with which he'd revealed what happened so far – he was a natural storyteller – he seemed to be having trouble getting out whatever came next. He seemed nervous, which made Michaela nervous too, and her heart sped up again. What did all this have to do with her?

"Angelo," she said, "if you don't tell me the rest of it right now, I'm going to dangle you over that cliff by your heel. Don't think I won't. I'm very motivated."

"Right. I'm sure you are. Believe me, I already feel like I'm hanging over a cliff. A lot depends on your reaction to what I'm about to tell you."

"Let's have it then."

"Okay. The stipulations of the investor, or investors – I'm

really not sure which – are these. First, they want to be anonymous to me, at least for now. That's not common, but it's doable. We'll use intermediaries, and I have people I trust for that. But the second one – it's about you. You have to be in on this with me. Either I'm supposed to hire you, or else give you a one third share, whichever you prefer. The investors will only put up their money if you're involved in the project."

He glanced at her and then turned to look out over the landscape as she processed the information.

Michaela was stunned. She stared at Angelo, expecting him to say more, then realized he was giving her time to form a response.

"Why?" she asked.

He turned back to look at her, palms up and shaking his head slowly.

"I have no idea. I asked, but they didn't say. They just said you don't know a thing about it, and I wasn't sure if I believed them, but I do now. That's right, isn't it? You didn't arrange for this to happen?"

"Oh, you can believe it. This is the first I've heard of it. And it's difficult to take in, so excuse me if I'm acting weird. I just… it doesn't make any sense."

"Right," he said.

They were silent for a time, watching the sun close in on the horizon.

Finally, Michaela said, "So what's next? I have to give you an answer? I need some time to think about it. More information. This is too strange, too sudden. I don't know what to think."

"I know. We should talk more, of course. But you're open to the possibility?"

"I'm not saying no. Not yet."

Michaela's head was buzzing, thoughts flying. This was bigger than anything she'd done before. She could bring in Roxanne to help. And Angelo seemed to be not nearly the asshole she'd thought he was. No worse than some of her clients. She could imagine working with him.

"Angelo," she said. "I don't think I can process any more now. Also, it's cold out here, and getting close to dinner. Why don't we go inside and help serve the meal. Then we can talk more. And why don't we ask Gyaltso to join us, and see what he has to say. I want to know just how full of shit he thinks the plan is this time."

Angelo nodded. They stood up together, and he reached around Michaela's shoulders to adjust his coat. He gave her shoulders a squeeze and leaned forward to kiss her cheek. She turned to say something, and their lips met, lingering for a moment before both pulled away. For an instant, all Michaela's thoughts vanished as she could feel only his lips on hers. Their eyes followed with a glance that seemed to say *anything is possible.*

Though unintentional, the kiss had been a promise. Whatever happened next, she thought, was going to be interesting.

53
Santa Fe

After reading the first page of the interview with Rennie, Dorothea flung the magazine onto the floor, where it landed atop a pile of rejected items: her purple iPod nano and matching purple fleece throw, a legal pad covered with crossed-out notes, a pink sparkle pen, the television remote, a pair of dark glasses, and Click-ee. She had been desperately trying to distract herself for the last two hours. It wasn't working.

"I still can't believe it, Click-ee," she said. "I just know someone made a huge mistake, and is gonna be in big trouble when they find out I was overlooked."

She picked up the plush dolphin by the tail and turned his face toward hers.

"*I* would have gone anyway. Even without an invitation," she said. "But Dirk said no. What the heck does he know? We should have gone without Dirk, shouldn't we, Click-ee?" She made kissing noises at the toy animal. "Yes, we should. You and me, Click-ee. Just you and me. Stupid Dirk could stay home."

She went looking for stupid Dirk and found him in his office, leaning back in his chair, eyes closed, his Bose noise cancelling headphones plugged into his computer. She pulled the device off his right ear and a song leaked out.

'I'm your captain, though I'm feeling mighty sick.'

Dirk sat up and opened his eyes.

"What's that you're listening to?" she asked. She didn't wait for an answer.

"It's not fair," she whined, for what had to be the two-hundredth time since they'd first gotten wind of the event. "I should be there. I'm *supposed* to be there. My invitation got lost in the mail."

Dirk took the earpiece from Dorothea's hand before it could snap back onto his ear, and removed the headphones.

'Can you hear me, can you hear me, or am I all alone?'

"I told you, Thea. I called and there was no mistake. We were not invited. Sounds like mostly big name celebrities."

"But I *am* a celebrity. I can understand them not asking you – you're nobody. But I was on *Ivy!*, and *everything*."

'I can feel the hand of a stranger, and it's tightening around my throat.'

"Could you *please* turn that dreadful song off? I'm just gonna scream if I hear one more word."

Dirk touched the keyboard and the headphones were silent.

"And I'm hungry," she said. "What are we going to eat?"

"Well, what do you want?" he asked.

"I want Suela to come back. I can't believe she left us. We were so good to her. At least she'd have left us something to heat up."

"Thea, you *fired* her. Remember? You screamed at her for coming in late, which she'd cleared with you ahead of time."

"Well, I didn't mean it. I thought that would be obvious. Of course I didn't want to fire her. The house isn't going to clean itself, is it? You're going to find someone new, right Dirk?"

He sighed. "Yes, Thea, I'll find us a new housekeeper."

"And what about dinner? Will you go get something?"

He looked longingly at the headphones in his hand.

"You know, Thea, I could really use a break right now. I'm kind of stressed out and don't feel like I should drive."

He didn't mention he had also just smoked half a joint, leaning out the window so Thea wouldn't notice the smell.

"Why don't you call Grass or Seabird, and see if one of them can bring something over for you. And have them get me a cheeseburger. With fries."

He settled the headphones back on his head and turned the music back on, loud enough for the noise to reach Dorothea.

She waited for him to say something more, but he merely closed his eyes and muttered, "Grand Funk Railroad."

She made a frustrated sound in her throat and flounced out of the room. She was on her own until he was ready to act like an adult again.

As much as she didn't want to, calling Grass or Seabird was probably her best option. They could bring over some Thai chicken, or an order of biryani from the Indian place. She'd even let them stay and eat with her. She could use the company to distract her from missing the most important, exciting event of the year.

After a few minutes, she located her cell phone next to the bathtub. Standing in the bathroom, she hit the speed dial for Grass, and was relieved to hear ringing on the other end. If it had gone straight to voicemail, she was going to scream.

"HELLO," someone yelled. Dorothea's volume was turned up, and the sound was so loud it hurt her ear. She pulled the phone away from her head.

"Hello, Grass? Are you there?"

"HELLO? THEA, IS THAT YOU? I'M SORRY, I CAN'T HEAR YOU. IT'S VERY LOUD HERE. HANG ON A MINUTE, I'LL GO OUTSIDE."

Thea waited. From the sound of it, Grass must be with a lot of people. Maybe she was in a restaurant already. Good. That could save time bringing food here to the house.

"Sorry, Thea, that's better. I can hear you now."

"Grass, sweetie, are you in a restaurant? Because Dirk fired the housekeeper and there's nothing to eat here. Could you be a dear and bring me over an order of … what type of food do they have where you are?"

"Here? Oh, Thea, I'm so sorry. I'm not in Santa Fe. I'm really sorry I can't help you out right now."

"Where are you? Albuquerque? I really don't want to wait that long. Oh, never mind, I'll try Seabird."

"Seabird is here too. I'm so sorry, Thea," she said again, "We only left for the weekend. We'll be back at work on Monday."

"I'll be dead of starvation by Monday," Thea said. "Where are you, anyway?"

"Oh, Thea, you wouldn't believe it. We're at the coolest party. It's that new restaurant opening in Santa Cruz, or near there. You've probably heard about it – it's called Eighth – and it's like, the highest, most sacred place I've ever been. The energy here is amazing. And you wouldn't believe all the famous people. Movie stars, big name teachers. Deepak, Eckhart. They even taped a segment for *Ivy!* earlier, out by this really cool stupa."

Dorothea gasped uncontrollably, and she started to black out. Her knees buckled and she collapsed onto the toilet.

This couldn't be happening, she thought. *I, Dorothea Light, teacher, Sha-Woman, and nearly Ascended Master, was passed over for the most significant gathering of spiritual teachers since the harmonic convergence, and yet somehow* Grass *is there. And* Seabird. *How is that possible? The dark forces of the universe must be taking over, for real. The world has truly turned inside out. How in the name of the Goddess are Grass and Seabird at that party and I'm not?*

"Are you … are you working? Serving drinks, or, or, parking cars, or … what?"

"Oh, no, Thea. We're here as guests. Michaela invited us. You remember Michaela, right?"

Michaela invited them? What did Michaela have to do with it? That woman has done nothing but cause me distress. Michaela was the worst thing ever to happen to me except for ... for... Guy. My horrible, awful brother. They must be working together, to undermine me. That's what I get for trying to do a little good in the world. The forces of evil have ganged up against me. I can feel the powerful negative energy, swirling around, right here and now. I don't deserve this. The forces of evil are just not fair.

Dorothea dropped the phone onto the bathroom rug, and put her head in her hands. Somewhere, very far away, she heard the tiny little sound of Grass saying, "Thea? Thea? Are you still there?" but the words didn't penetrate. She took a huge, ragged breath and closed her eyes until the phone became silent.

And when she opened them, Dorothea found herself in another place. A good, special place, where those mean old forces of evil couldn't touch her. A part of her realized she was staring down into a toilet bowl, but it didn't really matter.

Water. What a lovely shade of blue. It's where I belong – in the dolphin pool with my darling, beloved Calvin, my beautiful savior and protector. That's where I'll go. Into the water with Calvin. None of what happens here, in this unfair, stupid little life, matters. Calvin loves me, and as soon as I'm with him, he'll make everything all right.

Dorothea felt better. She began to sing quietly to herself.

"Somewhere. Beyond the sea. He's there, waiting for me. Happy we'll be, beyond the sea..."

It would just be Calvin, and her, and their little Click-ee, together forever. Everything was fine. Perfect. The stress was gone. She knew she was in the right place, and she intended to stay there. In fact, Dorothea planned to never move from where she was sitting right now, looking into the beautiful blue water. Never, ever again.

54
Santa Cruz Mountains

*T*he party was going great, but Michaela needed a break. She scanned the room for Angelo to tell him she was stepping outside for a few minutes, and found him sitting at a back corner booth with a group of men, all leaning over listening to some guy in a Miami Dolphins cap. She started toward him, but as she closed in, the group broke into snickering laughter and she changed her mind. From the looks of things, they were about ready to pull out cigars and grab any female ass within reach.

Michaela didn't mind. Angelo had turned out to be more down to earth and less flaky than she'd expected, but she still liked it when he would let loose and act macho with the guys. She quickly made her way past the clusters of guests, some at tables, others standing and talking in clusters. Appetizers and entrees had been cleared, but people were still nibbling desserts and sipping wine.

There was no doubt they were going to be as successful as Roxanne had predicted two years ago, when she first told Michaela about Eighth. And now Michaela had a major role in it. Not just designing the menus, as she'd hoped for at first. But as a partner, with Angelo and their talented and visionary new chef, who Angelo's psychic advisor told him was the reincarnation of the renowned nineteenth century epicure Antoine Carême.

And they had toned down the original pretentious concept of the restaurant. The ingredients still came from spiritually significant sources worldwide, but what was wrong with that? Most successful restaurants, in addition to the excellence of the food, went over the top in some way in order to stand out. And if they hadn't done it here, someone would have, sooner or later, done it somewhere else.

Most of all, though, Michaela could not possibly have imagined the personal journey she'd taken since first hearing about the place. She was such a mess back then. She'd lived with the constant feeling of being "less-than," both professionally and personally, and then in the spiritual paths she'd tried taking up.

She felt so much more comfortable now with the person she was, and the turns her life had taken. She had found a middle path for herself. For her practice, she still chanted and meditated around the stupa nearly every day. If she was out of town, she found someplace to walk in the woods or by water. And when life felt challenging or out of balance, she talked to Gyaltso, whom she had come to deeply respect and love. He had taken her in when she was lost and given her the chance to find herself. And then this new life had found her as well.

Once she had gotten over the shock of Angelo's revelation, she'd gladly thrown herself into making Eighth a reality. And while they were working together, she and Angelo had gotten personally closer too. She hadn't yet given up her house in Mill Valley, but she found herself staying most nights here with him.

And if that weren't enough, her clothing line was taking off. She had investors of her own and, now that Eighth was open, she was going to pull back to concentrate on developing her lines.

Passing through the restaurant, she scanned the dining

room one more time. The new sand painting was progressing well. Everything seemed to be going smoothly, so she slipped into the kitchen before anyone could ask her a question or start a conversation. She nodded to the staff as they cleaned up, and she headed for the back door to get some air.

A lock of hair fell into her face, and as she raised a hand to push it back, she accidentally nudged her diamond drop earring. It fell with a gentle clatter onto the floor. Michaela looked at her feet, but didn't see the earring. Damn. It must have slid under the stainless steel shelving next to her. She squatted down to reach underneath, and felt around, but didn't find it. She lowered her head to the floor to look. Ah! There it was, a little further back.

Michaela flattened herself as much as she could in order to reach it, her shoulder to the ground, and her face flat on the floor, looking in the other direction. She stretched her arm under the shelving as far as it would go and felt her fingers close around the errant earring. She knew the floor was immaculate, but still wished she wasn't being forced to lie on it in her good clothes.

"Gotcha, you little troublemaker," she said, and began pulling her arm out. As she did so, she caught a glimpse of something else out of place on the otherwise clean floor. It was on the underside of another set of shelves directly across from her, where a broom should have reached it but apparently hadn't.

Still kneeling, Michaela pushed her earring back into place and tugged to make sure it was secure. Then she reached across the floor for the other item. It was hard and round and small and cold and impossible.

She had only one thought: No way.

There could be no radishes in that kitchen. Radishes were not an ingredient in anything currently being served at Eighth. Michaela knew this for sure. She had written out the menu, and she was privy to all orders placed and received.

Not only that, but this particular specimen was an exact replica of THAT radish.

The radish that had changed her life.

Michaela sat on the floor of the kitchen at Eighth and stared at the radish, excitement mixed with confusion.

She wanted to run right to Angelo, and tell him the whole story. He would love the synchronicity of finding an identical radish on this night, closing the circle of one journey of self-discovery and beginning another. But she didn't want to interrupt his male bonding ritual. She'd tell him later.

She would keep the radish. Maybe she should meditate with it in front of her, or even do an incense session with it. That might allow her to go deeply into some aspect of the meaning of life. Or at least the meaning of her life. She could work with it every day and observe impermanence as it changed form, from a healthy fresh vegetable into a piece of rotting vegetation, and then into nothingness.

But what if this actually *was* the very radish she had lost. A magic radish that never wilted or rotted, disappearing and reappearing according to some deep unknowable universal force. Probably Michaela should keep it enclosed in a protective plastic case on her altar and see what happened next.

Or, in case it was neither magic nor the same radish, and really was going to go bad, maybe she should take it back to her studio and paint it, thereby preserving the image for herself forever. That way she would always have a reminder of the mystery of life, and how you really didn't know what could happen when you open up and trust the universe to take care of you.

Keeping her eyes on the radish, she stepped outside into the beautiful clear night and walked a few steps away from the restaurant, and off the gravel path. She took off her shoes and eased her feet onto the soft dirt, and said a silent thank you to whatever it was that had brought her to this point in her life, and would lead her on to whatever happened next. She didn't know who or what she was thanking, but it really made no difference.

Michaela closed her eyes. She breathed deeply. And then she ate the radish.

Addendum

From the New York Times "Style" section, Sunday June 15, wedding announcements:

Last Saturday, Robin Hannah Newman and Dhananjay Kamadev Ashvin exchanged vows in a lovely intimate ceremony on a private West Indies island. Guests flew in from all over the world, including the groom's family from Northern India, and the bride's parents from Venezuela, where they were doing volunteer work for the group AllOnePlanet.org.

Ms. Newman is the daughter of Jack and Kate Newman, well-known philanthropists. Ms. Newman's maternal great-great grandfather, Tyrannius Hermley, founded arms manufacturer Triton-Hermley-Evens Corporation in 1907, now known as THE International. The THE company no longer produces weapons.

Mr. Ashvin, known as D.K., or Duke, is the son of Roop and Aditi Ashvin. Until recently, the family were farmers in a remote area of Northern India. Duke Ashvin is currently rated the number two poker player in the world. He created the website YouCanPlay.com, an online course that many have called the best teaching system for poker ever invented. Mr. Ashvin credits his success to the spiritual leader known as, "Business Card Guru," subject of the most recent book by reclusive meditation teacher Rennie Morrow.

Mr. Morrow officiated at the ceremony. Before his unexpected semi-retirement, Mr. Morrow created a highly successful seminar series. He now limits his teaching to a small retreat center in Mendocino County, California, where he also distributes a brand of incense said to aid seekers in reaching a state of enlightenment. Despite positive reports from numerous users, researchers have not been able to validate these claims in laboratory studies.

The many celebrity guests included designer Michaela Thomason, a friend of both bride and groom, who created the bridal gown and bridesmaid dresses. In recent interviews, Ms Thomason credited the couple with anonymously backing the startup of Eighth, the highly lauded new restaurant she opened with partners Angelo (who goes by a single name) and celebrated Native American chef Anthony Isi.

Mr. and Mrs. Ashvin will divide their time between homes in Delhi, London, San Diego, and Las Vegas.

The End

Cary Jane Sparks lives in northern California with her husband, son, and Thunder the cat. In the process of organizing numerous workshops and conferences, she's encountered an entertaining and inspiring variety of seekers and teachers, upon whom absolutely none of the characters in this book are based.

caryjanesparks.com

Made in the USA
Charleston, SC
22 October 2011